BATMAN LI'L GOTHAM

Dustin Nguyen **Derek Fridolfs** Writers **Dustin Nguyen** Artist & Collection Cover Artist
Saida Temofonte Letterer BATMAN Created by **BOB KANE**

Sarah Gaydos **Kristy Quinn** Editors – Original Series **Rachel Pinnelas** Editor
Robbin Brosterman Design Director – Books **Louis Prandi** Publication Design
Hank Kanalz Senior VP – Vertigo & Integrated Publishing
Diane Nelson President **Dan DiDio** and **Jim Lee** Co-Publishers **Geoff Johns** Chief Creative Officer
John Rood Executive VP – Sales, Marketing & Business Development **Amy Genkins** Senior VP – Business & Legal Affairs
Nairi Gardiner Senior VP – Finance **Jeff Boison** VP – Publishing Planning **John Cunningham** VP – Marketing
Terri Cunningham VP – Editorial Administration **Amit Desai** Senior VP – Franchise Management **Alison Gill** Senior VP – Manufacturing & Operations
Bob Harras Senior VP – Editor-in-Chief, DC Comics **Jason James** VP – Interactive Marketing **Jay Kogan** VP – Business & Legal Affairs, Publishing
Jack Mahan VP – Business Affairs, Talent **Nick Napolitano** VP – Manufacturing Administration **Rich Palermo** VP – Business Affairs, Media
Courtney Simmons Senior VP – Publicity **Bob Wayne** Senior VP – Sales

BATMAN LI'L GOTHAM VOLUME 1
Published by DC Comics. Copyright © 2014 DC Comics. All Rights Reserved.
Originally published in single magazine form in BATMAN: LI'L GOTHAM 1-6 and online as BATMAN: LI'L GOTHAM Chapters 1-12. Copyright © 2013
DC Comics. All Rights Reserved. All characters, their distinctive likenesses and related elements featured in this publication are trademarks of DC Comics.
The stories, characters and incidents featured in this publication are entirely fictional. DC Comics does not read or accept unsolicited ideas, stories or artwork.
DC Comics, 1700 Broadway, New York, NY 10019. A Warner Bros. Entertainment Company.
Printed by RR Donnelley, Salem, VA, USA. 1/17/14. First Printing.
ISBN: 978-1-4012-4494-1

Library of Congress Cataloging-in-Publication Data

Nguyen, Dustin.
Batman Li'l Gotham. Volume 1 / Dustin Nguyen, Derek Fridolfs.
pages cm
Summary: Tales of adventure through the holidays featuring favorite Gotham City characters.
"Originally published in single magazine form in BATMAN: LI'L GOTHAM 1-6 and online as BATMAN: LI'L GOTHAM Chapters 1-12."
ISBN 978-1-4012-4494-1 (pbk.)
1. Graphic novels. [1. Graphic novels. 2. Superheroes—Fiction. 3. Holidays--Fiction.] I. Fridolfs, Derek. II. Title.
PZ7.7.N49Bat 2014
741.5'973—dc23

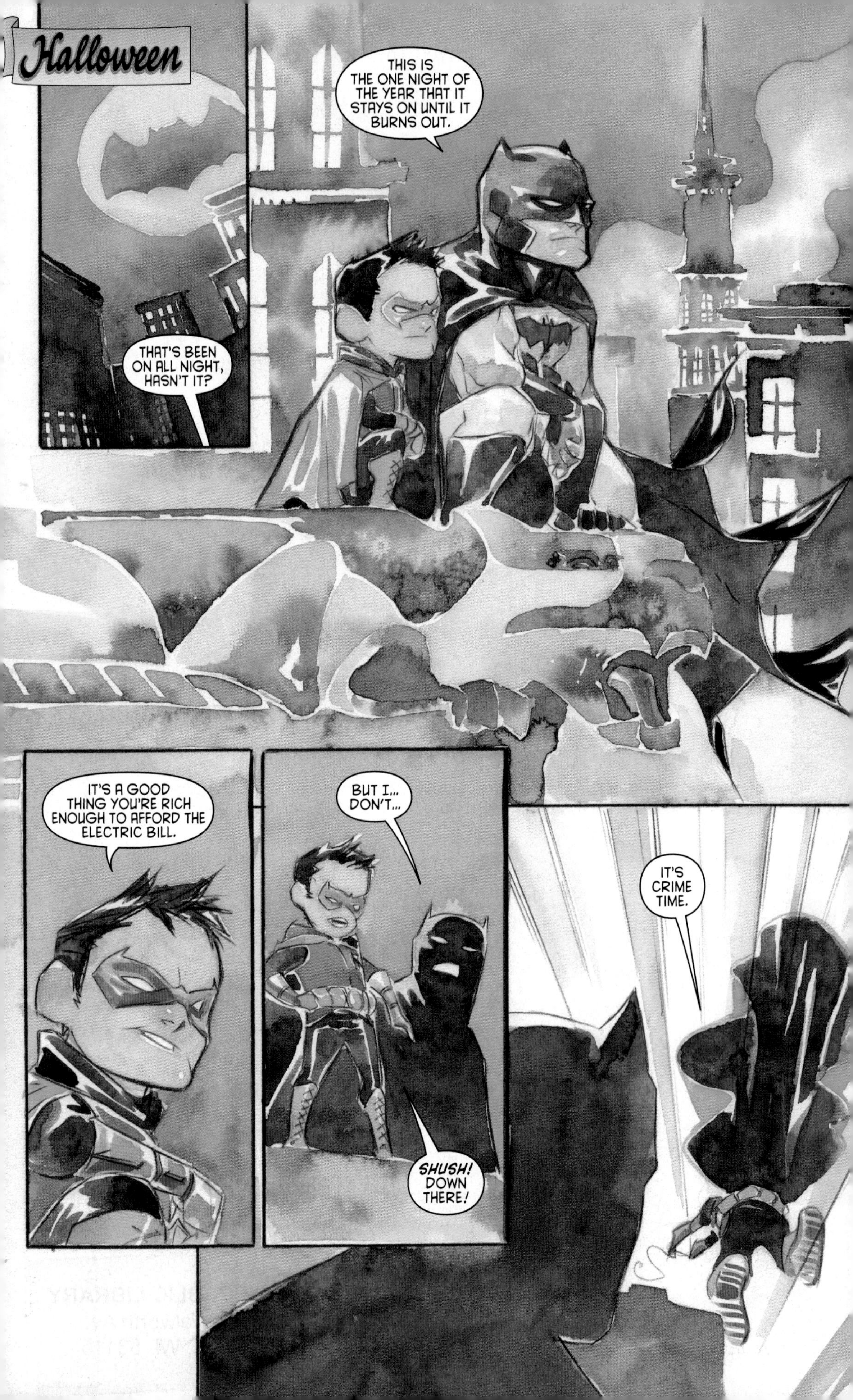
Halloween
THAT'S BEEN ON ALL NIGHT, HASN'T IT?
THIS IS THE ONE NIGHT OF THE YEAR THAT IT STAYS ON UNTIL IT BURNS OUT.
IT'S A GOOD THING YOU'RE RICH ENOUGH TO AFFORD THE ELECTRIC BILL.
BUT I... DON'T...
SHUSH! DOWN THERE!
IT'S CRIME TIME.

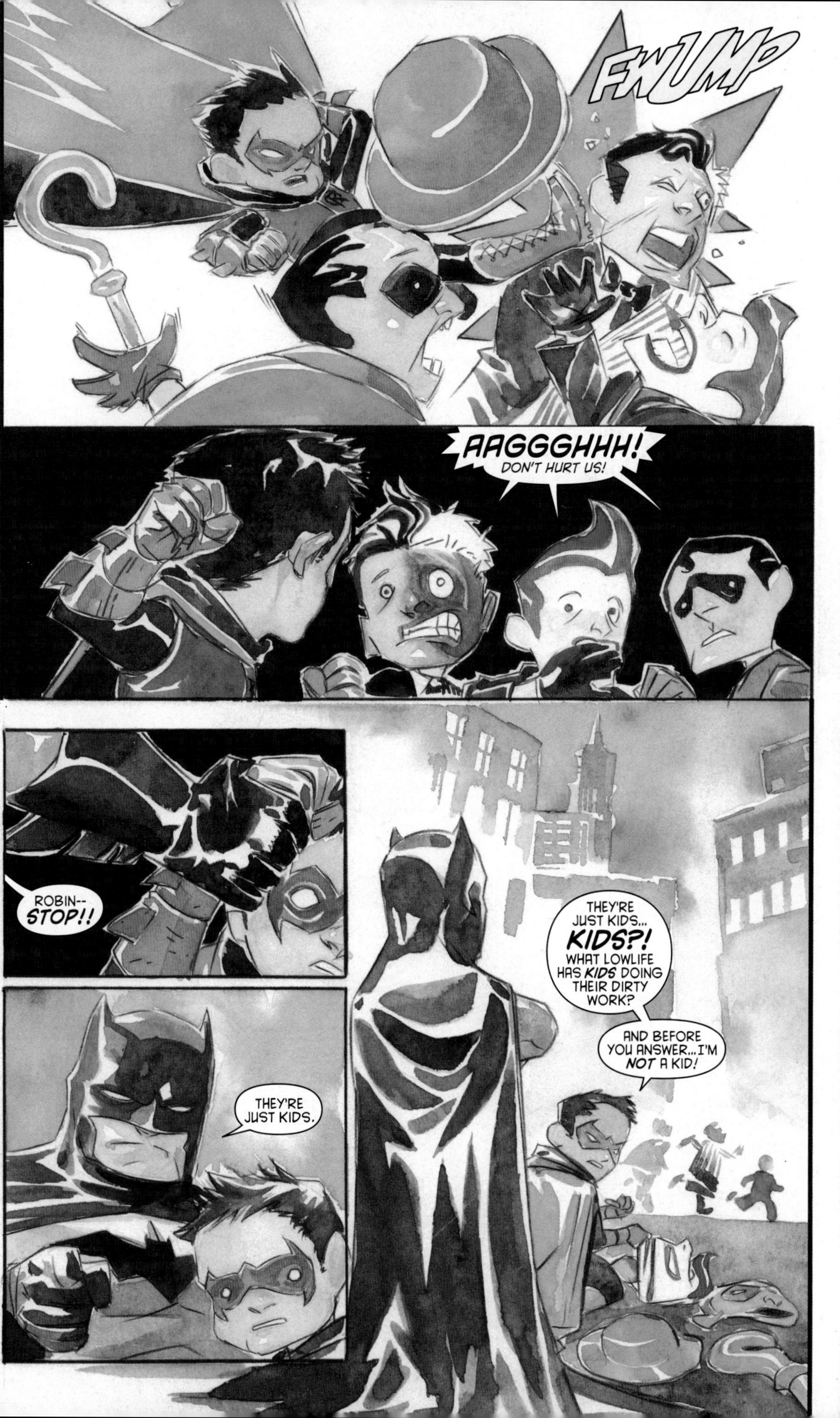

FWUMP
AAGGGHHH!
DON'T HURT US!
ROBIN--
STOP!!
THEY'RE
JUST KIDS.
THEY'RE
JUST KIDS...
KIDS?!
WHAT LOWLIFE
HAS KIDS DOING
THEIR DIRTY
WORK?
AND BEFORE
YOU ANSWER...I'M
NOT A KID!

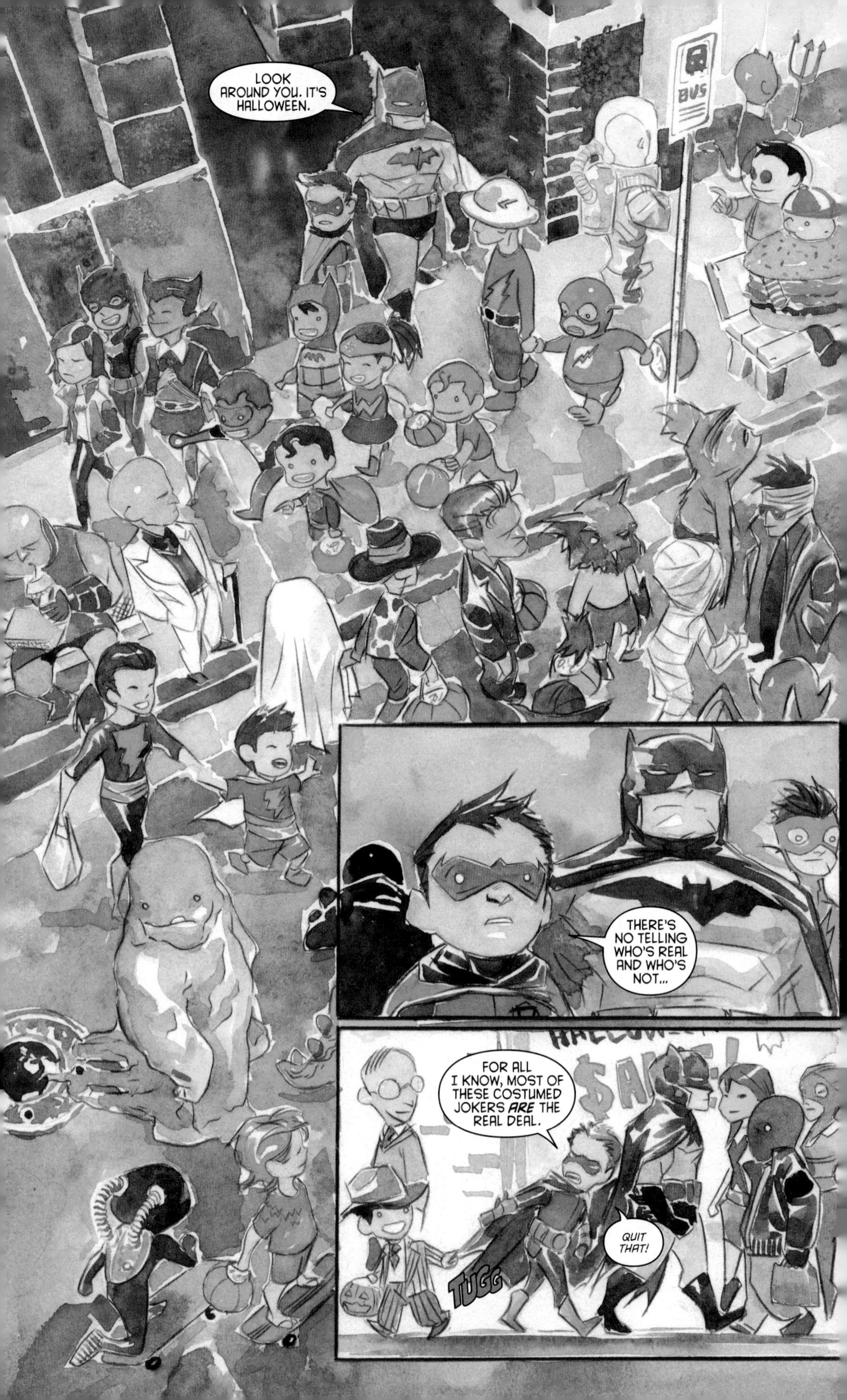
LOOK AROUND YOU. IT'S HALLOWEEN.
BUS
THERE'S NO TELLING WHO'S REAL AND WHO'S NOT...
FOR ALL I KNOW, MOST OF THESE COSTUMED JOKERS *ARE* THE REAL DEAL.
TUGG
QUIT THAT!

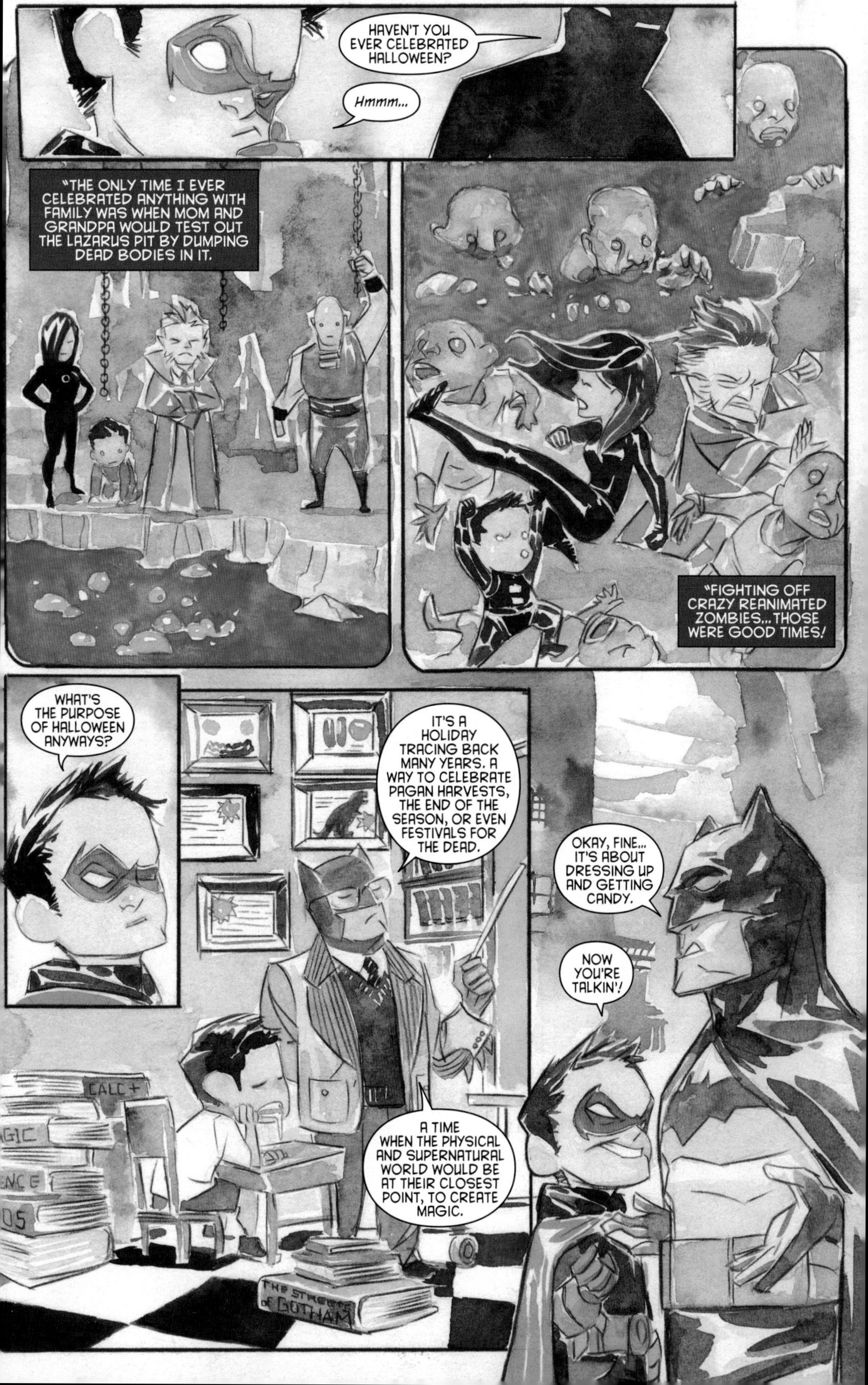
HAVEN'T YOU EVER CELEBRATED HALLOWEEN?
Hmmm...
"THE ONLY TIME I EVER CELEBRATED ANYTHING WITH FAMILY WAS WHEN MOM AND GRANDPA WOULD TEST OUT THE LAZARUS PIT BY DUMPING DEAD BODIES IN IT.
"FIGHTING OFF CRAZY REANIMATED ZOMBIES... THOSE WERE GOOD TIMES!
WHAT'S THE PURPOSE OF HALLOWEEN ANYWAYS?
IT'S A HOLIDAY TRACING BACK MANY YEARS. A WAY TO CELEBRATE PAGAN HARVESTS, THE END OF THE SEASON, OR EVEN FESTIVALS FOR THE DEAD.
A TIME WHEN THE PHYSICAL AND SUPERNATURAL WORLD WOULD BE AT THEIR CLOSEST POINT, TO CREATE MAGIC.
OKAY, FINE... IT'S ABOUT DRESSING UP AND GETTING CANDY.
NOW YOU'RE TALKIN'!
THE STREETS OF GOTHAM

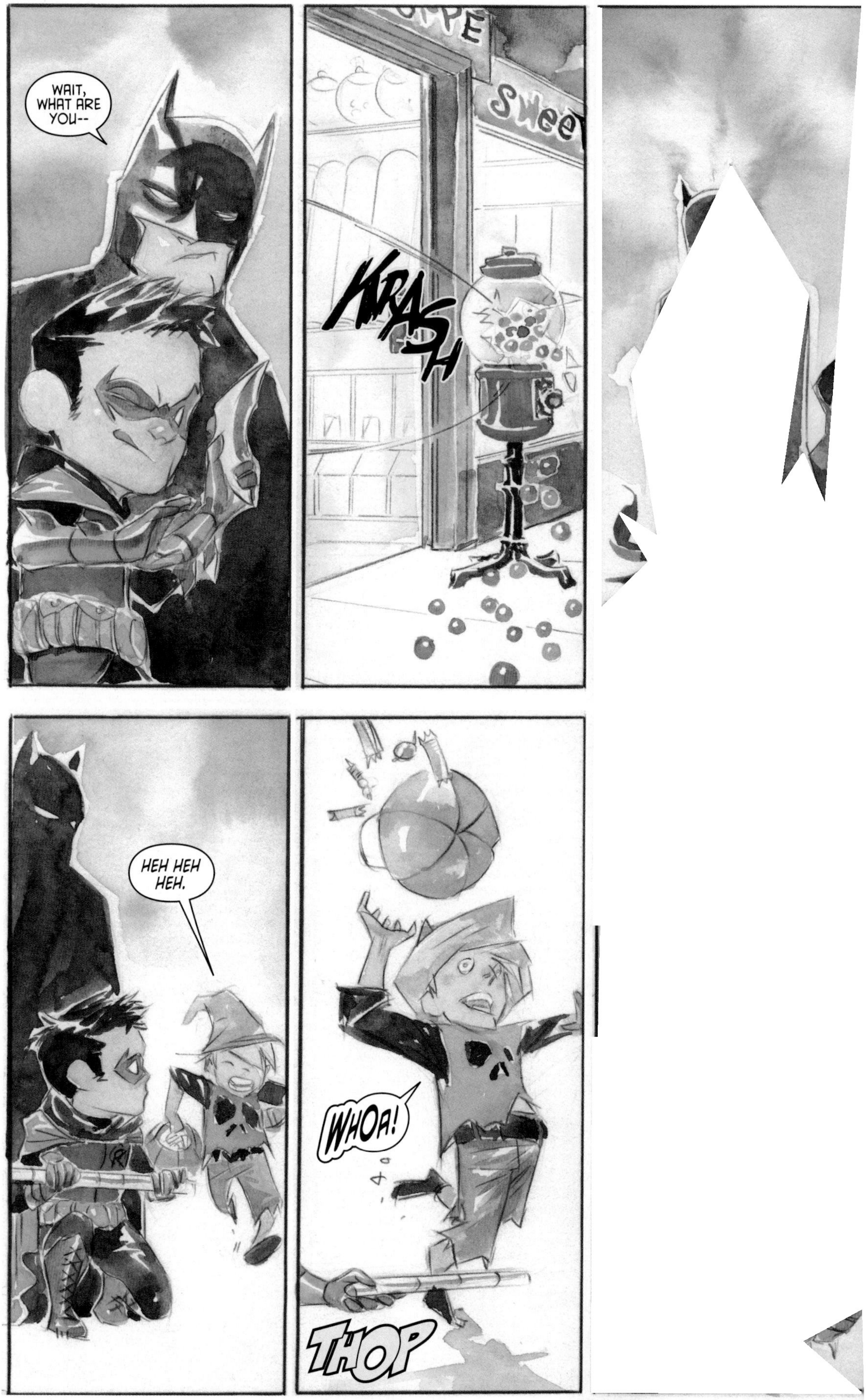
WAIT, WHAT ARE YOU--
SWEET
KRASH
HEH HEH HEH.
WHOA!
THOP

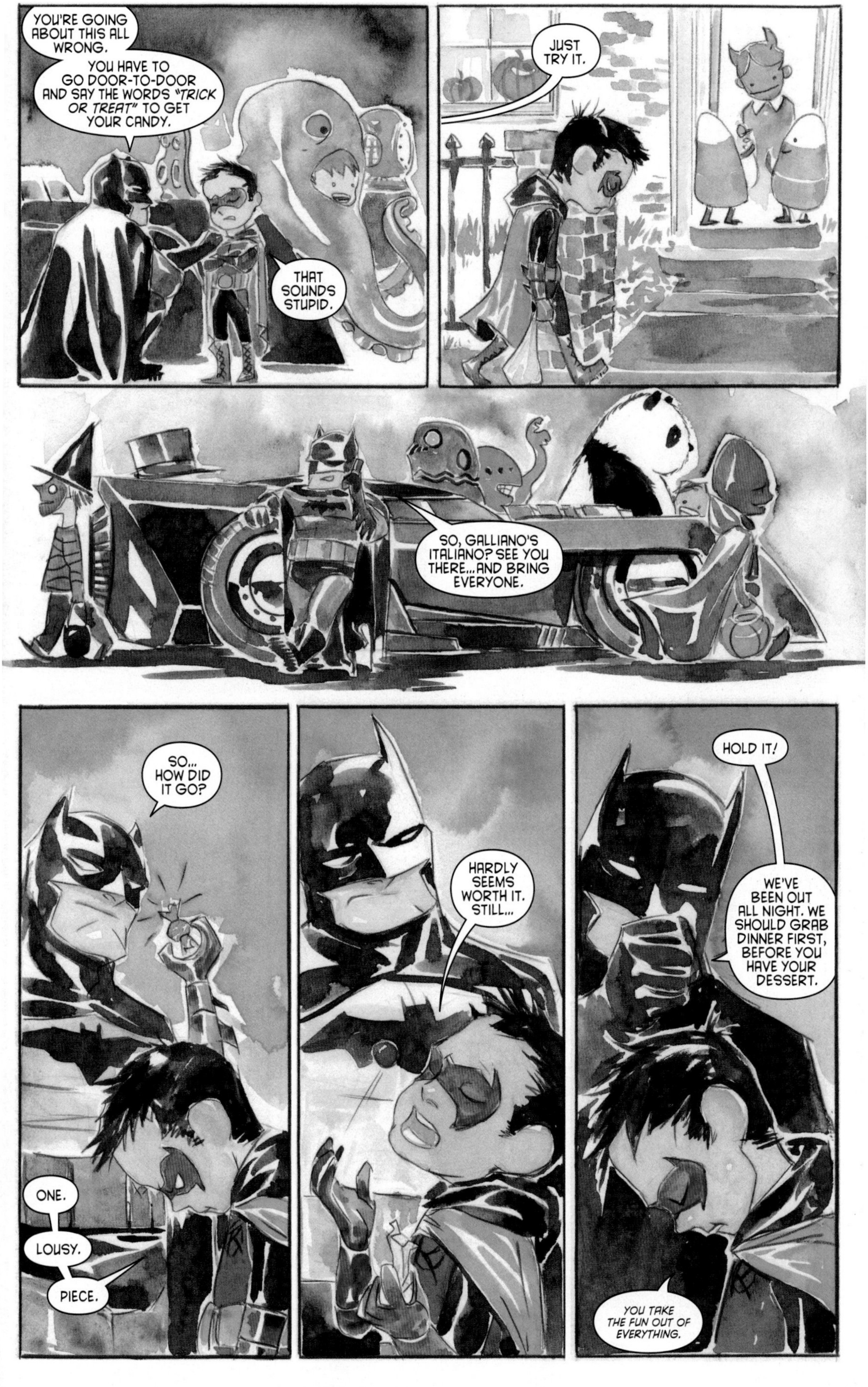
YOU'RE GOING ABOUT THIS ALL WRONG.
YOU HAVE TO GO DOOR-TO-DOOR AND SAY THE WORDS "TRICK OR TREAT" TO GET YOUR CANDY.
THAT SOUNDS STUPID.
JUST TRY IT.
SO, GALLIANO'S ITALIANO? SEE YOU THERE...AND BRING EVERYONE.
SO... HOW DID IT GO?
ONE.
LOUSY.
PIECE.
HARDLY SEEMS WORTH IT. STILL...
HOLD IT!
WE'VE BEEN OUT ALL NIGHT. WE SHOULD GRAB DINNER FIRST, BEFORE YOU HAVE YOUR DESSERT.
YOU TAKE THE FUN OUT OF EVERYTHING.

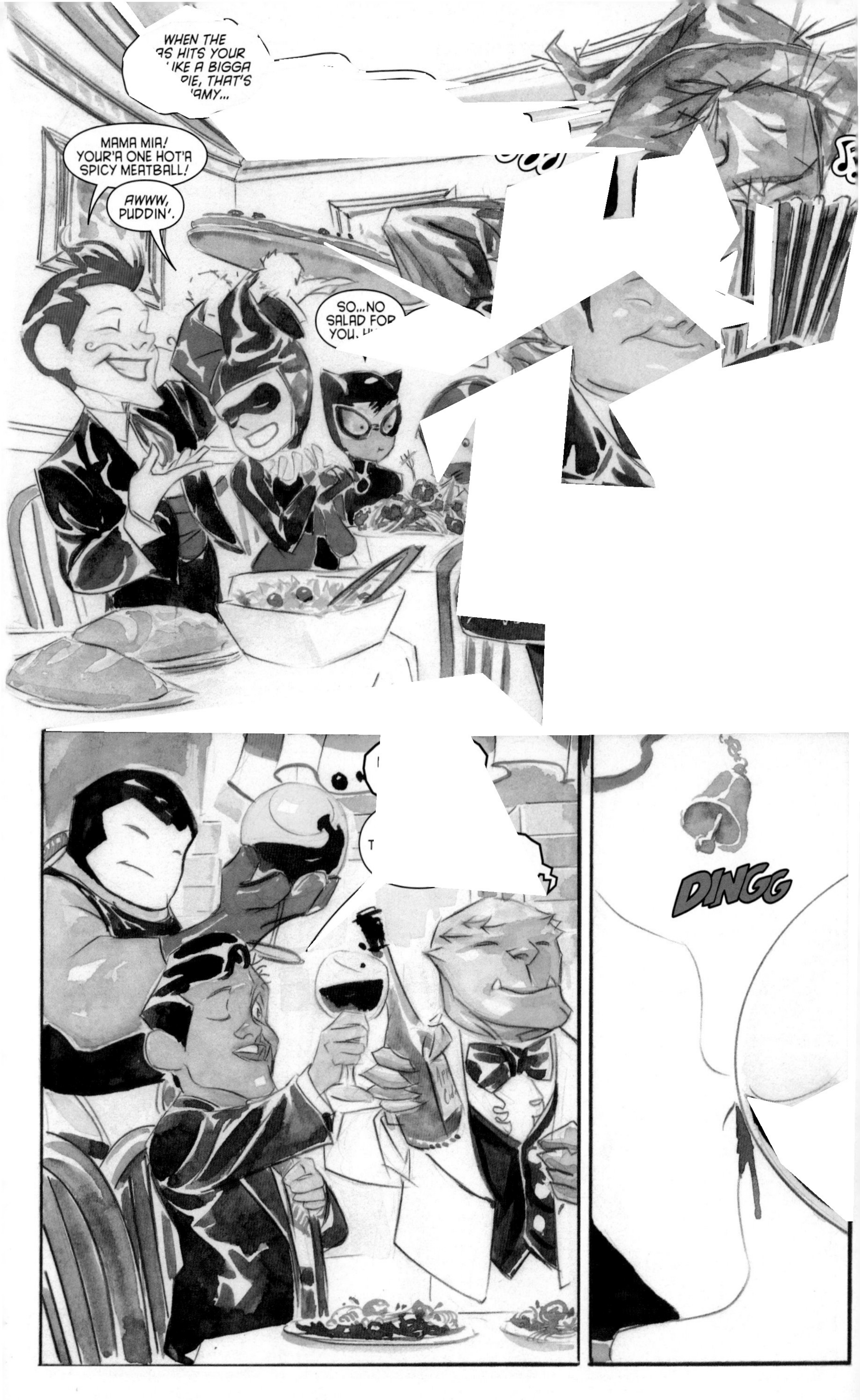
WHEN THE
HITS YOUR
IKE A BIGGA
PIE, THAT'S
MAMA MIA! YOUR'A ONE HOT'A SPICY MEATBALL!
AWWW, PUDDIN'.
SO...NO SALAD FOR
DINGG

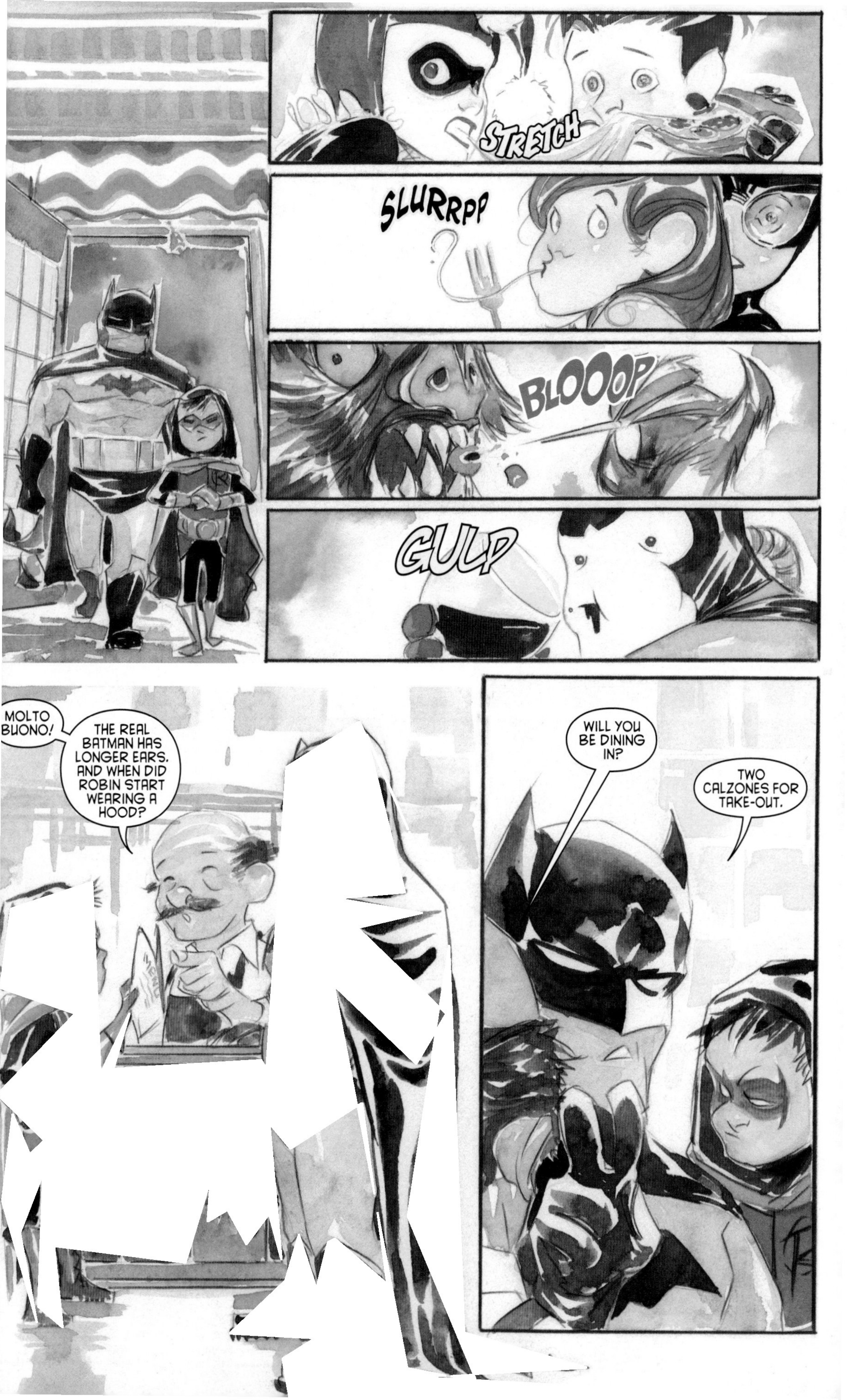
STRETCH
SLURRPP
BLOOOP
GULP
MOLTO BUONO!
THE REAL BATMAN HAS LONGER EARS. AND WHEN DID ROBIN START WEARING A HOOD?
WILL YOU BE DINING IN?
TWO CALZONES FOR TAKE-OUT.

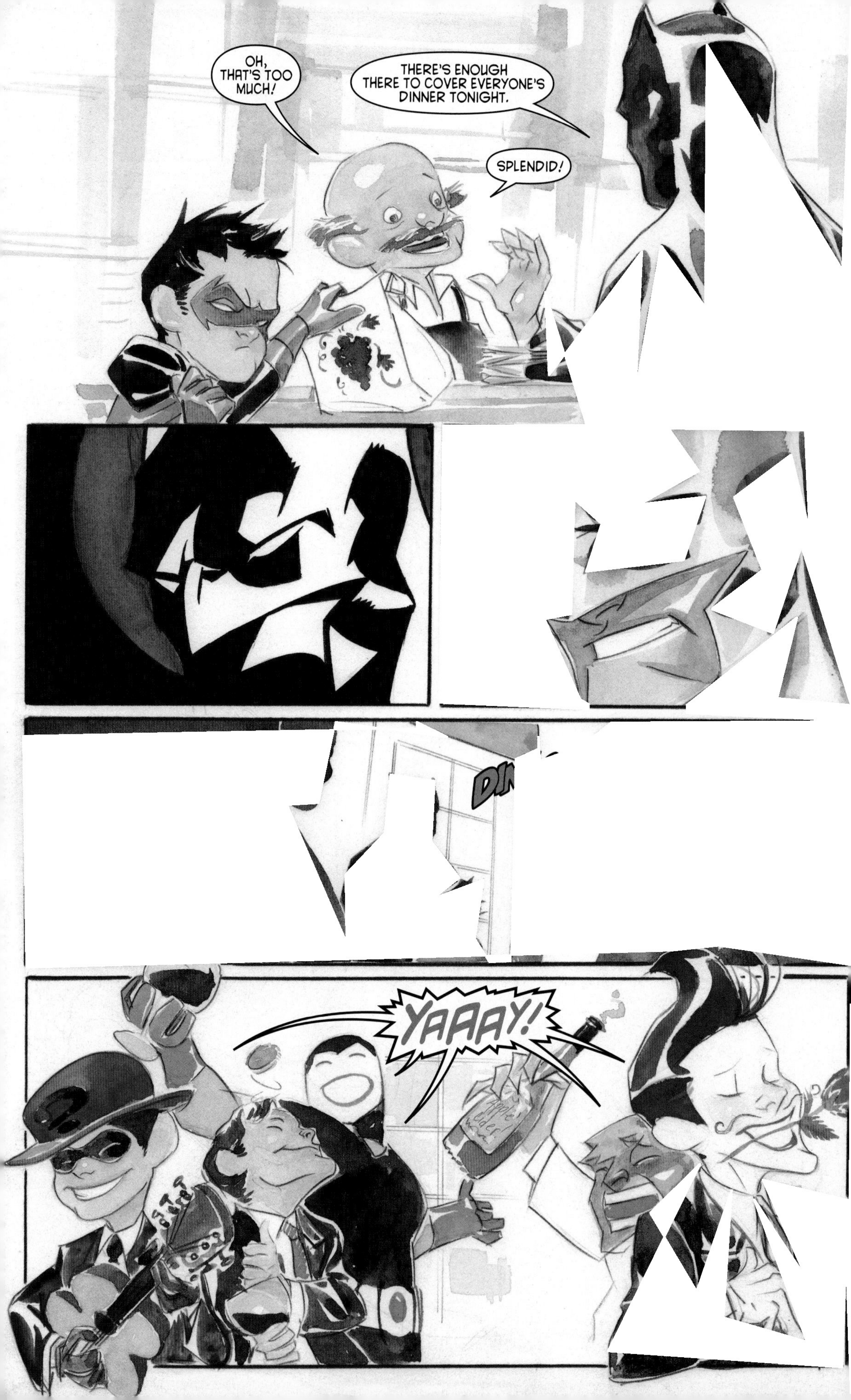
OH, THAT'S TOO MUCH!
THERE'S ENOUGH THERE TO COVER EVERYONE'S DINNER TONIGHT.
SPLENDID!
YAAAY!
Apple Cider

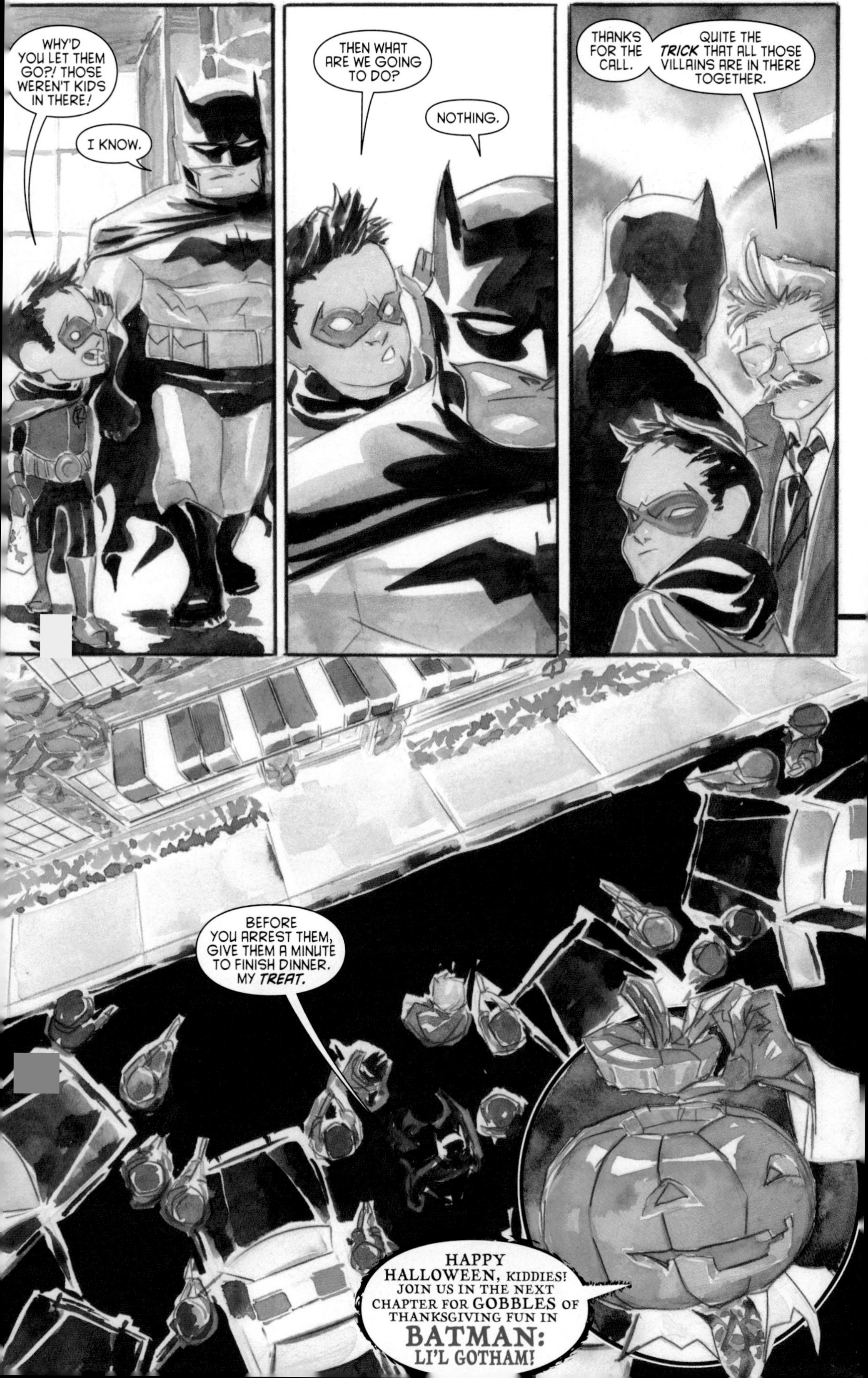

WHY'D YOU LET THEM GO?! THOSE WEREN'T KIDS IN THERE!
I KNOW.
THEN WHAT ARE WE GOING TO DO?
NOTHING.
THANKS FOR THE CALL.
QUITE THE *TRICK* THAT ALL THOSE VILLAINS ARE IN THERE TOGETHER.
BEFORE YOU ARREST THEM, GIVE THEM A MINUTE TO FINISH DINNER. MY *TREAT.*
HAPPY HALLOWEEN, KIDDIES! JOIN US IN THE NEXT CHAPTER FOR GOBBLES OF THANKSGIVING FUN IN BATMAN: LI'L GOTHAM!

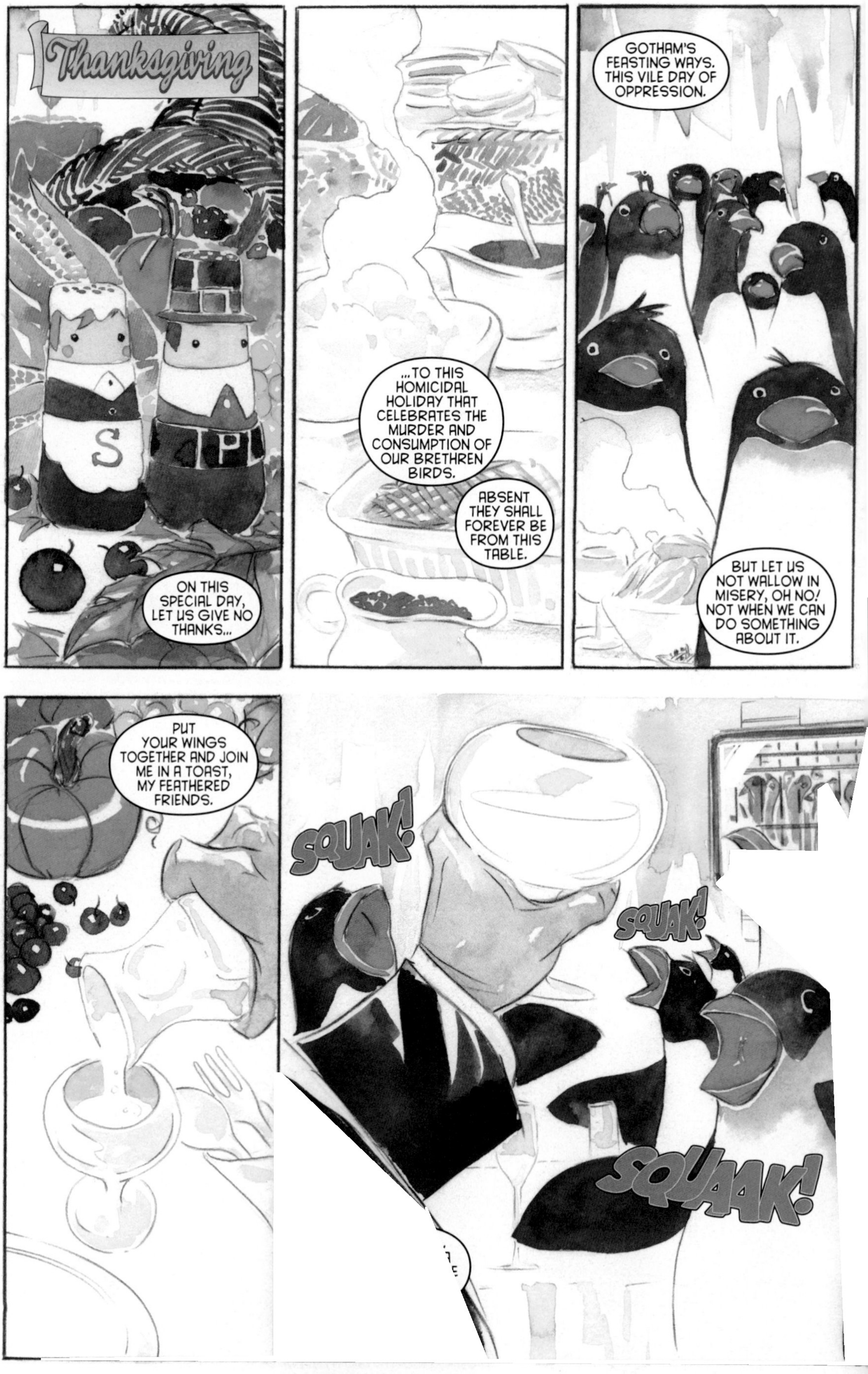

Thanksgiving
ON THIS SPECIAL DAY, LET US GIVE NO THANKS...
...TO THIS HOMICIDAL HOLIDAY THAT CELEBRATES THE MURDER AND CONSUMPTION OF OUR BRETHREN BIRDS.
ABSENT THEY SHALL FOREVER BE FROM THIS TABLE.
GOTHAM'S FEASTING WAYS. THIS VILE DAY OF OPPRESSION.
BUT LET US NOT WALLOW IN MISERY, OH NO! NOT WHEN WE CAN DO SOMETHING ABOUT IT.
PUT YOUR WINGS TOGETHER AND JOIN ME IN A TOAST, MY FEATHERED FRIENDS.
SQUAK!
SQUAK!
SQUAAK!

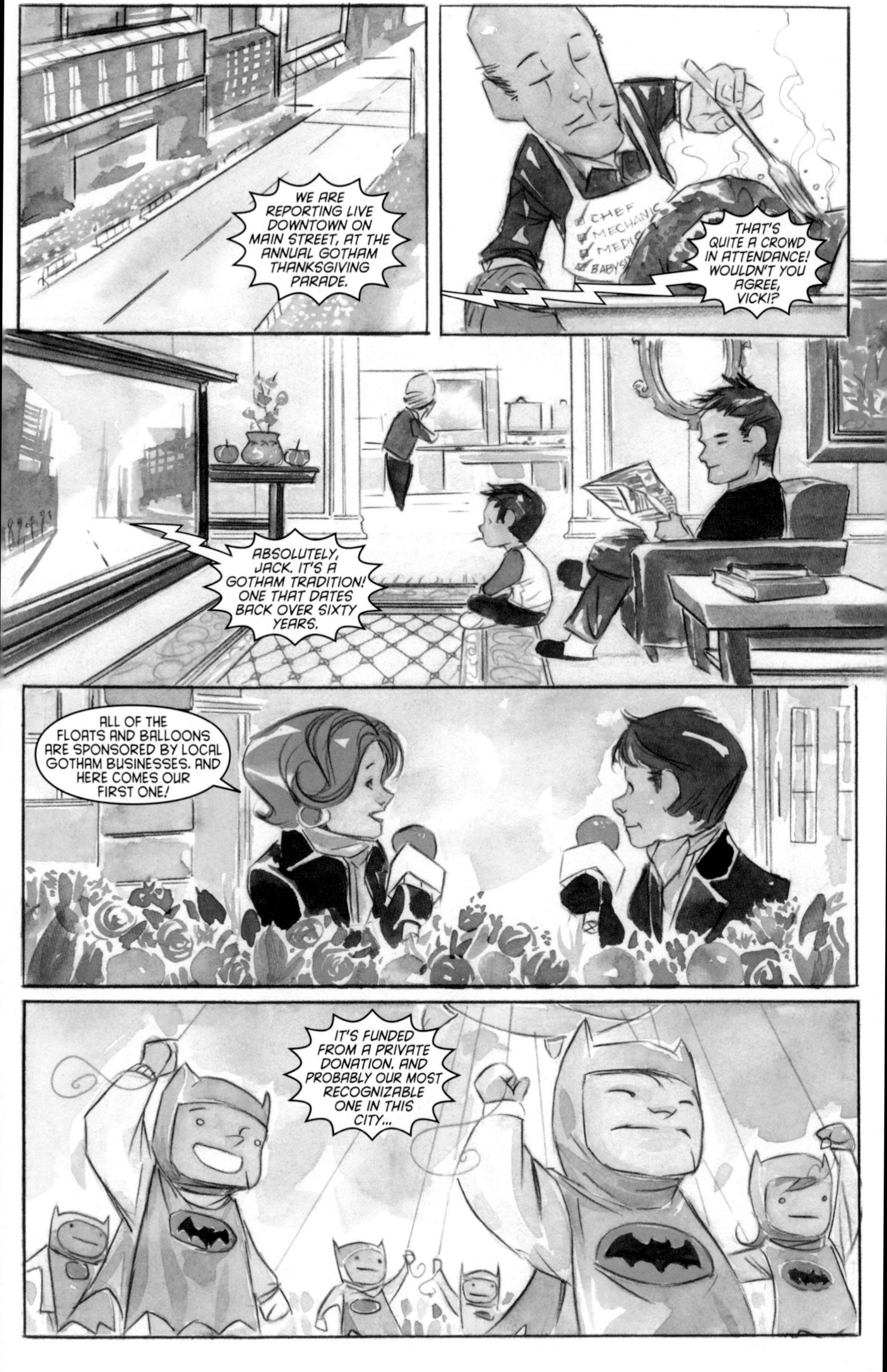
WE ARE REPORTING LIVE DOWNTOWN ON MAIN STREET, AT THE ANNUAL GOTHAM THANKSGIVING PARADE.
CHEF
MECHANIC
MEDIC
BABYS
THAT'S QUITE A CROWD IN ATTENDANCE! WOULDN'T YOU AGREE, VICKI?
ABSOLUTELY, JACK. IT'S A GOTHAM TRADITION! ONE THAT DATES BACK OVER SIXTY YEARS.
ALL OF THE FLOATS AND BALLOONS ARE SPONSORED BY LOCAL GOTHAM BUSINESSES. AND HERE COMES OUR FIRST ONE!
IT'S FUNDED FROM A PRIVATE DONATION. AND PROBABLY OUR MOST RECOGNIZABLE ONE IN THIS CITY...

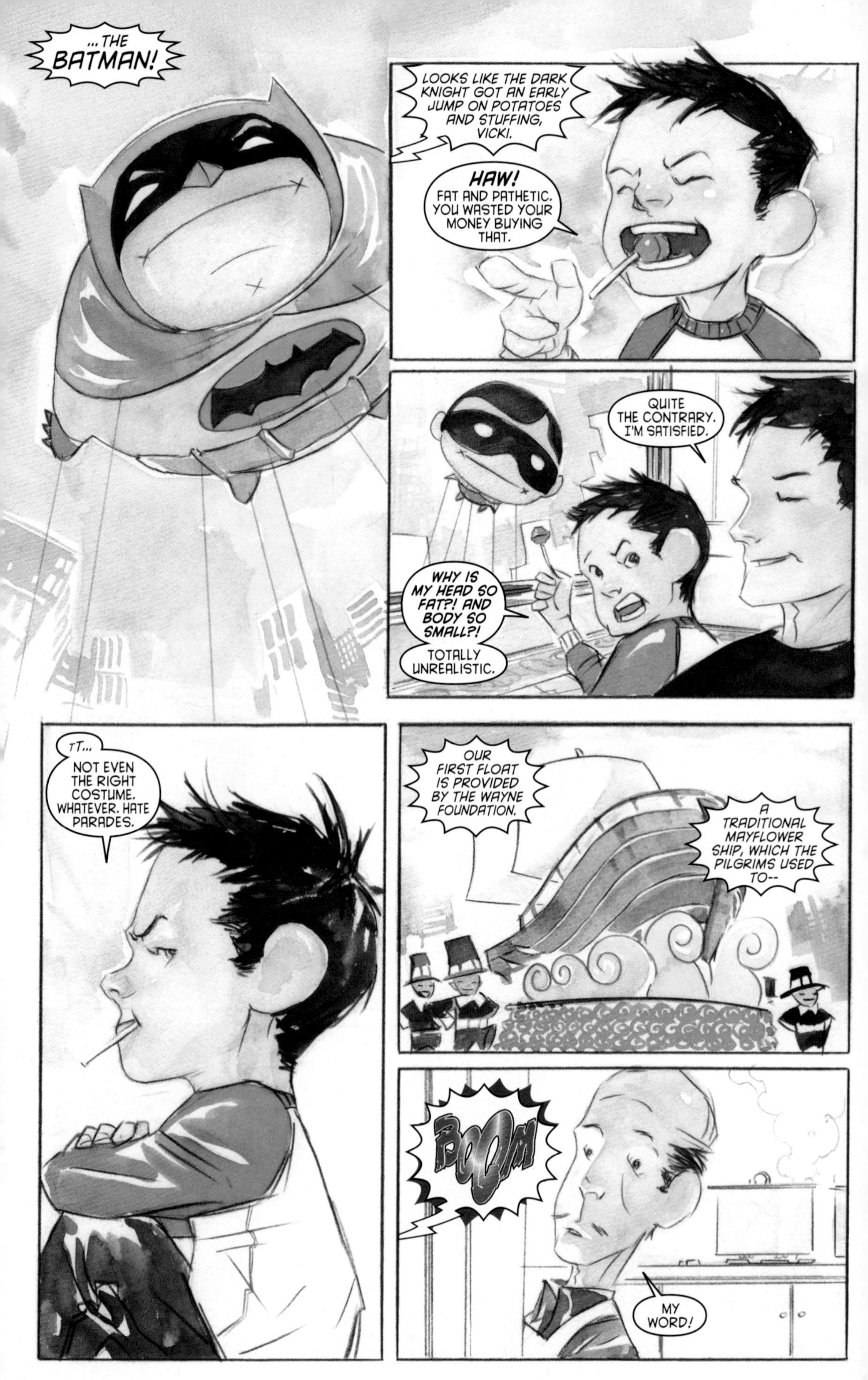
...THE BATMAN!
LOOKS LIKE THE DARK KNIGHT GOT AN EARLY JUMP ON POTATOES AND STUFFING, VICKI.
HAW! FAT AND PATHETIC. YOU WASTED YOUR MONEY BUYING THAT.
QUITE THE CONTRARY. I'M SATISFIED.
WHY IS MY HEAD SO FAT?! AND BODY SO SMALL?!
TOTALLY UNREALISTIC.
TT...
NOT EVEN THE RIGHT COSTUME. WHATEVER. HATE PARADES.
OUR FIRST FLOAT IS PROVIDED BY THE WAYNE FOUNDATION.
A TRADITIONAL MAYFLOWER SHIP, WHICH THE PILGRIMS USED TO--
BOOM
MY WORD!

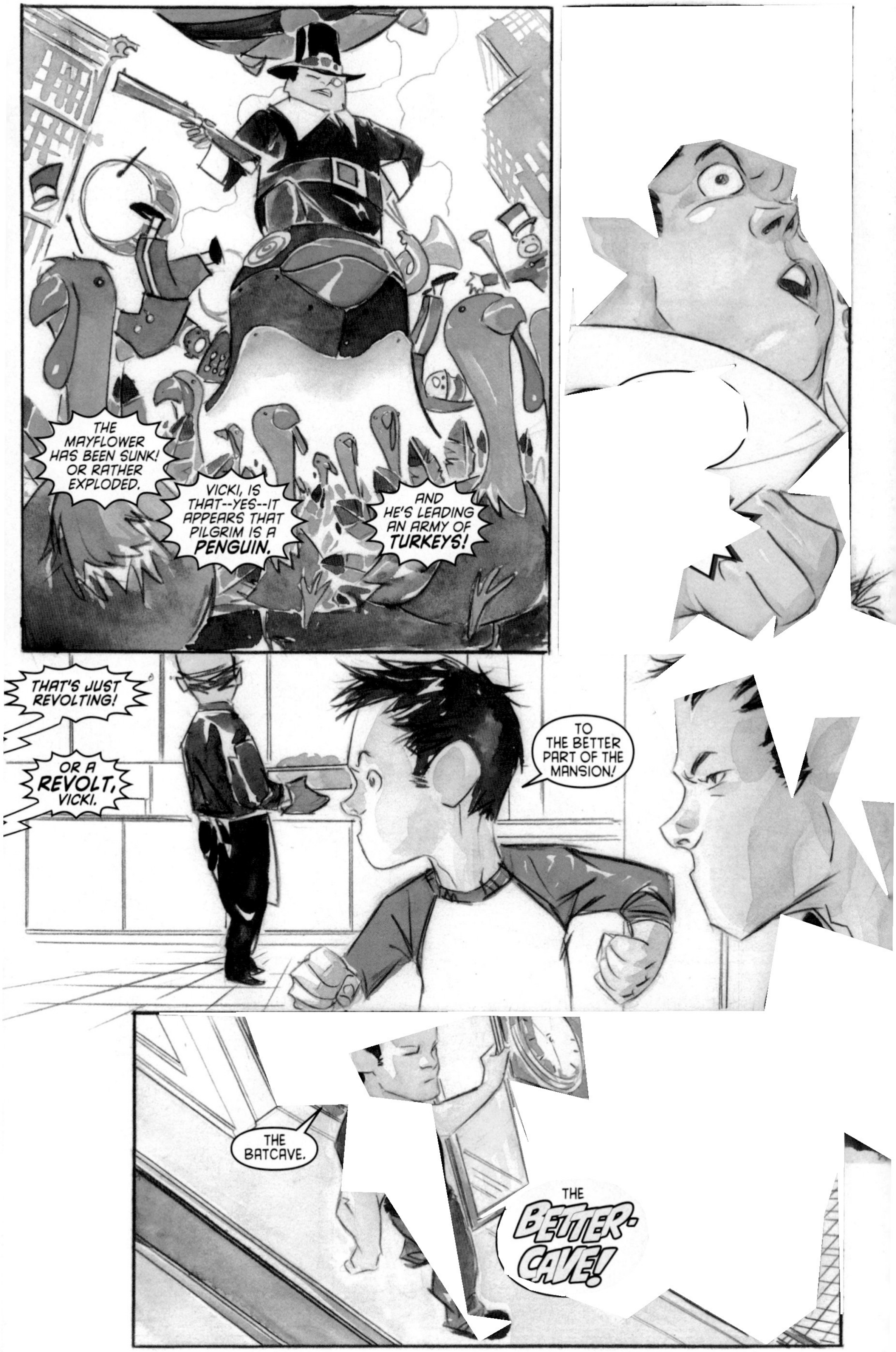
THE MAYFLOWER HAS BEEN SUNK! OR RATHER EXPLODED.
VICKI, IS THAT--YES--IT APPEARS THAT PILGRIM IS A PENGUIN.
AND HE'S LEADING AN ARMY OF TURKEYS!
THAT'S JUST REVOLTING!
OR A REVOLT, VICKI.
TO THE BETTER PART OF THE MANSION!
THE BATCAVE.
THE BETTER-CAVE!

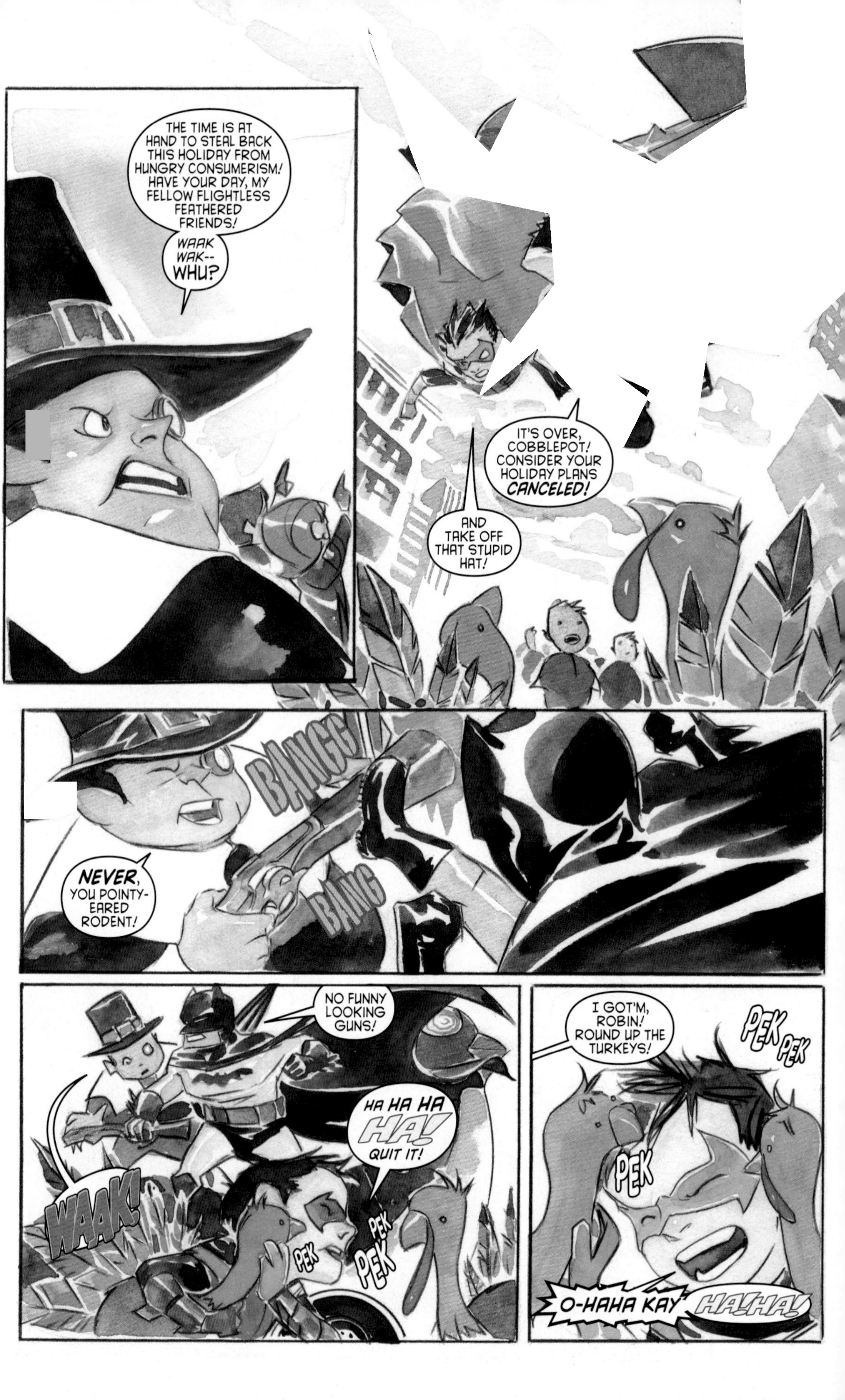
THE TIME IS AT HAND TO STEAL BACK THIS HOLIDAY FROM HUNGRY CONSUMERISM! HAVE YOUR DAY, MY FELLOW FLIGHTLESS FEATHERED FRIENDS!
WAAK WAK-- WHU?
IT'S OVER, COBBLEPOT! CONSIDER YOUR HOLIDAY PLANS CANCELED!
AND TAKE OFF THAT STUPID HAT!
BANGG
BANG
NEVER, YOU POINTY-EARED RODENT!
NO FUNNY LOOKING GUNS!
HA HA HA HA!
QUIT IT!
WAAK!
PEK
PEK PEK
I GOT'M, ROBIN! ROUND UP THE TURKEYS!
PEK PEK
PEK
O-HAHA KAY
HA!HA!

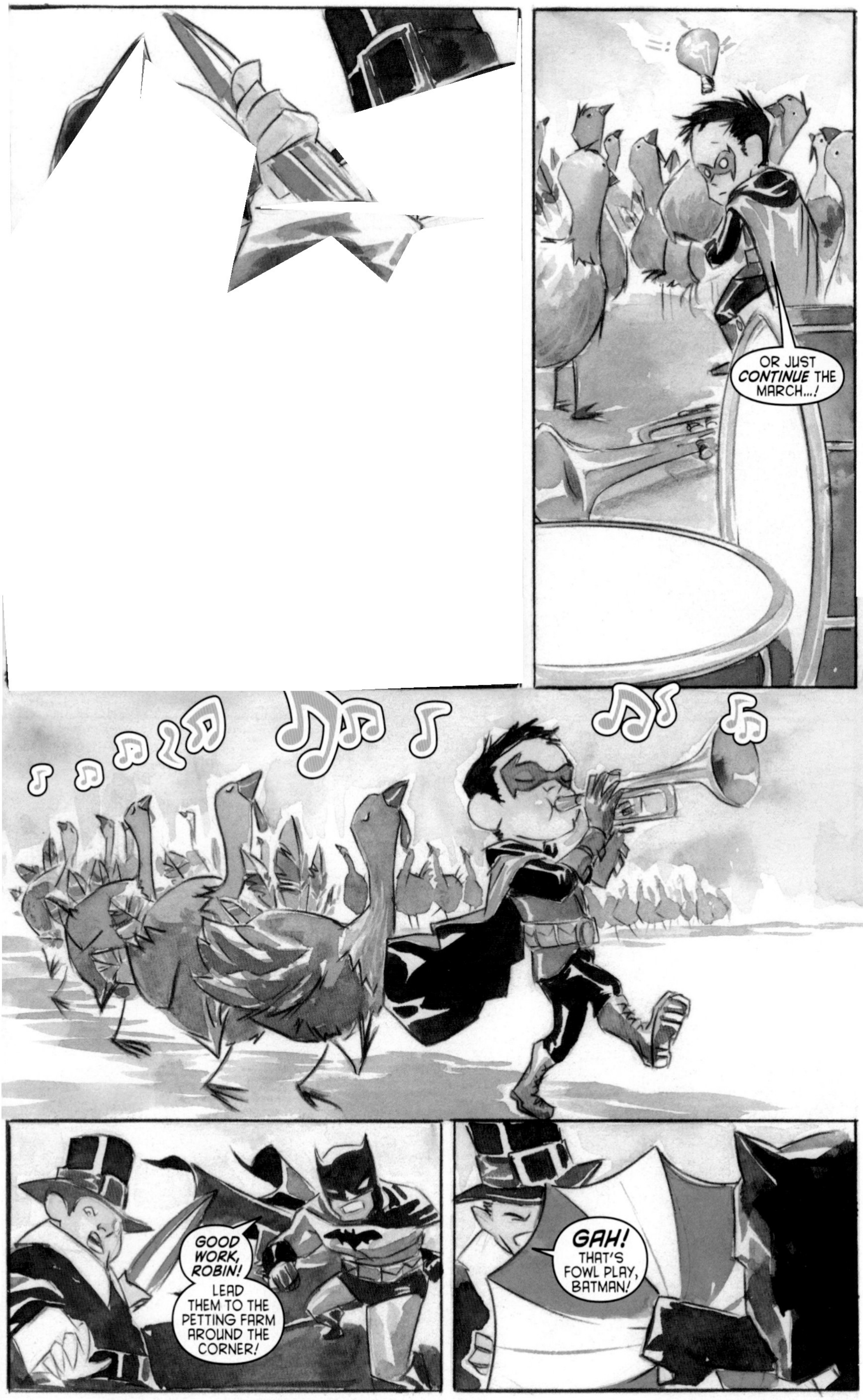
OR JUST CONTINUE THE MARCH...!
GOOD WORK, ROBIN!
LEAD THEM TO THE PETTING FARM AROUND THE CORNER!
GAH!
THAT'S FOWL PLAY, BATMAN!

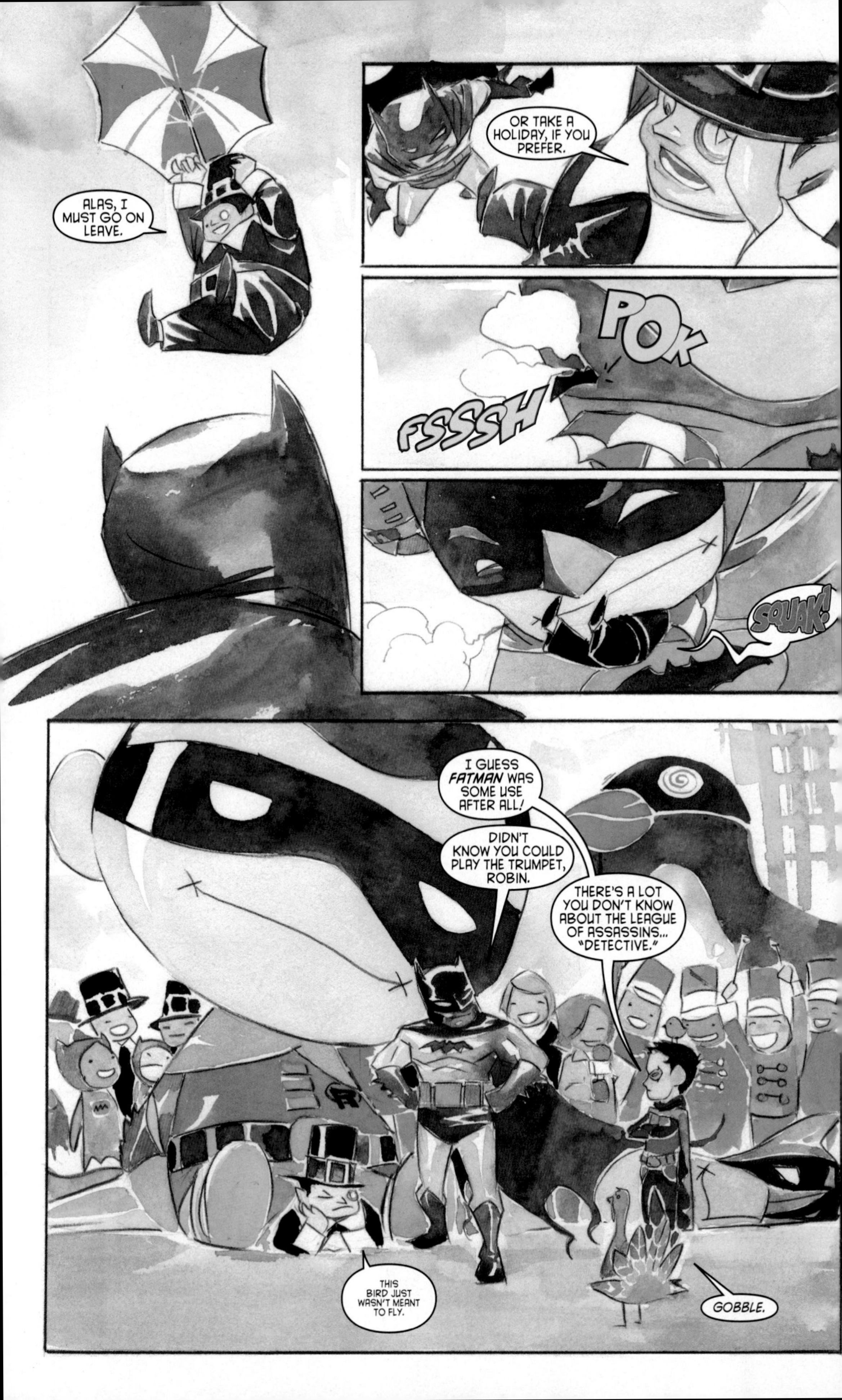
ALAS, I MUST GO ON LEAVE.
OR TAKE A HOLIDAY, IF YOU PREFER.
POK
FSSSH
SQUAK!
I GUESS FATMAN WAS SOME USE AFTER ALL!
DIDN'T KNOW YOU COULD PLAY THE TRUMPET, ROBIN.
THERE'S A LOT YOU DON'T KNOW ABOUT THE LEAGUE OF ASSASSINS... "DETECTIVE."
THIS BIRD JUST WASN'T MEANT TO FLY.
GOBBLE.

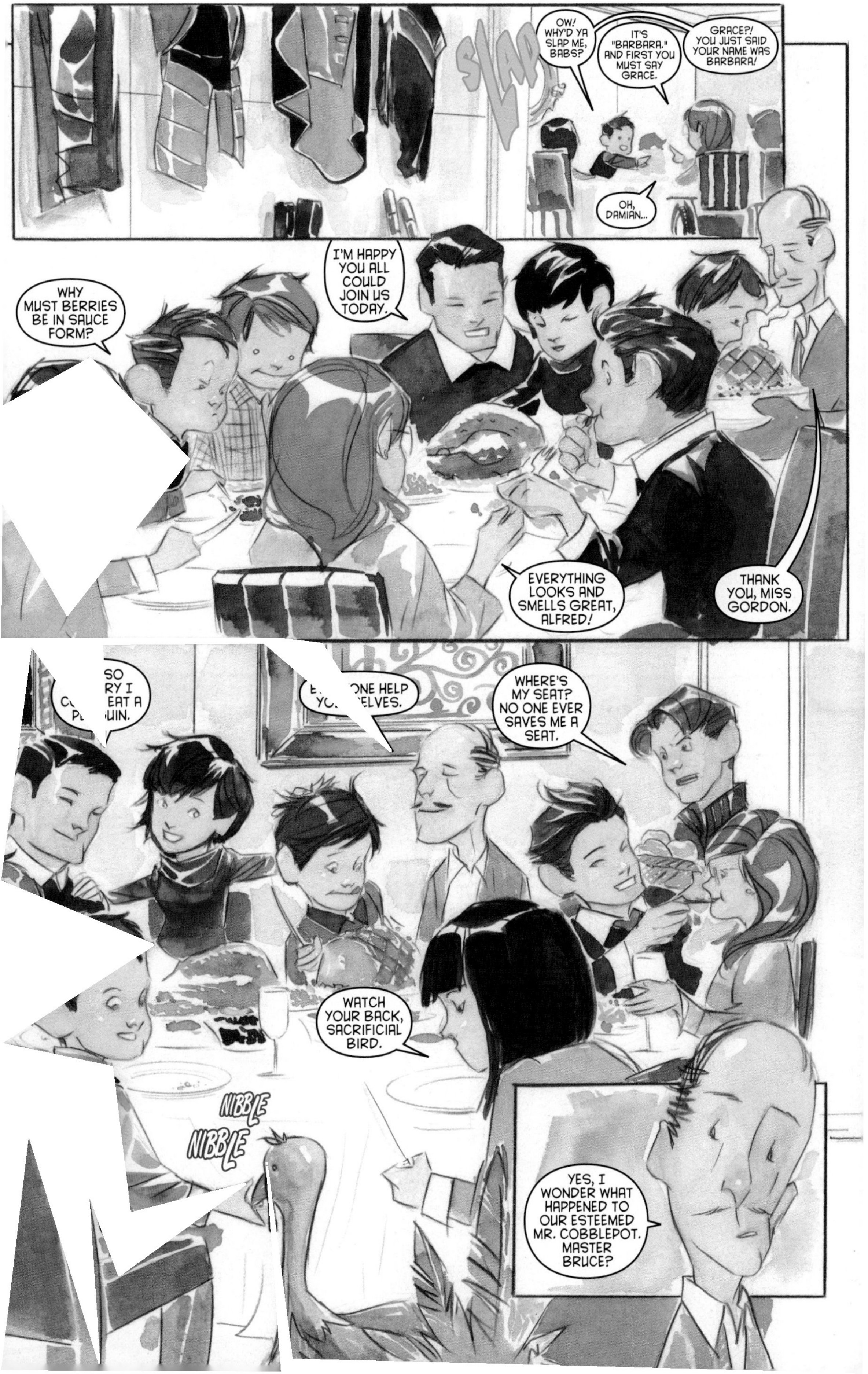
SLAP
OW! WHY'D YA SLAP ME, BABS?
IT'S "BARBARA." AND FIRST YOU MUST SAY GRACE.
GRACE?! YOU JUST SAID YOUR NAME WAS BARBARA!
OH, DAMIAN...
WHY MUST BERRIES BE IN SAUCE FORM?
I'M HAPPY YOU ALL COULD JOIN US TODAY.
EVERYTHING LOOKS AND SMELLS GREAT, ALFRED!
THANK YOU, MISS GORDON.
WHERE'S MY SEAT? NO ONE EVER SAVES ME A SEAT.
WATCH YOUR BACK, SACRIFICIAL BIRD.
NIBBLE
NIBBLE
YES, I WONDER WHAT HAPPENED TO OUR ESTEEMED MR. COBBLEPOT. MASTER BRUCE?

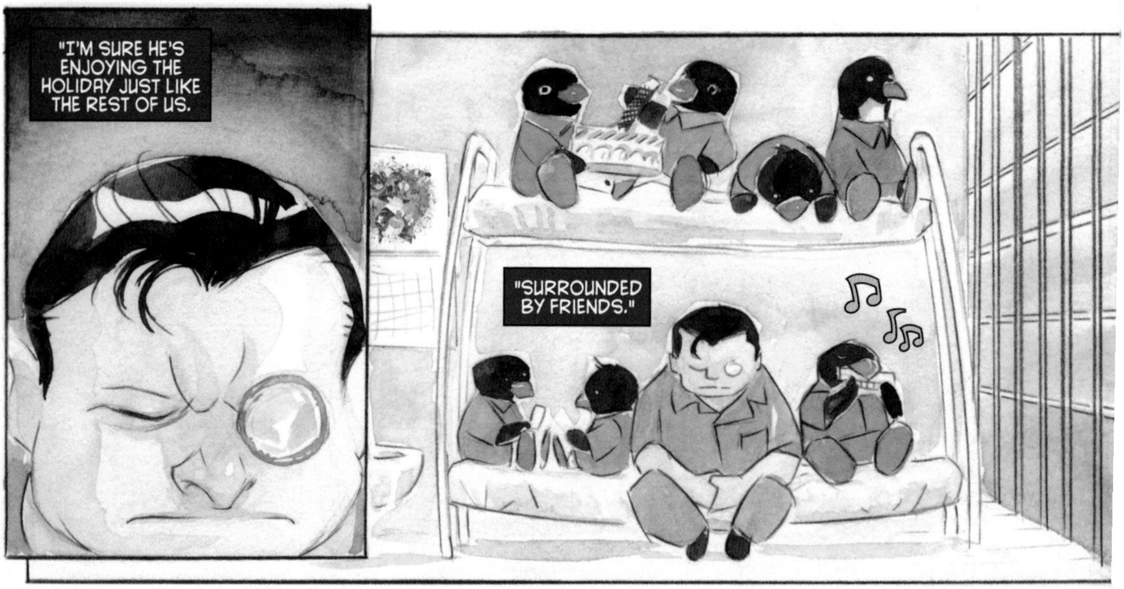
"I'M SURE HE'S ENJOYING THE HOLIDAY JUST LIKE THE REST OF US.
"SURROUNDED BY FRIENDS."

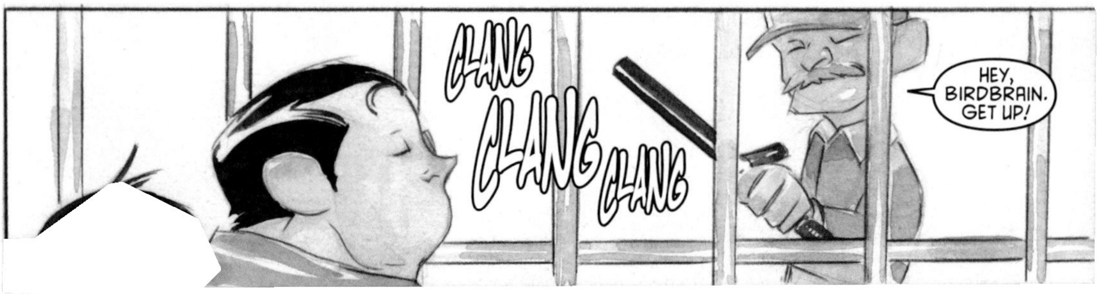
CLANG
CLANG
CLANG
HEY, BIRDBRAIN. GET UP!

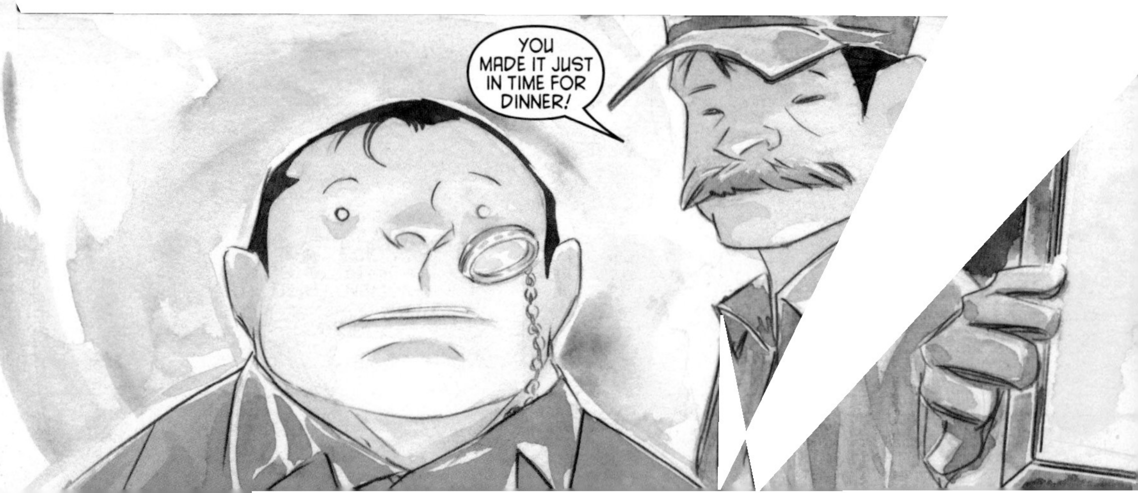
YOU MADE IT JUST IN TIME FOR DINNER!

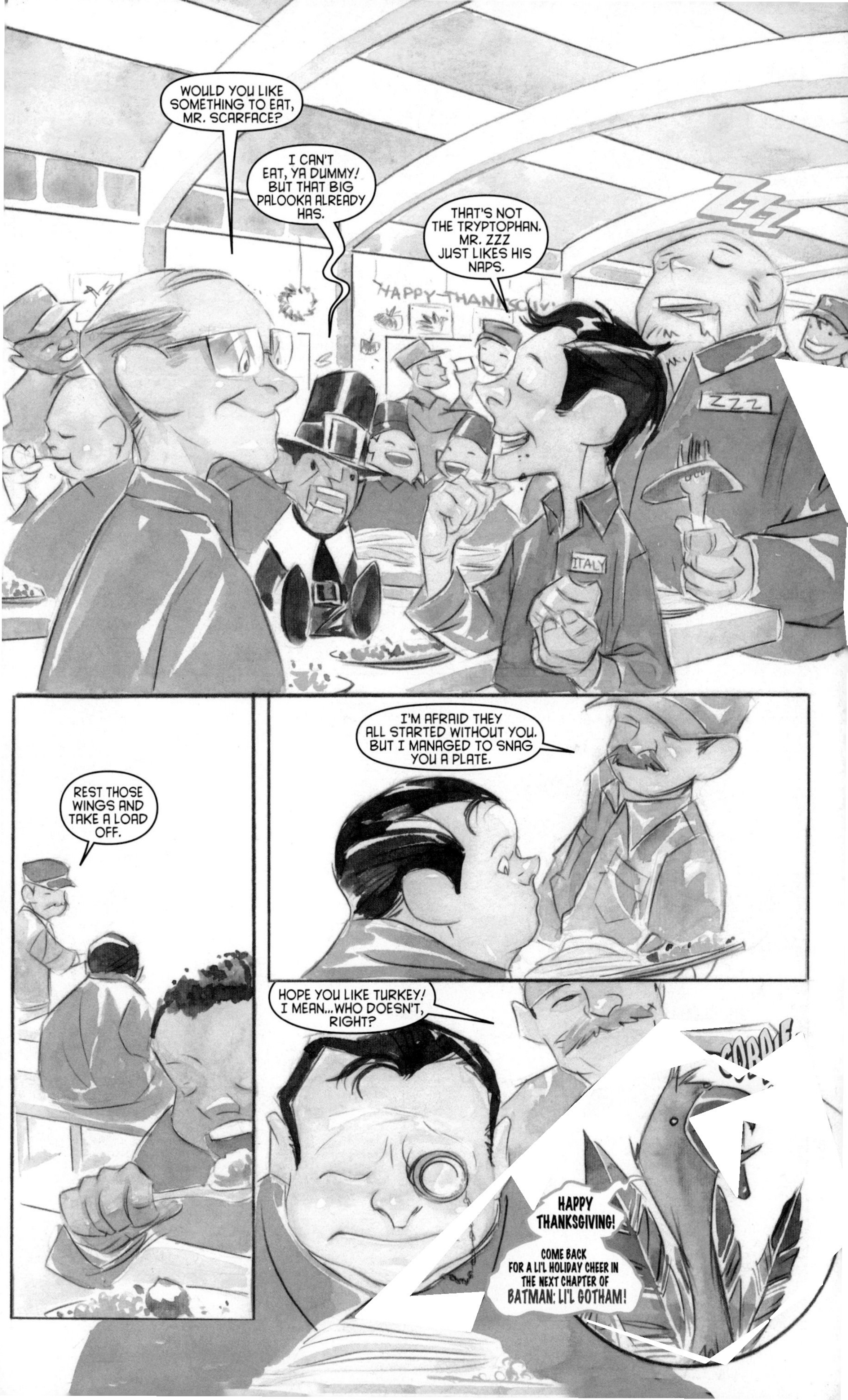
WOULD YOU LIKE SOMETHING TO EAT, MR. SCARFACE?
I CAN'T EAT, YA DUMMY! BUT THAT BIG PALOOKA ALREADY HAS.
THAT'S NOT THE TRYPTOPHAN. MR. ZZZ JUST LIKES HIS NAPS.
ZZZ
HAPPY THANKSGIV...
ZZZ
ITALY
REST THOSE WINGS AND TAKE A LOAD OFF.
I'M AFRAID THEY ALL STARTED WITHOUT YOU. BUT I MANAGED TO SNAG YOU A PLATE.
HOPE YOU LIKE TURKEY! I MEAN...WHO DOESN'T, RIGHT?
HAPPY THANKSGIVING!
COME BACK FOR A LI'L HOLIDAY CHEER IN THE NEXT CHAPTER OF BATMAN: LI'L GOTHAM!

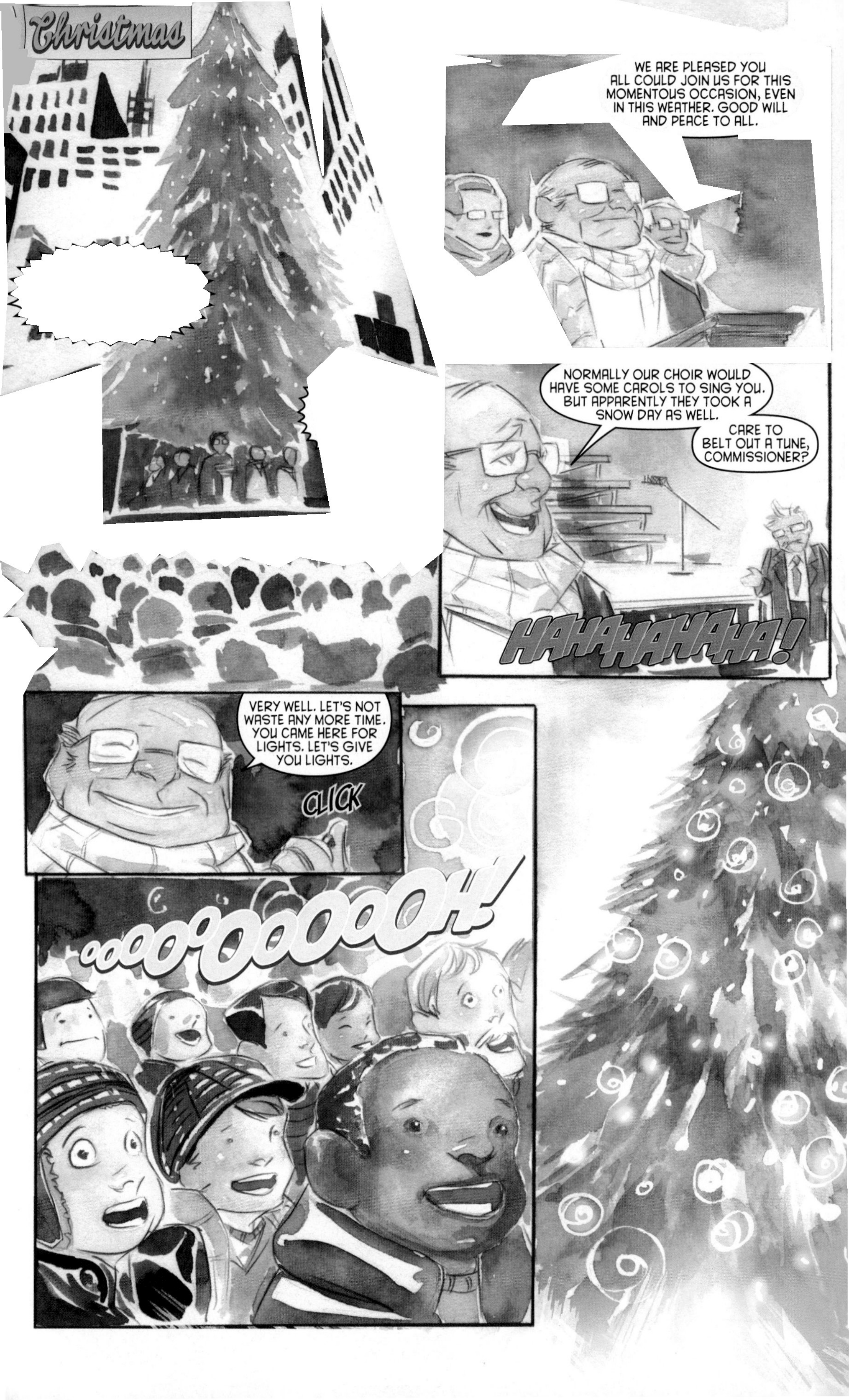
Christmas
WE ARE PLEASED YOU ALL COULD JOIN US FOR THIS MOMENTOUS OCCASION, EVEN IN THIS WEATHER. GOOD WILL AND PEACE TO ALL.
NORMALLY OUR CHOIR WOULD HAVE SOME CAROLS TO SING YOU. BUT APPARENTLY THEY TOOK A SNOW DAY AS WELL.
CARE TO BELT OUT A TUNE, COMMISSIONER?
HAHAHAHAHAHA!
VERY WELL. LET'S NOT WASTE ANY MORE TIME. YOU CAME HERE FOR LIGHTS. LET'S GIVE YOU LIGHTS.
CLICK
oooOoOOOOOOH!

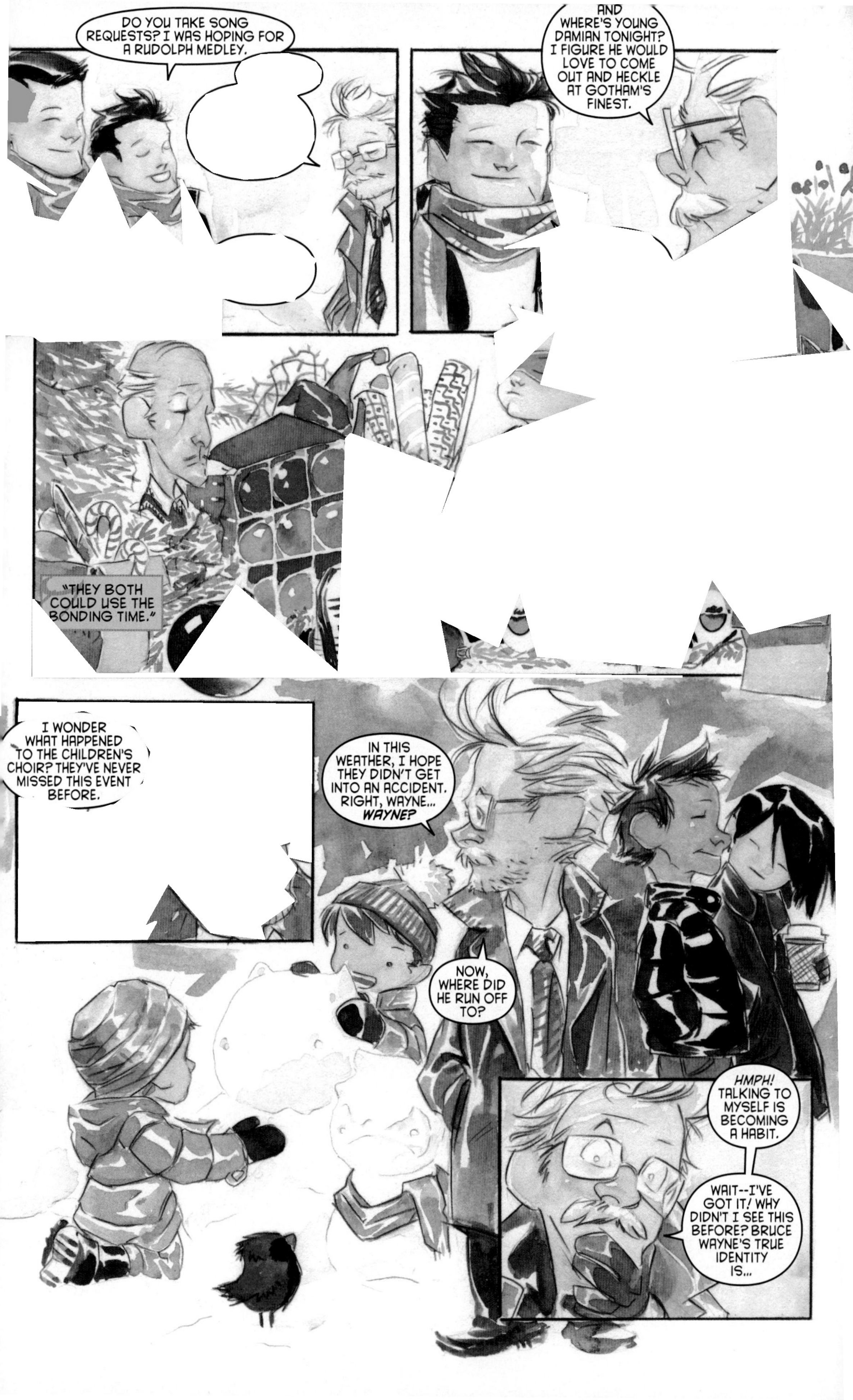
DO YOU TAKE SONG REQUESTS? I WAS HOPING FOR A RUDOLPH MEDLEY.
AND WHERE'S YOUNG DAMIAN TONIGHT? I FIGURE HE WOULD LOVE TO COME OUT AND HECKLE AT GOTHAM'S FINEST.
"THEY BOTH COULD USE THE BONDING TIME."
I WONDER WHAT HAPPENED TO THE CHILDREN'S CHOIR? THEY'VE NEVER MISSED THIS EVENT BEFORE.
IN THIS WEATHER, I HOPE THEY DIDN'T GET INTO AN ACCIDENT. RIGHT, WAYNE... WAYNE?
NOW, WHERE DID HE RUN OFF TO?
HMPH! TALKING TO MYSELF IS BECOMING A HABIT.
WAIT--I'VE GOT IT! WHY DIDN'T I SEE THIS BEFORE? BRUCE WAYNE'S TRUE IDENTITY IS...

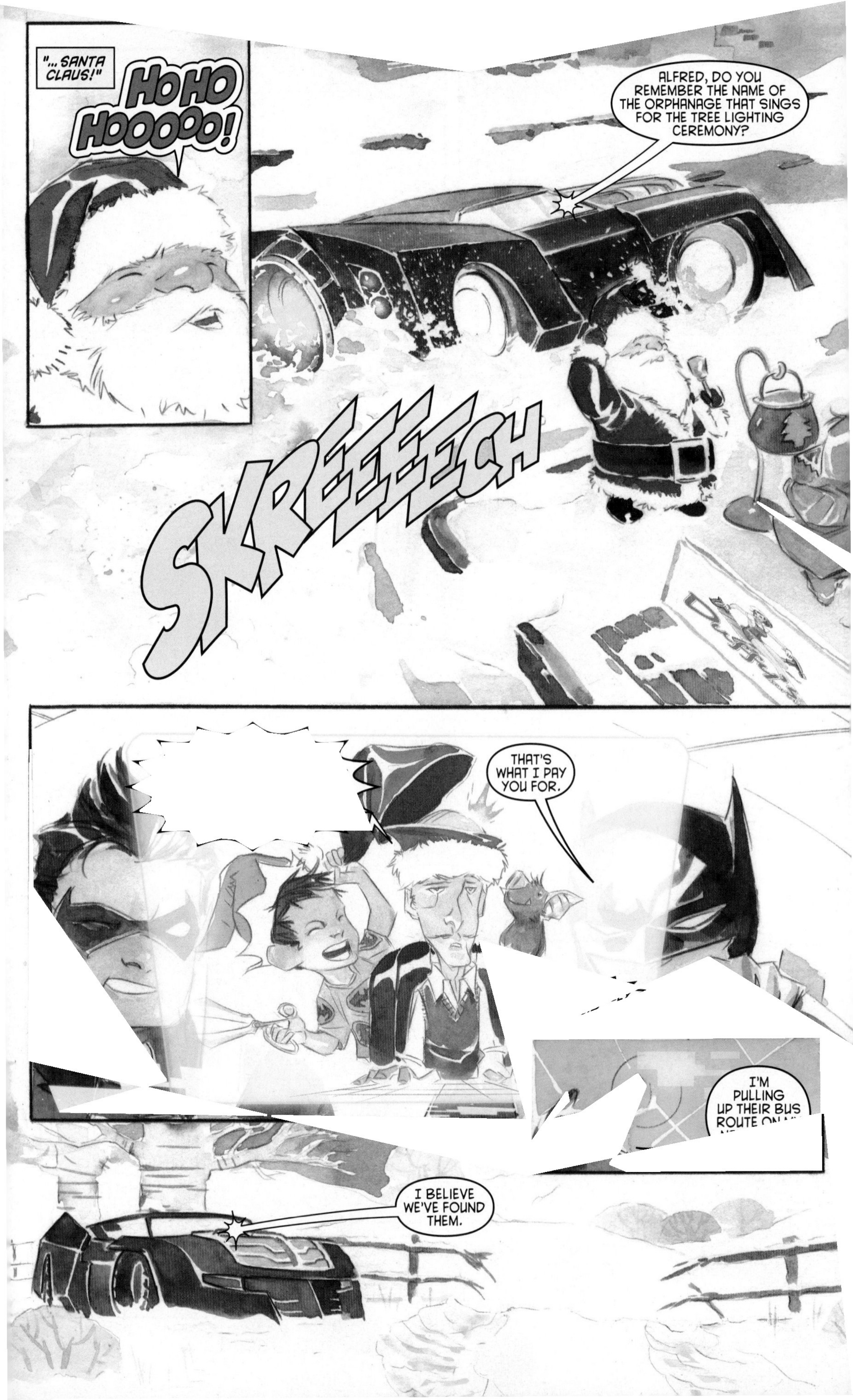
"... SANTA CLAUS!"
HO HO HOOOOOO!
ALFRED, DO YOU REMEMBER THE NAME OF THE ORPHANAGE THAT SINGS FOR THE TREE LIGHTING CEREMONY?
SKREEEECH
THAT'S WHAT I PAY YOU FOR.
I'M PULLING UP THEIR BUS ROUTE
I BELIEVE WE'VE FOUND THEM.

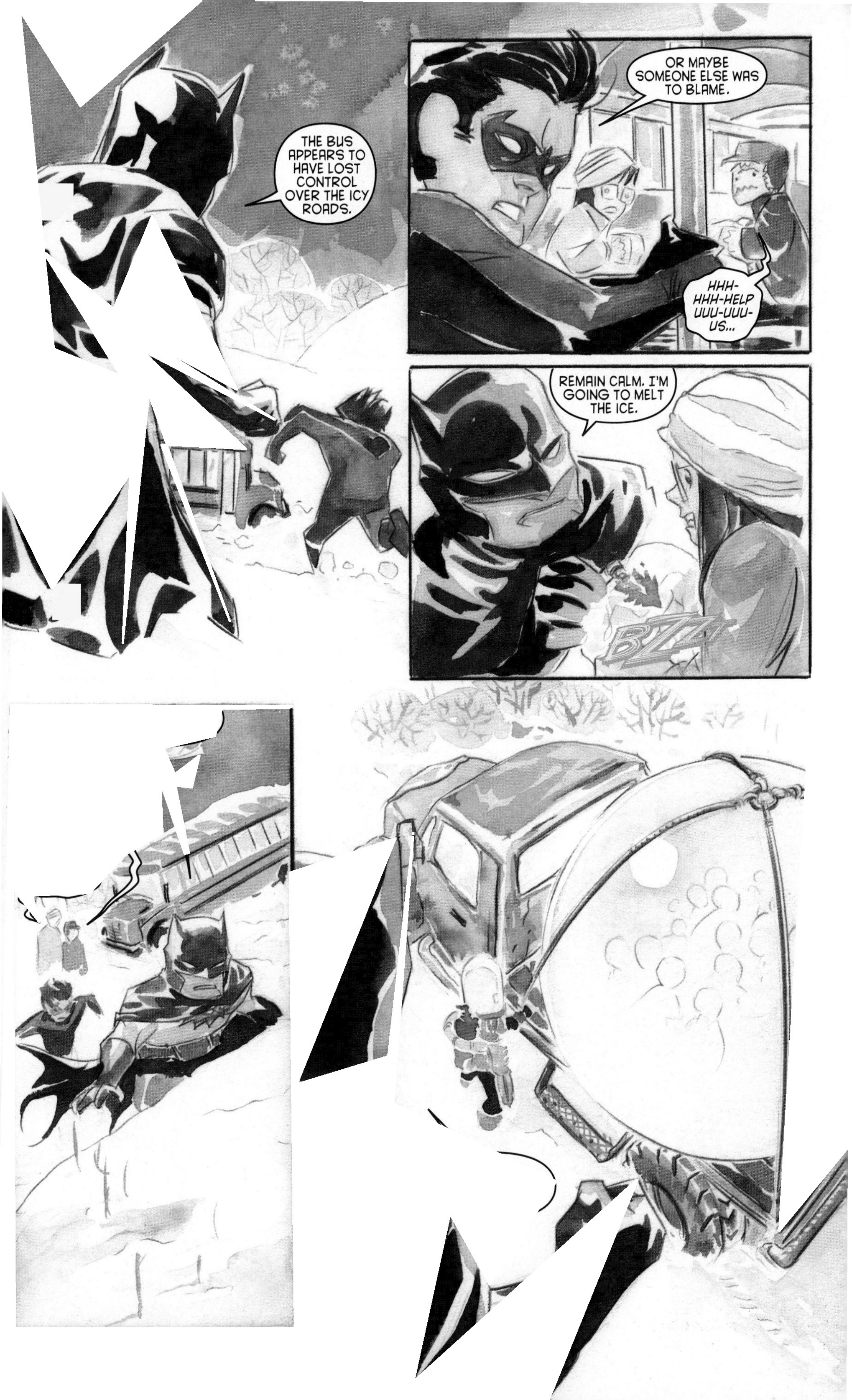
THE BUS APPEARS TO HAVE LOST CONTROL OVER THE ICY ROADS.
OR MAYBE SOMEONE ELSE WAS TO BLAME.
HHH-HHH-HELP UUU-UUU-US...
REMAIN CALM. I'M GOING TO MELT THE ICE.
BZZT

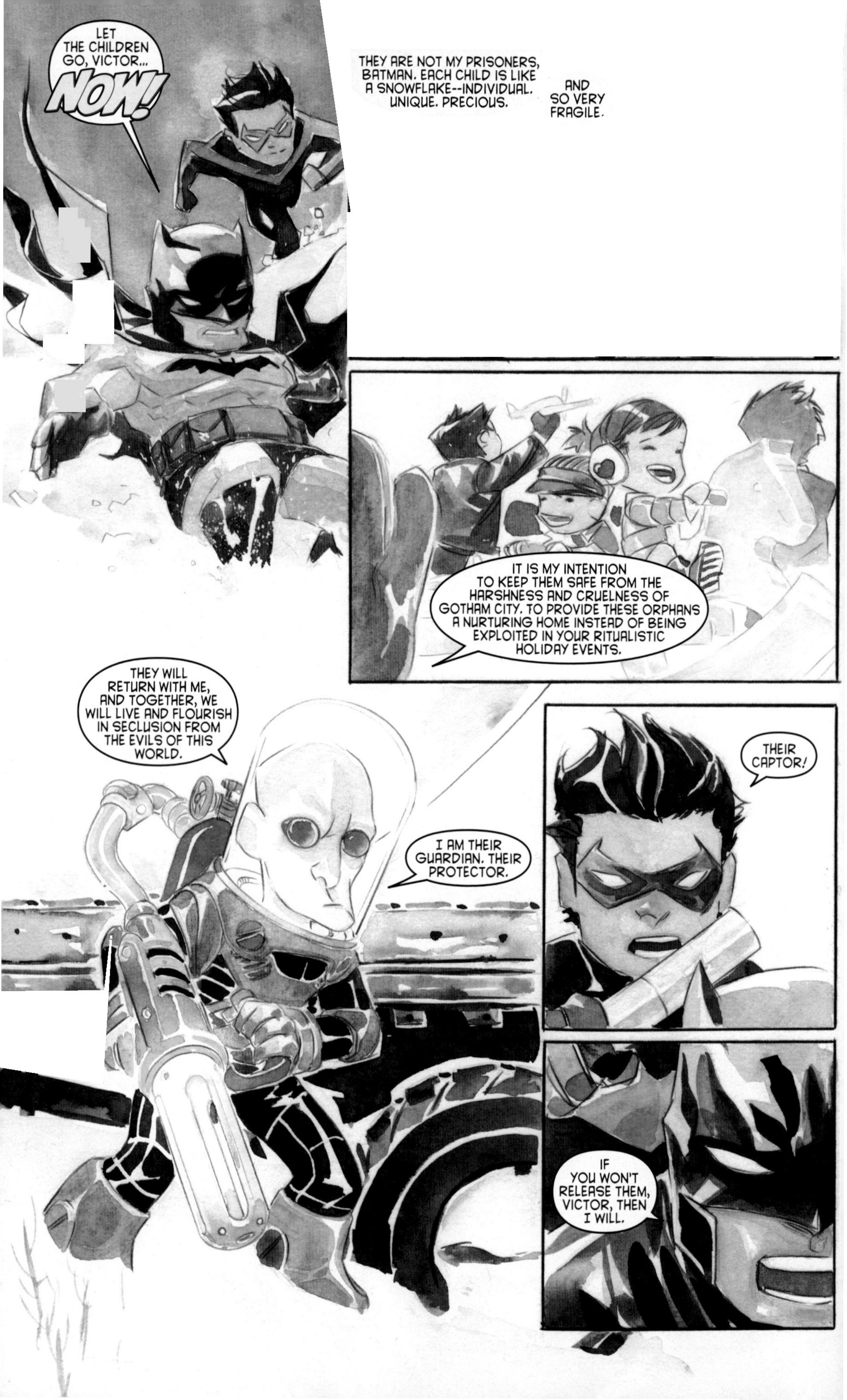
LET THE CHILDREN GO, VICTOR... NOW!
THEY ARE NOT MY PRISONERS, BATMAN. EACH CHILD IS LIKE A SNOWFLAKE--INDIVIDUAL. UNIQUE. PRECIOUS.
AND SO VERY FRAGILE.
IT IS MY INTENTION TO KEEP THEM SAFE FROM THE HARSHNESS AND CRUELNESS OF GOTHAM CITY. TO PROVIDE THESE ORPHANS A NURTURING HOME INSTEAD OF BEING EXPLOITED IN YOUR RITUALISTIC HOLIDAY EVENTS.
THEY WILL RETURN WITH ME, AND TOGETHER, WE WILL LIVE AND FLOURISH IN SECLUSION FROM THE EVILS OF THIS WORLD.
THEIR CAPTOR!
I AM THEIR GUARDIAN. THEIR PROTECTOR.
IF YOU WON'T RELEASE THEM, VICTOR, THEN I WILL.

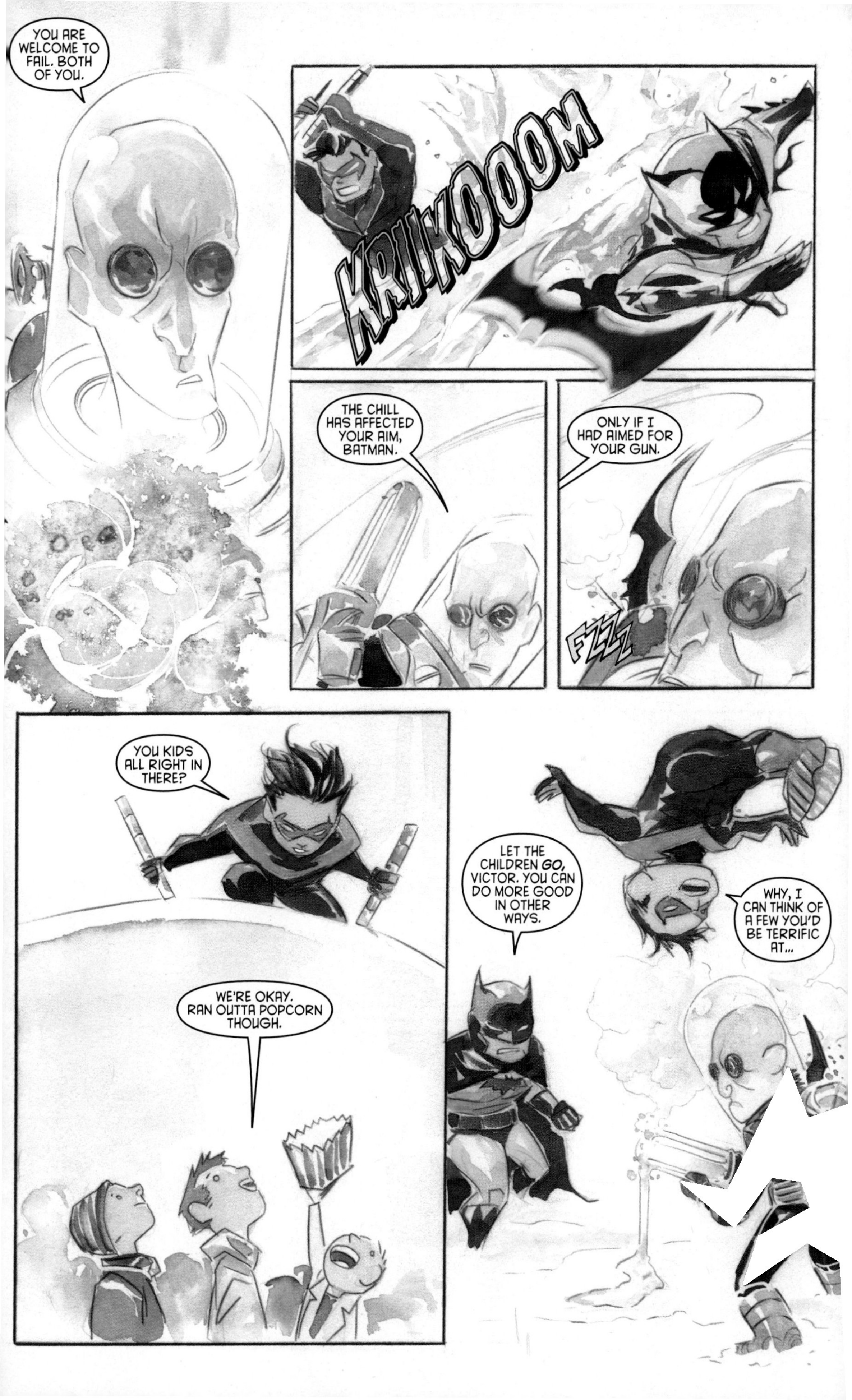
YOU ARE WELCOME TO FAIL. BOTH OF YOU.
KRIIKOOOM
THE CHILL HAS AFFECTED YOUR AIM, BATMAN.
ONLY IF I HAD AIMED FOR YOUR GUN.
FZZZ
YOU KIDS ALL RIGHT IN THERE?
WE'RE OKAY. RAN OUTTA POPCORN THOUGH.
LET THE CHILDREN GO, VICTOR. YOU CAN DO MORE GOOD IN OTHER WAYS.
WHY, I CAN THINK OF A FEW YOU'D BE TERRIFIC AT...

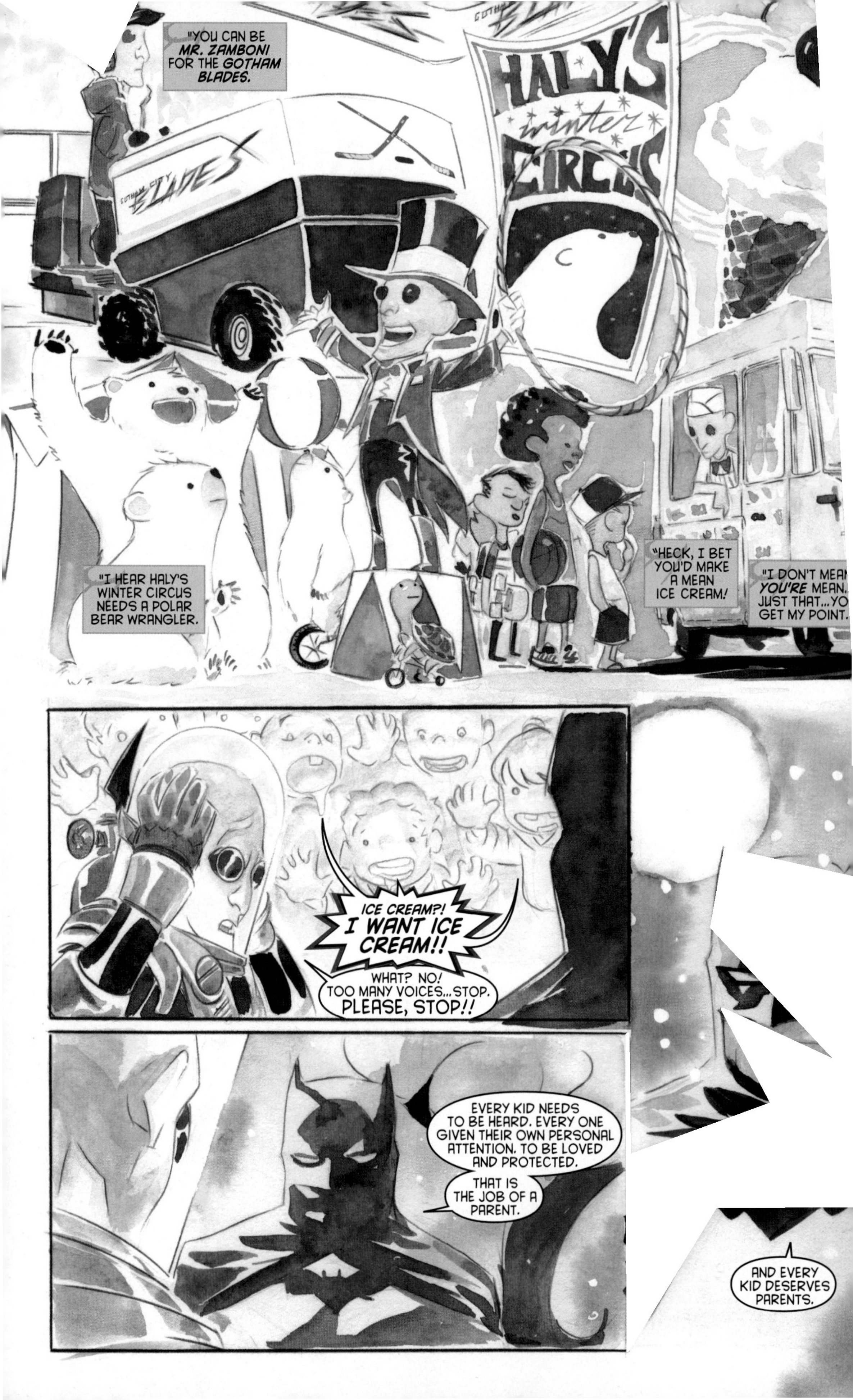

"YOU CAN BE *MR. ZAMBONI* FOR THE *GOTHAM BLADES.*
GOTHAM CITY BLADES
HALY'S winter CIRCUS
"I HEAR HALY'S WINTER CIRCUS NEEDS A POLAR BEAR WRANGLER.
"HECK, I BET YOU'D MAKE A MEAN ICE CREAM!
"I DON'T MEAN *YOU'RE* MEAN... JUST THAT...YO GET MY POINT.
ICE CREAM?! I WANT ICE CREAM!!
WHAT? NO! TOO MANY VOICES... STOP. PLEASE, STOP!!
EVERY KID NEEDS TO BE HEARD. EVERY ONE GIVEN THEIR OWN PERSONAL ATTENTION. TO BE LOVED AND PROTECTED.
THAT IS THE JOB OF A PARENT.
AND EVERY KID DESERVES PARENTS.

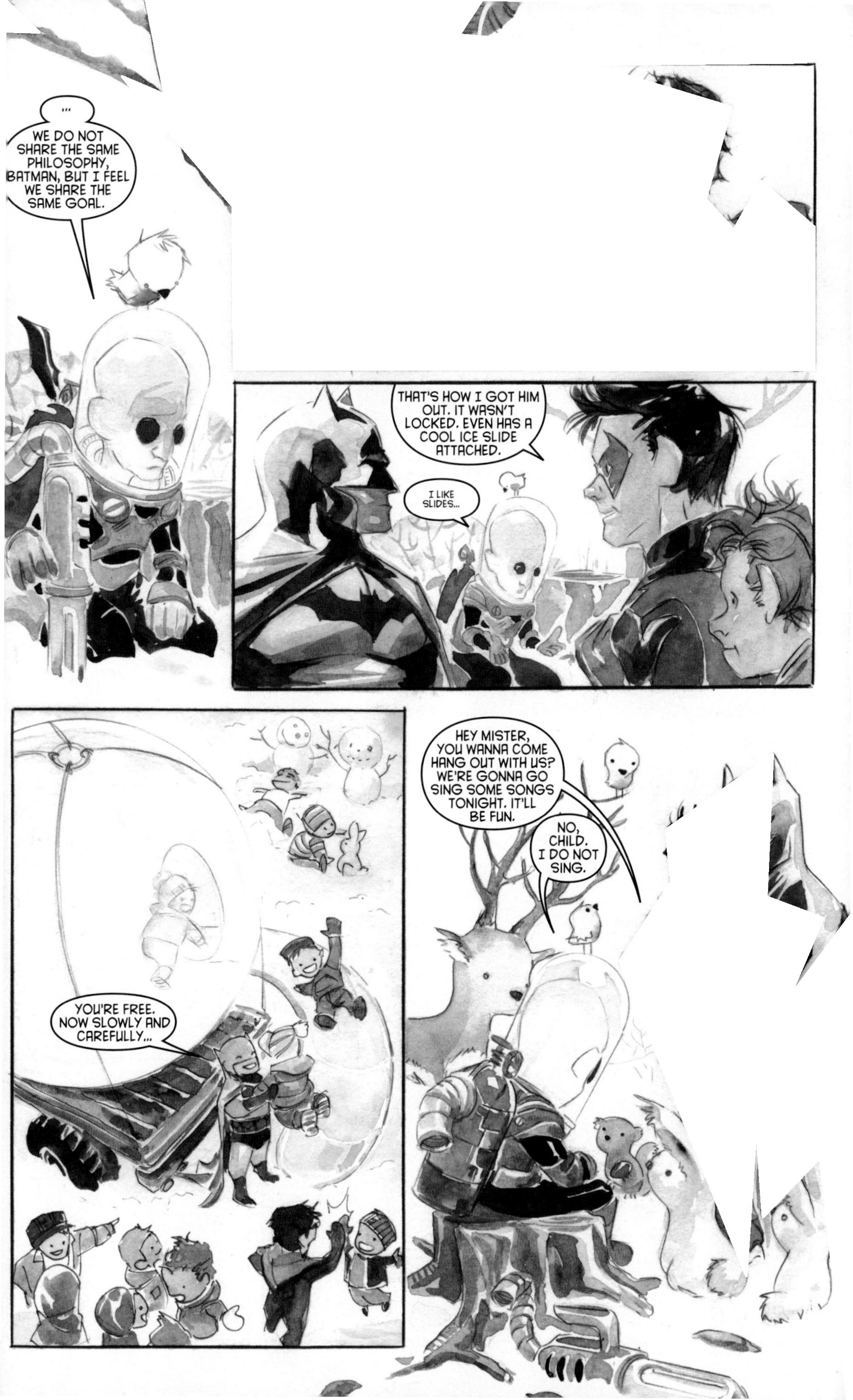
...
WE DO NOT SHARE THE SAME PHILOSOPHY, BATMAN, BUT I FEEL WE SHARE THE SAME GOAL.
THAT'S HOW I GOT HIM OUT. IT WASN'T LOCKED. EVEN HAS A COOL ICE SLIDE ATTACHED.
I LIKE SLIDES...
YOU'RE FREE. NOW SLOWLY AND CAREFULLY...
HEY MISTER, YOU WANNA COME HANG OUT WITH US? WE'RE GONNA GO SING SOME SONGS TONIGHT. IT'LL BE FUN.
NO, CHILD. I DO NOT SING.

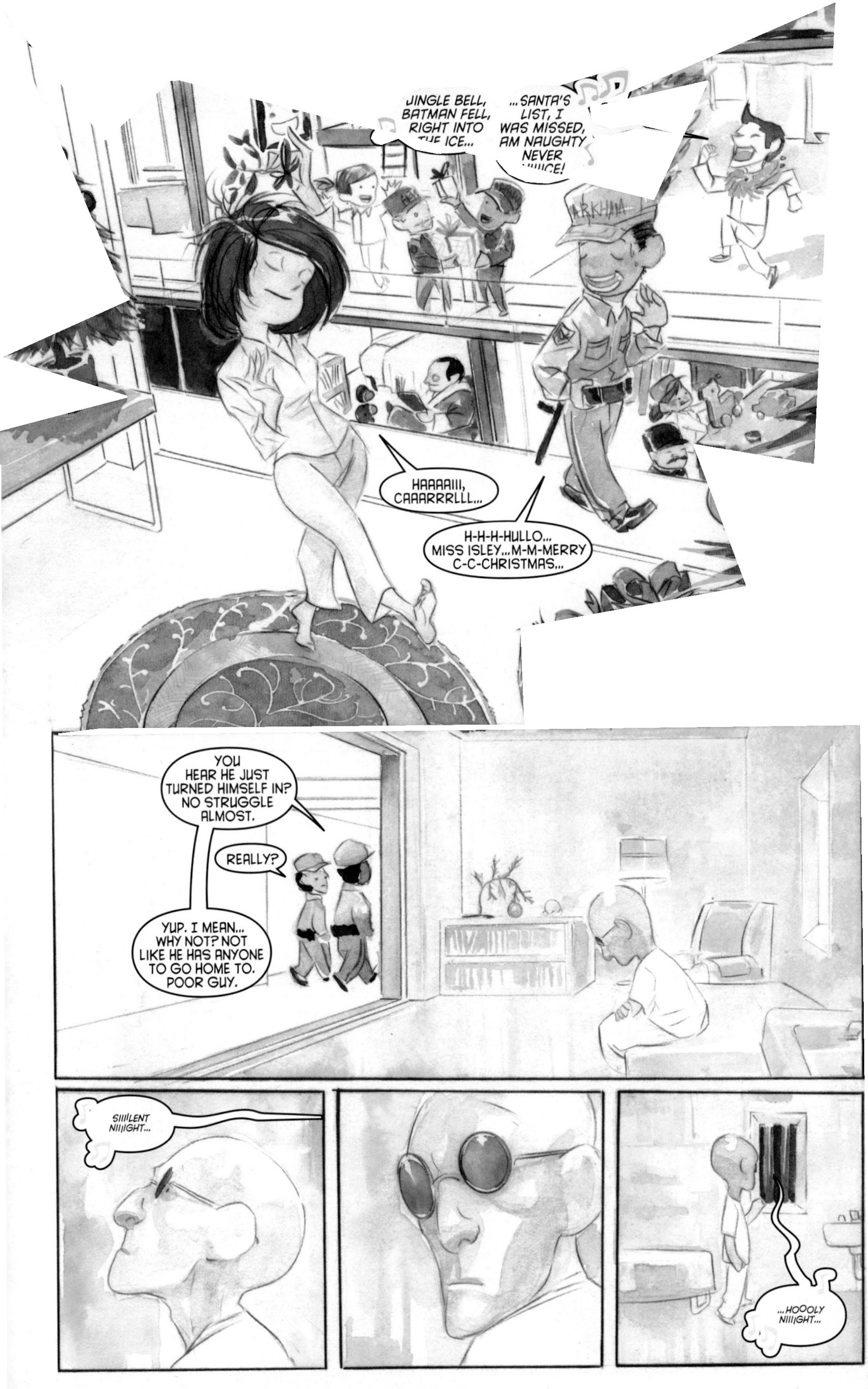
JINGLE BELL, BATMAN FELL, RIGHT INTO ICE...
...SANTA'S LIST, I WAS MISSED, AM NAUGHTY NEVER
HAAAAIII, CAAARRRLLL...
H-H-H-HULLO... MISS ISLEY...M-M-MERRY C-C-CHRISTMAS...
YOU HEAR HE JUST TURNED HIMSELF IN? NO STRUGGLE ALMOST.
REALLY?
YUP. I MEAN... WHY NOT? NOT LIKE HE HAS ANYONE TO GO HOME TO. POOR GUY.
SIIIILENT NIIIIGHT...
...HOOOLY NIIIIGHT...

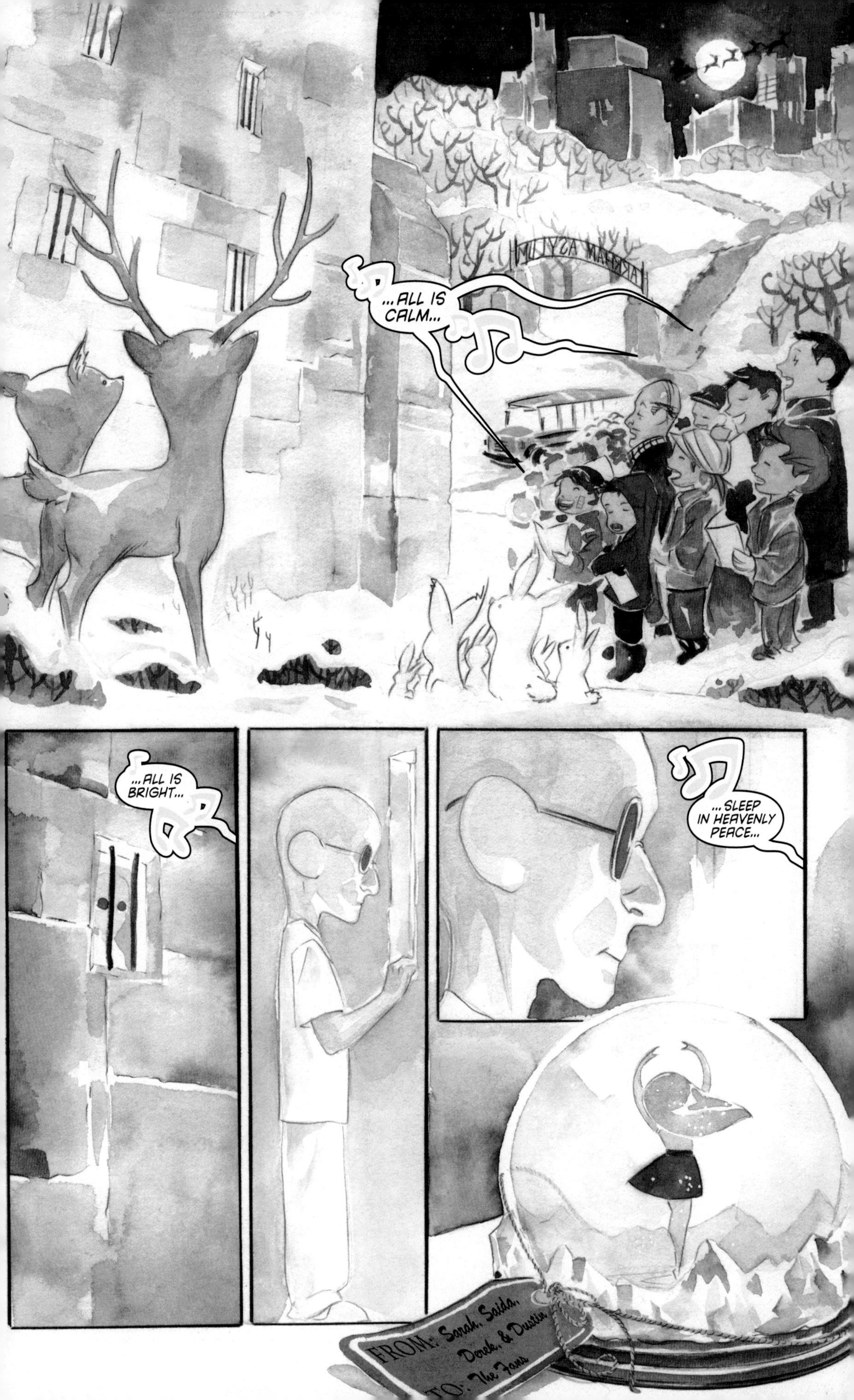
...ALL IS CALM...
...ALL IS BRIGHT...
...SLEEP IN HEAVENLY PEACE...
FROM: Sarah, Saida, Derek, & Dustin
TO: The Fans

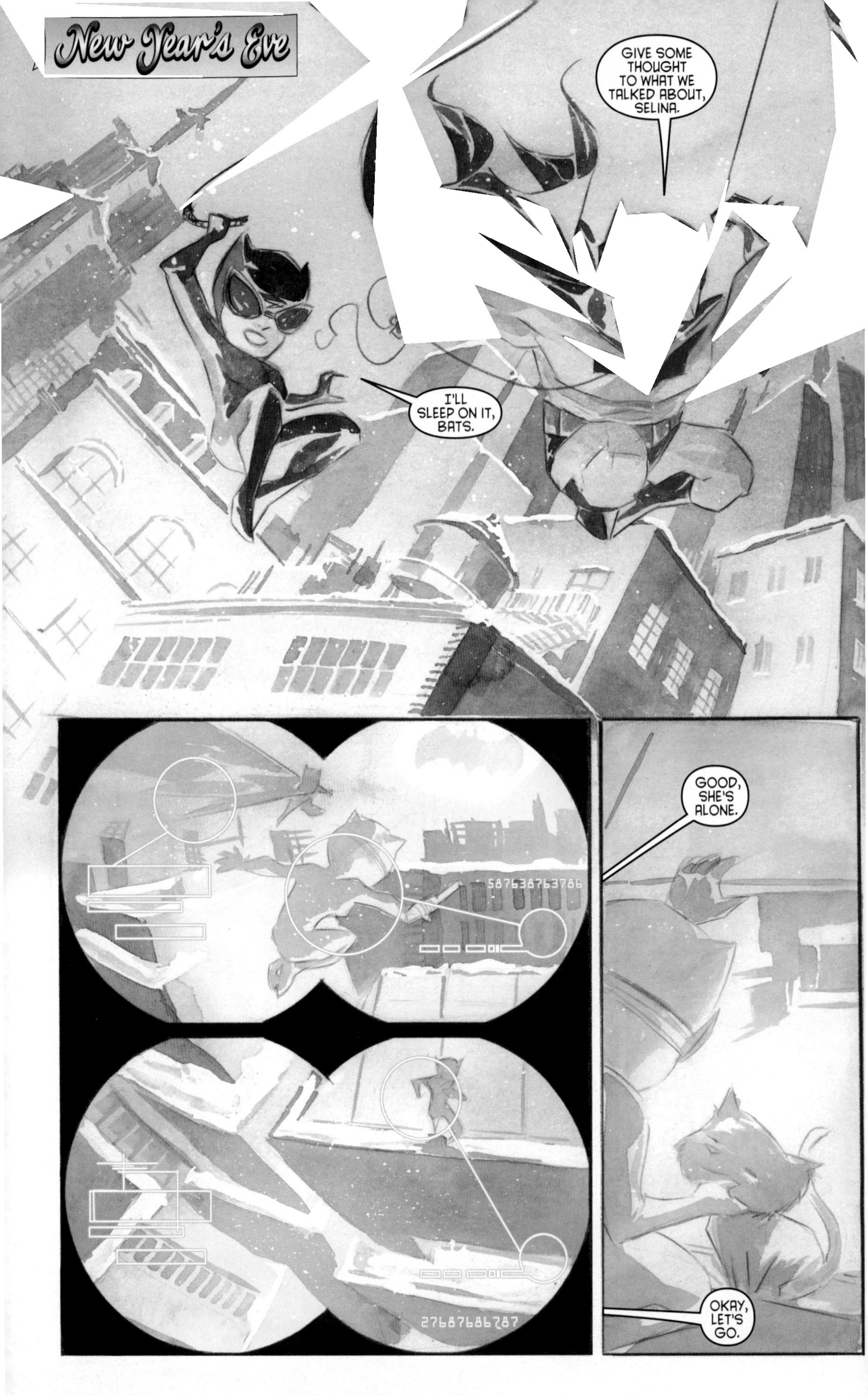

New Year's Eve
GIVE SOME THOUGHT TO WHAT WE TALKED ABOUT, SELINA.
I'LL SLEEP ON IT, BATS.
587638763786
27687686787
GOOD, SHE'S ALONE.
OKAY, LET'S GO.

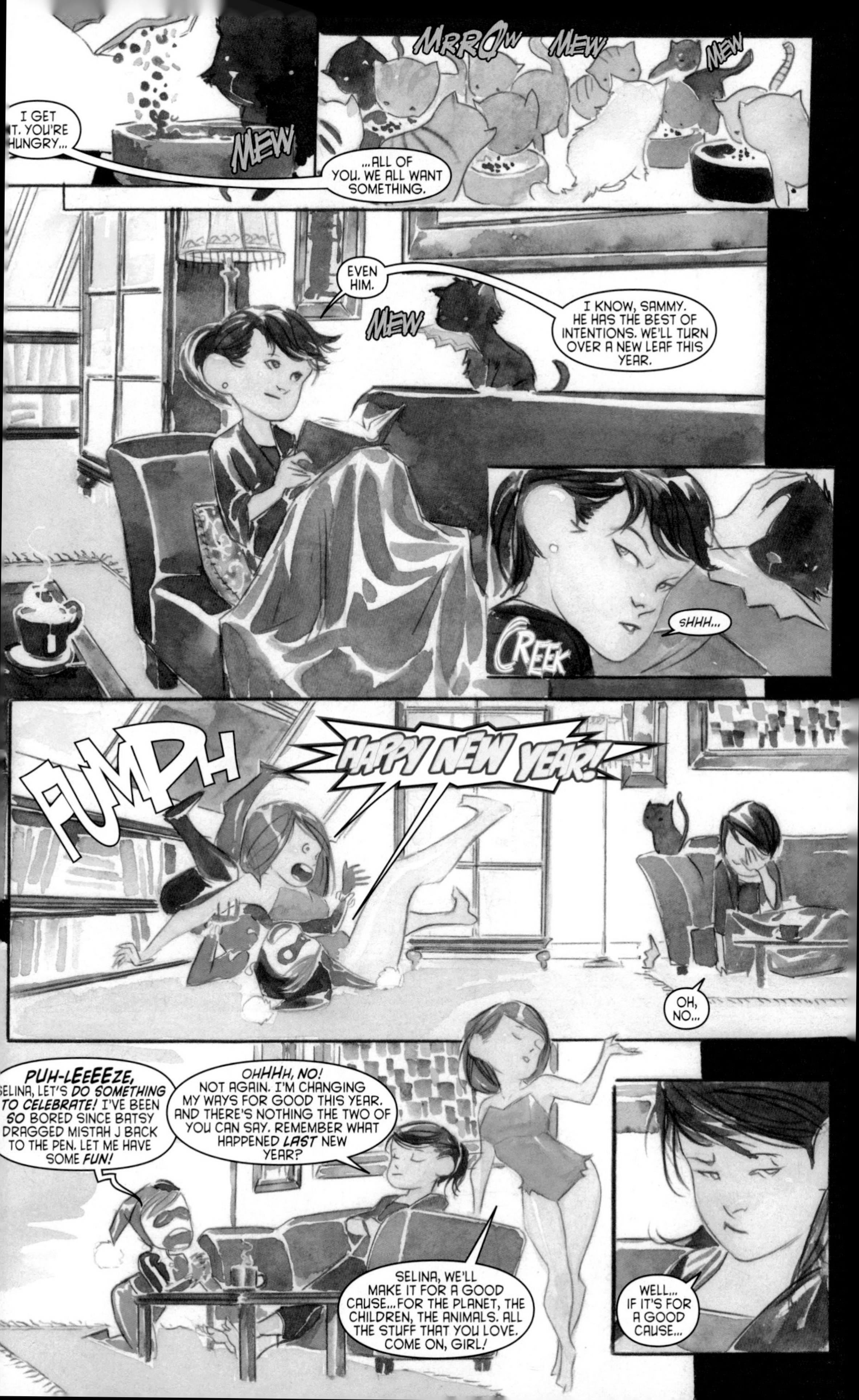

MRROW
MEW
MEW
I GET IT. YOU'RE HUNGRY...
MEW
...ALL OF YOU. WE ALL WANT SOMETHING.
EVEN HIM.
MEW
I KNOW, SAMMY. HE HAS THE BEST OF INTENTIONS. WE'LL TURN OVER A NEW LEAF THIS YEAR.
CREEK
SHHH...
FUMPH
HAPPY NEW YEAR!
OH, NO...
PUH-LEEEEZE, SELINA, LET'S DO SOMETHING TO CELEBRATE! I'VE BEEN SO BORED SINCE BATSY DRAGGED MISTAH J BACK TO THE PEN. LET ME HAVE SOME FUN!
OHHHH, NO! NOT AGAIN. I'M CHANGING MY WAYS FOR GOOD THIS YEAR. AND THERE'S NOTHING THE TWO OF YOU CAN SAY. REMEMBER WHAT HAPPENED LAST NEW YEAR?
SELINA, WE'LL MAKE IT FOR A GOOD CAUSE...FOR THE PLANET, THE CHILDREN, THE ANIMALS. ALL THE STUFF THAT YOU LOVE. COME ON, GIRL!
WELL... IF IT'S FOR A GOOD CAUSE...

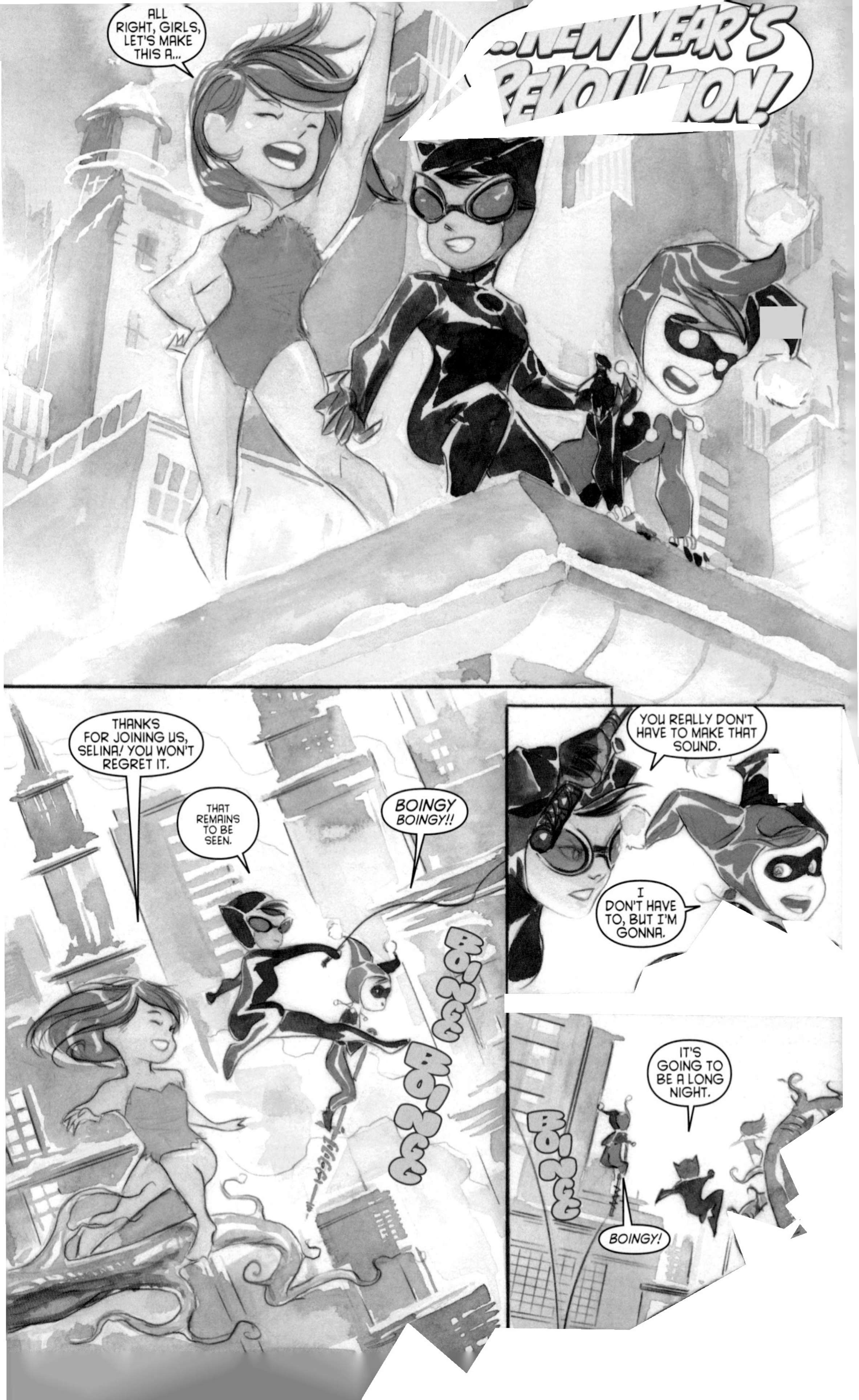
ALL RIGHT, GIRLS, LET'S MAKE THIS A...
...NEW YEAR'S REVOLUTION!
THANKS FOR JOINING US, SELINA! YOU WON'T REGRET IT.
THAT REMAINS TO BE SEEN.
BOINGY BOINGY!!
BOINGG
BOINGG
YOU REALLY DON'T HAVE TO MAKE THAT SOUND.
I DON'T HAVE TO, BUT I'M GONNA.
IT'S GOING TO BE A LONG NIGHT.
BOINGG
BOINGY!

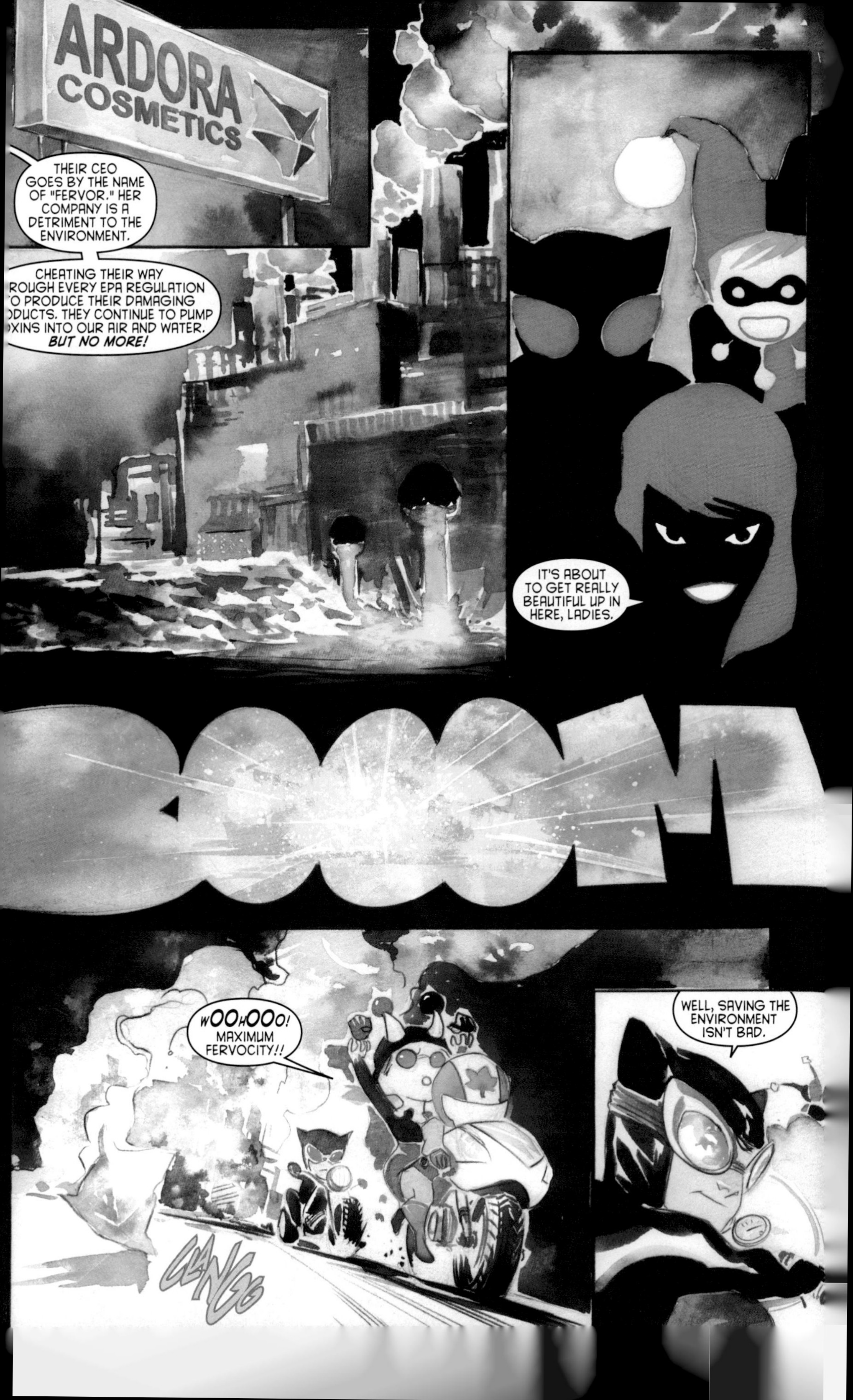
ARDORA COSMETICS
THEIR CEO GOES BY THE NAME OF "FERVOR." HER COMPANY IS A DETRIMENT TO THE ENVIRONMENT.
CHEATING THEIR WAY ROUGH EVERY EPA REGULATION O PRODUCE THEIR DAMAGING ODUCTS. THEY CONTINUE TO PUMP OXINS INTO OUR AIR AND WATER. BUT NO MORE!
IT'S ABOUT TO GET REALLY BEAUTIFUL UP IN HERE, LADIES.
BOOOM
WOOHOOO! MAXIMUM FERVOCITY!!
WELL, SAVING THE ENVIRONMENT ISN'T BAD.
CLANGG

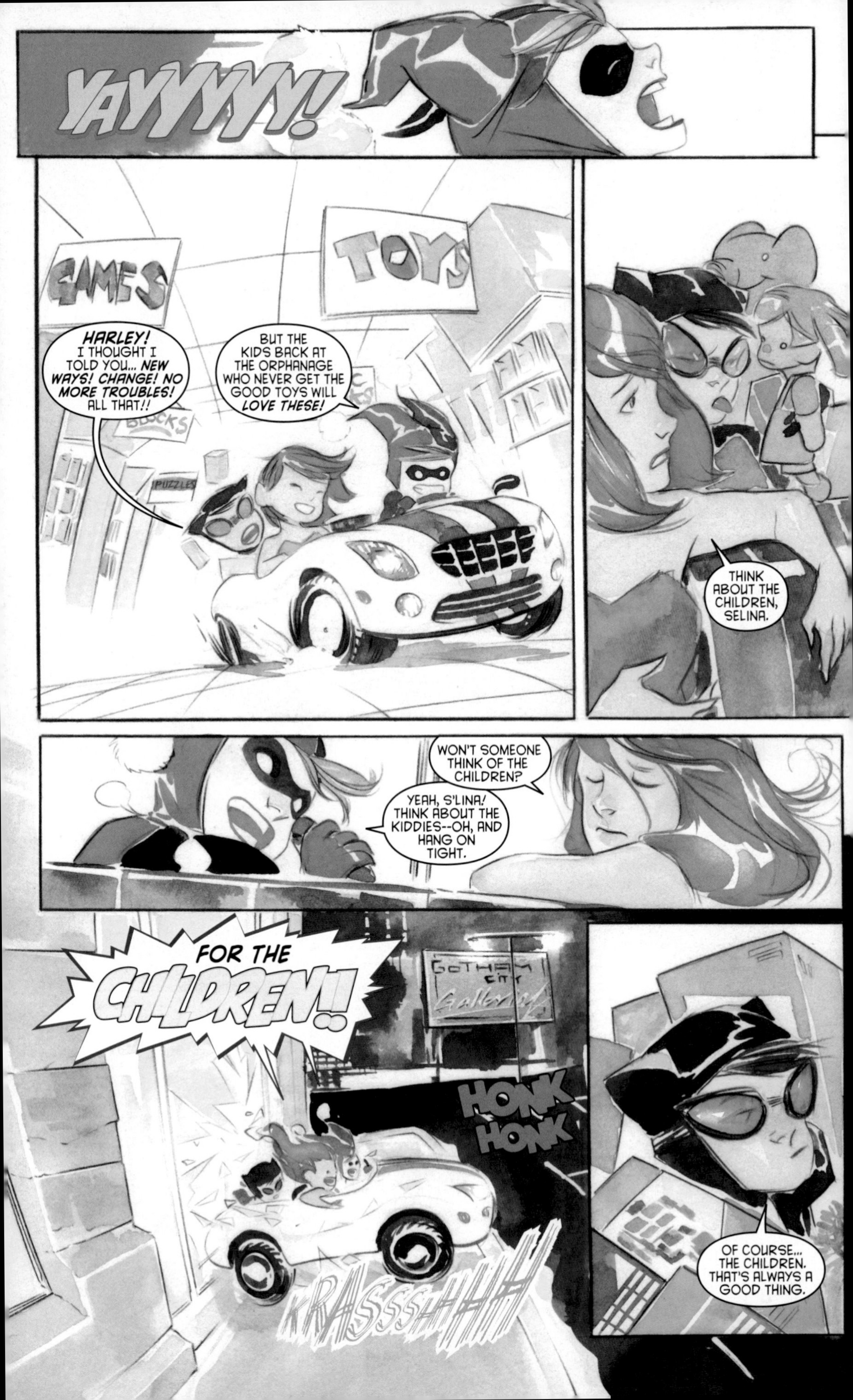
YAYYYYY!
GAMES
TOYS
HARLEY! I THOUGHT I TOLD YOU... NEW WAYS! CHANGE! NO MORE TROUBLES! ALL THAT!!
BUT THE KIDS BACK AT THE ORPHANAGE WHO NEVER GET THE GOOD TOYS WILL LOVE THESE!
BLOCKS
PUZZLES
THINK ABOUT THE CHILDREN, SELINA.
WON'T SOMEONE THINK OF THE CHILDREN?
YEAH, S'LINA! THINK ABOUT THE KIDDIES--OH, AND HANG ON TIGHT.
FOR THE CHILDREN!!
GOTHAM CITY Galleria
HONK HONK
KRASSSSHHHH
OF COURSE... THE CHILDREN. THAT'S ALWAYS A GOOD THING.

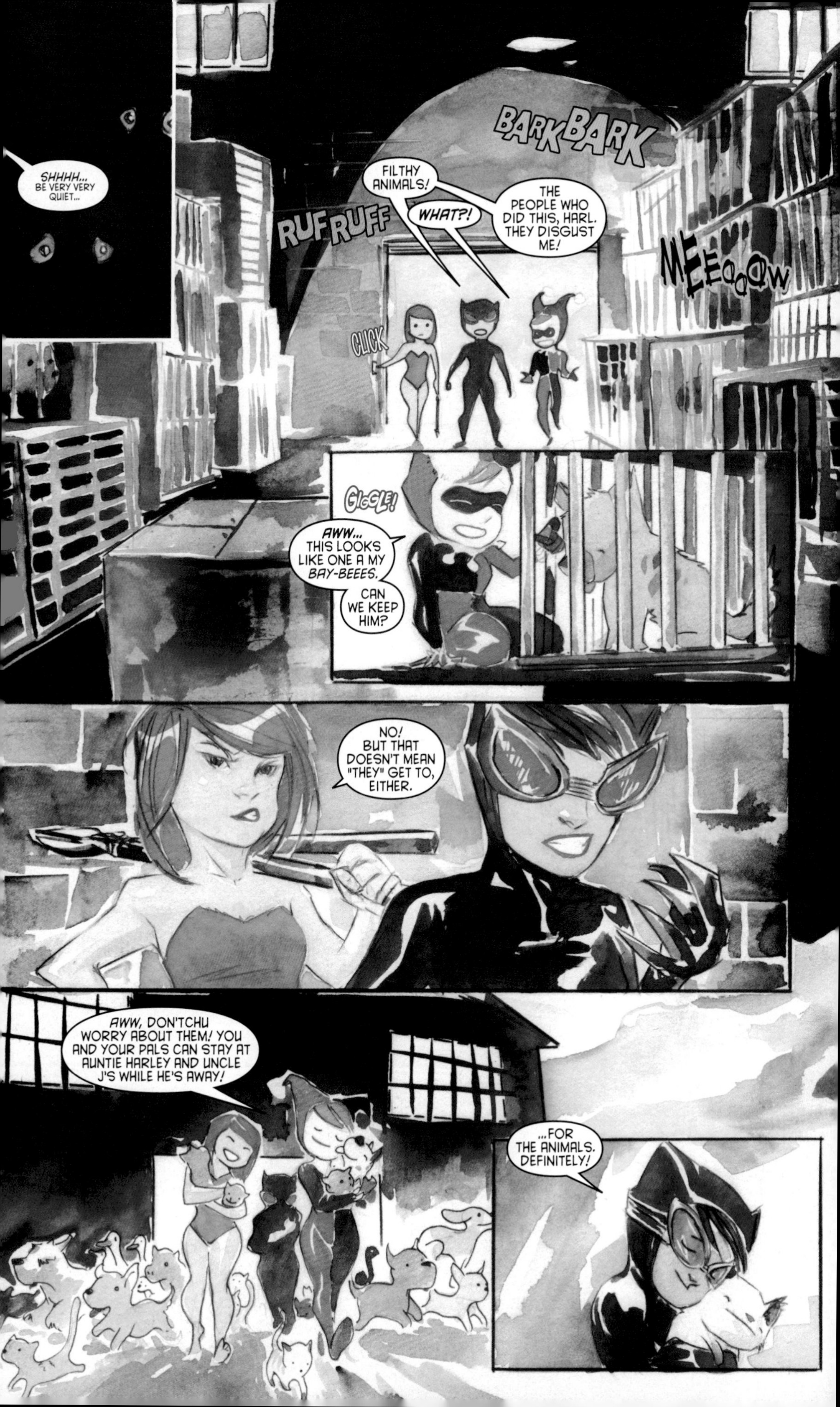
SHHHH... BE VERY VERY QUIET...
BARK BARK
FILTHY ANIMALS!
RUF RUFF
WHAT?!
THE PEOPLE WHO DID THIS, HARL. THEY DISGUST ME!
MEEOOW
CLICK
GIGGLE!
AWW... THIS LOOKS LIKE ONE A MY BAY-BEEES.
CAN WE KEEP HIM?
NO! BUT THAT DOESN'T MEAN "THEY" GET TO, EITHER.
AWW, DON'TCHU WORRY ABOUT THEM! YOU AND YOUR PALS CAN STAY AT AUNTIE HARLEY AND UNCLE J'S WHILE HE'S AWAY!
...FOR THE ANIMALS. DEFINITELY!

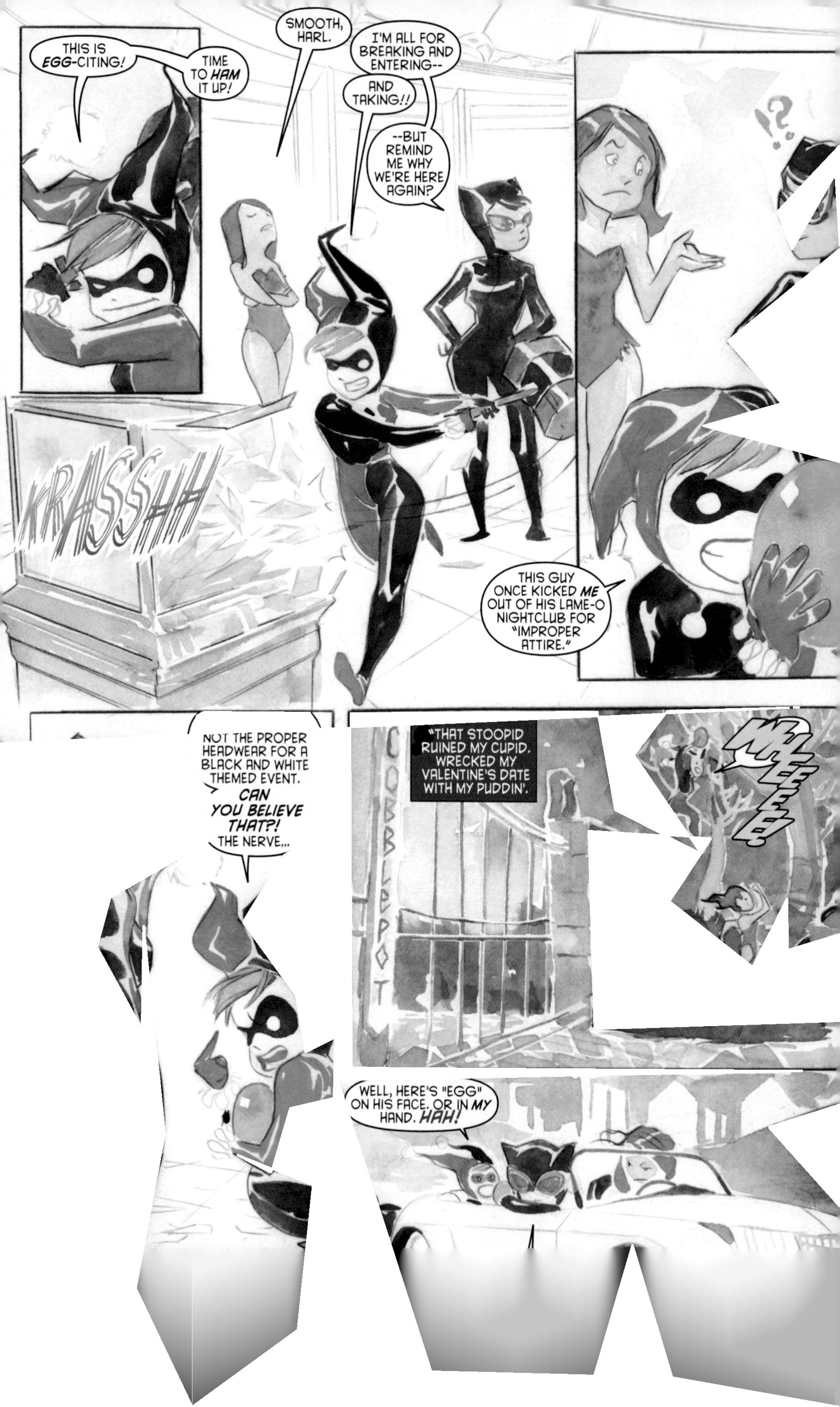
THIS IS EGG-CITING!
TIME TO HAM IT UP!
SMOOTH, HARL.
I'M ALL FOR BREAKING AND ENTERING--
AND TAKING!!
--BUT REMIND ME WHY WE'RE HERE AGAIN?
KRASSHH
!?
THIS GUY ONCE KICKED ME OUT OF HIS LAME-O NIGHTCLUB FOR "IMPROPER ATTIRE."
NOT THE PROPER HEADWEAR FOR A BLACK AND WHITE THEMED EVENT. CAN YOU BELIEVE THAT?! THE NERVE...
"THAT STOOPID RUINED MY CUPID. WRECKED MY VALENTINE'S DATE WITH MY PUDDIN'.
COBBLEPOT
WHEEEEE!
WELL, HERE'S "EGG" ON HIS FACE. OR IN MY HAND. HAH!

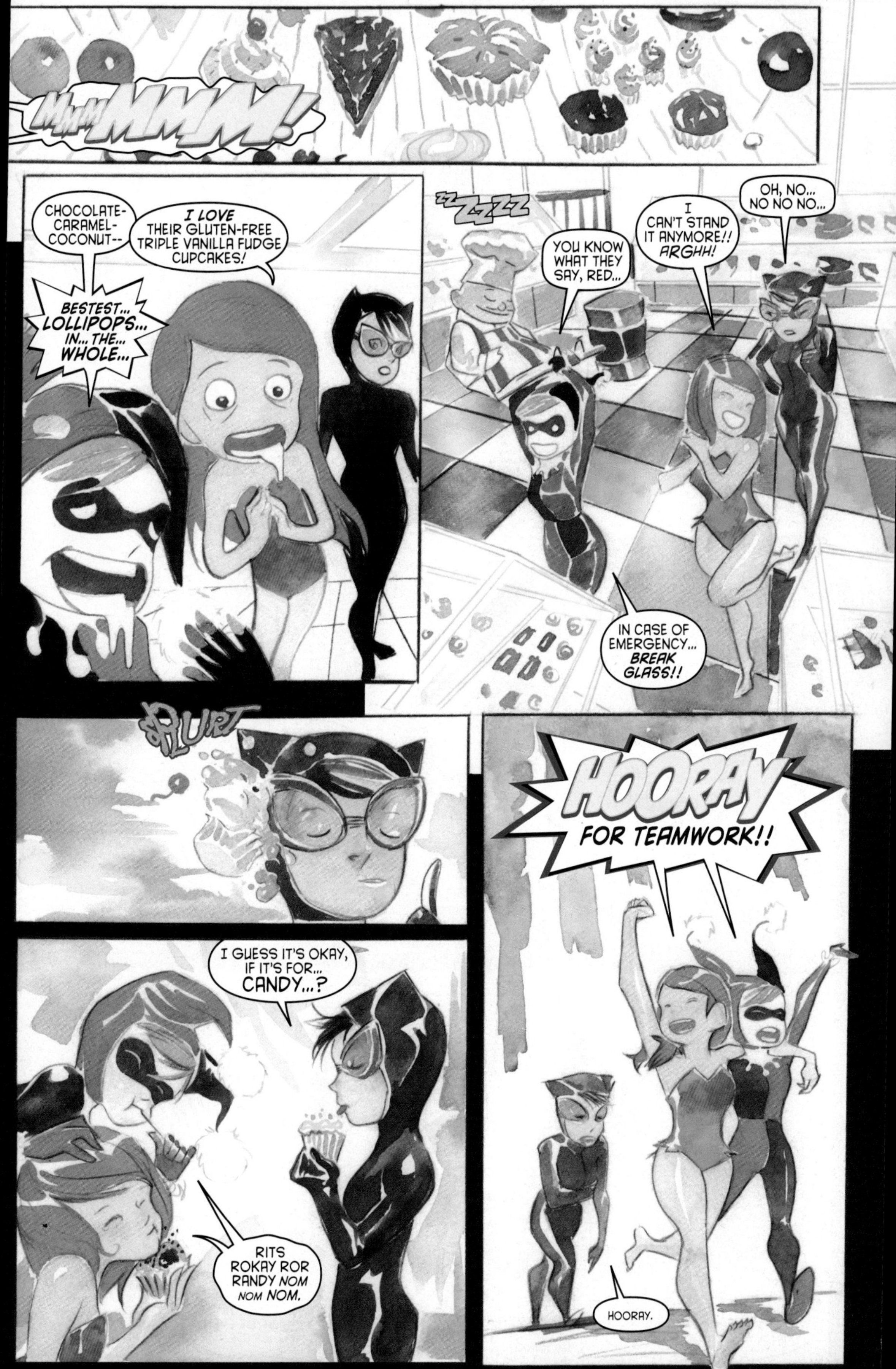
MMMMMMM!
CHOCOLATE-CARAMEL-COCONUT--
I LOVE THEIR GLUTEN-FREE TRIPLE VANILLA FUDGE CUPCAKES!
BESTEST... LOLLIPOPS... IN... THE... WHOLE...
ZZZZZZ
YOU KNOW WHAT THEY SAY, RED...
I CAN'T STAND IT ANYMORE!! ARGHH!
OH, NO... NO NO NO...
IN CASE OF EMERGENCY... BREAK GLASS!!
SPLURT
HOORAY FOR TEAMWORK!!
I GUESS IT'S OKAY, IF IT'S FOR... CANDY...?
RITS ROKAY ROR RANDY NOM NOM NOM.
HOORAY.

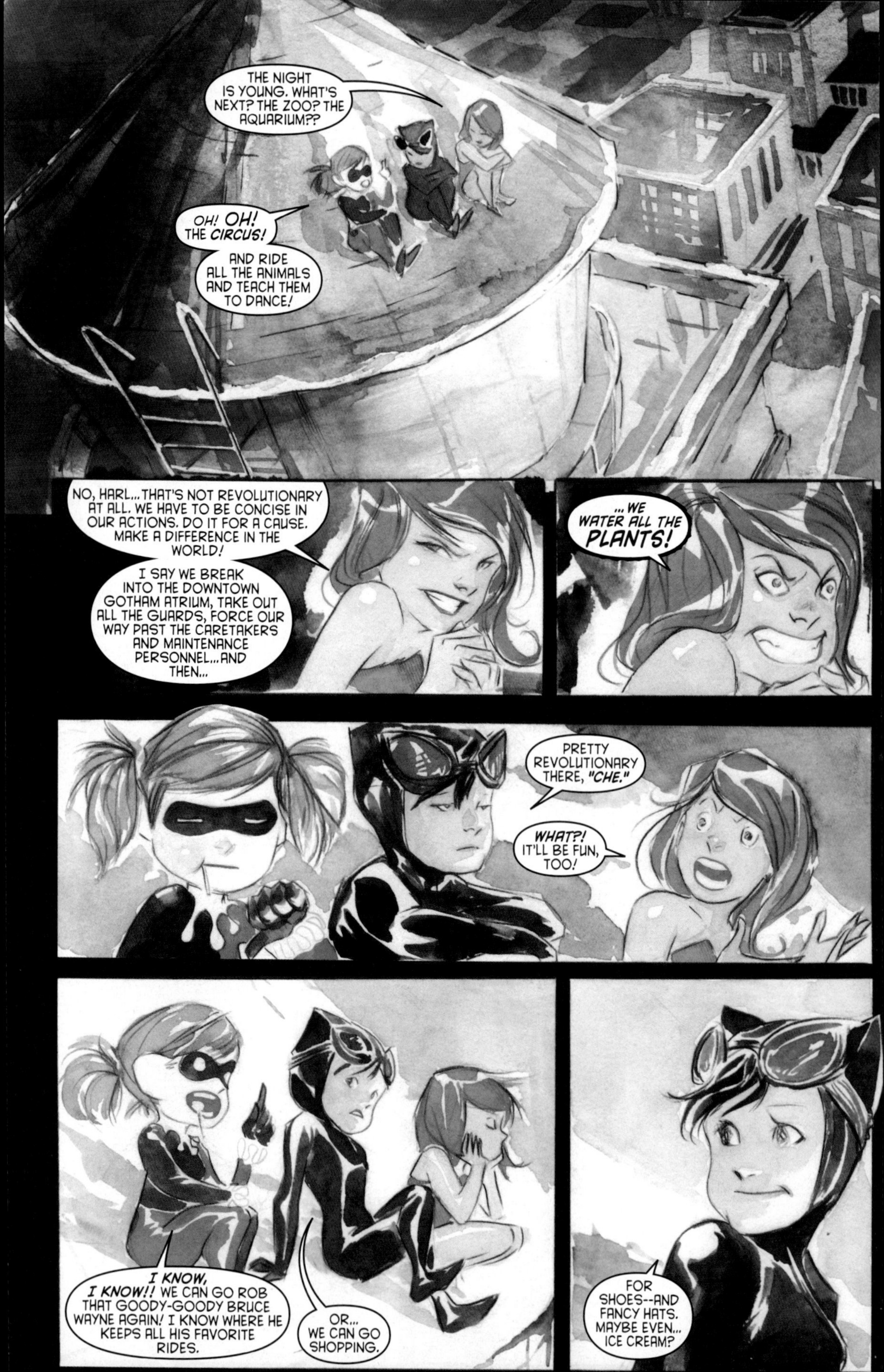
THE NIGHT IS YOUNG. WHAT'S NEXT? THE ZOO? THE AQUARIUM??
OH! OH! THE CIRCUS!
AND RIDE ALL THE ANIMALS AND TEACH THEM TO DANCE!
NO, HARL...THAT'S NOT REVOLUTIONARY AT ALL. WE HAVE TO BE CONCISE IN OUR ACTIONS. DO IT FOR A CAUSE. MAKE A DIFFERENCE IN THE WORLD!
I SAY WE BREAK INTO THE DOWNTOWN GOTHAM ATRIUM, TAKE OUT ALL THE GUARDS, FORCE OUR WAY PAST THE CARETAKERS AND MAINTENANCE PERSONNEL...AND THEN...
...WE WATER ALL THE PLANTS!
PRETTY REVOLUTIONARY THERE, "CHE."
WHAT?! IT'LL BE FUN, TOO!
I KNOW, I KNOW!! WE CAN GO ROB THAT GOODY-GOODY BRUCE WAYNE AGAIN! I KNOW WHERE HE KEEPS ALL HIS FAVORITE RIDES.
OR... WE CAN GO SHOPPING.
FOR SHOES--AND FANCY HATS. MAYBE EVEN... ICE CREAM?

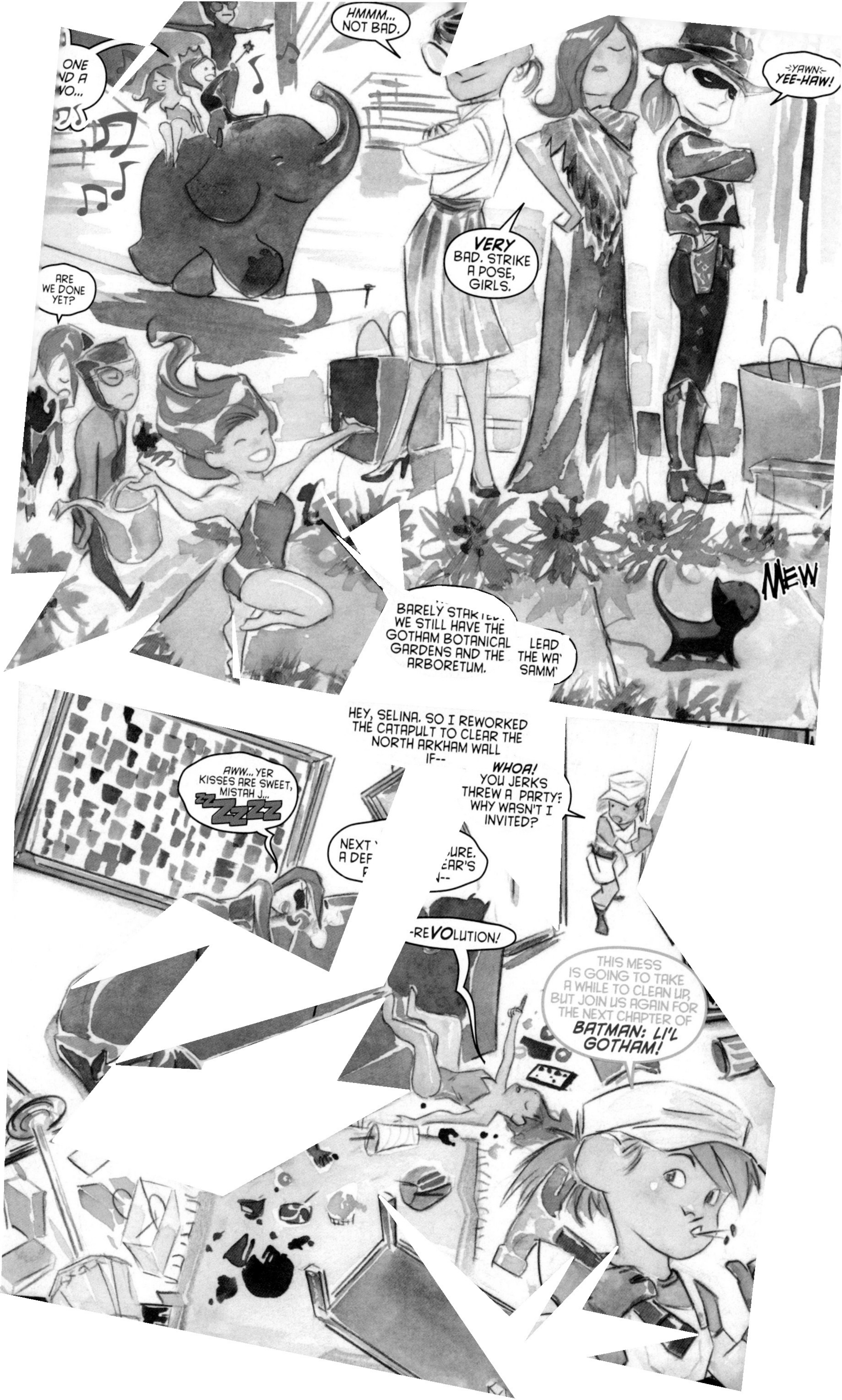

ONE
ND A
VO...
HMMM... NOT BAD.
YAWN YEE-HAW!
VERY BAD. STRIKE A POSE, GIRLS.
ARE WE DONE YET?
MEW
BARELY STARTED. WE STILL HAVE THE GOTHAM BOTANICAL GARDENS AND THE ARBORETUM.
LEAD THE WA SAMM
HEY, SELINA. SO I REWORKED THE CATAPULT TO CLEAR THE NORTH ARKHAM WALL IF--
AWW... YER KISSES ARE SWEET, MISTAH J... ZZZZZ
WHOA! YOU JERKS THREW A PARTY?! WHY WASN'T I INVITED?
NEXT ... URE. A DEF ... EAR'S ... N--
-REVOLUTION!
THIS MESS IS GOING TO TAKE A WHILE TO CLEAN UP, BUT JOIN US AGAIN FOR THE NEXT CHAPTER OF BATMAN: LI'L GOTHAM!

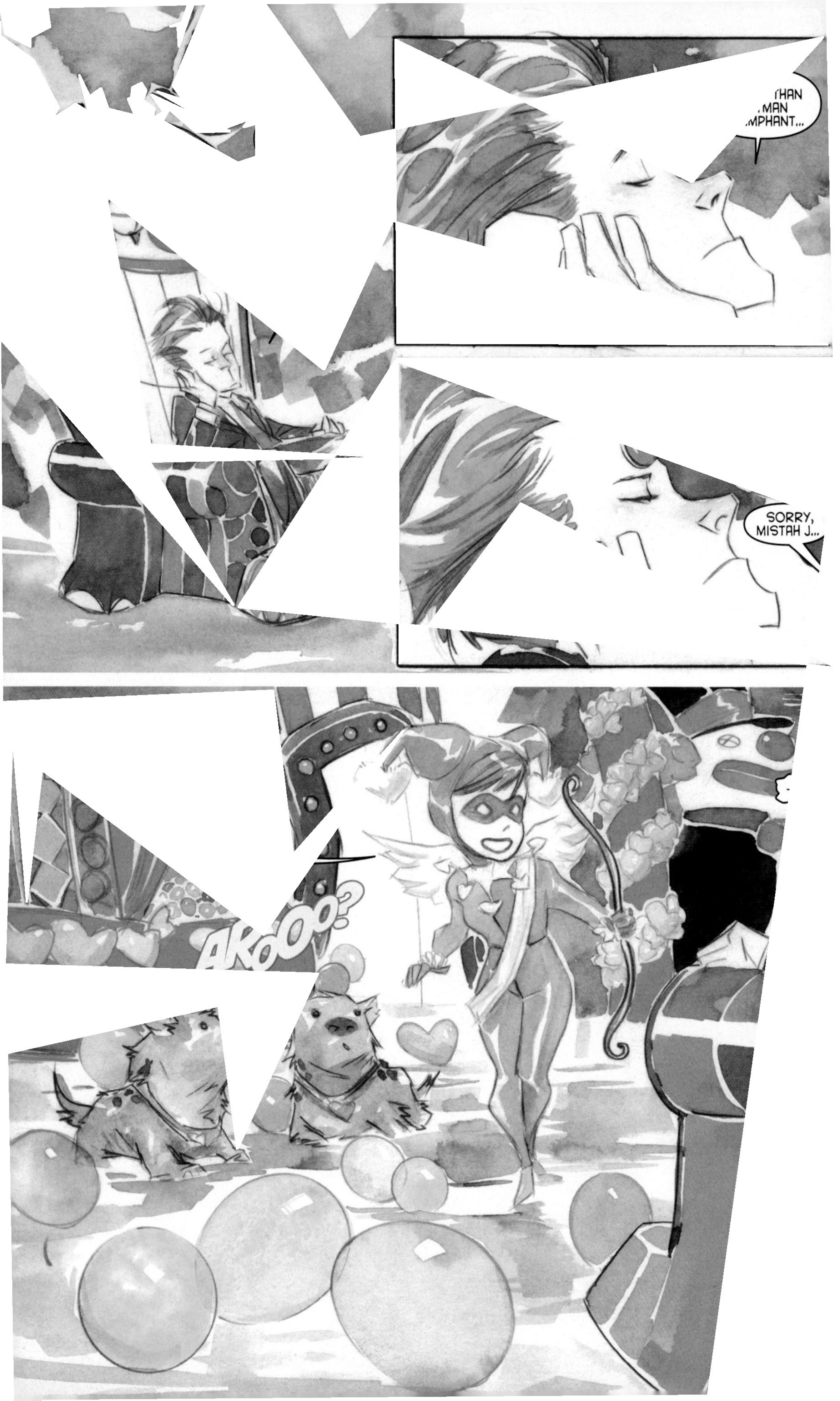

THAN
MAN
MPHANT...
SORRY,
MISTAH J...
AKOOO?

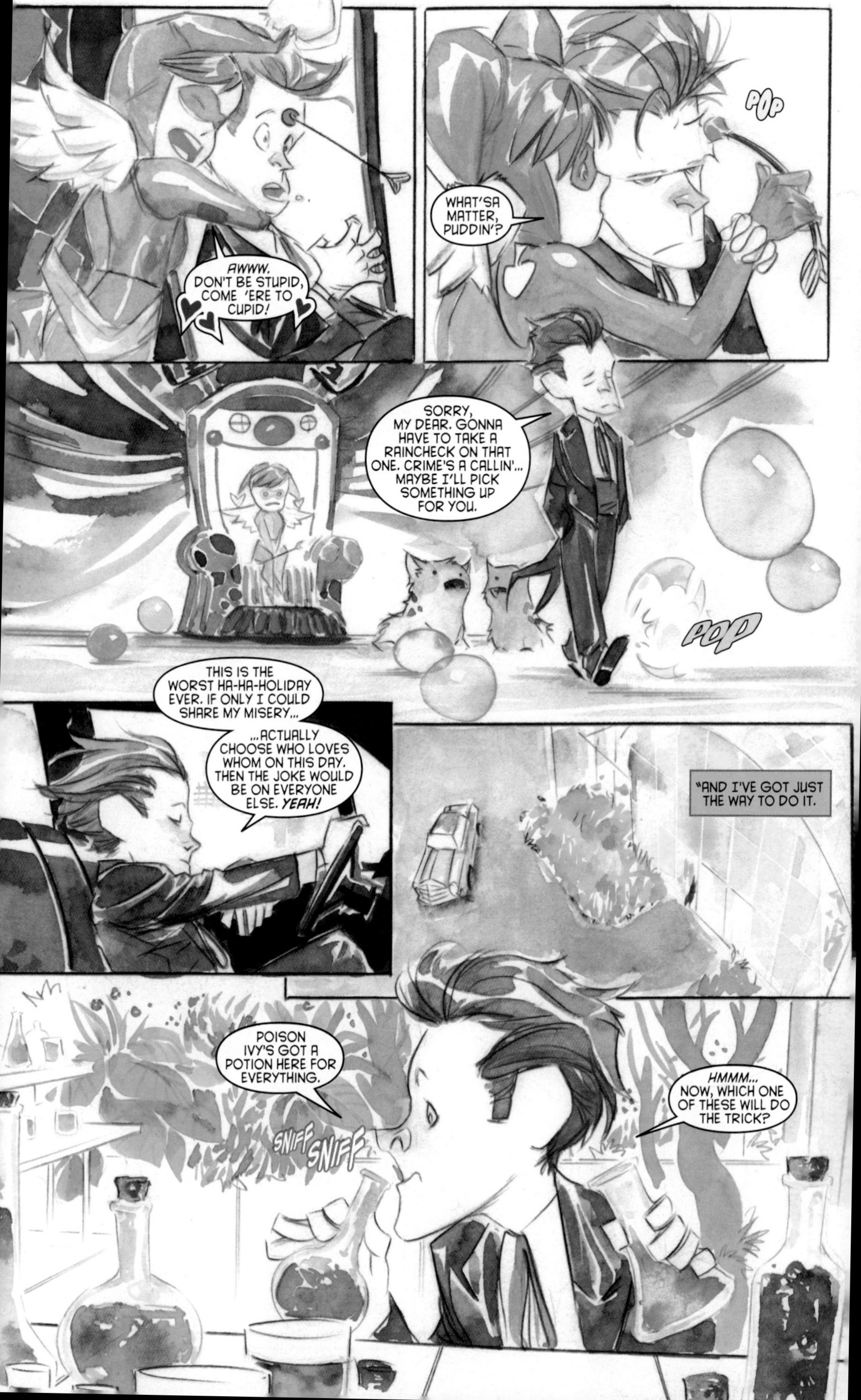
AWWW. DON'T BE STUPID, COME 'ERE TO CUPID!
WHAT'SA MATTER, PUDDIN'?
POP
SORRY, MY DEAR. GONNA HAVE TO TAKE A RAINCHECK ON THAT ONE. CRIME'S A CALLIN'... MAYBE I'LL PICK SOMETHING UP FOR YOU.
POP
THIS IS THE WORST HA-HA-HOLIDAY EVER. IF ONLY I COULD SHARE MY MISERY...
...ACTUALLY CHOOSE WHO LOVES WHOM ON THIS DAY. THEN THE JOKE WOULD BE ON EVERYONE ELSE. YEAH!
"AND I'VE GOT JUST THE WAY TO DO IT.
POISON IVY'S GOT A POTION HERE FOR EVERYTHING.
SNIFF SNIFF
HMMM... NOW, WHICH ONE OF THESE WILL DO THE TRICK?

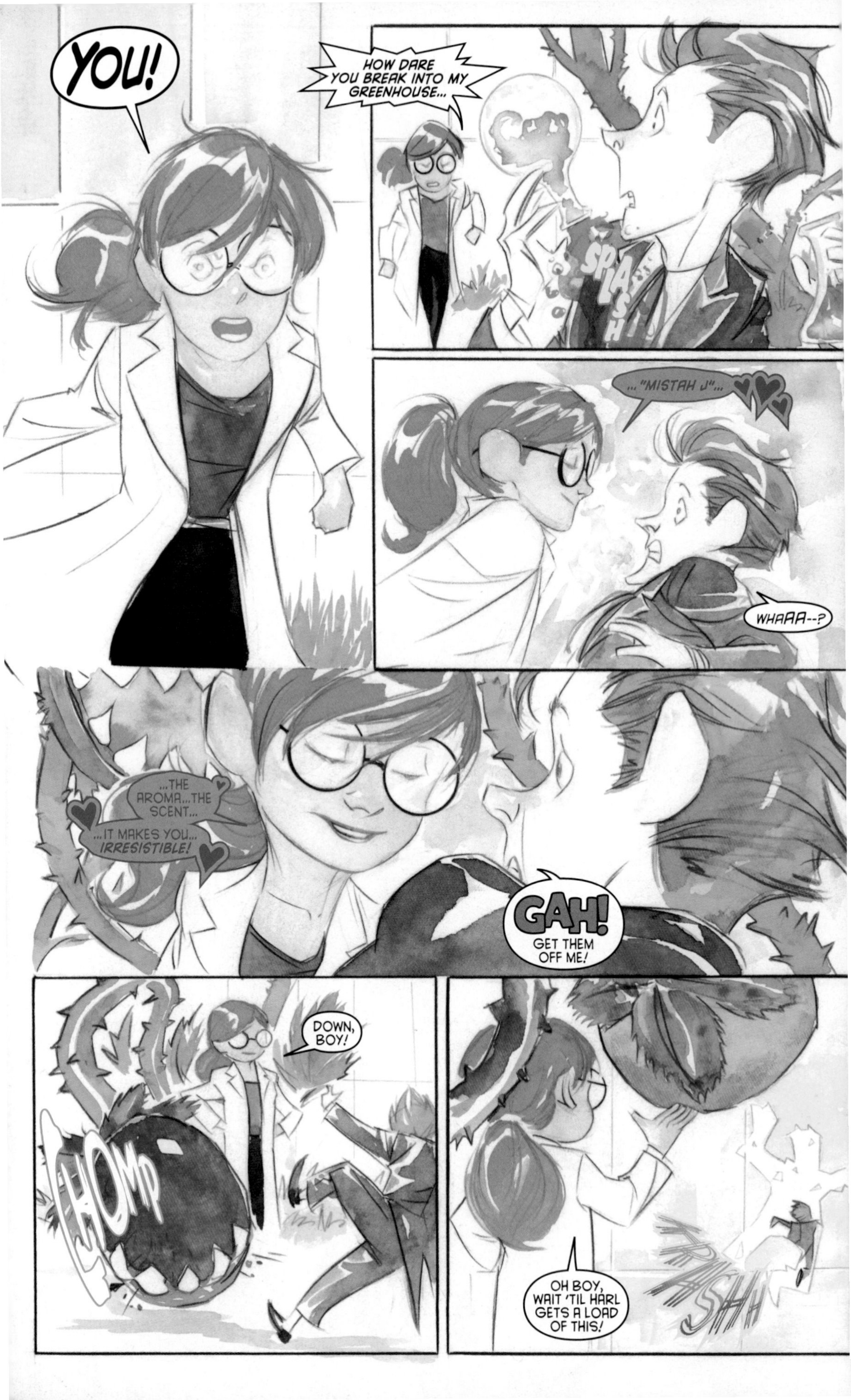
YOU!
HOW DARE YOU BREAK INTO MY GREENHOUSE...
SPLASH
..."MISTAH J"...
WHAAA--?
...THE AROMA...THE SCENT...
...IT MAKES YOU... IRRESISTIBLE!
GAH! GET THEM OFF ME!
DOWN, BOY!
CHOMP
OH BOY, WAIT 'TIL HARL GETS A LOAD OF THIS!

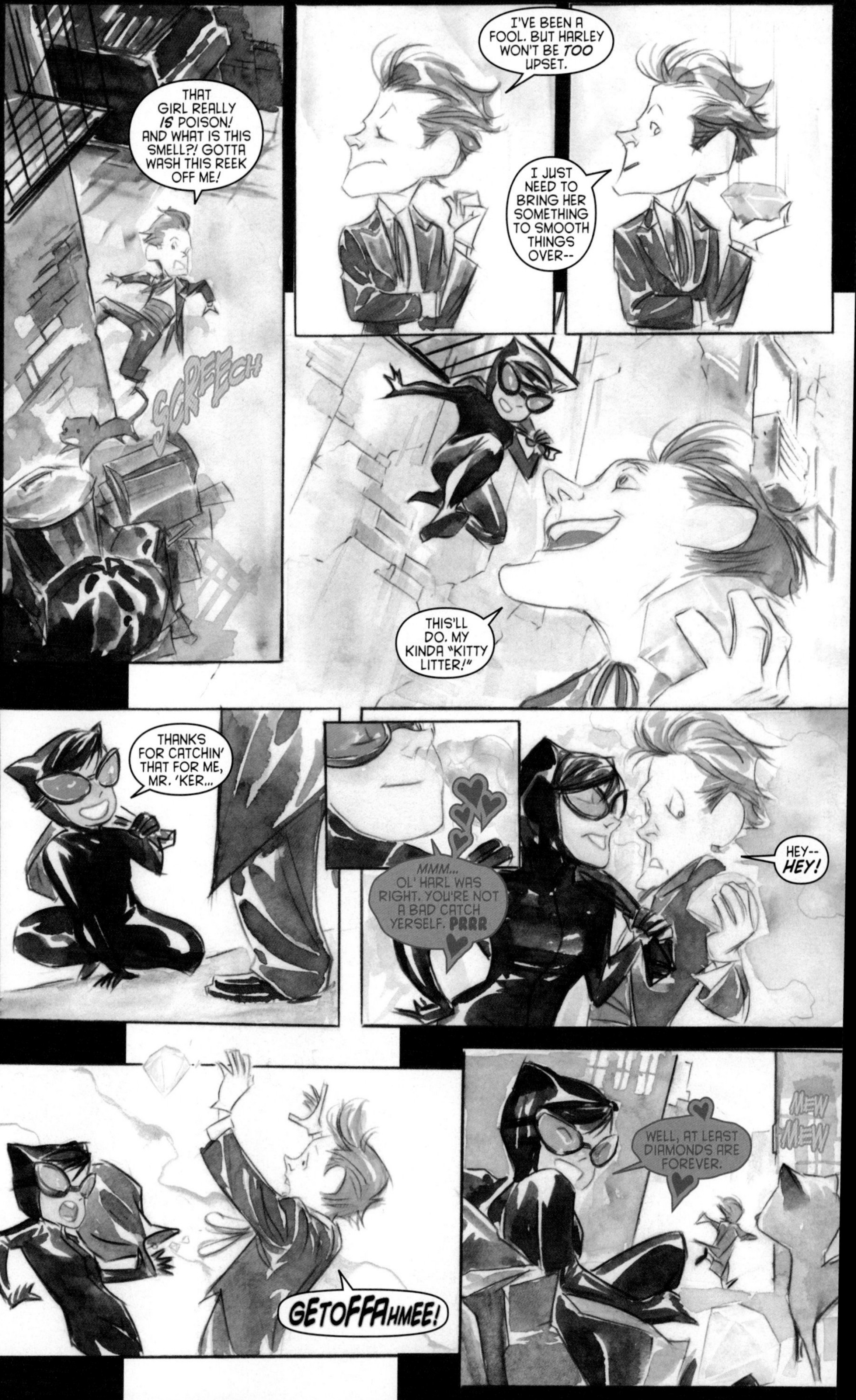

THAT GIRL REALLY IS POISON! AND WHAT IS THIS SMELL?! GOTTA WASH THIS REEK OFF ME!
SCREECH
I'VE BEEN A FOOL. BUT HARLEY WON'T BE TOO UPSET.
I JUST NEED TO BRING HER SOMETHING TO SMOOTH THINGS OVER--
THIS'LL DO. MY KINDA "KITTY LITTER!"
THANKS FOR CATCHIN' THAT FOR ME, MR. 'KER...
MMM... OL' HARL WAS RIGHT. YOU'RE NOT A BAD CATCH YERSELF. PRRR
HEY-- HEY!
GETOFFAHMEE!
WELL, AT LEAST DIAMONDS ARE FOREVER.
MEW MEW

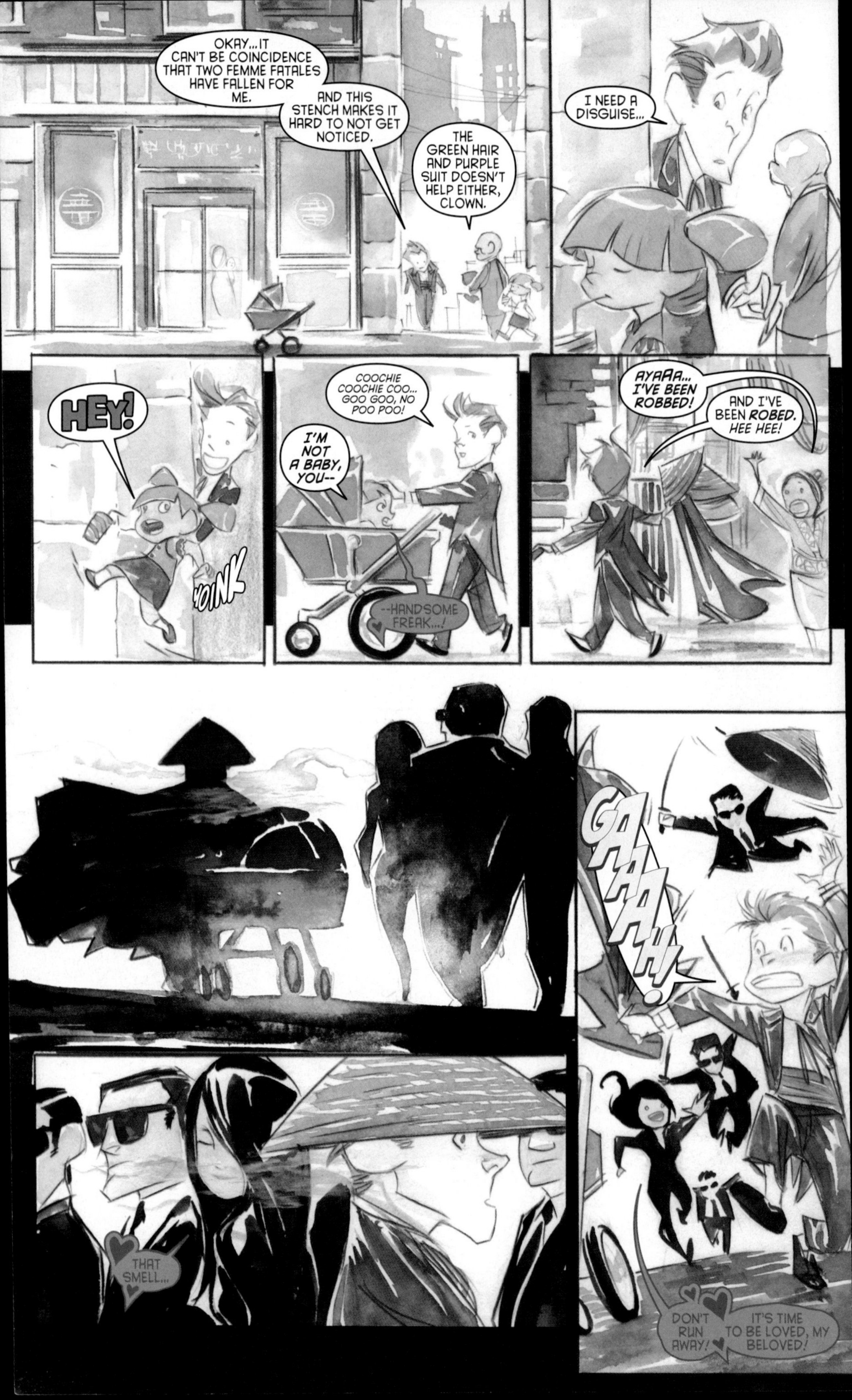
OKAY...IT CAN'T BE COINCIDENCE THAT TWO FEMME FATALES HAVE FALLEN FOR ME.
AND THIS STENCH MAKES IT HARD TO NOT GET NOTICED.
THE GREEN HAIR AND PURPLE SUIT DOESN'T HELP EITHER, CLOWN.
I NEED A DISGUISE...
HEY!
YOINK
COOCHIE COOCHIE COO... GOO GOO, NO POO POO!
I'M NOT A BABY, YOU--
--HANDSOME FREAK...!
AYAAA... I'VE BEEN ROBBED!
AND I'VE BEEN ROBED. HEE HEE!
THAT SMELL...
GAAAAH!
DON'T RUN AWAY!
IT'S TIME TO BE LOVED, MY BELOVED!

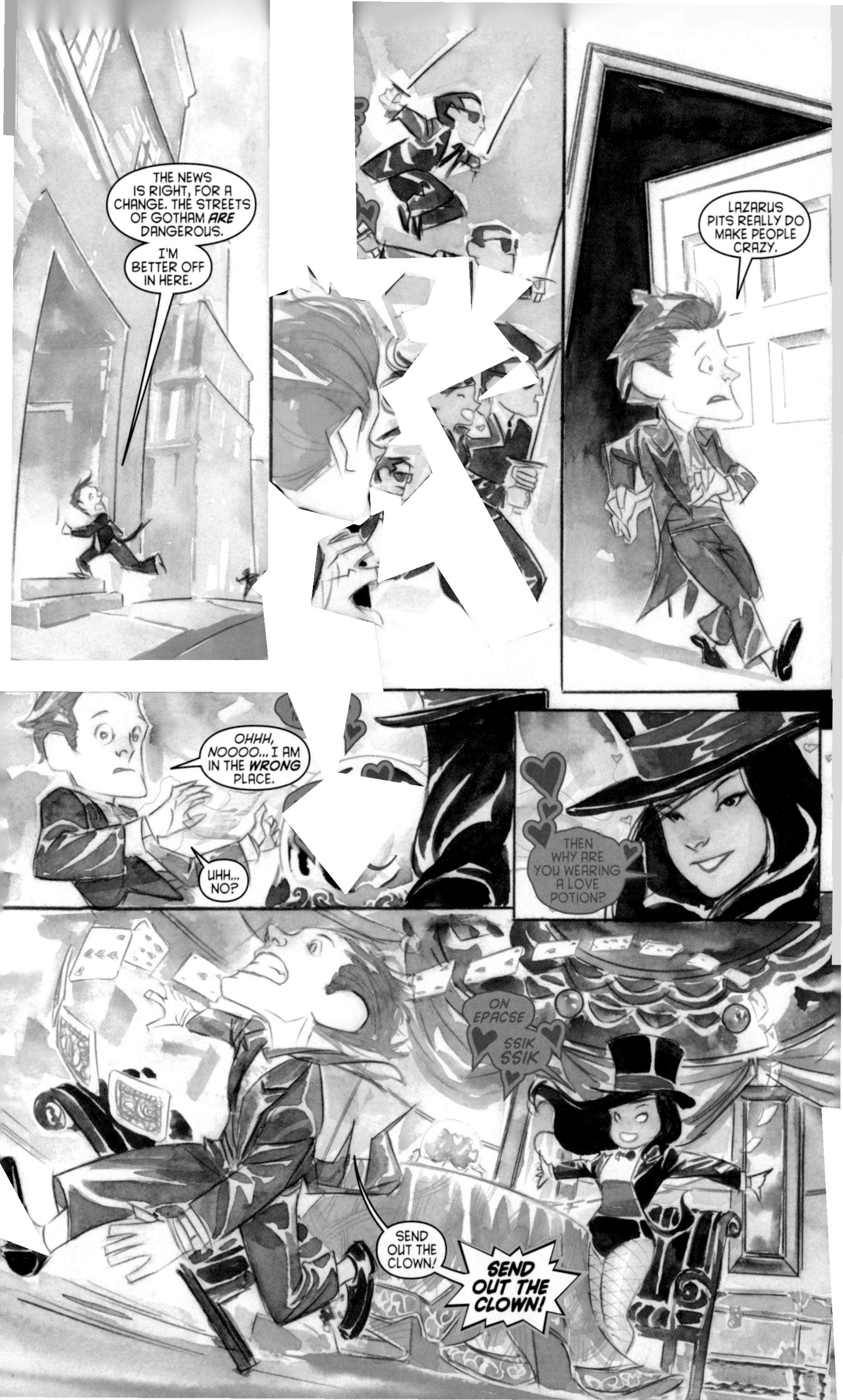
THE NEWS IS RIGHT, FOR A CHANGE. THE STREETS OF GOTHAM *ARE* DANGEROUS.
I'M BETTER OFF IN HERE.
LAZARUS PITS REALLY DO MAKE PEOPLE CRAZY.
OHHH, NOOOO... I AM IN THE *WRONG* PLACE.
UHH... NO?
THEN WHY ARE YOU WEARING A LOVE POTION?
ON EPACSE
SSIK SSIK
SEND OUT THE CLOWN!
SEND OUT THE CLOWN!

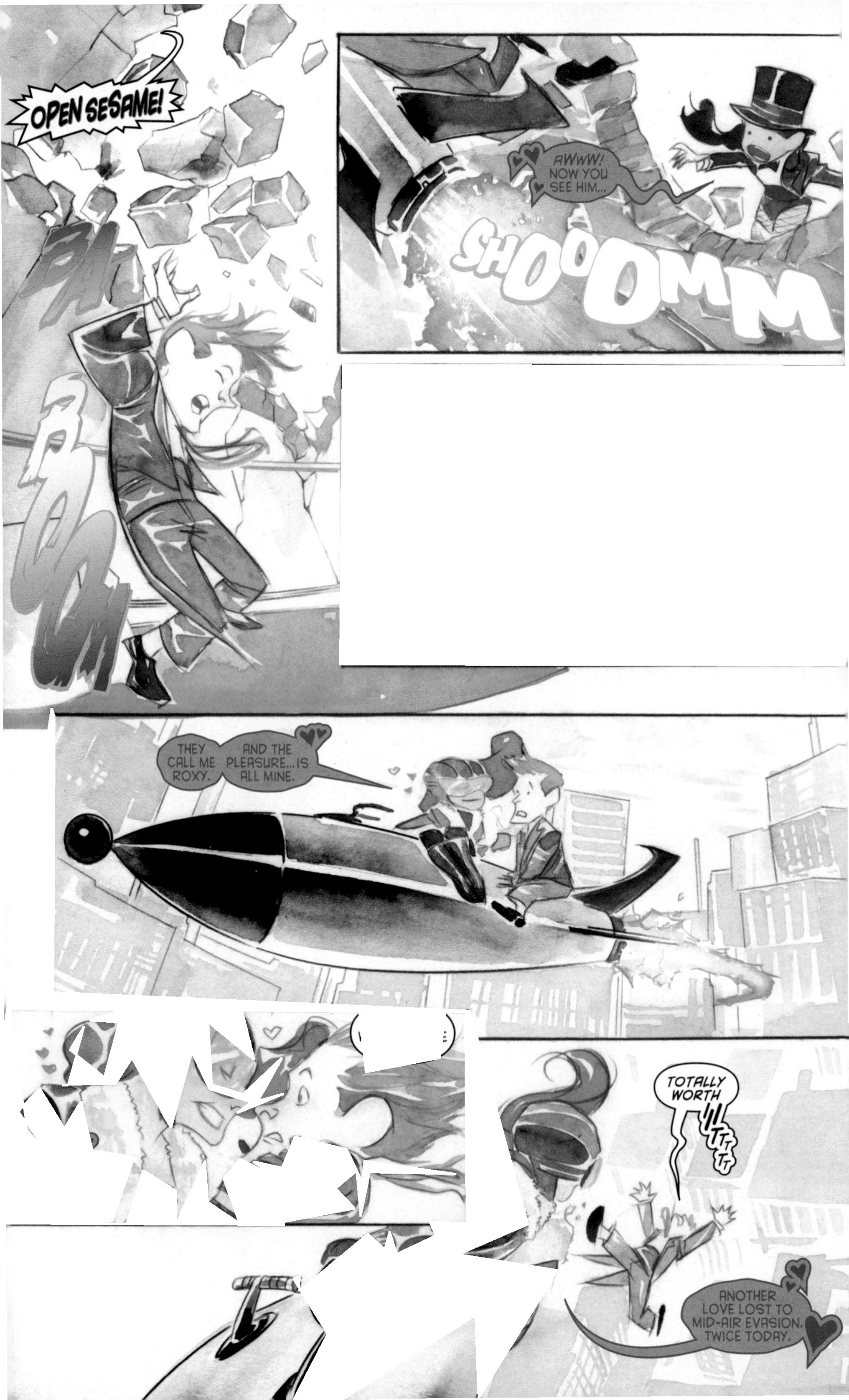
OPEN SESAME!
BAM
BOOM
AWWW! NOW YOU SEE HIM...
SHOOOMMM
THEY CALL ME ROXY.
AND THE PLEASURE...IS ALL MINE.
TOTALLY WORTH IIIITTTTT
ANOTHER LOVE LOST TO MID-AIR EVASION. TWICE TODAY.

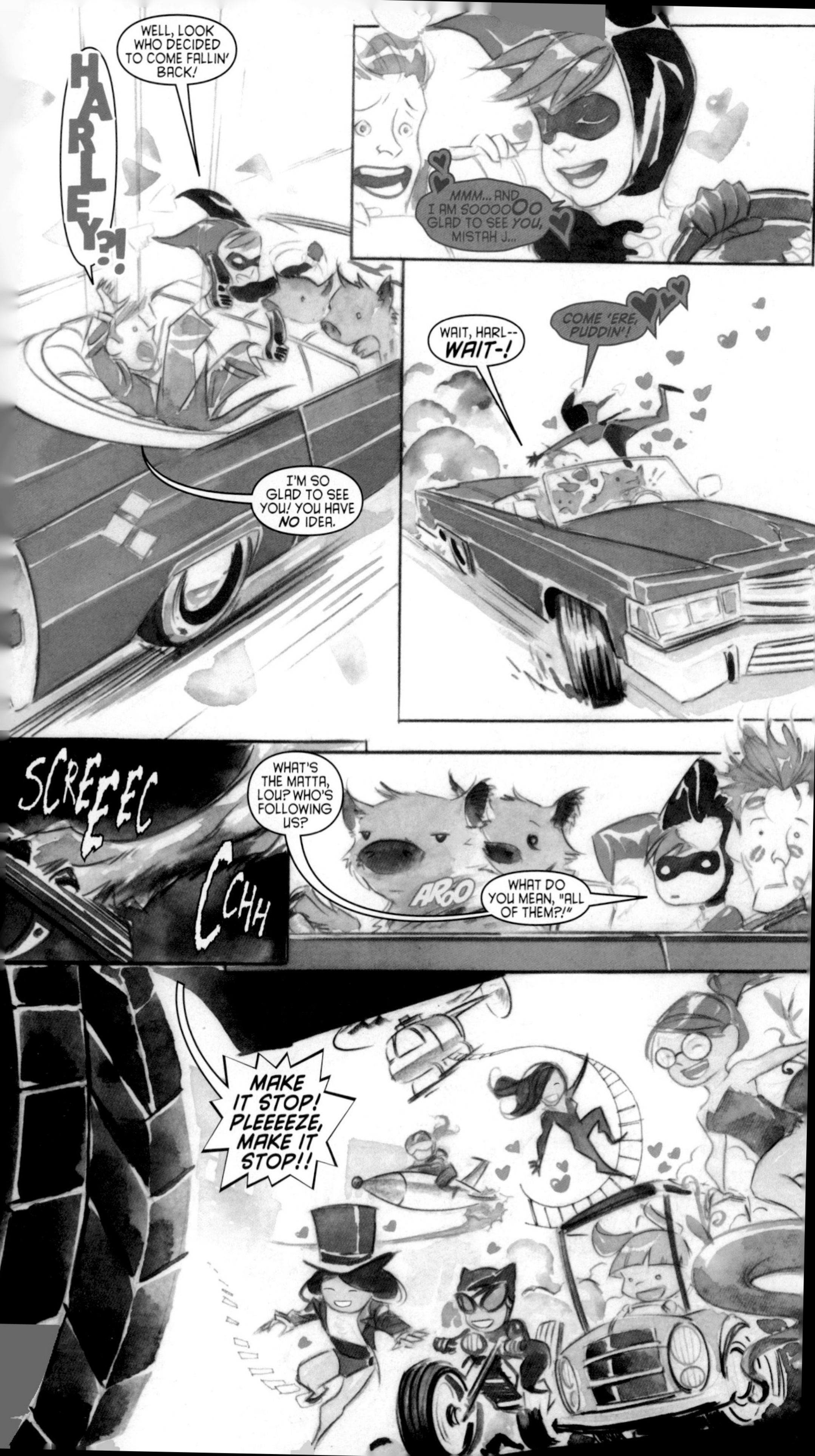

WELL, LOOK WHO DECIDED TO COME FALLIN' BACK!
HARLEY?!
MMM... AND I AM SOOOOOOO GLAD TO SEE YOU, MISTAH J...
I'M SO GLAD TO SEE YOU! YOU HAVE NO IDEA.
WAIT, HARL-- WAIT-!
COME 'ERE, PUDDIN'!
SCREEEC
CCHH
WHAT'S THE MATTA, LOU? WHO'S FOLLOWING US?
AROO
WHAT DO YOU MEAN, "ALL OF THEM?!"
MAKE IT STOP! PLEEEEZE, MAKE IT STOP!!

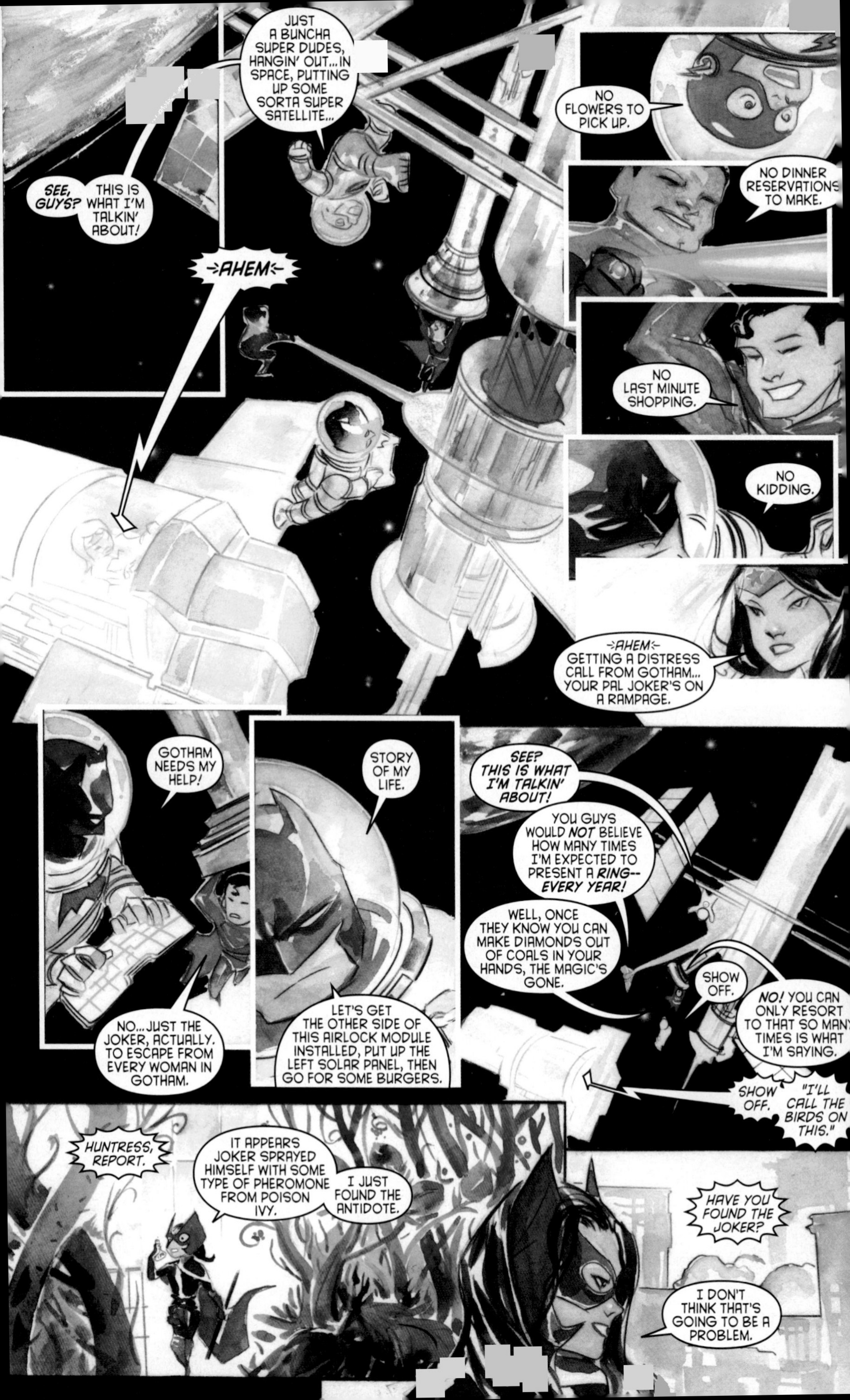
SEE, GUYS?
THIS IS WHAT I'M TALKIN' ABOUT!
JUST A BUNCHA SUPER DUDES, HANGIN' OUT... IN SPACE, PUTTING UP SOME SORTA SUPER SATELLITE...
NO FLOWERS TO PICK UP.
NO DINNER RESERVATIONS TO MAKE.
NO LAST MINUTE SHOPPING.
NO KIDDING.
AHEM
AHEM
GETTING A DISTRESS CALL FROM GOTHAM... YOUR PAL JOKER'S ON A RAMPAGE.
GOTHAM NEEDS MY HELP!
NO... JUST THE JOKER, ACTUALLY. TO ESCAPE FROM EVERY WOMAN IN GOTHAM.
STORY OF MY LIFE.
LET'S GET THE OTHER SIDE OF THIS AIRLOCK MODULE INSTALLED, PUT UP THE LEFT SOLAR PANEL, THEN GO FOR SOME BURGERS.
SEE? THIS IS WHAT I'M TALKIN' ABOUT!
YOU GUYS WOULD NOT BELIEVE HOW MANY TIMES I'M EXPECTED TO PRESENT A RING-- EVERY YEAR!
WELL, ONCE THEY KNOW YOU CAN MAKE DIAMONDS OUT OF COALS IN YOUR HANDS, THE MAGIC'S GONE.
SHOW OFF.
NO! YOU CAN ONLY RESORT TO THAT SO MANY TIMES IS WHAT I'M SAYING.
SHOW OFF.
"I'LL CALL THE BIRDS ON THIS."
HUNTRESS, REPORT.
IT APPEARS JOKER SPRAYED HIMSELF WITH SOME TYPE OF PHEROMONE FROM POISON IVY.
I JUST FOUND THE ANTIDOTE.
HAVE YOU FOUND THE JOKER?
I DON'T THINK THAT'S GOING TO BE A PROBLEM.

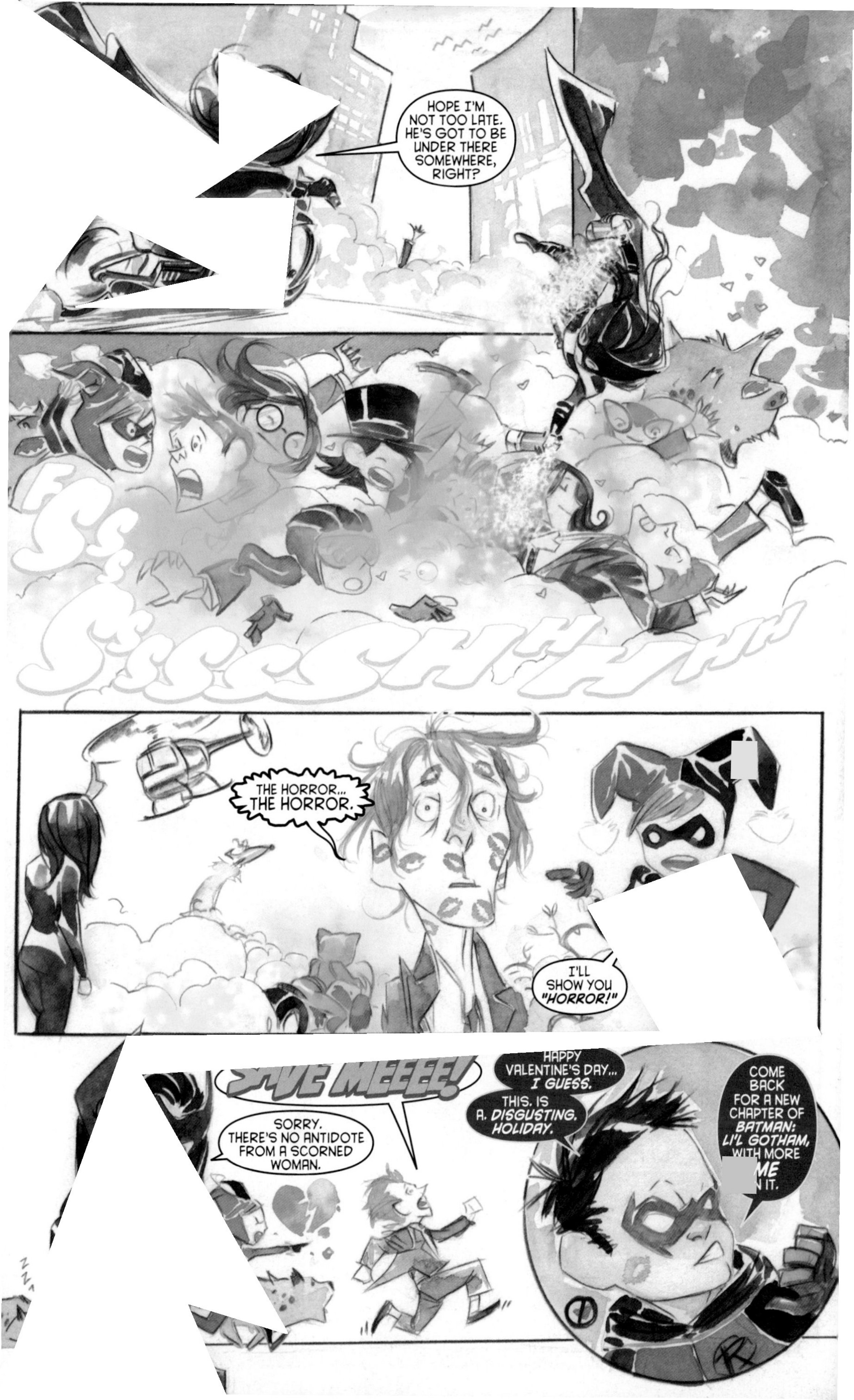
HOPE I'M NOT TOO LATE. HE'S GOT TO BE UNDER THERE SOMEWHERE, RIGHT?
THE HORROR... THE HORROR.
I'LL SHOW YOU "HORROR!"
VE MEEEE!
SORRY. THERE'S NO ANTIDOTE FROM A SCORNED WOMAN.
HAPPY VALENTINE'S DAY... I GUESS.
THIS. IS A. DISGUSTING. HOLIDAY.
COME BACK FOR A NEW CHAPTER OF BATMAN: LI'L GOTHAM, WITH MORE
ME
N IT.

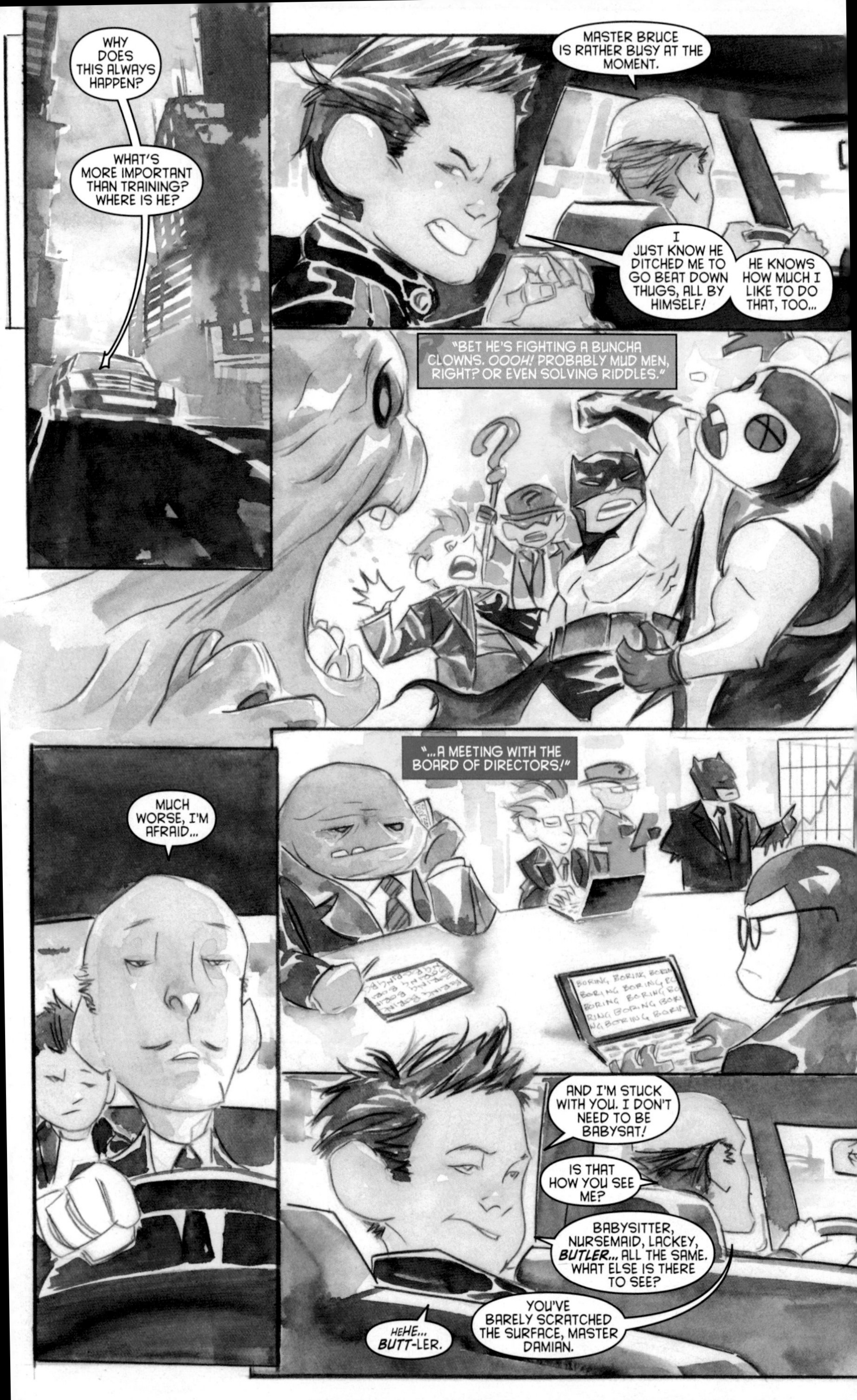
WHY DOES THIS ALWAYS HAPPEN?
WHAT'S MORE IMPORTANT THAN TRAINING? WHERE IS HE?
MASTER BRUCE IS RATHER BUSY AT THE MOMENT.
I JUST KNOW HE DITCHED ME TO GO BEAT DOWN THUGS, ALL BY HIMSELF!
HE KNOWS HOW MUCH I LIKE TO DO THAT, TOO...
"BET HE'S FIGHTING A BUNCHA CLOWNS. *OOOH!* PROBABLY MUD MEN, RIGHT? OR EVEN SOLVING RIDDLES."
MUCH WORSE, I'M AFRAID...
"...A MEETING WITH THE BOARD OF DIRECTORS!"
AND I'M STUCK WITH YOU. I DON'T NEED TO BE BABYSAT!
IS THAT HOW YOU SEE ME?
BABYSITTER, NURSEMAID, LACKEY, ***BUTLER***... ALL THE SAME. WHAT ELSE IS THERE TO SEE?
HEHE... ***BUTT*-LER.**
YOU'VE BARELY SCRATCHED THE SURFACE, MASTER DAMIAN.

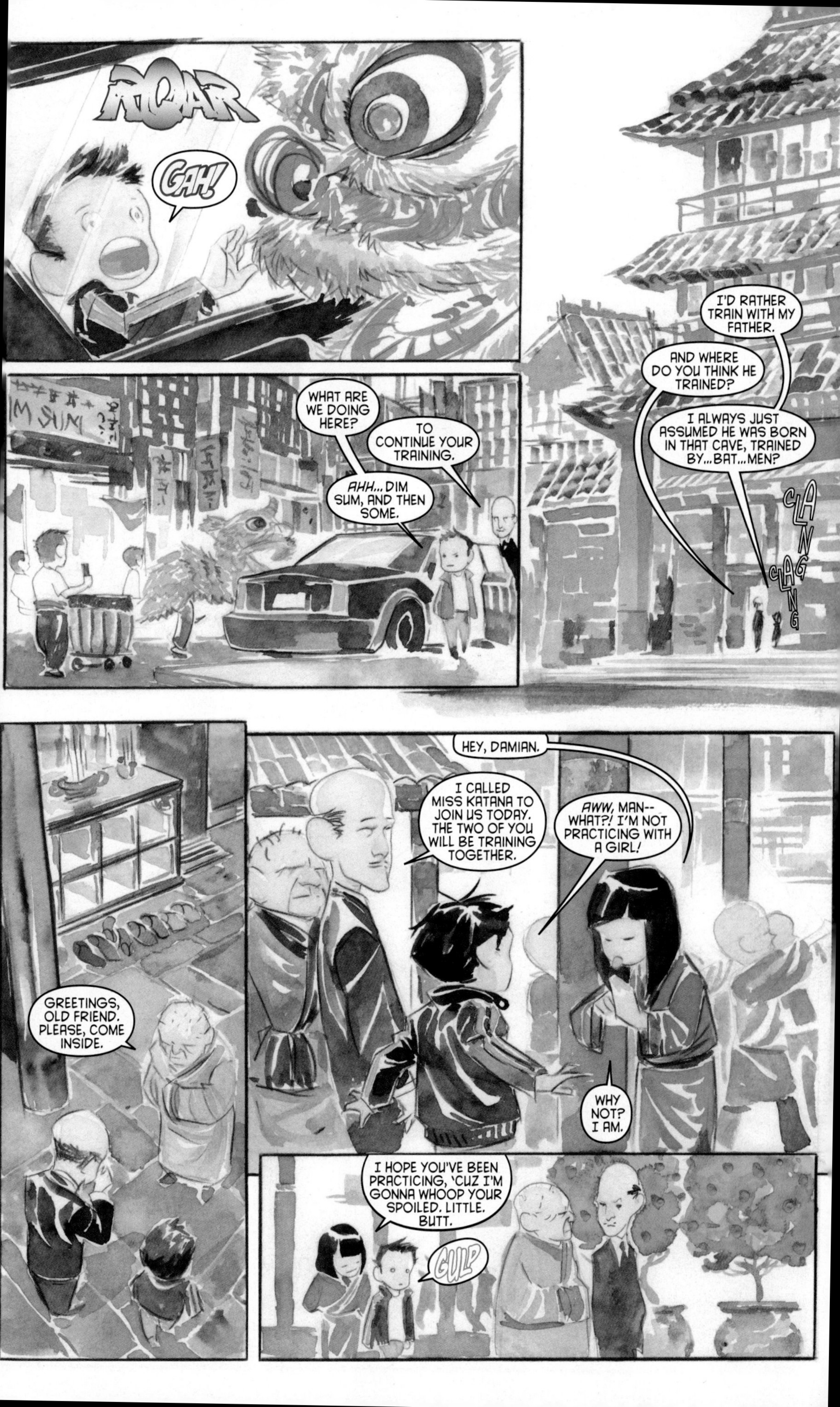
ROAR
GAH!
WHAT ARE WE DOING HERE?
TO CONTINUE YOUR TRAINING.
AHH... DIM SUM, AND THEN SOME.
I'D RATHER TRAIN WITH MY FATHER.
AND WHERE DO YOU THINK HE TRAINED?
I ALWAYS JUST ASSUMED HE WAS BORN IN THAT CAVE, TRAINED BY...BAT...MEN?
CLANG
CLANG
GREETINGS, OLD FRIEND. PLEASE, COME INSIDE.
HEY, DAMIAN.
I CALLED MISS KATANA TO JOIN US TODAY. THE TWO OF YOU WILL BE TRAINING TOGETHER.
AWW, MAN-- WHAT?! I'M NOT PRACTICING WITH A GIRL!
WHY NOT? I AM.
I HOPE YOU'VE BEEN PRACTICING, 'CUZ I'M GONNA WHOOP YOUR SPOILED. LITTLE. BUTT.
GULP

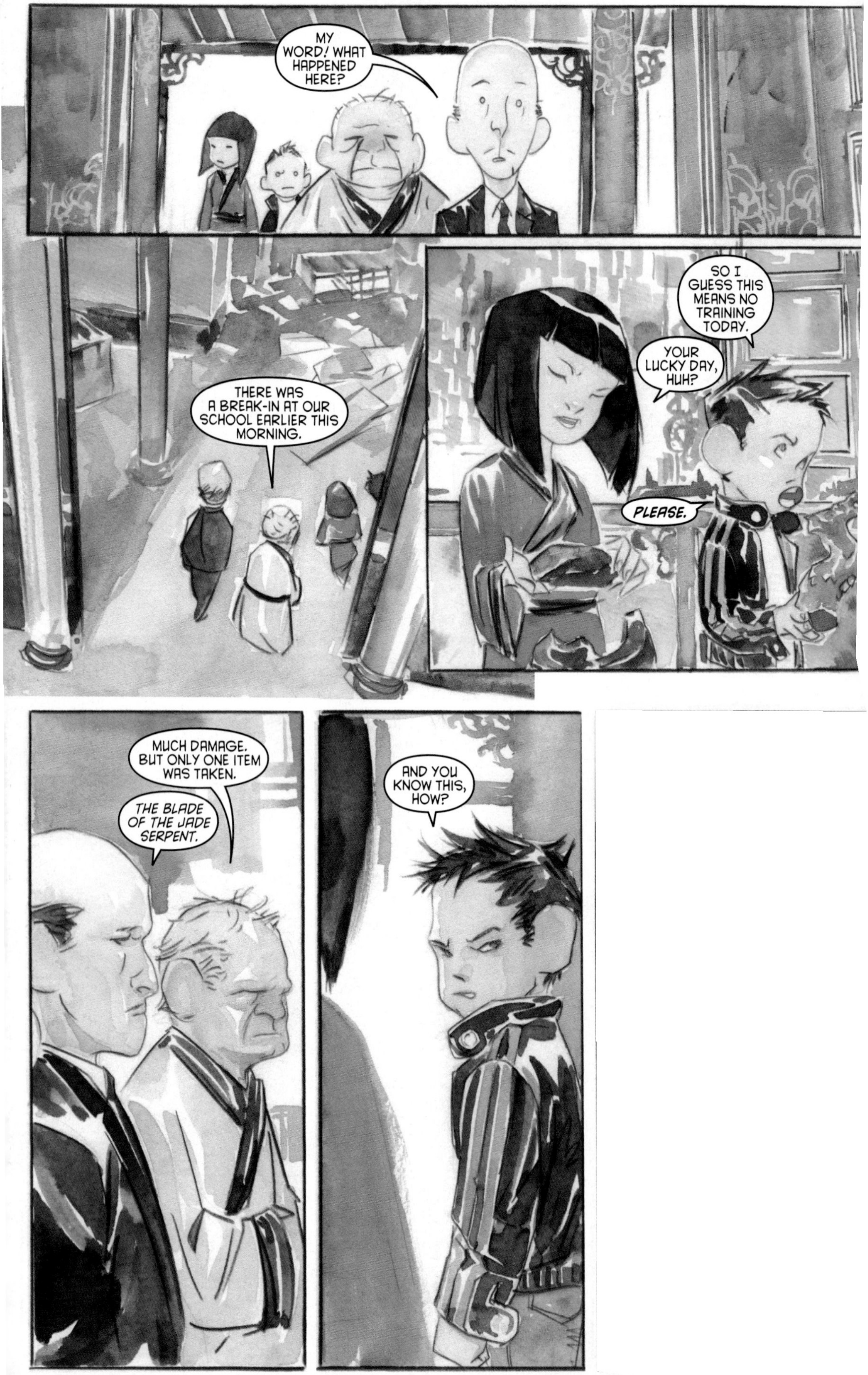

MY WORD! WHAT HAPPENED HERE?
THERE WAS A BREAK-IN AT OUR SCHOOL EARLIER THIS MORNING.
SO I GUESS THIS MEANS NO TRAINING TODAY.
YOUR LUCKY DAY, HUH?
PLEASE.
MUCH DAMAGE. BUT ONLY ONE ITEM WAS TAKEN.
THE BLADE OF THE JADE SERPENT.
AND YOU KNOW THIS, HOW?

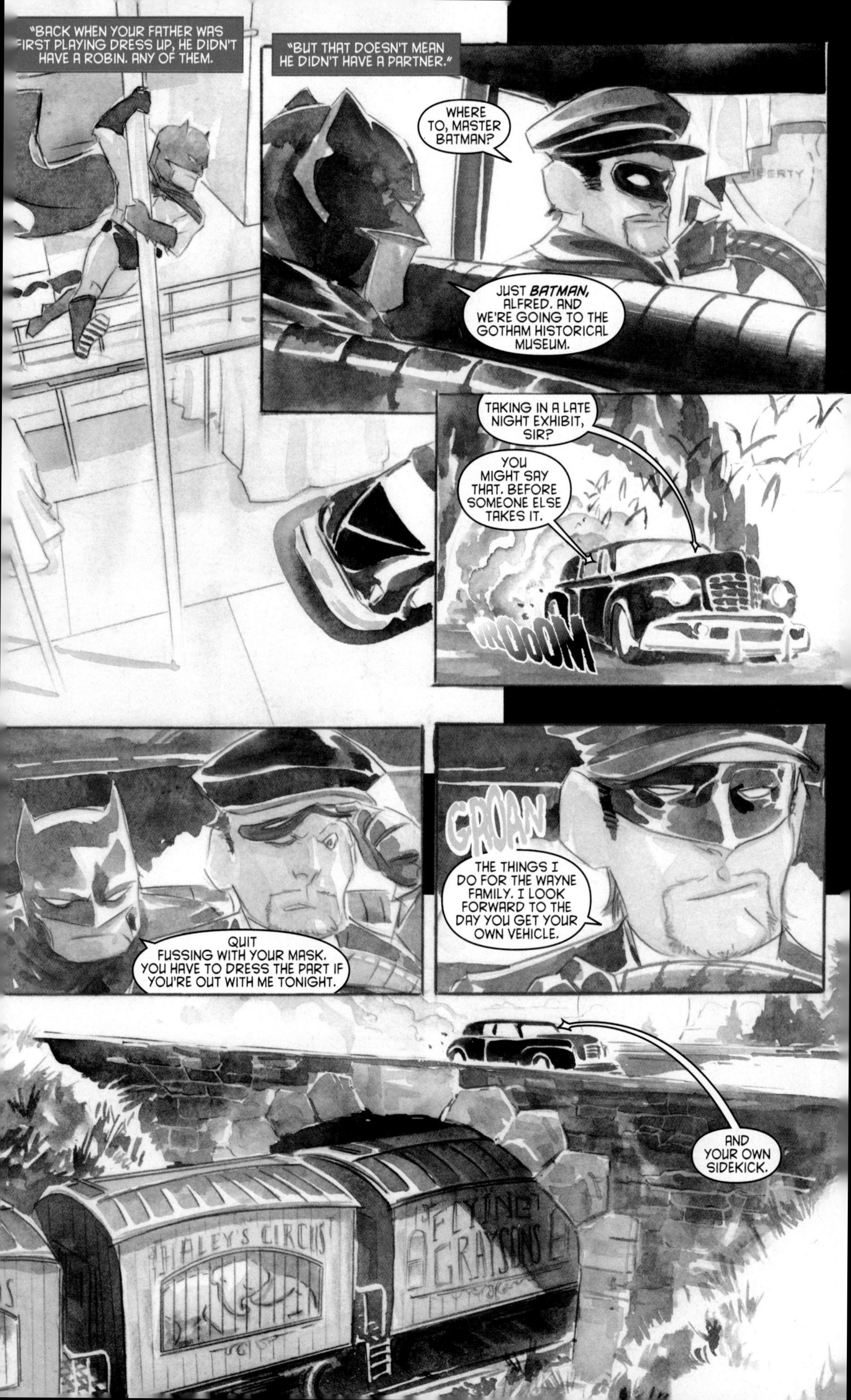
"BACK WHEN YOUR FATHER WAS FIRST PLAYING DRESS UP, HE DIDN'T HAVE A ROBIN. ANY OF THEM.
"BUT THAT DOESN'T MEAN HE DIDN'T HAVE A PARTNER."
WHERE TO, MASTER BATMAN?
JUST BATMAN, ALFRED. AND WE'RE GOING TO THE GOTHAM HISTORICAL MUSEUM.
TAKING IN A LATE NIGHT EXHIBIT, SIR?
YOU MIGHT SAY THAT. BEFORE SOMEONE ELSE TAKES IT.
VROOOM
QUIT FUSSING WITH YOUR MASK. YOU HAVE TO DRESS THE PART IF YOU'RE OUT WITH ME TONIGHT.
GROAN
THE THINGS I DO FOR THE WAYNE FAMILY. I LOOK FORWARD TO THE DAY YOU GET YOUR OWN VEHICLE.
AND YOUR OWN SIDEKICK.
HALEY'S CIRCUS
FLYING GRAYSONS

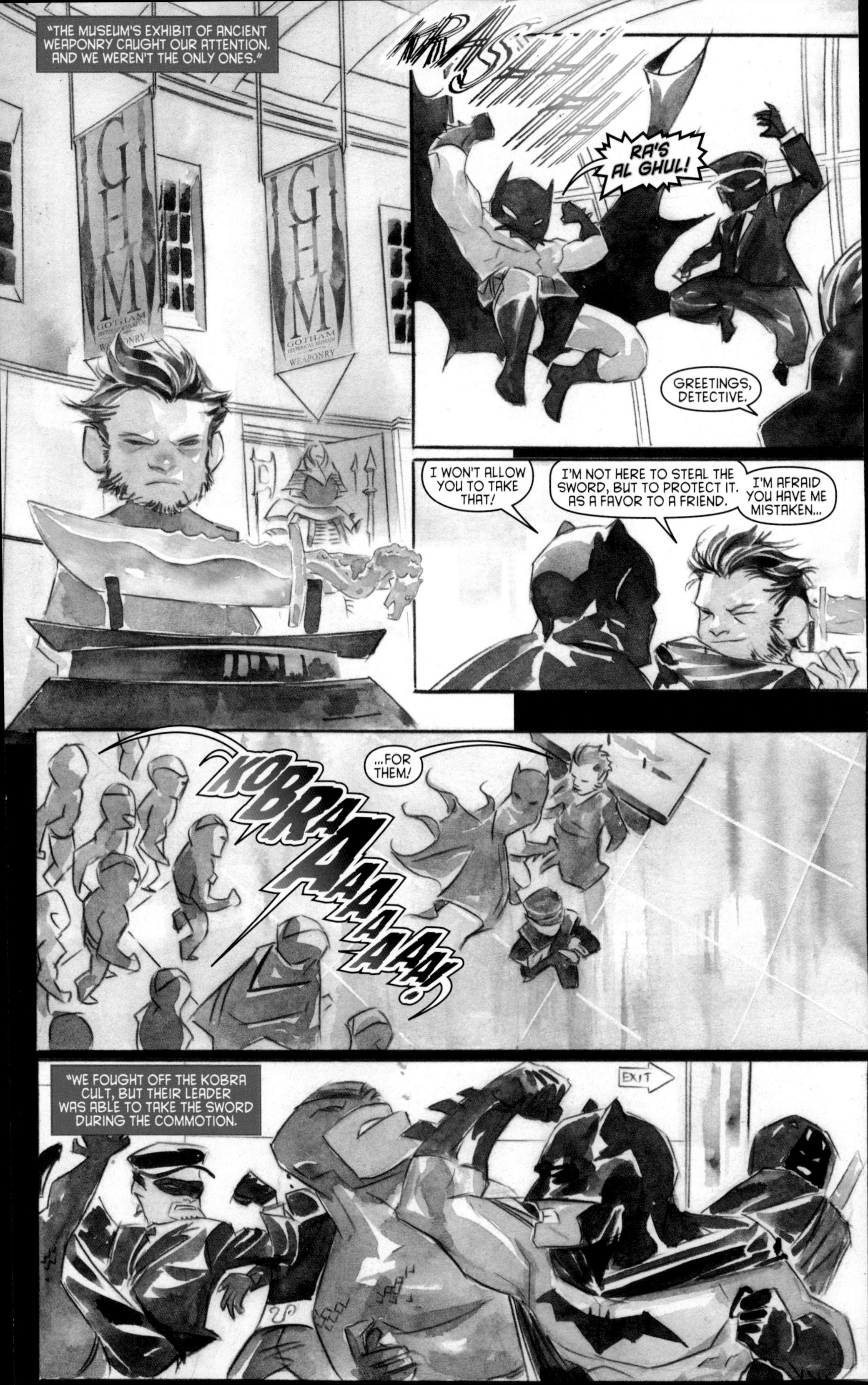
"THE MUSEUM'S EXHIBIT OF ANCIENT WEAPONRY CAUGHT OUR ATTENTION. AND WE WEREN'T THE ONLY ONES."
GHM GOTHAM HISTORICAL MUSEUM WEAPONRY
GHM GOTHAM HISTORICAL MUSEUM WEAPONRY
KRASHHH
RA'S AL GHUL!
GREETINGS, DETECTIVE.
I WON'T ALLOW YOU TO TAKE THAT!
I'M AFRAID YOU HAVE ME MISTAKEN...
I'M NOT HERE TO STEAL THE SWORD, BUT TO PROTECT IT. AS A FAVOR TO A FRIEND.
...FOR THEM!
KOBRAAAAAAA!
"WE FOUGHT OFF THE KOBRA CULT, BUT THEIR LEADER WAS ABLE TO TAKE THE SWORD DURING THE COMMOTION.
EXIT

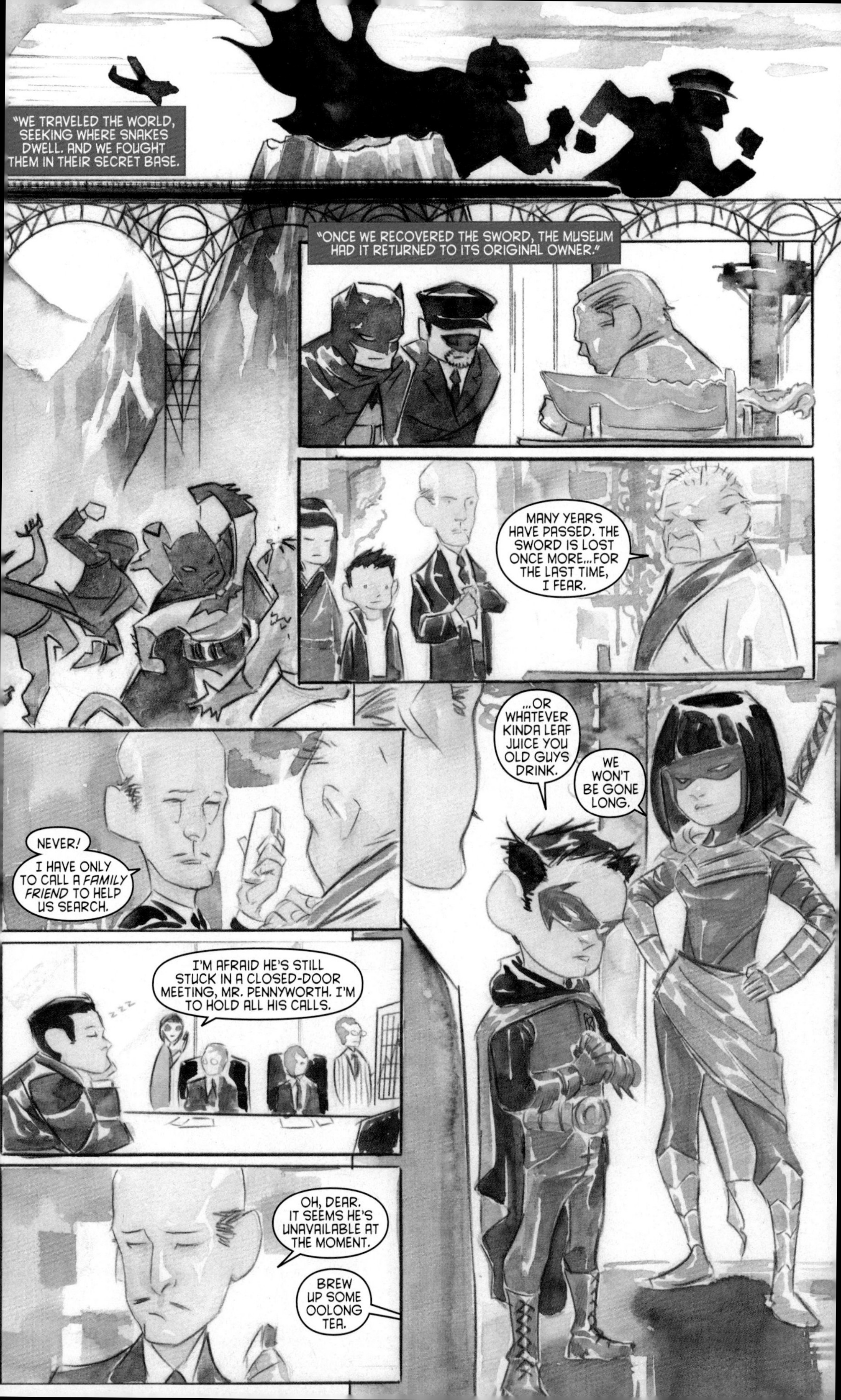
"WE TRAVELED THE WORLD, SEEKING WHERE SNAKES DWELL. AND WE FOUGHT THEM IN THEIR SECRET BASE.
"ONCE WE RECOVERED THE SWORD, THE MUSEUM HAD IT RETURNED TO ITS ORIGINAL OWNER."
MANY YEARS HAVE PASSED. THE SWORD IS LOST ONCE MORE...FOR THE LAST TIME, I FEAR.
NEVER!
I HAVE ONLY TO CALL A *FAMILY FRIEND* TO HELP US SEARCH.
I'M AFRAID HE'S STILL STUCK IN A CLOSED-DOOR MEETING, MR. PENNYWORTH. I'M TO HOLD ALL HIS CALLS.
ZZZ
OH, DEAR. IT SEEMS HE'S UNAVAILABLE AT THE MOMENT.
BREW UP SOME OOLONG TEA.
...OR WHATEVER KINDA LEAF JUICE YOU OLD GUYS DRINK.
WE WON'T BE GONE LONG.

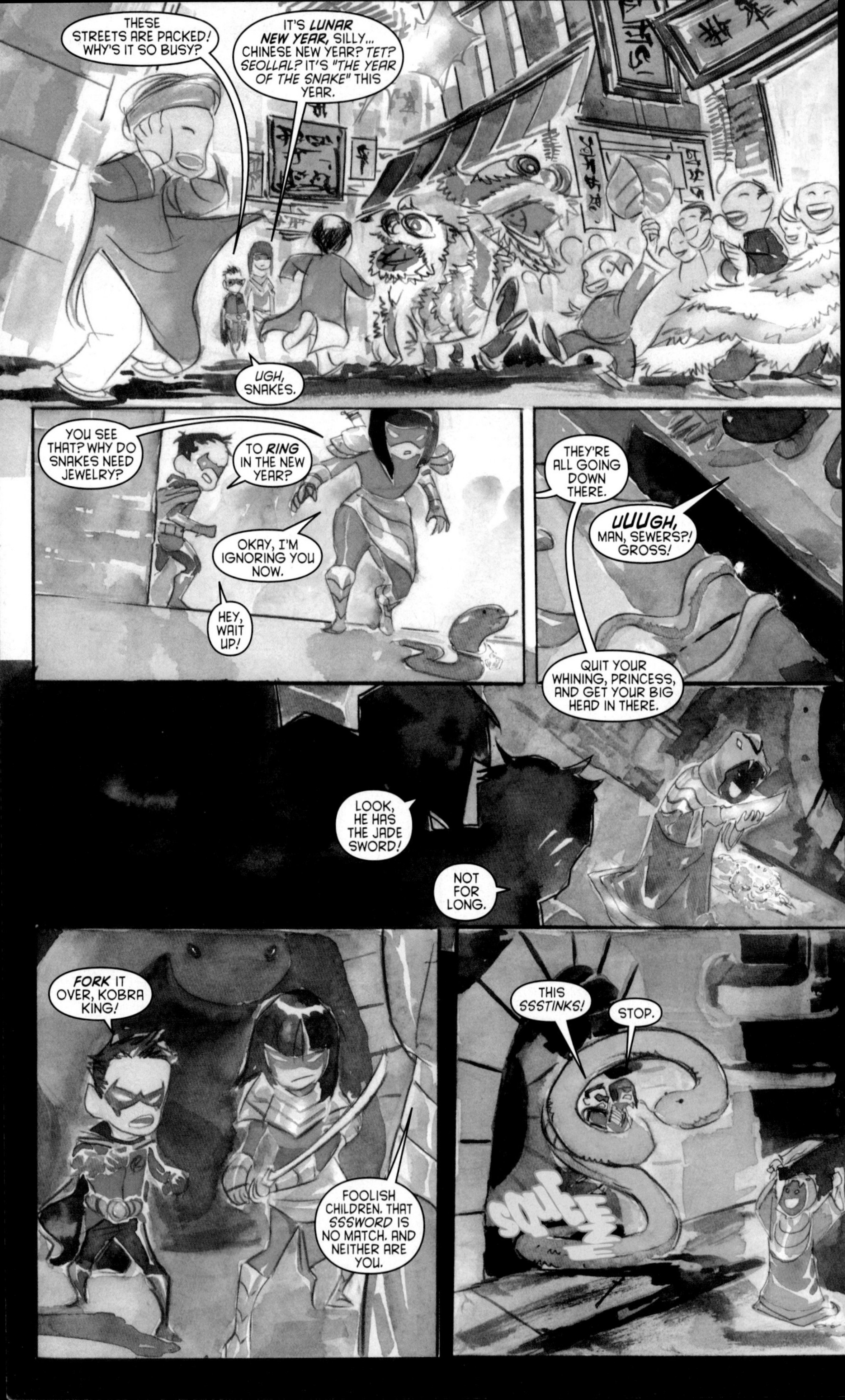
THESE STREETS ARE PACKED! WHY'S IT SO BUSY?
IT'S LUNAR NEW YEAR, SILLY... CHINESE NEW YEAR? TET? SEOLLAL? IT'S "THE YEAR OF THE SNAKE" THIS YEAR.
UGH, SNAKES.
YOU SEE THAT? WHY DO SNAKES NEED JEWELRY?
TO RING IN THE NEW YEAR?
OKAY, I'M IGNORING YOU NOW.
HEY, WAIT UP!
THEY'RE ALL GOING DOWN THERE.
UUUGH, MAN, SEWERS?! GROSS!
QUIT YOUR WHINING, PRINCESS, AND GET YOUR BIG HEAD IN THERE.
LOOK, HE HAS THE JADE SWORD!
NOT FOR LONG.
FORK IT OVER, KOBRA KING!
FOOLISH CHILDREN. THAT SSSWORD IS NO MATCH. AND NEITHER ARE YOU.
THIS SSSTINKS!
STOP.

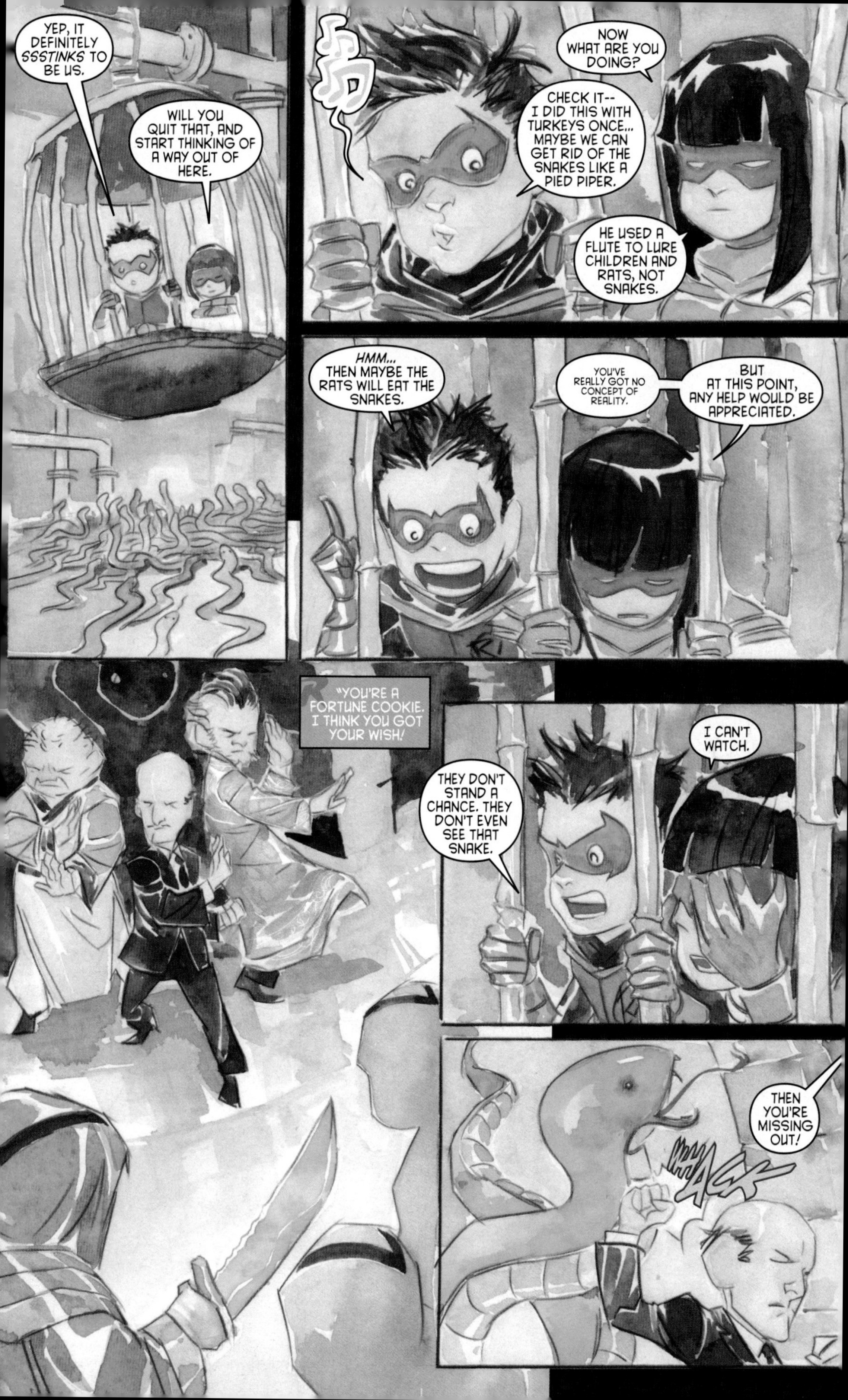
YEP, IT DEFINITELY SSSTINKS TO BE US.
WILL YOU QUIT THAT, AND START THINKING OF A WAY OUT OF HERE.
NOW WHAT ARE YOU DOING?
CHECK IT-- I DID THIS WITH TURKEYS ONCE... MAYBE WE CAN GET RID OF THE SNAKES LIKE A PIED PIPER.
HE USED A FLUTE TO LURE CHILDREN AND RATS, NOT SNAKES.
HMM... THEN MAYBE THE RATS WILL EAT THE SNAKES.
YOU'VE REALLY GOT NO CONCEPT OF REALITY.
BUT AT THIS POINT, ANY HELP WOULD BE APPRECIATED.
"YOU'RE A FORTUNE COOKIE. I THINK YOU GOT YOUR WISH!
I CAN'T WATCH.
THEY DON'T STAND A CHANCE. THEY DON'T EVEN SEE THAT SNAKE.
THEN YOU'RE MISSING OUT!
WHACK

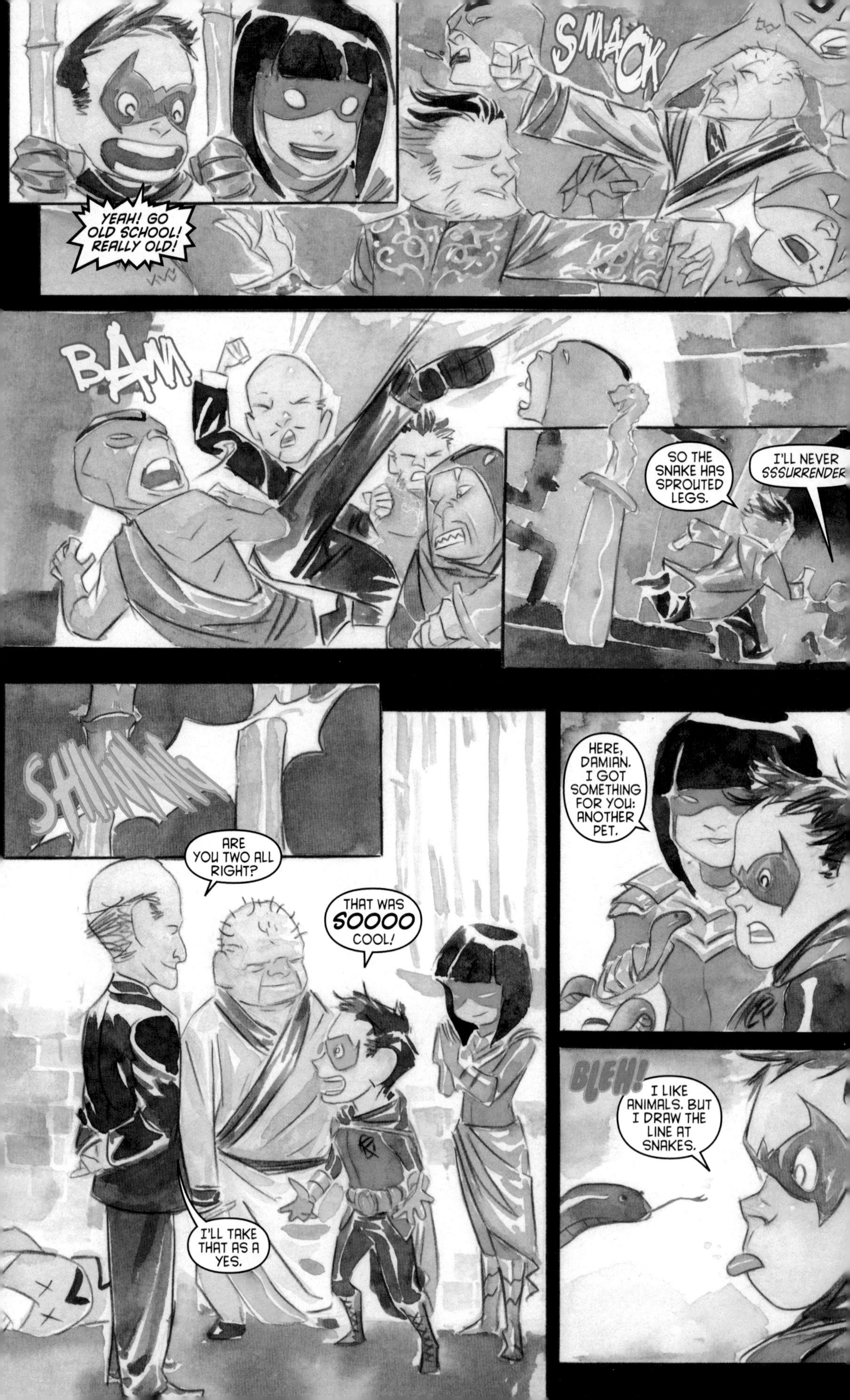
YEAH! GO OLD SCHOOL! REALLY OLD!
SMACK
BAM
SO THE SNAKE HAS SPROUTED LEGS.
I'LL NEVER SSSURRENDER
SHINNNG
ARE YOU TWO ALL RIGHT?
THAT WAS SOOOO COOL!
I'LL TAKE THAT AS A YES.
HERE, DAMIAN. I GOT SOMETHING FOR YOU: ANOTHER PET.
BLEH!
I LIKE ANIMALS. BUT I DRAW THE LINE AT SNAKES.

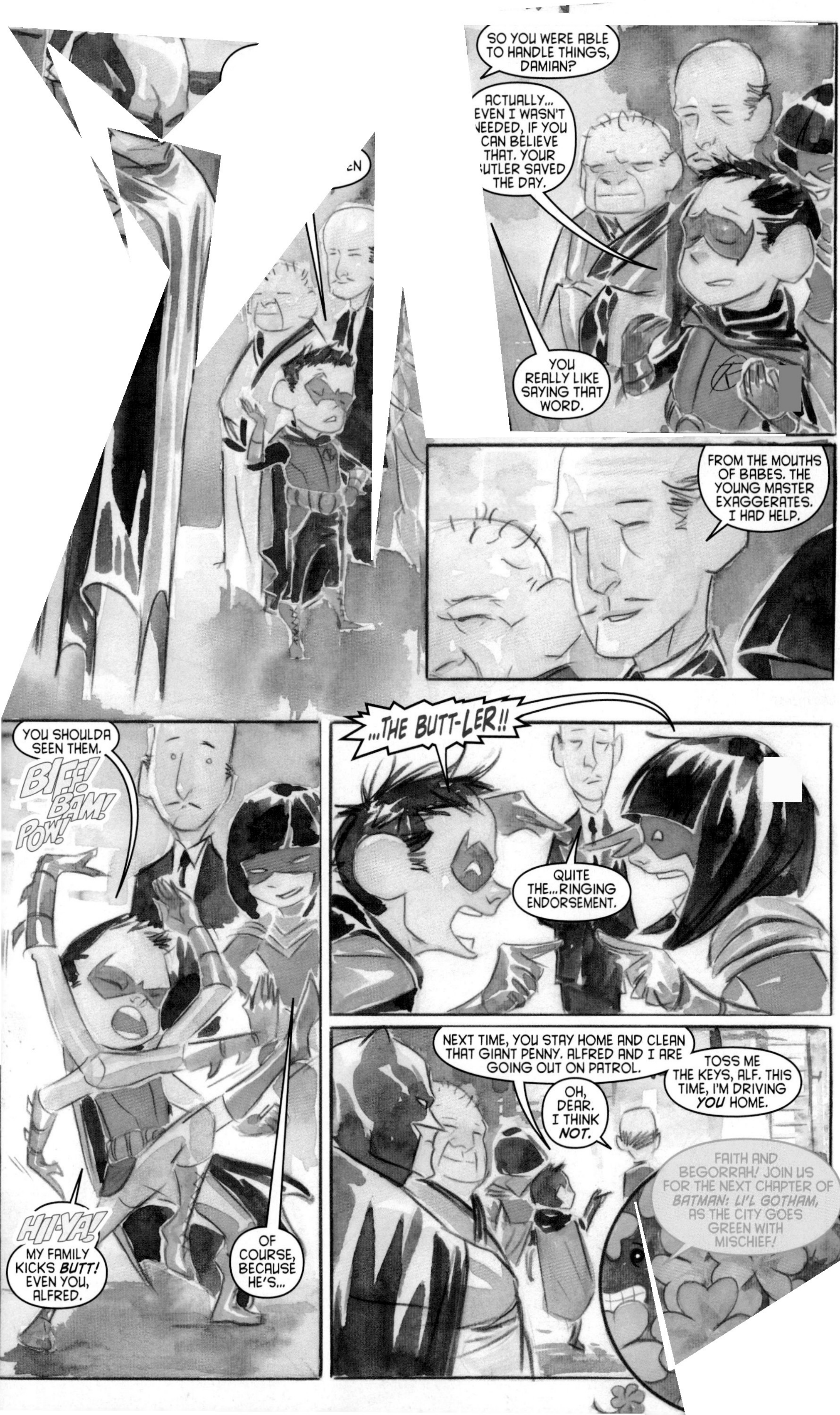
SO YOU WERE ABLE TO HANDLE THINGS, DAMIAN?
ACTUALLY... EVEN I WASN'T NEEDED, IF YOU CAN BELIEVE THAT. YOUR BUTLER SAVED THE DAY.
YOU REALLY LIKE SAYING THAT WORD.
FROM THE MOUTHS OF BABES. THE YOUNG MASTER EXAGGERATES. I HAD HELP.
YOU SHOULDA SEEN THEM.
BIFF! BAM! POW!
HI-YA!
MY FAMILY KICKS *BUTT*! EVEN YOU, ALFRED.
OF COURSE, BECAUSE HE'S...
...THE BUTT-LER!!
QUITE THE...RINGING ENDORSEMENT.
NEXT TIME, YOU STAY HOME AND CLEAN THAT GIANT PENNY. ALFRED AND I ARE GOING OUT ON PATROL.
OH, DEAR. I THINK *NOT*.
TOSS ME THE KEYS, ALF. THIS TIME, I'M DRIVING *YOU* HOME.
FAITH AND BEGORRAH! JOIN US FOR THE NEXT CHAPTER OF *BATMAN: LI'L GOTHAM*, AS THE CITY GOES GREEN WITH MISCHIEF!

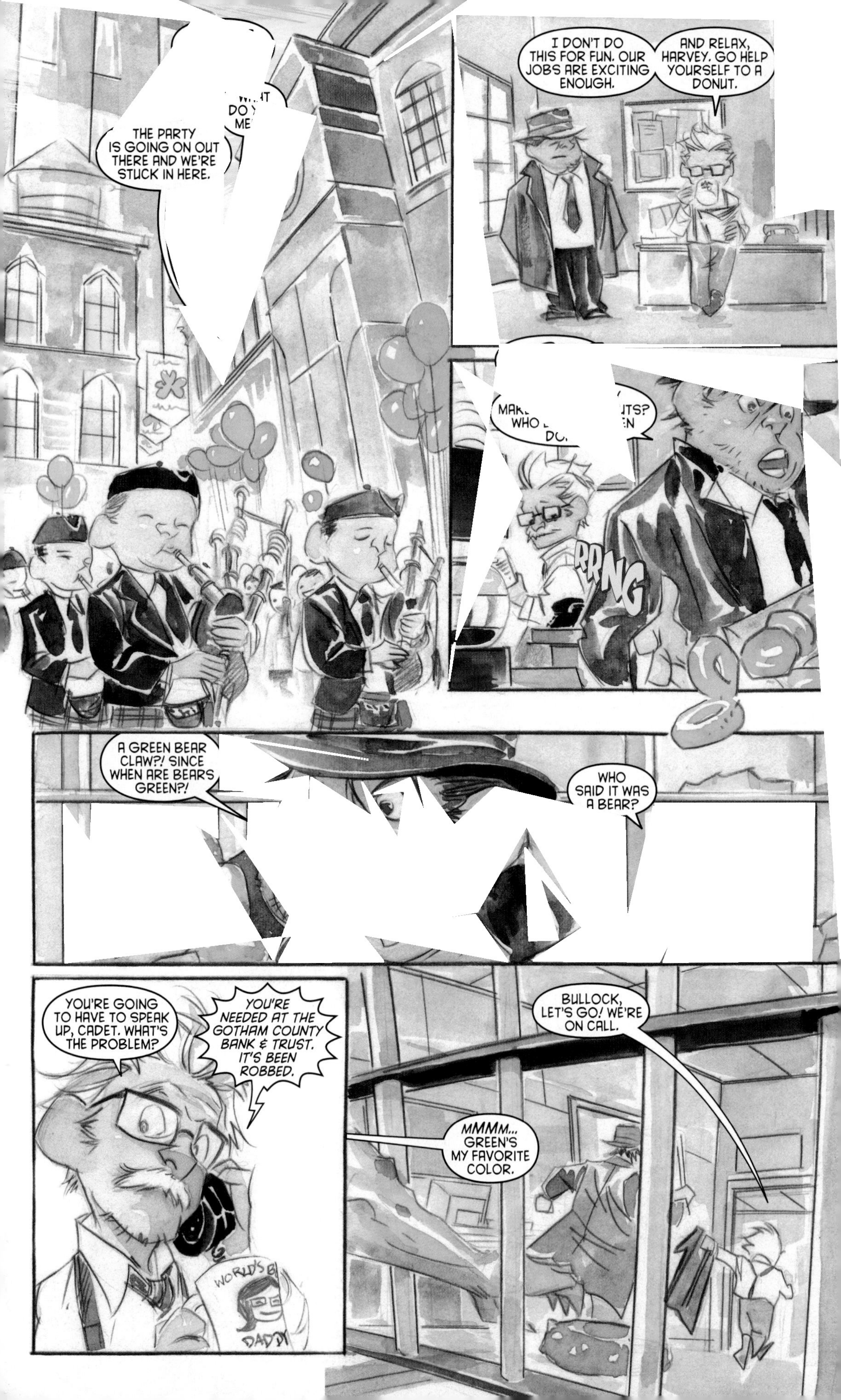
THE PARTY IS GOING ON OUT THERE AND WE'RE STUCK IN HERE.
I DON'T DO THIS FOR FUN. OUR JOBS ARE EXCITING ENOUGH.
AND RELAX, HARVEY. GO HELP YOURSELF TO A DONUT.
RRNG
A GREEN BEAR CLAW?! SINCE WHEN ARE BEARS GREEN?!
WHO SAID IT WAS A BEAR?
YOU'RE GOING TO HAVE TO SPEAK UP, CADET. WHAT'S THE PROBLEM?
YOU'RE NEEDED AT THE GOTHAM COUNTY BANK & TRUST. IT'S BEEN ROBBED.
BULLOCK, LET'S GO! WE'RE ON CALL.
MMMM... GREEN'S MY FAVORITE COLOR.
DADDY

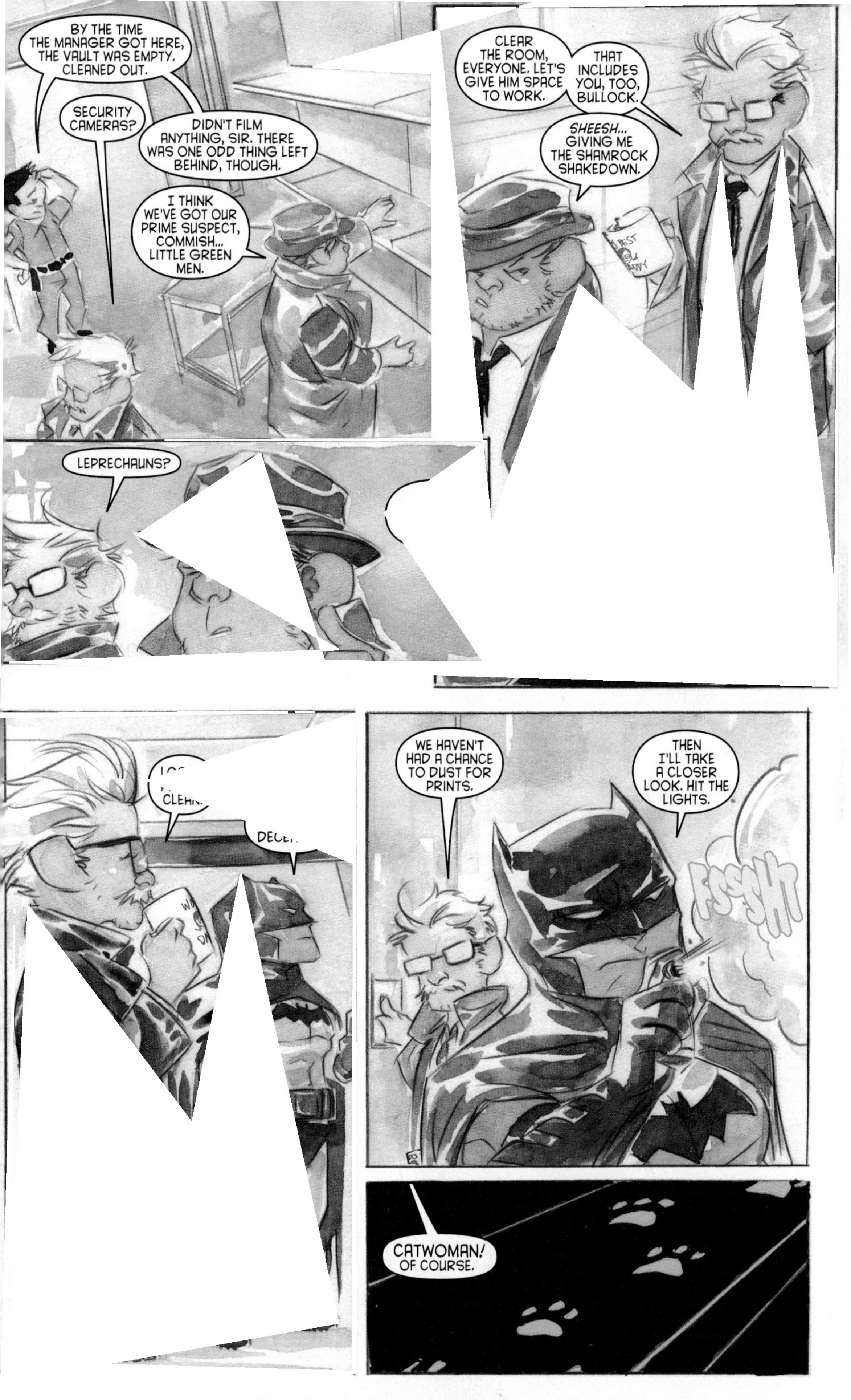

BY THE TIME THE MANAGER GOT HERE, THE VAULT WAS EMPTY. CLEANED OUT.
SECURITY CAMERAS?
DIDN'T FILM ANYTHING, SIR. THERE WAS ONE ODD THING LEFT BEHIND, THOUGH.
I THINK WE'VE GOT OUR PRIME SUSPECT, COMMISH... LITTLE GREEN MEN.
CLEAR THE ROOM, EVERYONE. LET'S GIVE HIM SPACE TO WORK.
THAT INCLUDES YOU, TOO, BULLOCK.
SHEESH... GIVING ME THE SHAMROCK SHAKEDOWN.
LEPRECHAUNS?
WE HAVEN'T HAD A CHANCE TO DUST FOR PRINTS.
THEN I'LL TAKE A CLOSER LOOK. HIT THE LIGHTS.
FSSSHT
CATWOMAN! OF COURSE.

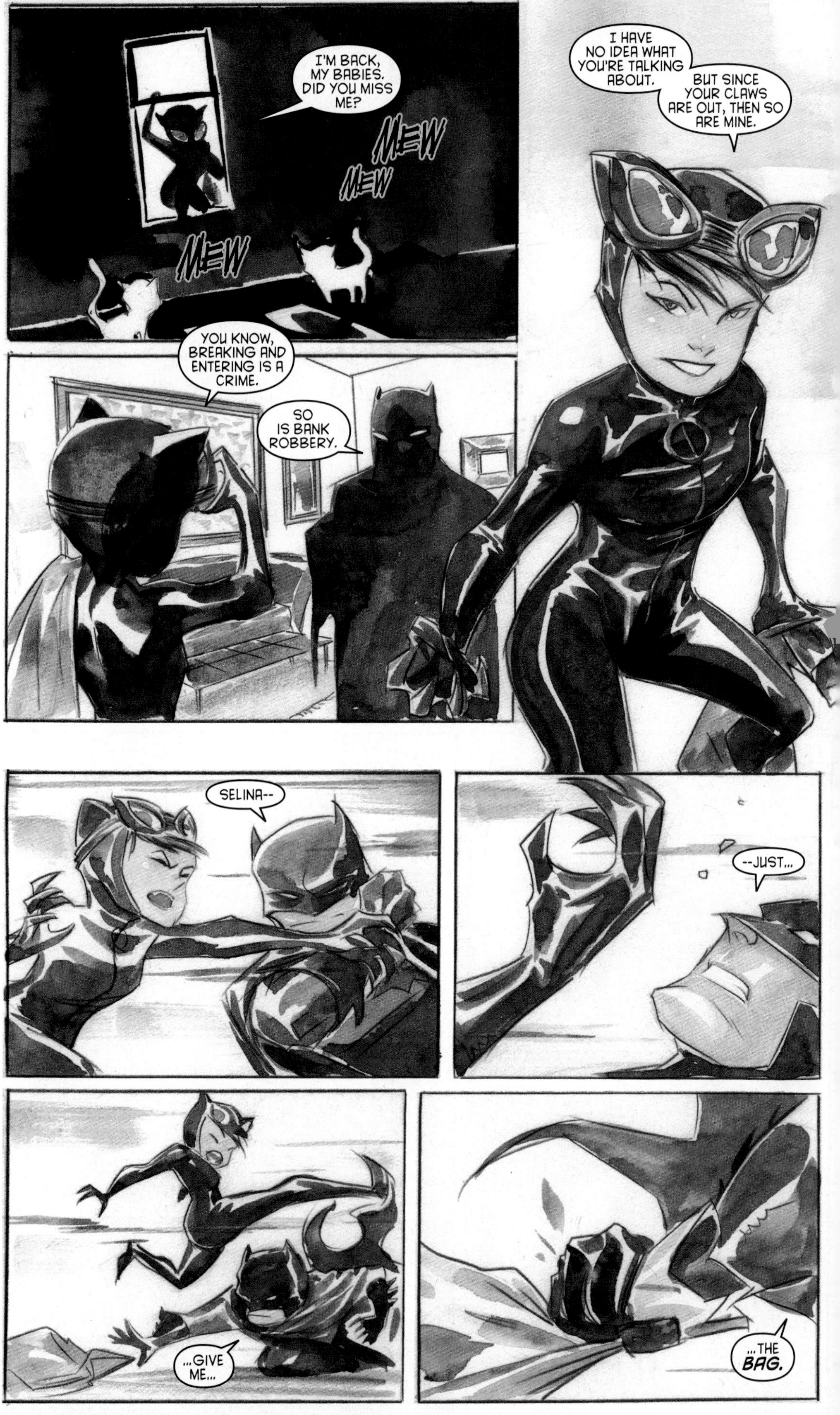
I'M BACK, MY BABIES. DID YOU MISS ME?
MEW
MEW
MEW
I HAVE NO IDEA WHAT YOU'RE TALKING ABOUT.
BUT SINCE YOUR CLAWS ARE OUT, THEN SO ARE MINE.
YOU KNOW, BREAKING AND ENTERING IS A CRIME.
SO IS BANK ROBBERY.
SELINA--
--JUST...
...GIVE ME...
...THE BAG.

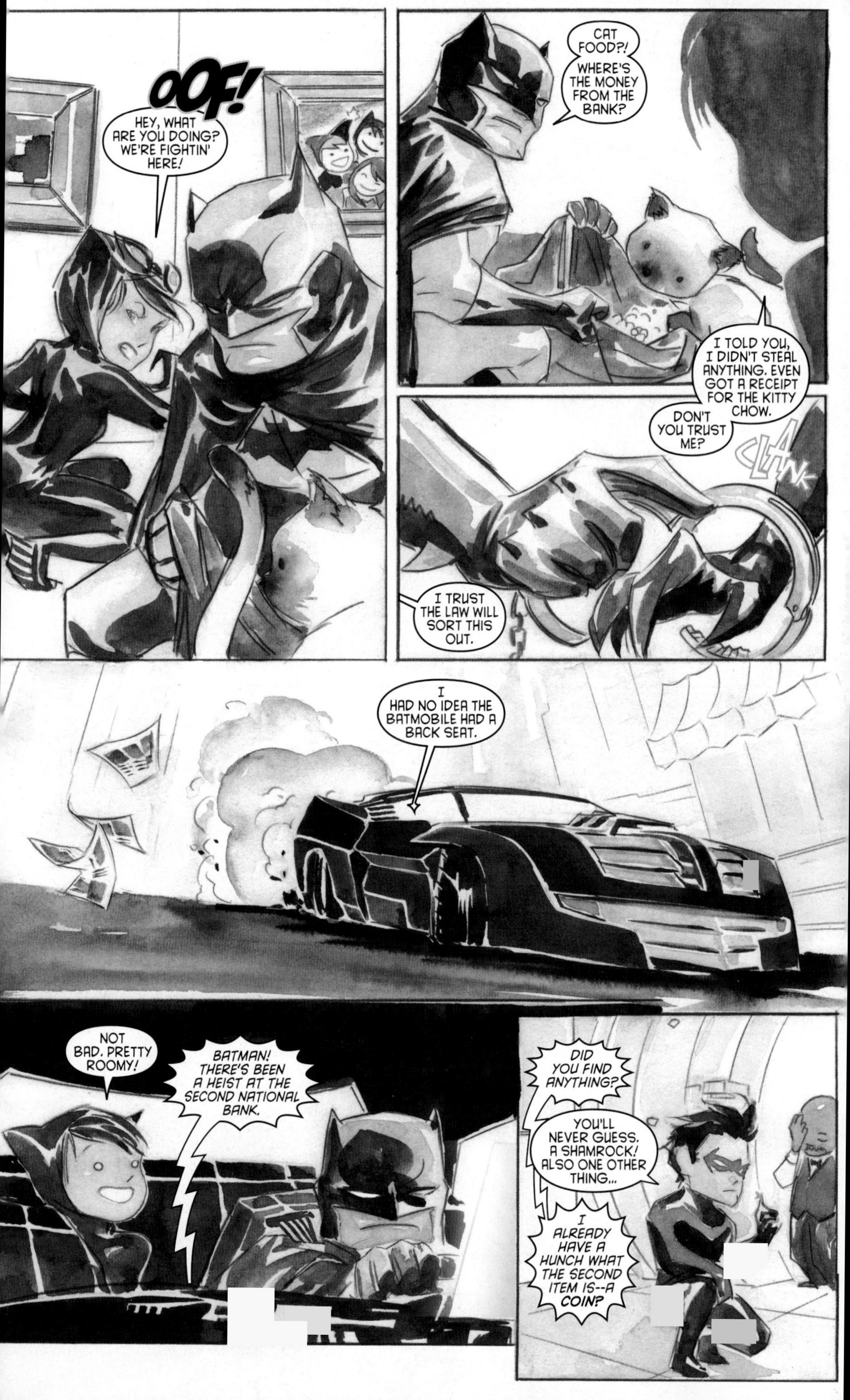
OOF!
HEY, WHAT ARE YOU DOING? WE'RE FIGHTIN' HERE!
CAT FOOD?! WHERE'S THE MONEY FROM THE BANK?
I TOLD YOU, I DIDN'T STEAL ANYTHING. EVEN GOT A RECEIPT FOR THE KITTY CHOW.
DON'T YOU TRUST ME?
CLANK
I TRUST THE LAW WILL SORT THIS OUT.
I HAD NO IDEA THE BATMOBILE HAD A BACK SEAT.
NOT BAD. PRETTY ROOMY!
BATMAN! THERE'S BEEN A HEIST AT THE SECOND NATIONAL BANK.
DID YOU FIND ANYTHING?
YOU'LL NEVER GUESS. A SHAMROCK! ALSO ONE OTHER THING...
I ALREADY HAVE A HUNCH WHAT THE SECOND ITEM IS--A COIN?

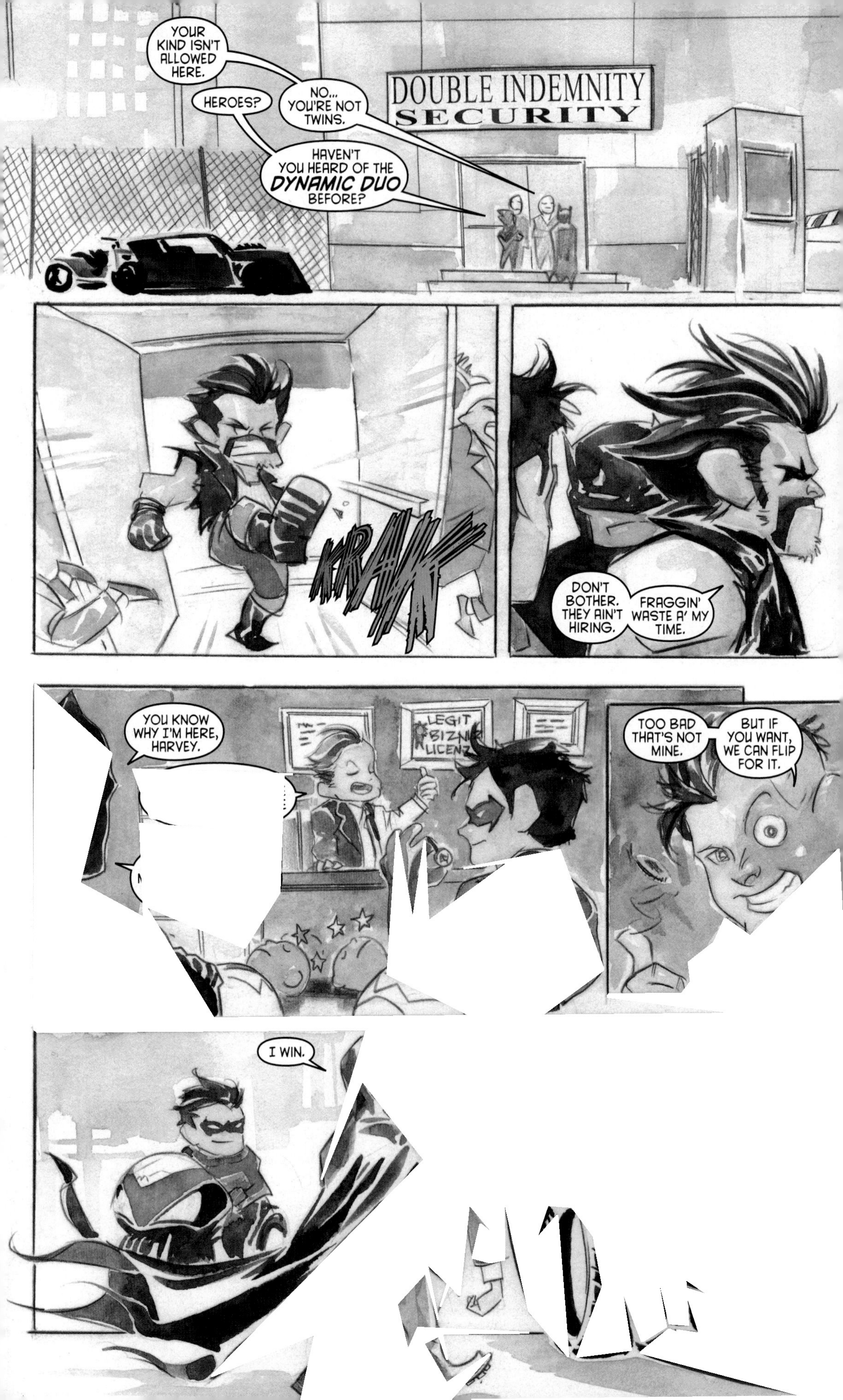

YOUR KIND ISN'T ALLOWED HERE.
HEROES?
NO... YOU'RE NOT TWINS.
HAVEN'T YOU HEARD OF THE DYNAMIC DUO BEFORE?
DOUBLE INDEMNITY SECURITY
KRAAK
DON'T BOTHER. THEY AIN'T HIRING.
FRAGGIN' WASTE A' MY TIME.
YOU KNOW WHY I'M HERE, HARVEY.
LEGIT BIZNI LICENZ
TOO BAD THAT'S NOT MINE.
BUT IF YOU WANT, WE CAN FLIP FOR IT.
I WIN.

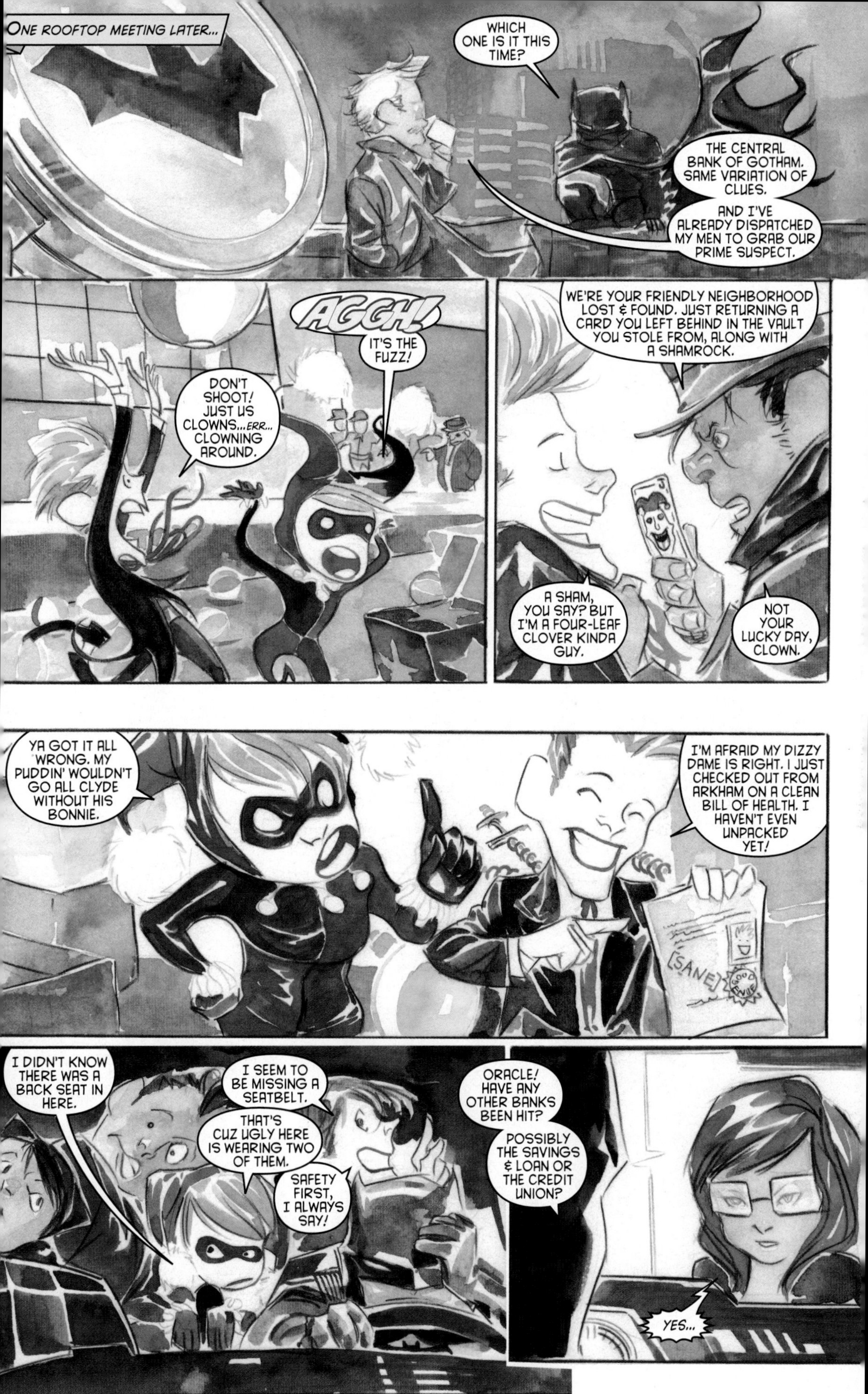
ONE ROOFTOP MEETING LATER...
WHICH ONE IS IT THIS TIME?
THE CENTRAL BANK OF GOTHAM. SAME VARIATION OF CLUES.
AND I'VE ALREADY DISPATCHED MY MEN TO GRAB OUR PRIME SUSPECT.
AGGH!
IT'S THE FUZZ!
DON'T SHOOT! JUST US CLOWNS...ERR... CLOWNING AROUND.
WE'RE YOUR FRIENDLY NEIGHBORHOOD LOST & FOUND. JUST RETURNING A CARD YOU LEFT BEHIND IN THE VAULT YOU STOLE FROM, ALONG WITH A SHAMROCK.
A SHAM, YOU SAY? BUT I'M A FOUR-LEAF CLOVER KINDA GUY.
NOT YOUR LUCKY DAY, CLOWN.
YA GOT IT ALL WRONG. MY PUDDIN' WOULDN'T GO ALL CLYDE WITHOUT HIS BONNIE.
I'M AFRAID MY DIZZY DAME IS RIGHT. I JUST CHECKED OUT FROM ARKHAM ON A CLEAN BILL OF HEALTH. I HAVEN'T EVEN UNPACKED YET!
SANE
I DIDN'T KNOW THERE WAS A BACK SEAT IN HERE.
I SEEM TO BE MISSING A SEATBELT.
THAT'S CUZ UGLY HERE IS WEARING TWO OF THEM.
SAFETY FIRST, I ALWAYS SAY!
ORACLE! HAVE ANY OTHER BANKS BEEN HIT?
POSSIBLY THE SAVINGS & LOAN OR THE CREDIT UNION?
YES...

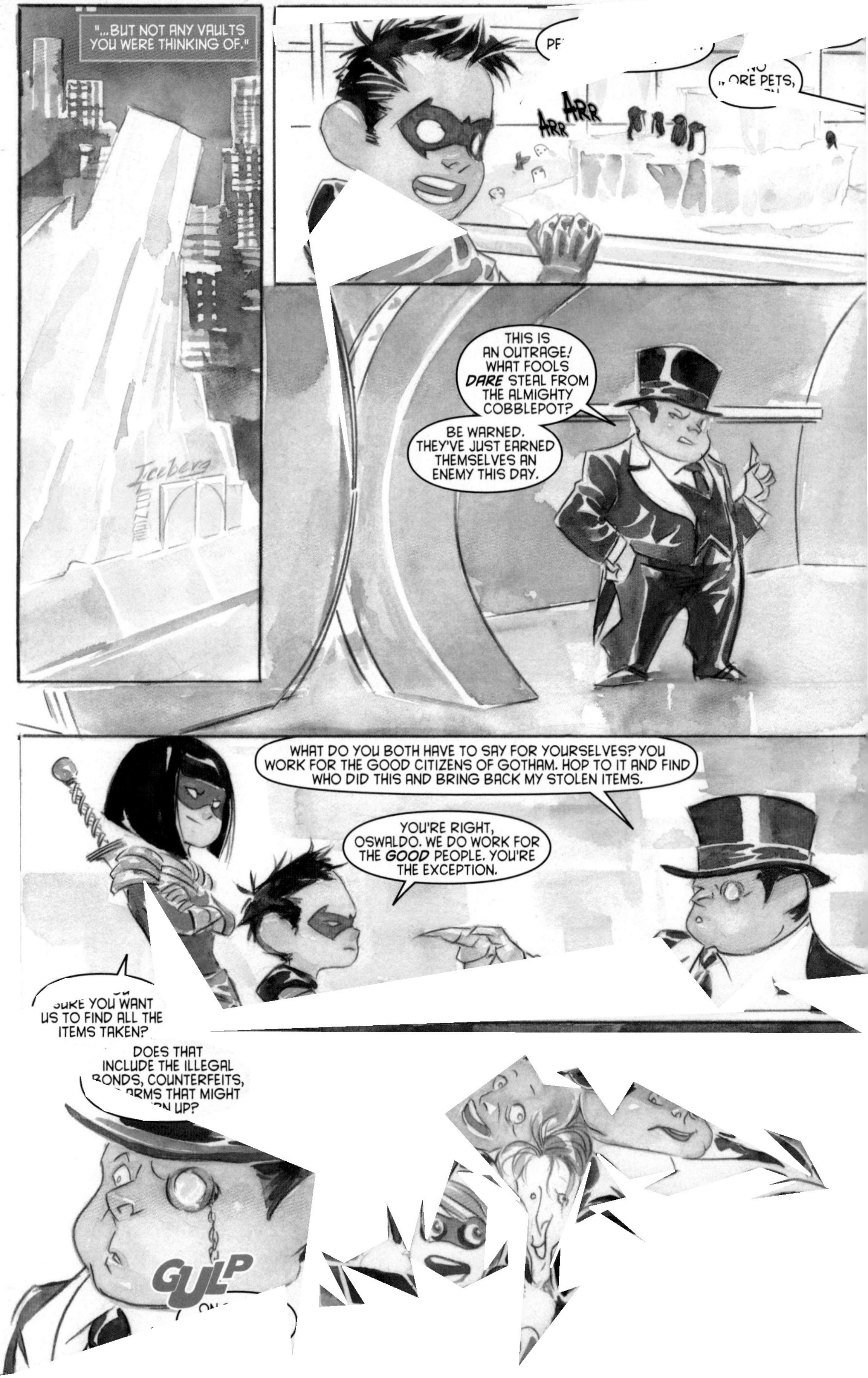

"...BUT NOT ANY VAULTS YOU WERE THINKING OF."
ARR ARR
Iceberg
THIS IS AN OUTRAGE! WHAT FOOLS DARE STEAL FROM THE ALMIGHTY COBBLEPOT?
BE WARNED. THEY'VE JUST EARNED THEMSELVES AN ENEMY THIS DAY.
WHAT DO YOU BOTH HAVE TO SAY FOR YOURSELVES? YOU WORK FOR THE GOOD CITIZENS OF GOTHAM. HOP TO IT AND FIND WHO DID THIS AND BRING BACK MY STOLEN ITEMS.
YOU'RE RIGHT, OSWALDO. WE DO WORK FOR THE GOOD PEOPLE. YOU'RE THE EXCEPTION.
US TO FIND ALL THE ITEMS TAKEN?
DOES THAT INCLUDE THE ILLEGAL BONDS, COUNTERFEITS,
GULP

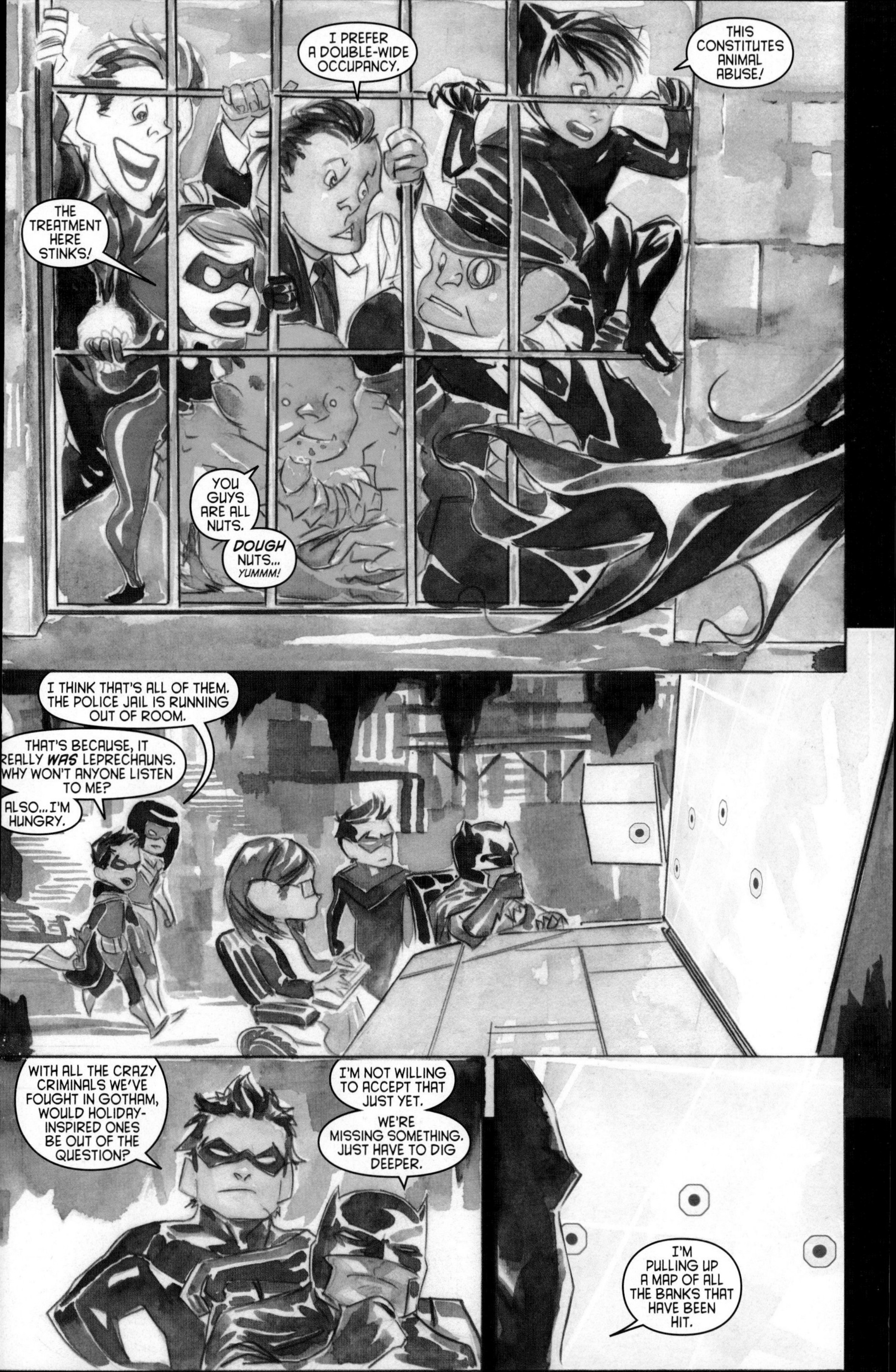

I PREFER A DOUBLE-WIDE OCCUPANCY.
THIS CONSTITUTES ANIMAL ABUSE!
THE TREATMENT HERE STINKS!
YOU GUYS ARE ALL NUTS.
DOUGH NUTS... YUMMM!
I THINK THAT'S ALL OF THEM. THE POLICE JAIL IS RUNNING OUT OF ROOM.
THAT'S BECAUSE, IT REALLY WAS LEPRECHAUNS. WHY WON'T ANYONE LISTEN TO ME?
ALSO...I'M HUNGRY.
WITH ALL THE CRAZY CRIMINALS WE'VE FOUGHT IN GOTHAM, WOULD HOLIDAY-INSPIRED ONES BE OUT OF THE QUESTION?
I'M NOT WILLING TO ACCEPT THAT JUST YET.
WE'RE MISSING SOMETHING. JUST HAVE TO DIG DEEPER.
I'M PULLING UP A MAP OF ALL THE BANKS THAT HAVE BEEN HIT.

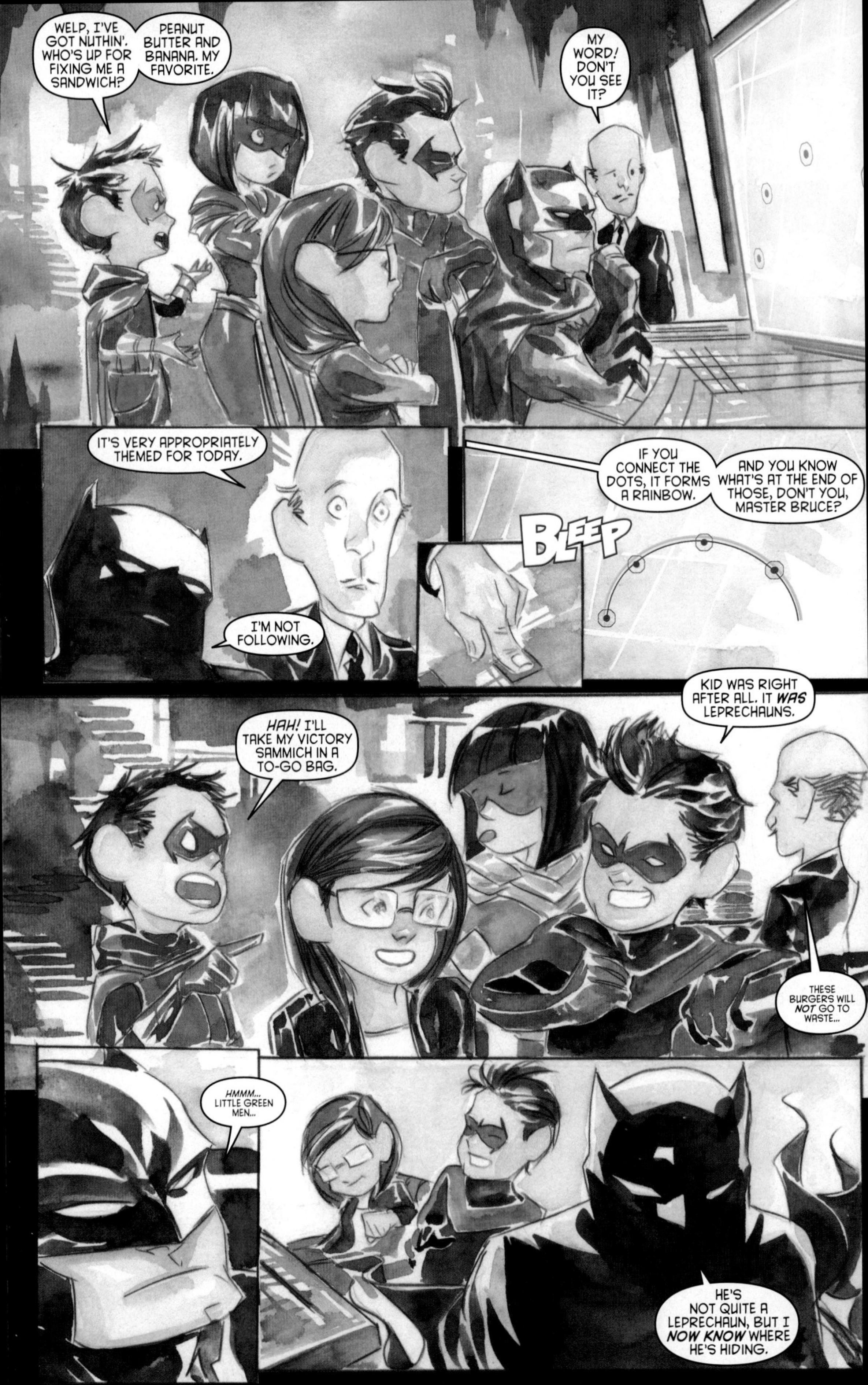
WELP, I'VE GOT NUTHIN'. WHO'S UP FOR FIXING ME A SANDWICH?
PEANUT BUTTER AND BANANA. MY FAVORITE.
MY WORD! DON'T YOU SEE IT?
IT'S VERY APPROPRIATELY THEMED FOR TODAY.
I'M NOT FOLLOWING.
IF YOU CONNECT THE DOTS, IT FORMS A RAINBOW.
AND YOU KNOW WHAT'S AT THE END OF THOSE, DON'T YOU, MASTER BRUCE?
BLEEP
HAH! I'LL TAKE MY VICTORY SAMMICH IN A TO-GO BAG.
KID WAS RIGHT AFTER ALL. IT WAS LEPRECHAUNS.
THESE BURGERS WILL NOT GO TO WASTE...
HMMM... LITTLE GREEN MEN...
HE'S NOT QUITE A LEPRECHAUN, BUT I NOW KNOW WHERE HE'S HIDING.

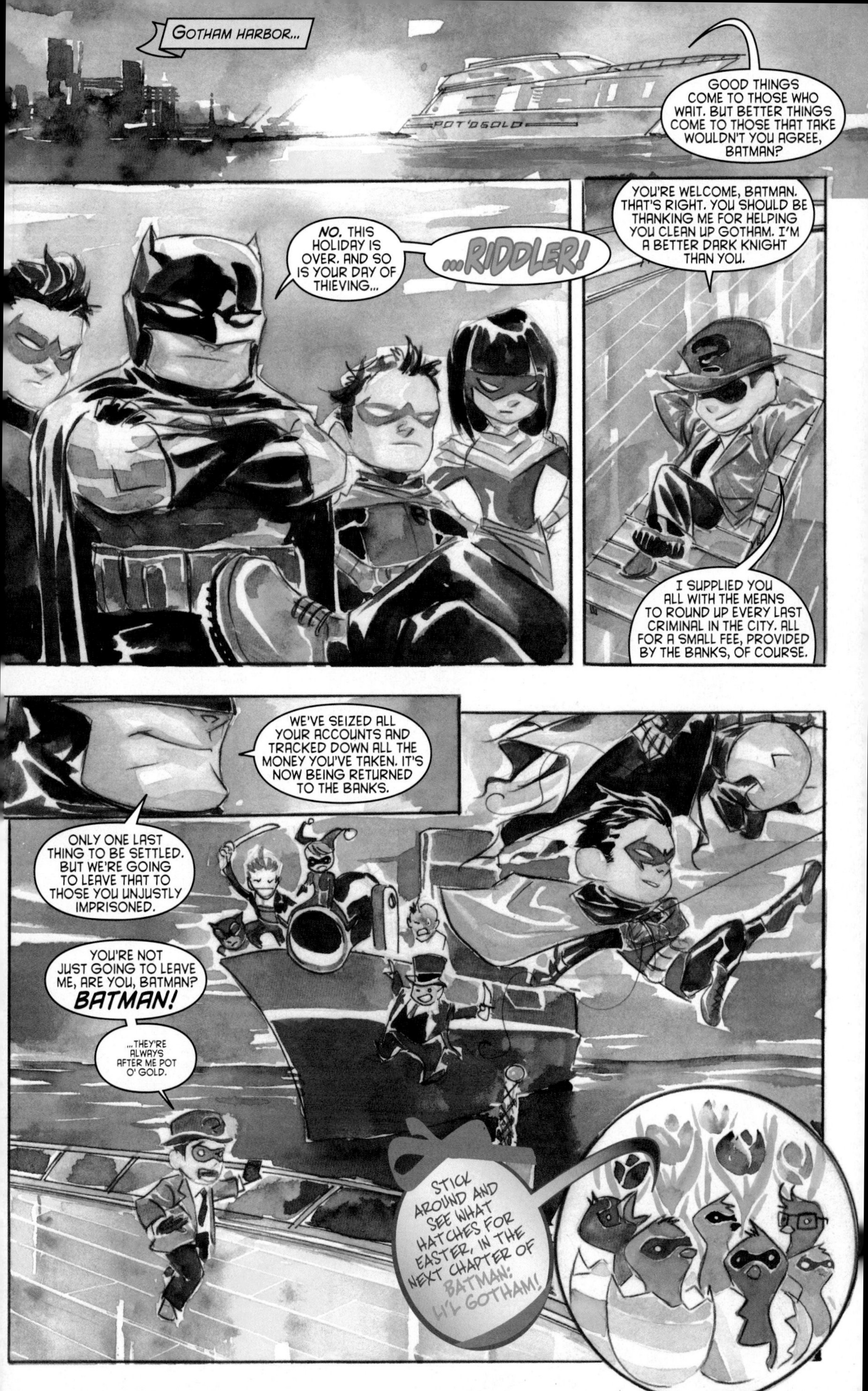
GOTHAM HARBOR...
POT 'O GOLD
GOOD THINGS COME TO THOSE WHO WAIT. BUT BETTER THINGS COME TO THOSE THAT TAKE WOULDN'T YOU AGREE, BATMAN?
NO. THIS HOLIDAY IS OVER. AND SO IS YOUR DAY OF THIEVING...
...RIDDLER!
YOU'RE WELCOME, BATMAN. THAT'S RIGHT. YOU SHOULD BE THANKING ME FOR HELPING YOU CLEAN UP GOTHAM. I'M A BETTER DARK KNIGHT THAN YOU.
I SUPPLIED YOU ALL WITH THE MEANS TO ROUND UP EVERY LAST CRIMINAL IN THE CITY. ALL FOR A SMALL FEE, PROVIDED BY THE BANKS, OF COURSE.
WE'VE SEIZED ALL YOUR ACCOUNTS AND TRACKED DOWN ALL THE MONEY YOU'VE TAKEN. IT'S NOW BEING RETURNED TO THE BANKS.
ONLY ONE LAST THING TO BE SETTLED. BUT WE'RE GOING TO LEAVE THAT TO THOSE YOU UNJUSTLY IMPRISONED.
YOU'RE NOT JUST GOING TO LEAVE ME, ARE YOU, BATMAN? BATMAN!
...THEY'RE ALWAYS AFTER ME POT O' GOLD.
STICK AROUND AND SEE WHAT HATCHES FOR EASTER, IN THE NEXT CHAPTER OF BATMAN: LI'L GOTHAM!

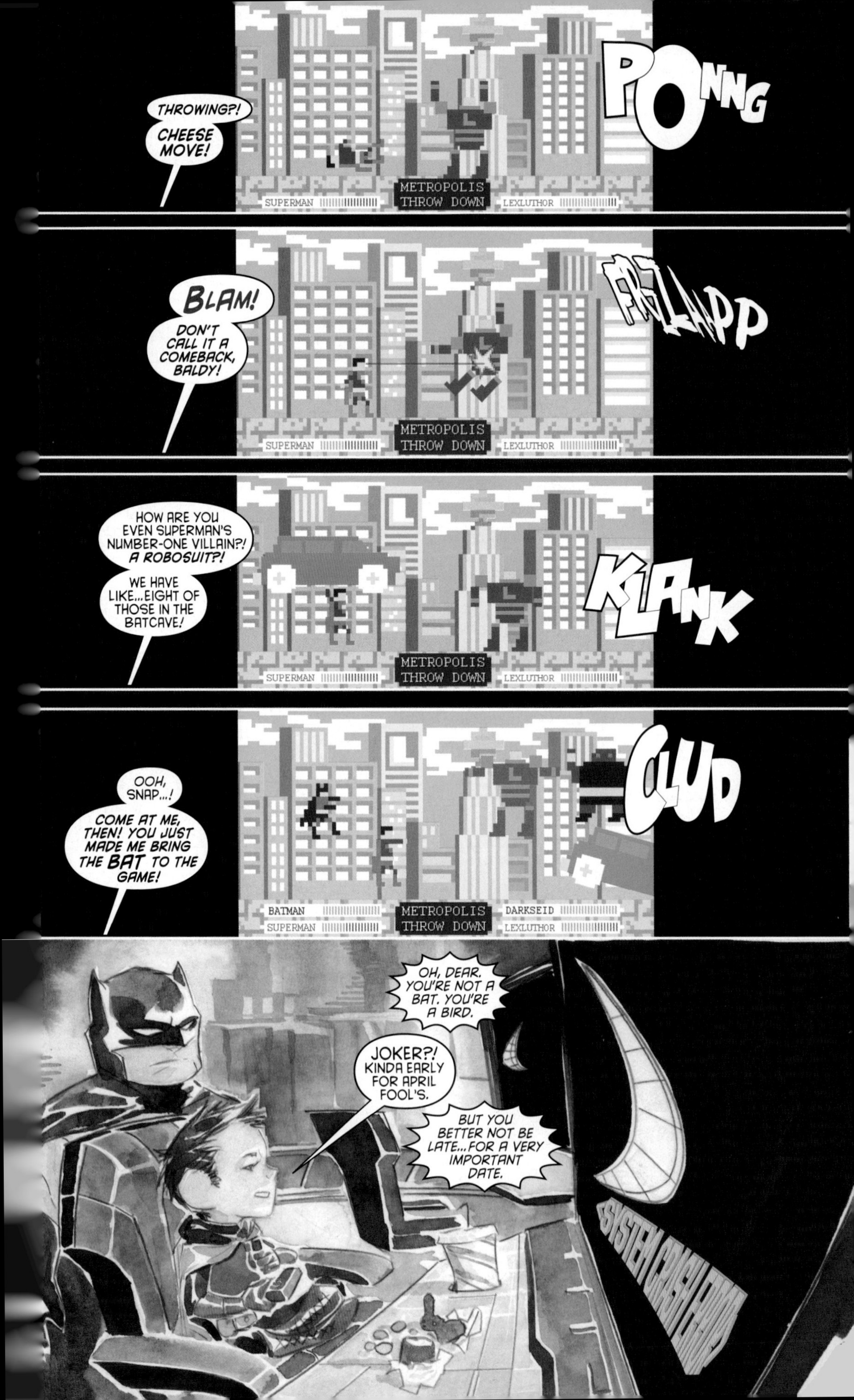
THROWING?! CHEESE MOVE!
PONNG
METROPOLIS THROW DOWN
SUPERMAN
LEXLUTHOR
BLAM! DON'T CALL IT A COMEBACK, BALDY!
FRZLAPP
METROPOLIS THROW DOWN
SUPERMAN
LEXLUTHOR
HOW ARE YOU EVEN SUPERMAN'S NUMBER-ONE VILLAIN?! A ROBOSUIT?!
WE HAVE LIKE...EIGHT OF THOSE IN THE BATCAVE!
KLANK
METROPOLIS THROW DOWN
SUPERMAN
LEXLUTHOR
OOH, SNAP...!
COME AT ME, THEN! YOU JUST MADE ME BRING THE BAT TO THE GAME!
CLUD
BATMAN
SUPERMAN
METROPOLIS THROW DOWN
DARKSEID
LEXLUTHOR
OH, DEAR. YOU'RE NOT A BAT. YOU'RE A BIRD.
JOKER?! KINDA EARLY FOR APRIL FOOL'S.
BUT YOU BETTER NOT BE LATE...FOR A VERY IMPORTANT DATE.
SYSTEM CRASH ERROR

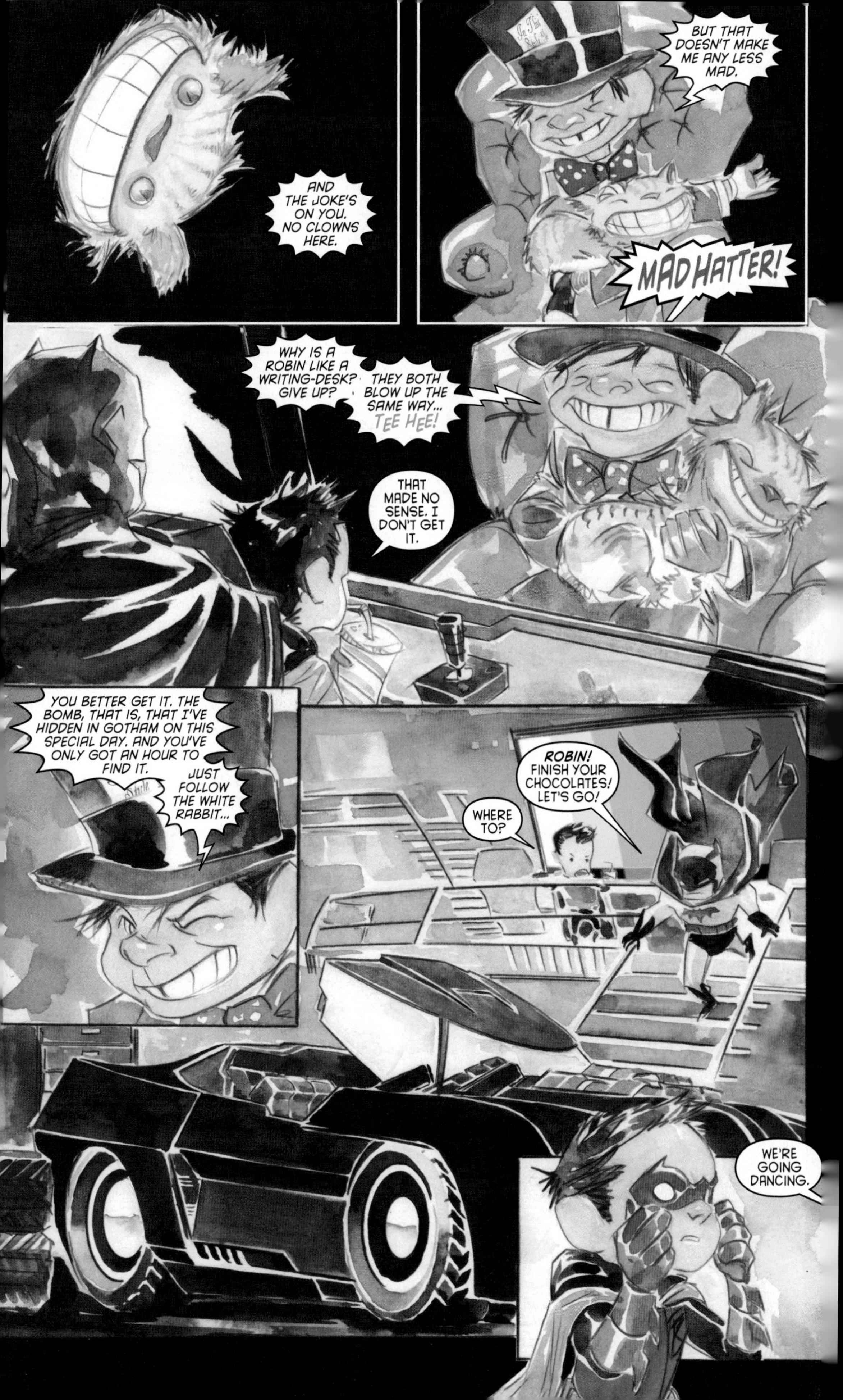
AND THE JOKE'S ON YOU. NO CLOWNS HERE.
BUT THAT DOESN'T MAKE ME ANY LESS MAD.
MAD HATTER!
WHY IS A ROBIN LIKE A WRITING-DESK? GIVE UP?
THEY BOTH BLOW UP THE SAME WAY... TEE HEE!
THAT MADE NO SENSE. I DON'T GET IT.
YOU BETTER GET IT. THE BOMB, THAT IS, THAT I'VE HIDDEN IN GOTHAM ON THIS SPECIAL DAY. AND YOU'VE ONLY GOT AN HOUR TO FIND IT.
JUST FOLLOW THE WHITE RABBIT...
ROBIN! FINISH YOUR CHOCOLATES! LET'S GO!
WHERE TO?
WE'RE GOING DANCING.

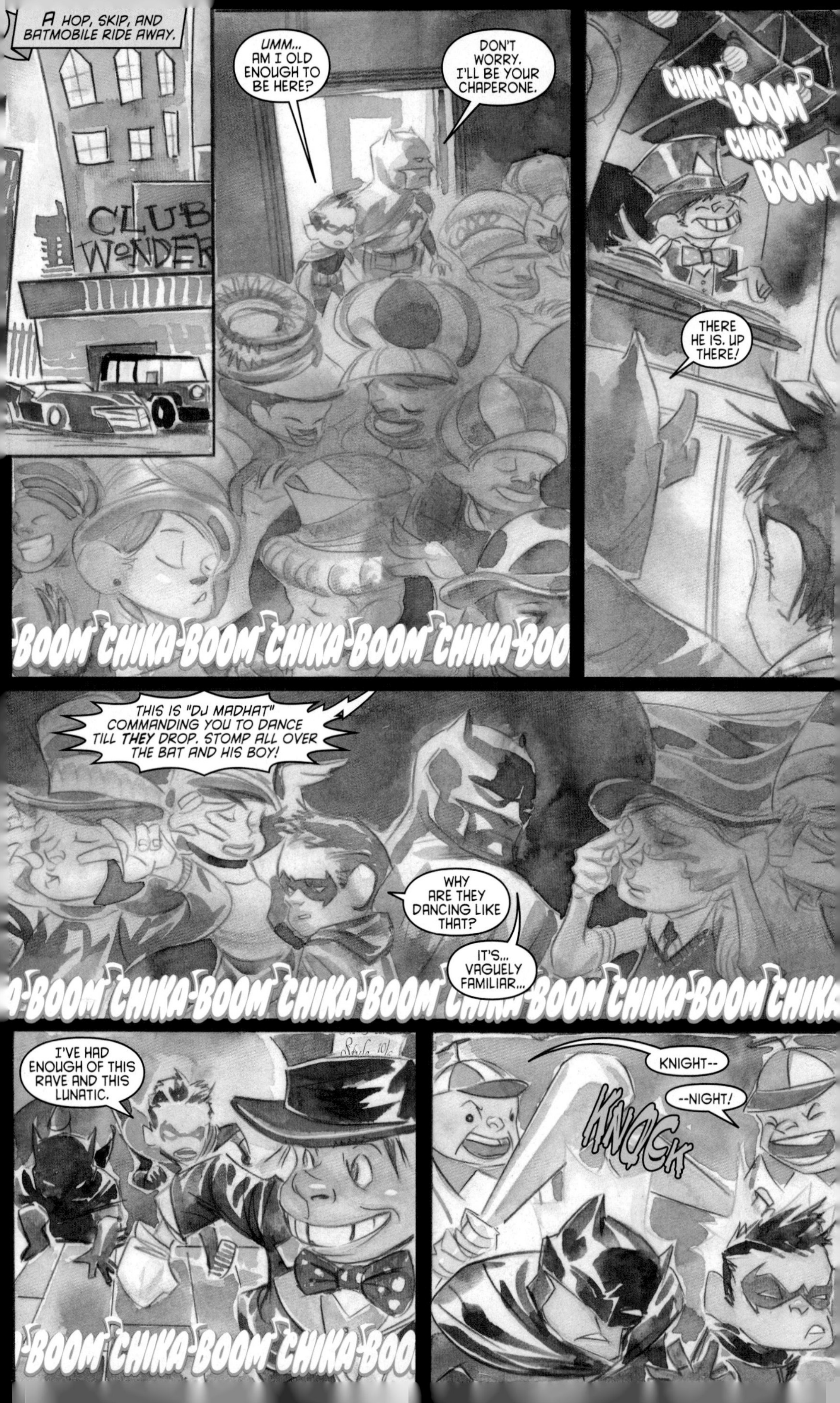
A HOP, SKIP, AND BATMOBILE RIDE AWAY.
CLUB WONDER
UMM... AM I OLD ENOUGH TO BE HERE?
DON'T WORRY. I'LL BE YOUR CHAPERONE.
-BOOM CHIKA-BOOM CHIKA-BOOM CHIKA-BOO
CHIKA-BOOM CHIKA-BOOM
THERE HE IS. UP THERE!
THIS IS "DJ MADHAT" COMMANDING YOU TO DANCE TILL THEY DROP. STOMP ALL OVER THE BAT AND HIS BOY!
WHY ARE THEY DANCING LIKE THAT?
IT'S... VAGUELY FAMILIAR...
-BOOM CHIKA-BOOM CHIKA-BOOM CHIKA-BOOM CHIKA
I'VE HAD ENOUGH OF THIS RAVE AND THIS LUNATIC.
-BOOM CHIKA-BOOM CHIKA-BOO
KNIGHT--
--NIGHT!
KNOCK

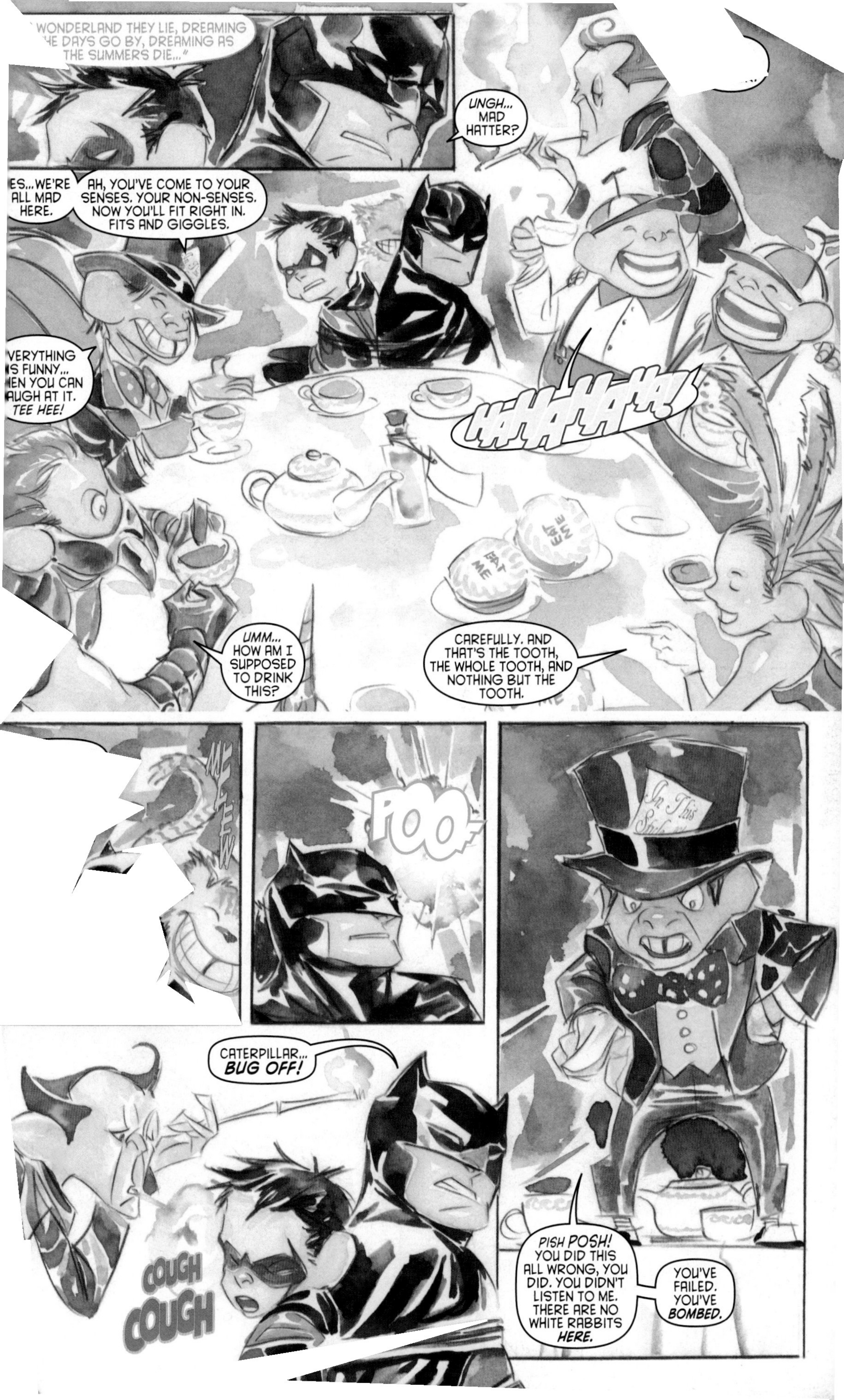

WONDERLAND THEY LIE, DREAMING AS THE DAYS GO BY, DREAMING AS THE SUMMERS DIE..."
UNGH... MAD HATTER?
ES... WE'RE ALL MAD HERE.
AH, YOU'VE COME TO YOUR SENSES. YOUR NON-SENSES. NOW YOU'LL FIT RIGHT IN. FITS AND GIGGLES.
VERYTHING IS FUNNY... HEN YOU CAN AUGH AT IT. TEE HEE!
HAHAHAHA!
EAT ME
EAT ME
UMM... HOW AM I SUPPOSED TO DRINK THIS?
CAREFULLY. AND THAT'S THE TOOTH, THE WHOLE TOOTH, AND NOTHING BUT THE TOOTH.
POOF
CATERPILLAR... BUG OFF!
COUGH COUGH
PISH POSH! YOU DID THIS ALL WRONG, YOU DID. YOU DIDN'T LISTEN TO ME. THERE ARE NO WHITE RABBITS HERE.
YOU'VE FAILED. YOU'VE BOMBED.

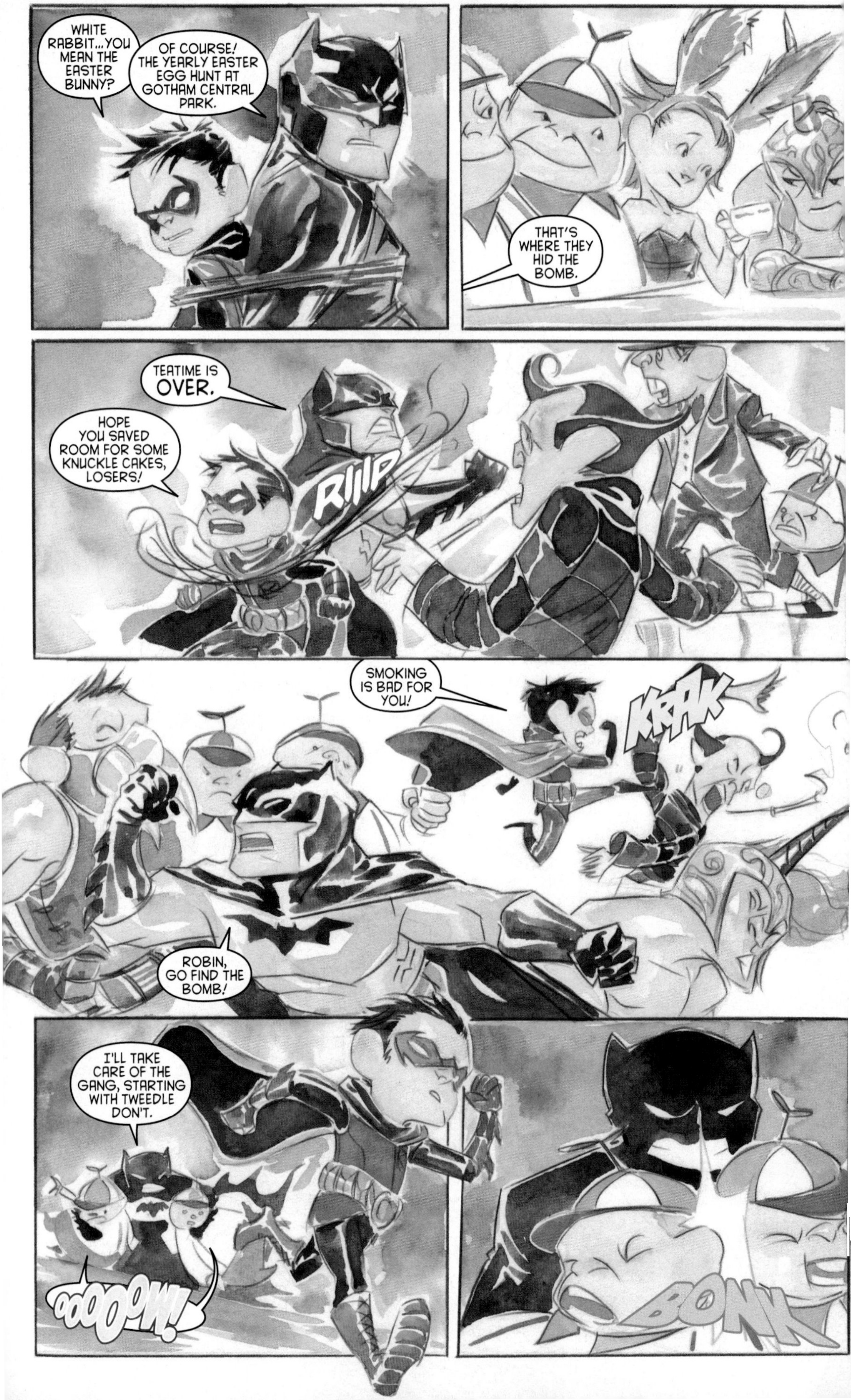

WHITE RABBIT...YOU MEAN THE EASTER BUNNY?
OF COURSE! THE YEARLY EASTER EGG HUNT AT GOTHAM CENTRAL PARK.
THAT'S WHERE THEY HID THE BOMB.
TEATIME IS OVER.
HOPE YOU SAVED ROOM FOR SOME KNUCKLE CAKES, LOSERS!
RIIIP
SMOKING IS BAD FOR YOU!
KRAK
ROBIN, GO FIND THE BOMB!
I'LL TAKE CARE OF THE GANG, STARTING WITH TWEEDLE DON'T.
oooOOOW!
BONK

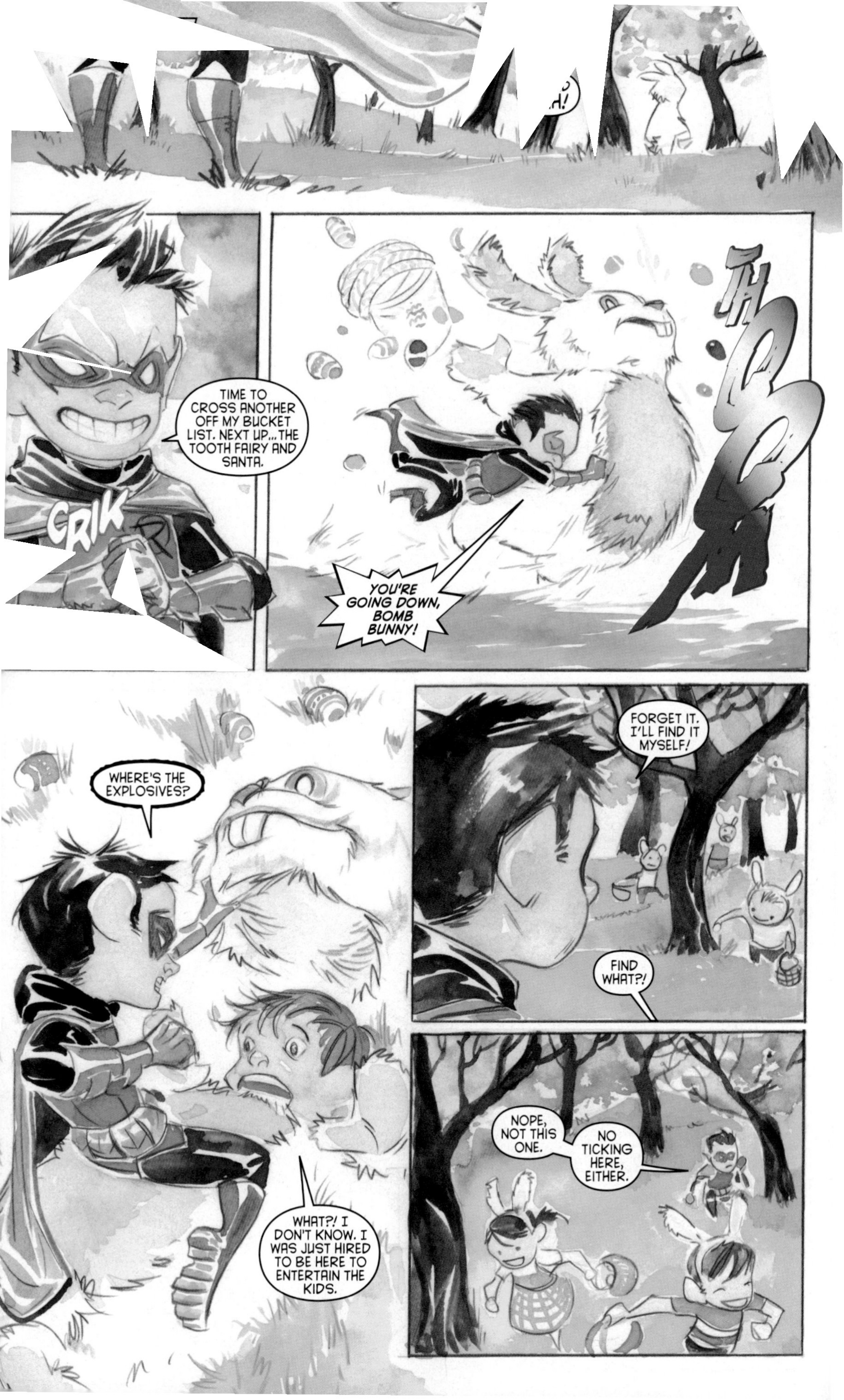
TIME TO CROSS ANOTHER OFF MY BUCKET LIST. NEXT UP... THE TOOTH FAIRY AND SANTA.
CRIK
YOU'RE GOING DOWN, BOMB BUNNY!
WHERE'S THE EXPLOSIVES?
WHAT?! I DON'T KNOW. I WAS JUST HIRED TO BE HERE TO ENTERTAIN THE KIDS.
FORGET IT. I'LL FIND IT MYSELF!
FIND WHAT?!
NOPE, NOT THIS ONE.
NO TICKING HERE, EITHER.

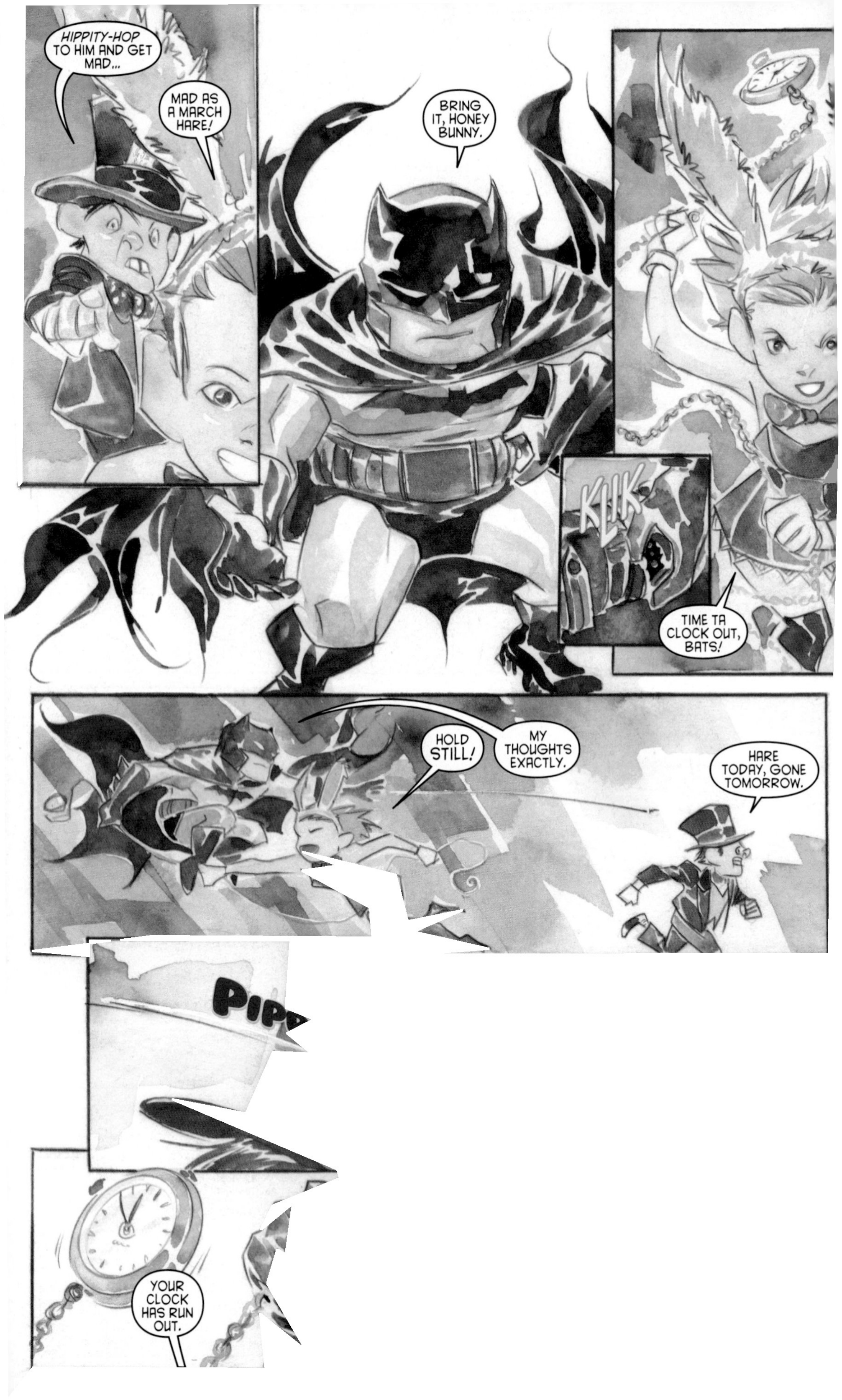
HIPPITY-HOP TO HIM AND GET MAD...
MAD AS A MARCH HARE!
BRING IT, HONEY BUNNY.
KLIK
TIME TA CLOCK OUT, BATS!
HOLD STILL!
MY THOUGHTS EXACTLY.
HARE TODAY, GONE TOMORROW.
PIPP
YOUR CLOCK HAS RUN OUT.

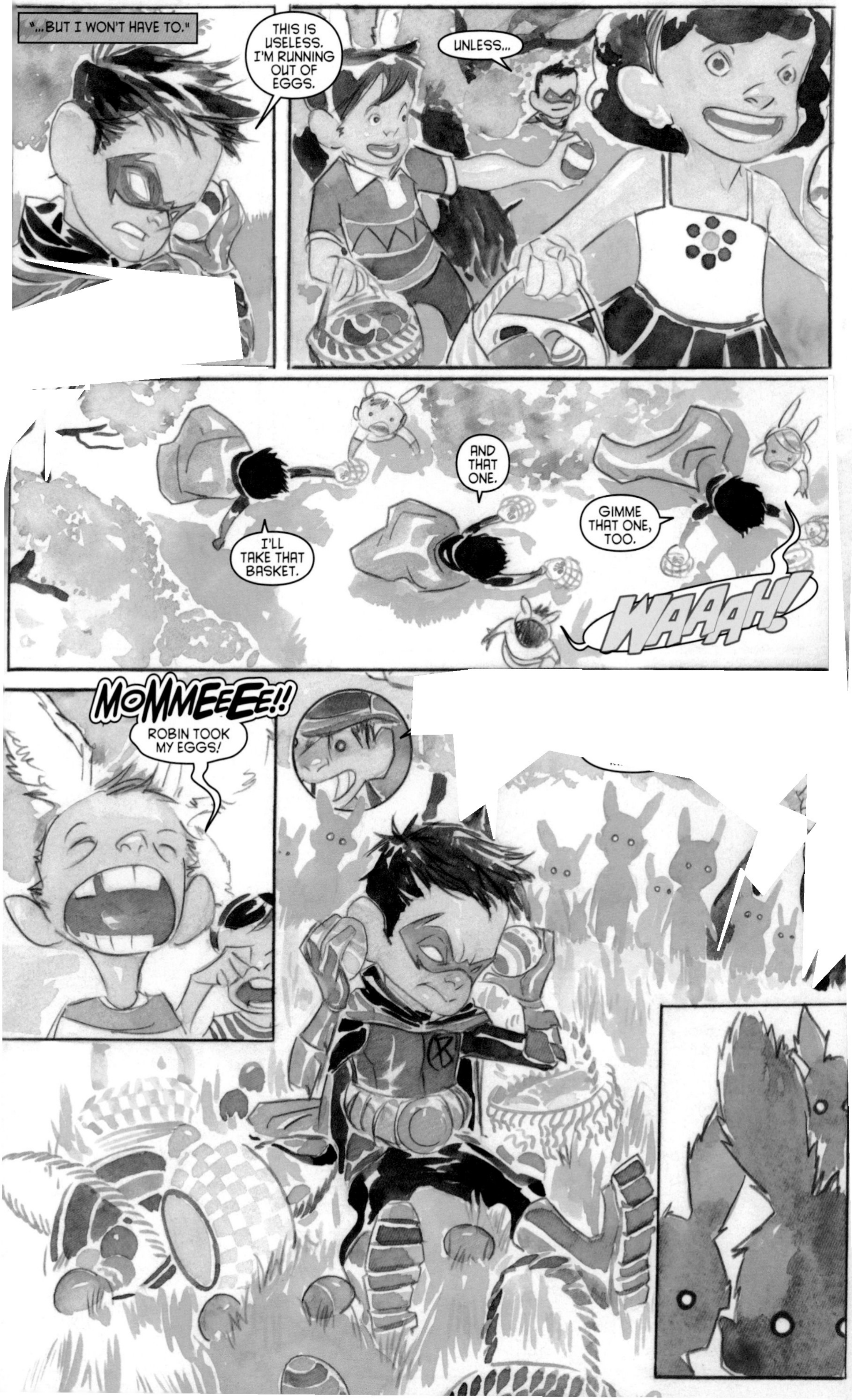
"...BUT I WON'T HAVE TO."
THIS IS USELESS. I'M RUNNING OUT OF EGGS.
UNLESS...
I'LL TAKE THAT BASKET.
AND THAT ONE.
GIMME THAT ONE, TOO.
WAAAH!
MOMMEEEE!!
ROBIN TOOK MY EGGS!

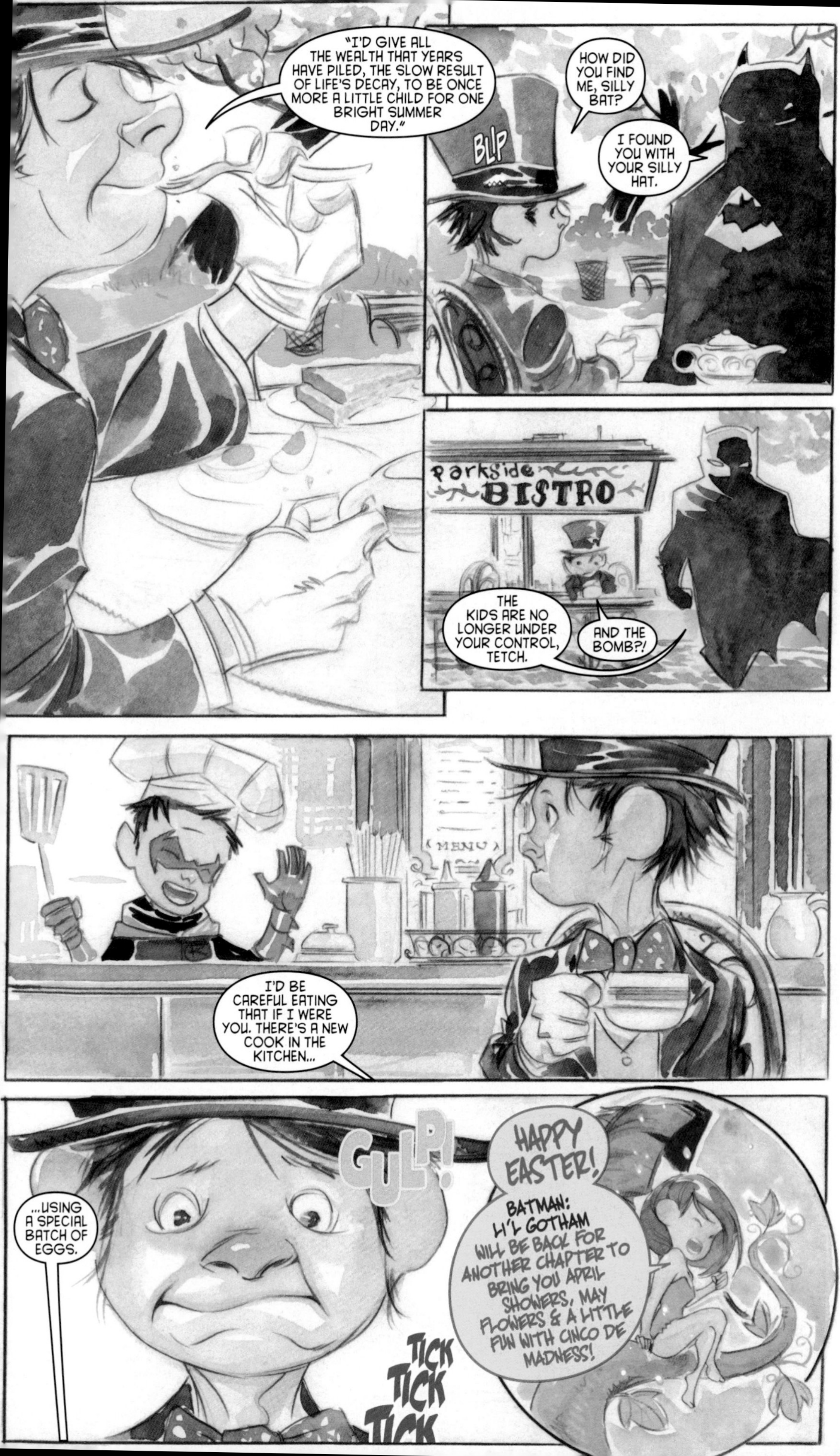
"I'D GIVE ALL THE WEALTH THAT YEARS HAVE PILED, THE SLOW RESULT OF LIFE'S DECAY, TO BE ONCE MORE A LITTLE CHILD FOR ONE BRIGHT SUMMER DAY."
BLIP
HOW DID YOU FIND ME, SILLY BAT?
I FOUND YOU WITH YOUR SILLY HAT.
Parkside BISTRO
THE KIDS ARE NO LONGER UNDER YOUR CONTROL, TETCH.
AND THE BOMB?!
MENU
I'D BE CAREFUL EATING THAT IF I WERE YOU. THERE'S A NEW COOK IN THE KITCHEN...
...USING A SPECIAL BATCH OF EGGS.
GULP!
HAPPY EASTER!
BATMAN: LI'L GOTHAM WILL BE BACK FOR ANOTHER CHAPTER TO BRING YOU APRIL SHOWERS, MAY FLOWERS & A LITTLE FUN WITH CINCO DE MADNESS!
TICK
TICK
TICK

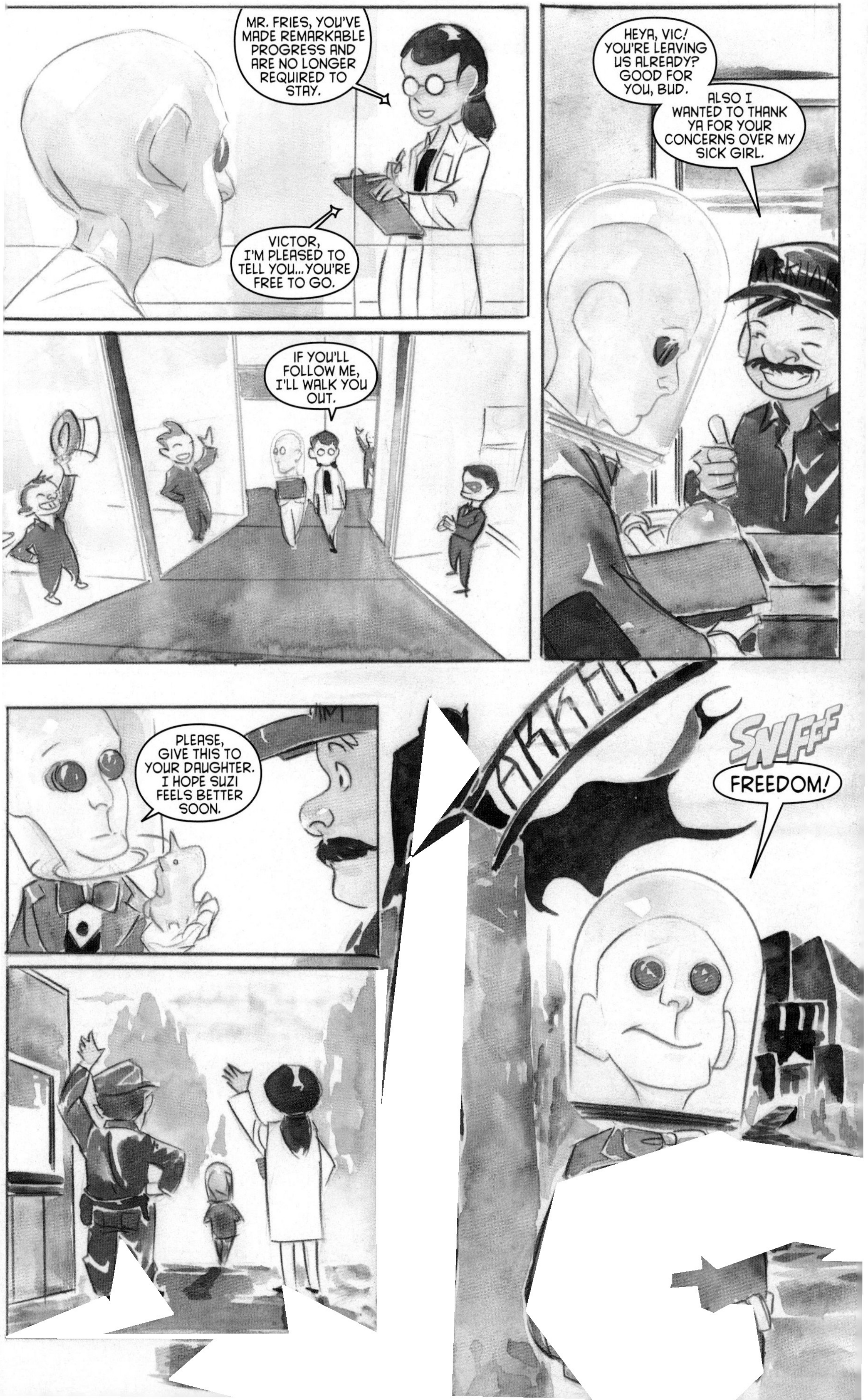
MR. FRIES, YOU'VE MADE REMARKABLE PROGRESS AND ARE NO LONGER REQUIRED TO STAY.
VICTOR, I'M PLEASED TO TELL YOU...YOU'RE FREE TO GO.
HEYA, VIC! YOU'RE LEAVING US ALREADY? GOOD FOR YOU, BUD.
ALSO I WANTED TO THANK YA FOR YOUR CONCERNS OVER MY SICK GIRL.
IF YOU'LL FOLLOW ME, I'LL WALK YOU OUT.
PLEASE, GIVE THIS TO YOUR DAUGHTER. I HOPE SUZI FEELS BETTER SOON.
SNIFFF
FREEDOM!

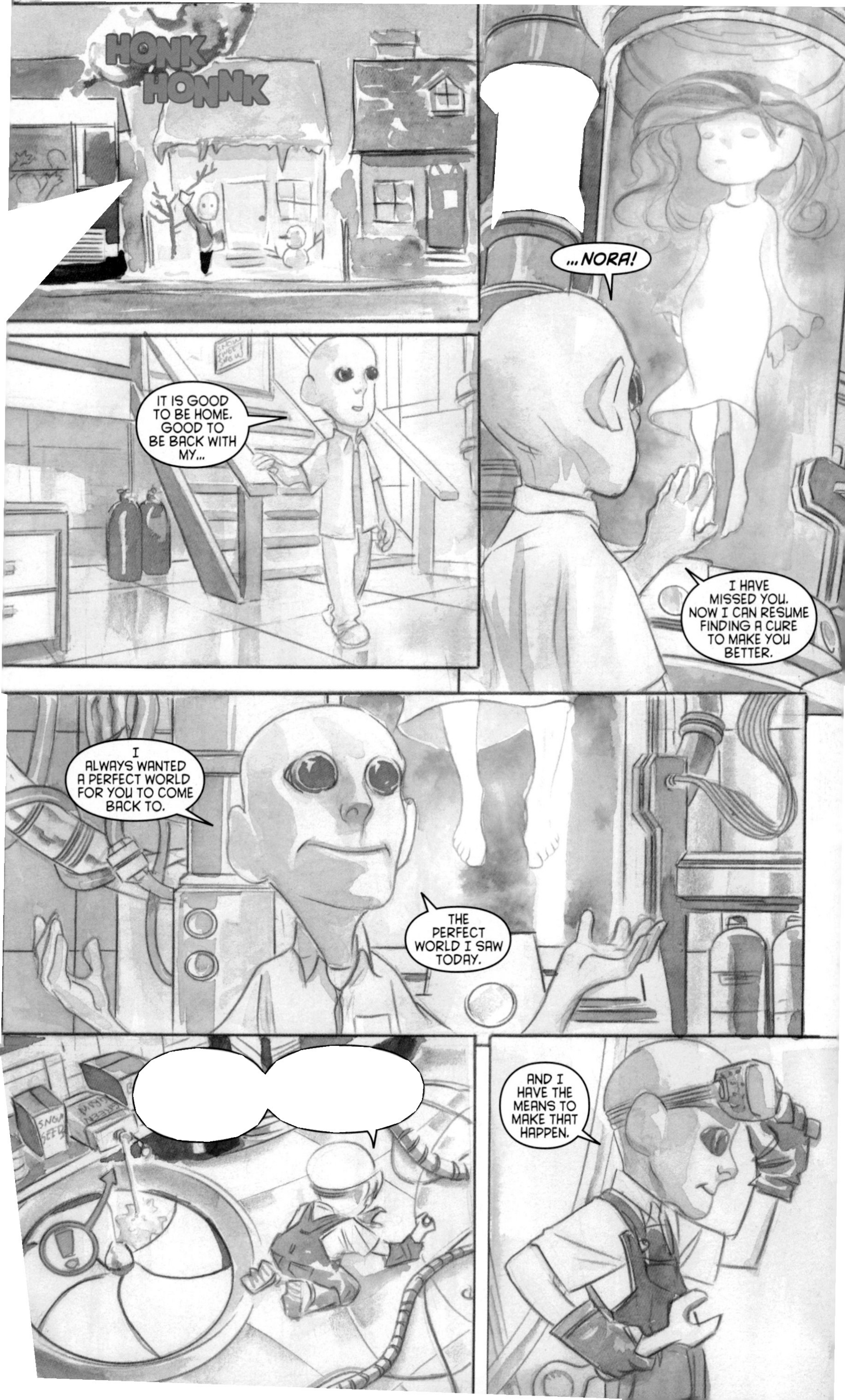
HONK HONNK
...NORA!
IT IS GOOD TO BE HOME. GOOD TO BE BACK WITH MY...
I HAVE MISSED YOU. NOW I CAN RESUME FINDING A CURE TO MAKE YOU BETTER.
I ALWAYS WANTED A PERFECT WORLD FOR YOU TO COME BACK TO.
THE PERFECT WORLD I SAW TODAY.
AND I HAVE THE MEANS TO MAKE THAT HAPPEN.

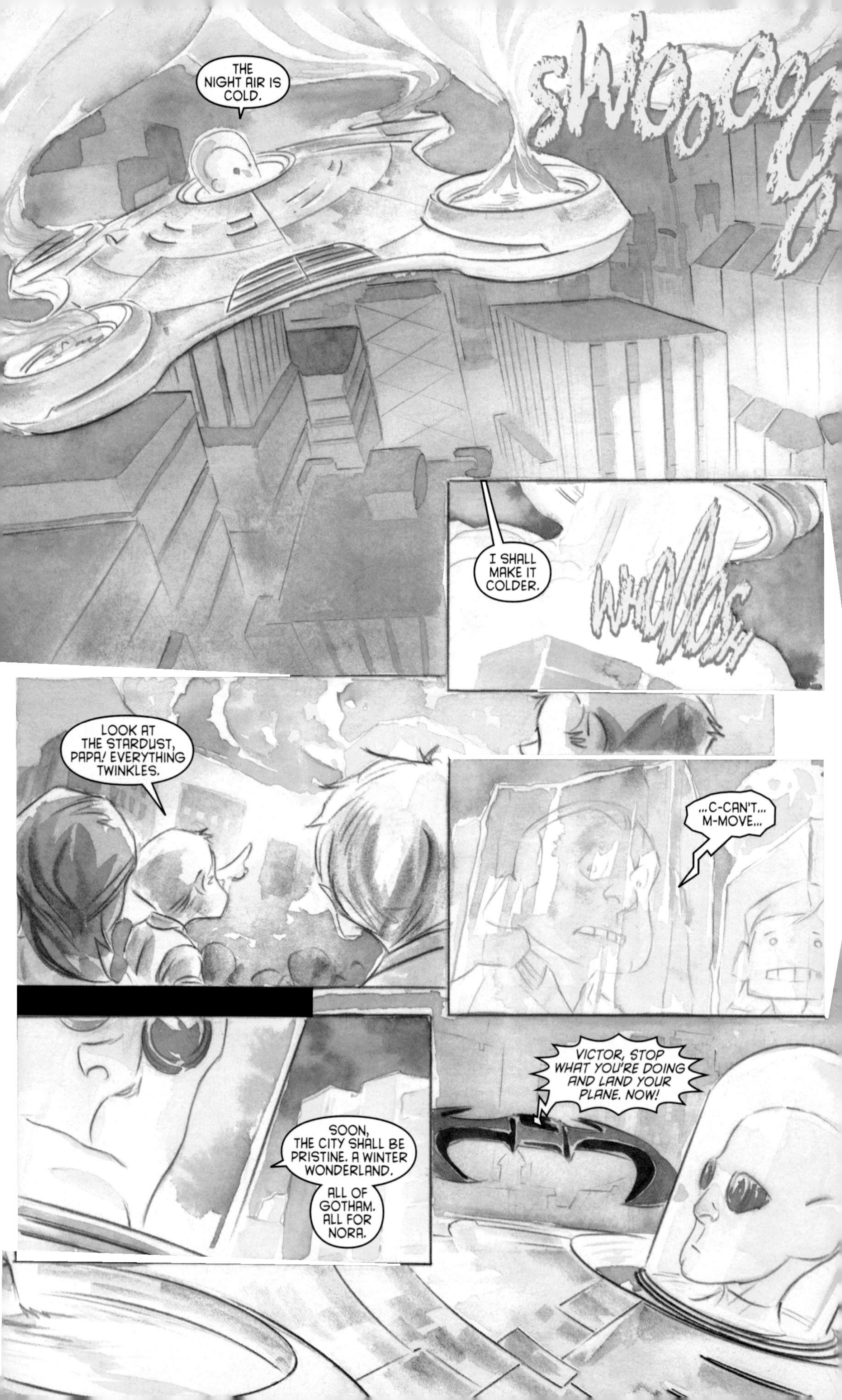
THE NIGHT AIR IS COLD.
I SHALL MAKE IT COLDER.
LOOK AT THE STARDUST, PAPA! EVERYTHING TWINKLES.
...C-CAN'T... M-MOVE...
SOON, THE CITY SHALL BE PRISTINE. A WINTER WONDERLAND.
ALL OF GOTHAM. ALL FOR NORA.
VICTOR, STOP WHAT YOU'RE DOING AND LAND YOUR PLANE. NOW!

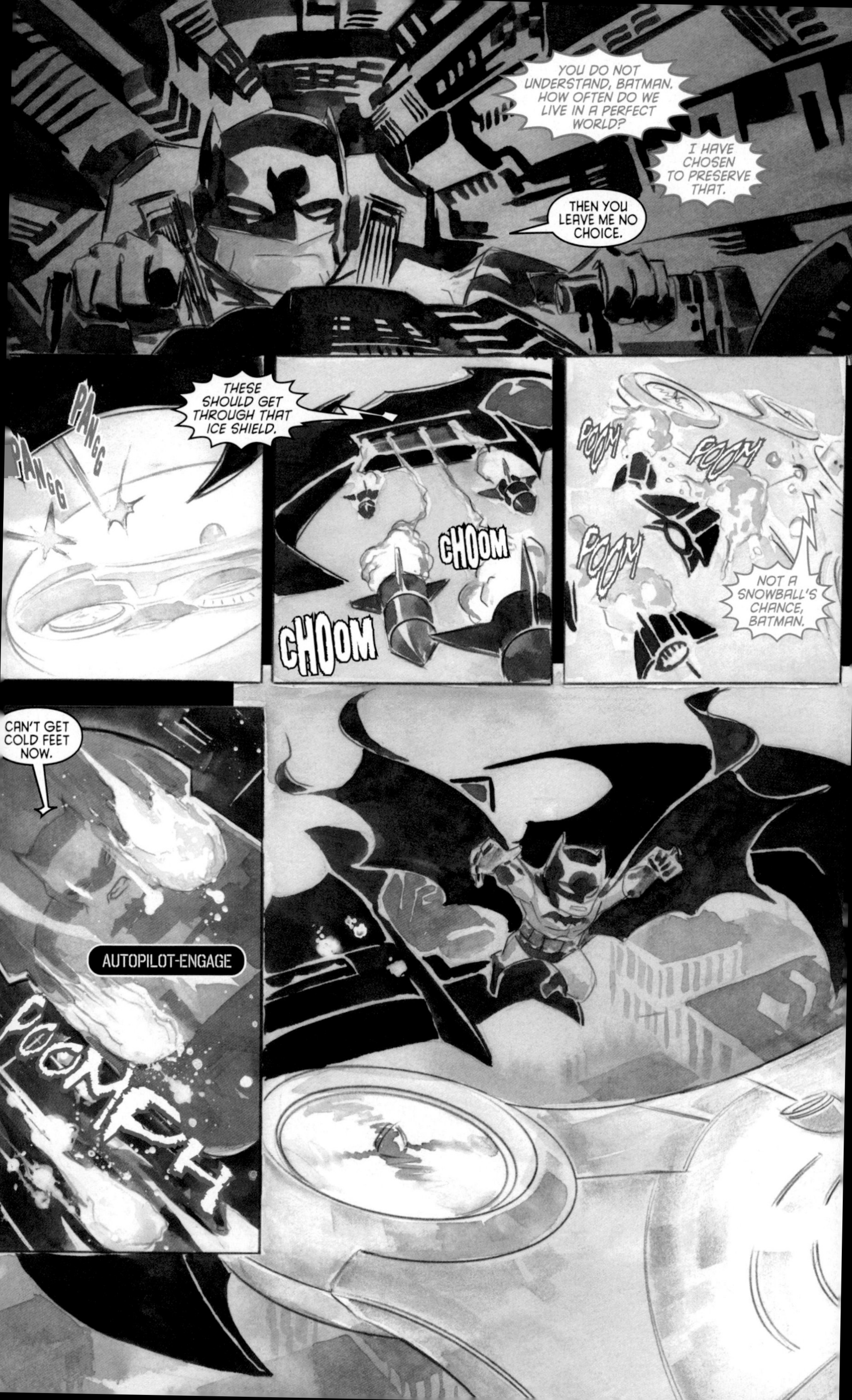
YOU DO NOT UNDERSTAND, BATMAN. HOW OFTEN DO WE LIVE IN A PERFECT WORLD?
I HAVE CHOSEN TO PRESERVE THAT.
THEN YOU LEAVE ME NO CHOICE.
PANGG
PANGG
THESE SHOULD GET THROUGH THAT ICE SHIELD.
CHOOM
CHOOM
POOM
POOM
POOM
NOT A SNOWBALL'S CHANCE, BATMAN.
CAN'T GET COLD FEET NOW.
AUTOPILOT-ENGAGE
POOMPH

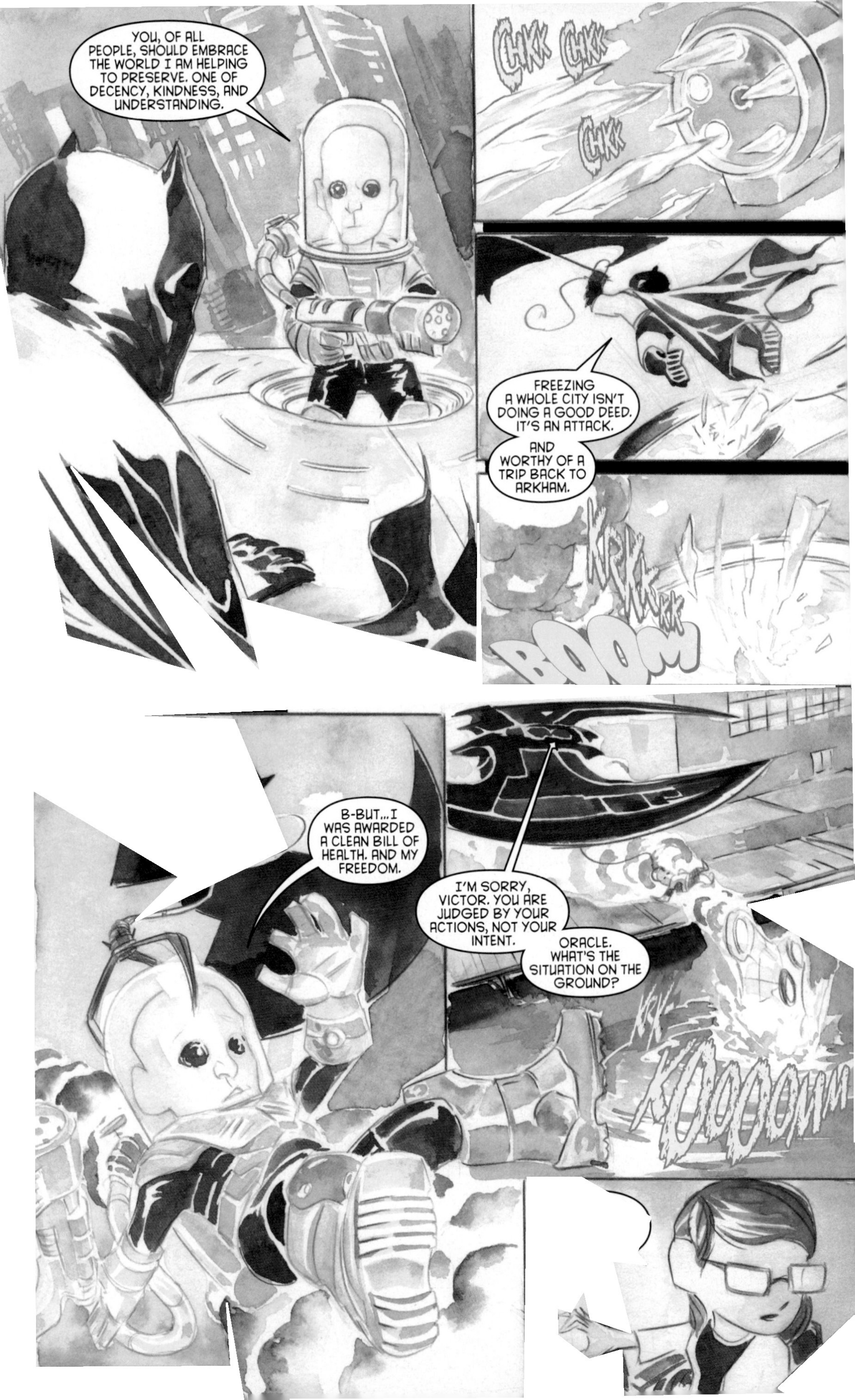
YOU, OF ALL PEOPLE, SHOULD EMBRACE THE WORLD I AM HELPING TO PRESERVE. ONE OF DECENCY, KINDNESS, AND UNDERSTANDING.
CHKK CHKK
CHKK
FREEZING A WHOLE CITY ISN'T DOING A GOOD DEED. IT'S AN ATTACK.
AND WORTHY OF A TRIP BACK TO ARKHAM.
KRAK
BOOM
B-BUT...I WAS AWARDED A CLEAN BILL OF HEALTH. AND MY FREEDOM.
I'M SORRY, VICTOR. YOU ARE JUDGED BY YOUR ACTIONS, NOT YOUR INTENT.
ORACLE. WHAT'S THE SITUATION ON THE GROUND?

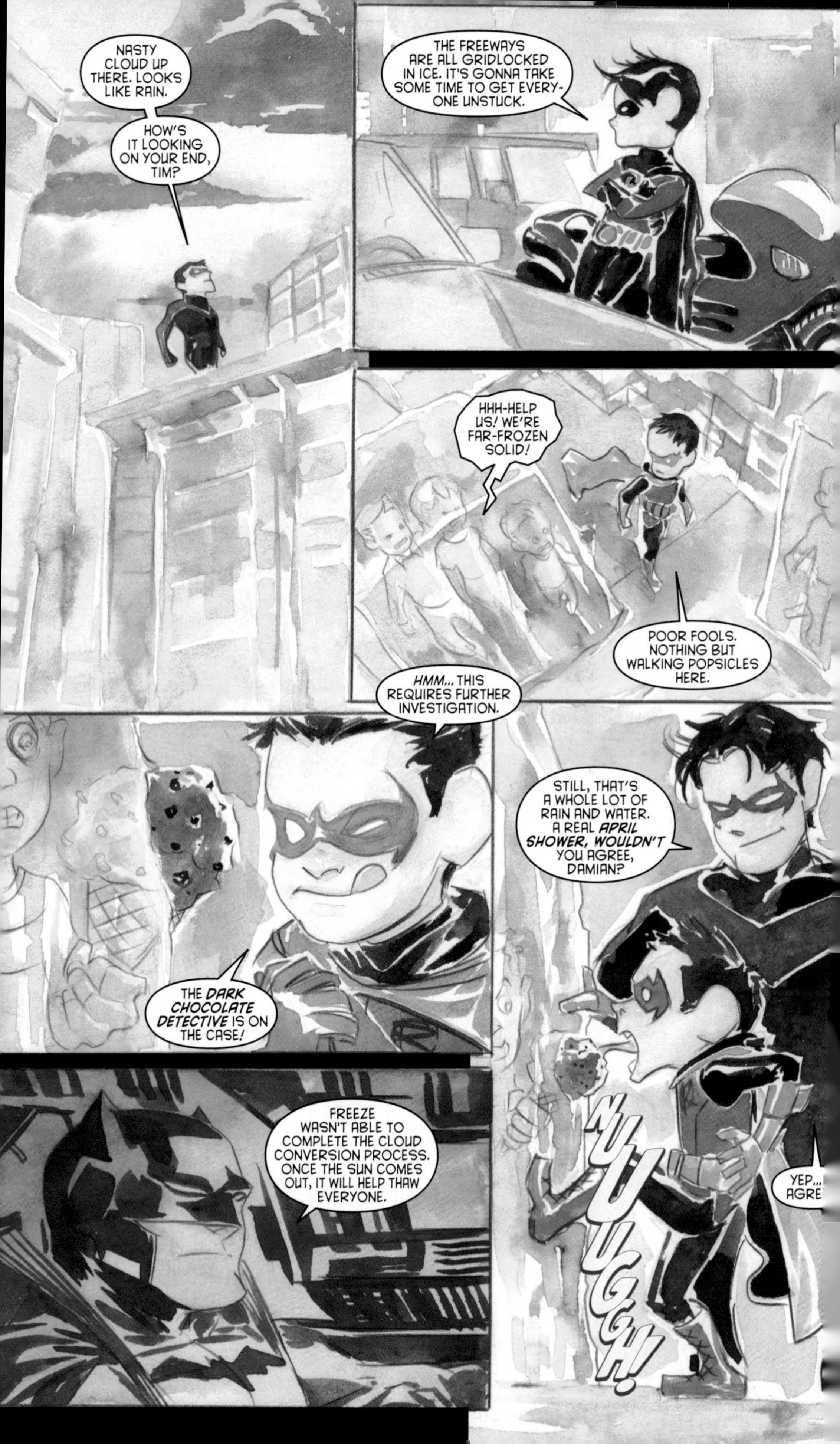
NASTY CLOUD UP THERE. LOOKS LIKE RAIN.
HOW'S IT LOOKING ON YOUR END, TIM?
THE FREEWAYS ARE ALL GRIDLOCKED IN ICE. IT'S GONNA TAKE SOME TIME TO GET EVERY-ONE UNSTUCK.
HHH-HELP US! WE'RE FAR-FROZEN SOLID!
POOR FOOLS. NOTHING BUT WALKING POPSICLES HERE.
HMM... THIS REQUIRES FURTHER INVESTIGATION.
THE DARK CHOCOLATE DETECTIVE IS ON THE CASE!
STILL, THAT'S A WHOLE LOT OF RAIN AND WATER. A REAL APRIL SHOWER, WOULDN'T YOU AGREE, DAMIAN?
FREEZE WASN'T ABLE TO COMPLETE THE CLOUD CONVERSION PROCESS. ONCE THE SUN COMES OUT, IT WILL HELP THAW EVERYONE.
NUUUGGH!
YEP... AGRE

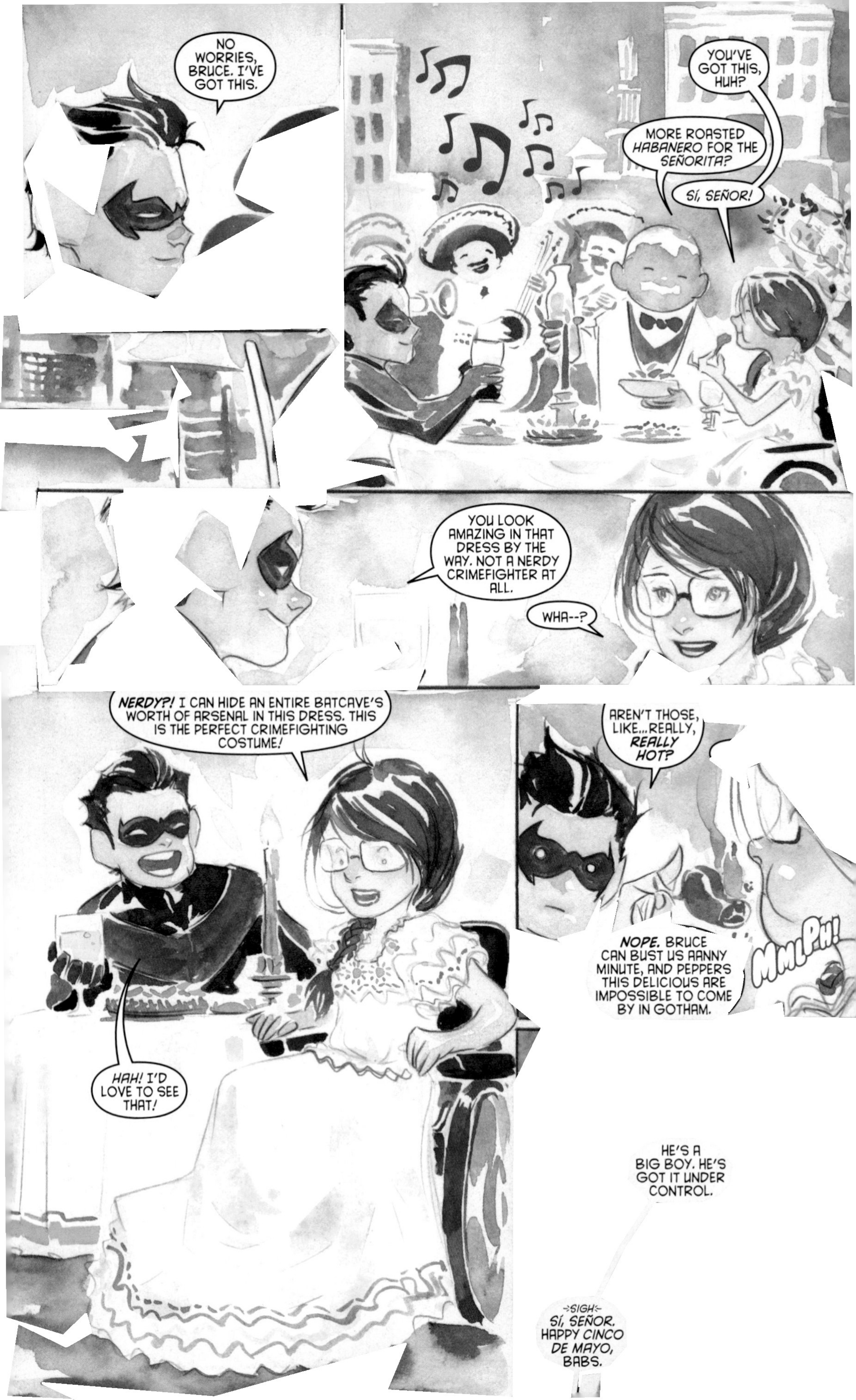
NO WORRIES, BRUCE. I'VE GOT THIS.
YOU'VE GOT THIS, HUH?
MORE ROASTED *HABANERO* FOR THE *SEÑORITA?*
SÍ, SEÑOR!
YOU LOOK AMAZING IN THAT DRESS BY THE WAY. NOT A NERDY CRIMEFIGHTER AT ALL.
WHA--?
NERDY?! I CAN HIDE AN ENTIRE BATCAVE'S WORTH OF ARSENAL IN THIS DRESS. THIS IS THE PERFECT CRIMEFIGHTING COSTUME!
HAH! I'D LOVE TO SEE THAT!
AREN'T THOSE, LIKE...REALLY, ***REALLY HOT?***
NOPE. BRUCE CAN BUST US AANNY MINUTE, AND PEPPERS THIS DELICIOUS ARE IMPOSSIBLE TO COME BY IN GOTHAM.
MMLPH!
HE'S A BIG BOY. HE'S GOT IT UNDER CONTROL.
SIGH
SÍ, SEÑOR. HAPPY CINCO DE MAYO, BABS.

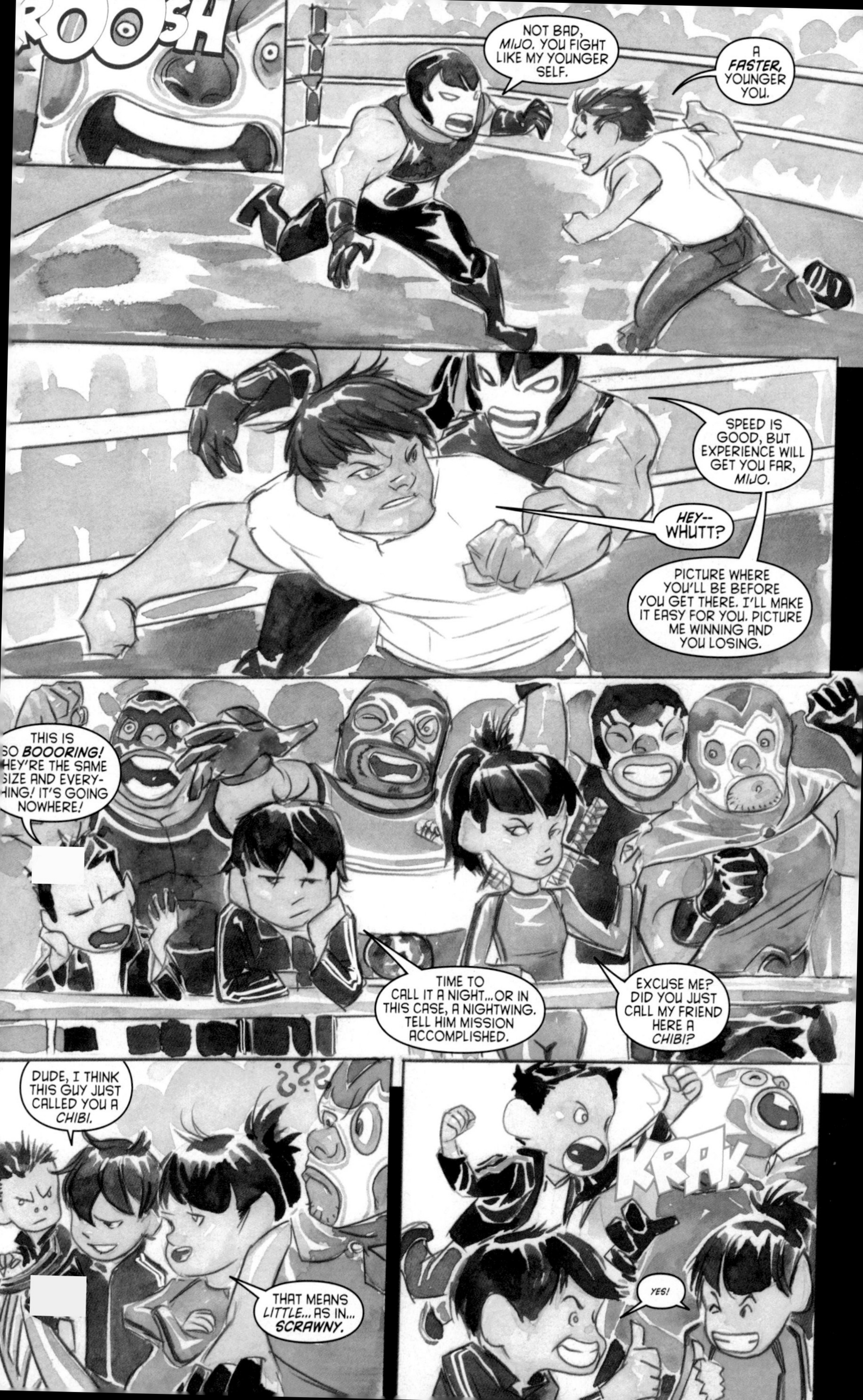
ROOSH
NOT BAD, MIJO. YOU FIGHT LIKE MY YOUNGER SELF.
A FASTER, YOUNGER YOU.
SPEED IS GOOD, BUT EXPERIENCE WILL GET YOU FAR, MIJO.
HEY-- WHUTT?
PICTURE WHERE YOU'LL BE BEFORE YOU GET THERE. I'LL MAKE IT EASY FOR YOU. PICTURE ME WINNING AND YOU LOSING.
THIS IS SO BOOORING! HEY'RE THE SAME SIZE AND EVERY-HING! IT'S GOING NOWHERE!
TIME TO CALL IT A NIGHT... OR IN THIS CASE, A NIGHTWING. TELL HIM MISSION ACCOMPLISHED.
EXCUSE ME? DID YOU JUST CALL MY FRIEND HERE A CHIBI?
DUDE, I THINK THIS GUY JUST CALLED YOU A CHIBI.
¿??
THAT MEANS LITTLE... AS IN... SCRAWNY.
KRAK
YES!

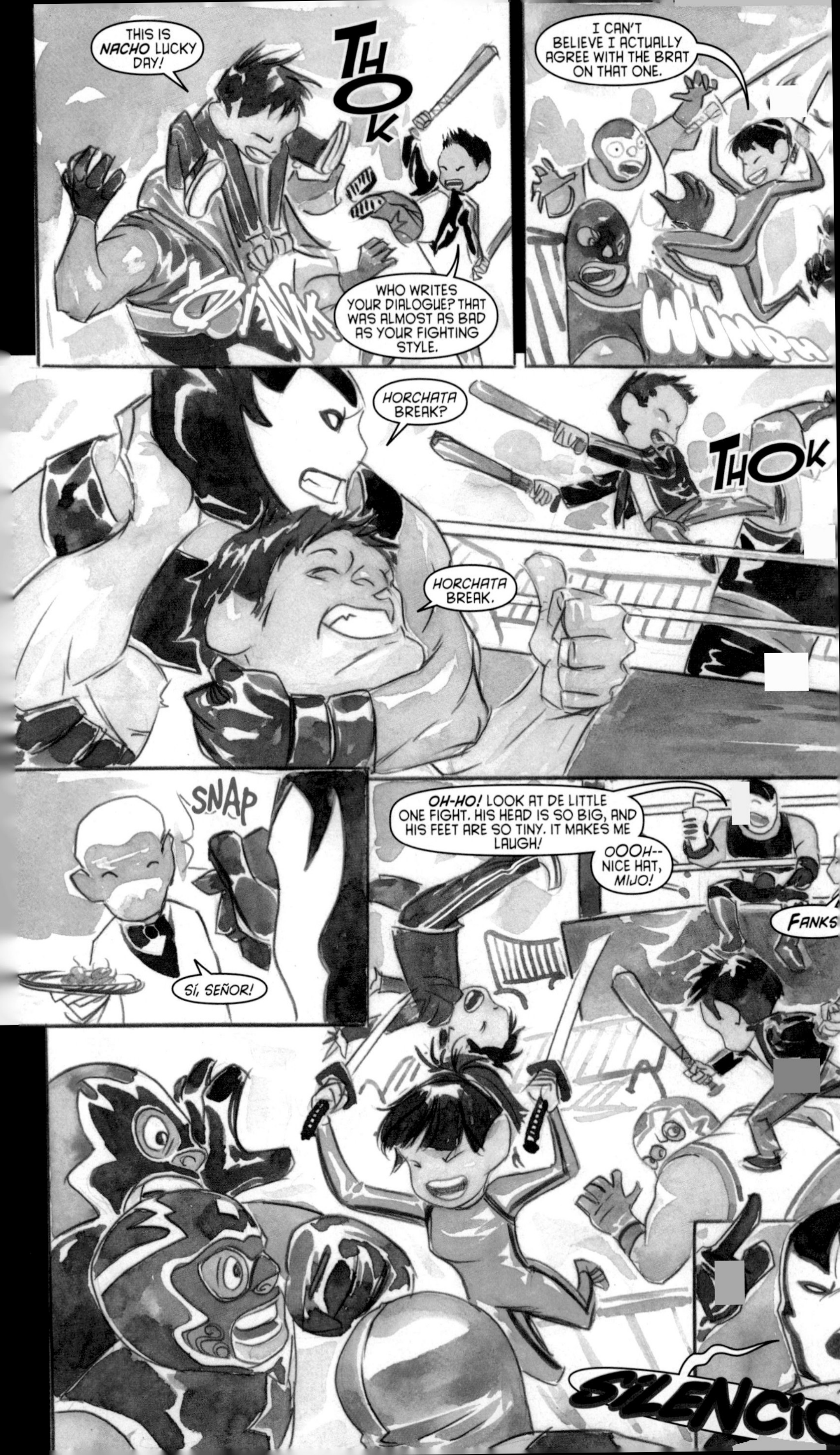
THIS IS NACHO LUCKY DAY!
THOK
WHO WRITES YOUR DIALOGUE? THAT WAS ALMOST AS BAD AS YOUR FIGHTING STYLE.
I CAN'T BELIEVE I ACTUALLY AGREE WITH THE BRAT ON THAT ONE.
WUMPH
HORCHATA BREAK?
HORCHATA BREAK.
THOK
SNAP
SÍ, SEÑOR!
OH-HO! LOOK AT DE LITTLE ONE FIGHT. HIS HEAD IS SO BIG, AND HIS FEET ARE SO TINY. IT MAKES ME LAUGH!
OOOH-- NICE HAT, MIJO!
FANKS
SILENCIO

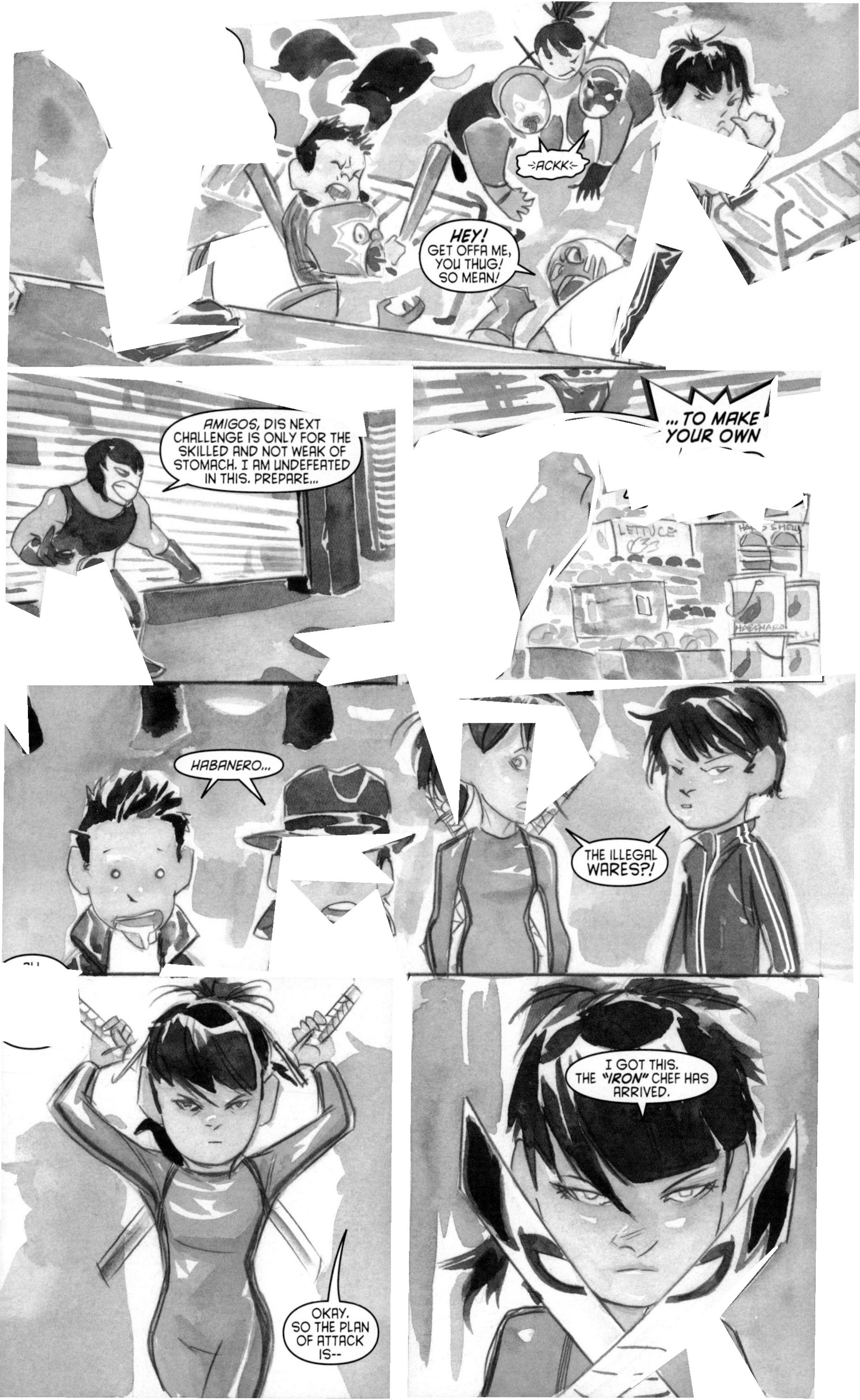

-ACKK-
HEY! GET OFFA ME, YOU THUG! SO MEAN!
AMIGOS, DIS NEXT CHALLENGE IS ONLY FOR THE SKILLED AND NOT WEAK OF STOMACH. I AM UNDEFEATED IN THIS. PREPARE...
...TO MAKE YOUR OWN
LETTUCE
HABANERO...
THE ILLEGAL WARES?!
OKAY. SO THE PLAN OF ATTACK IS--
I GOT THIS. THE "IRON" CHEF HAS ARRIVED.

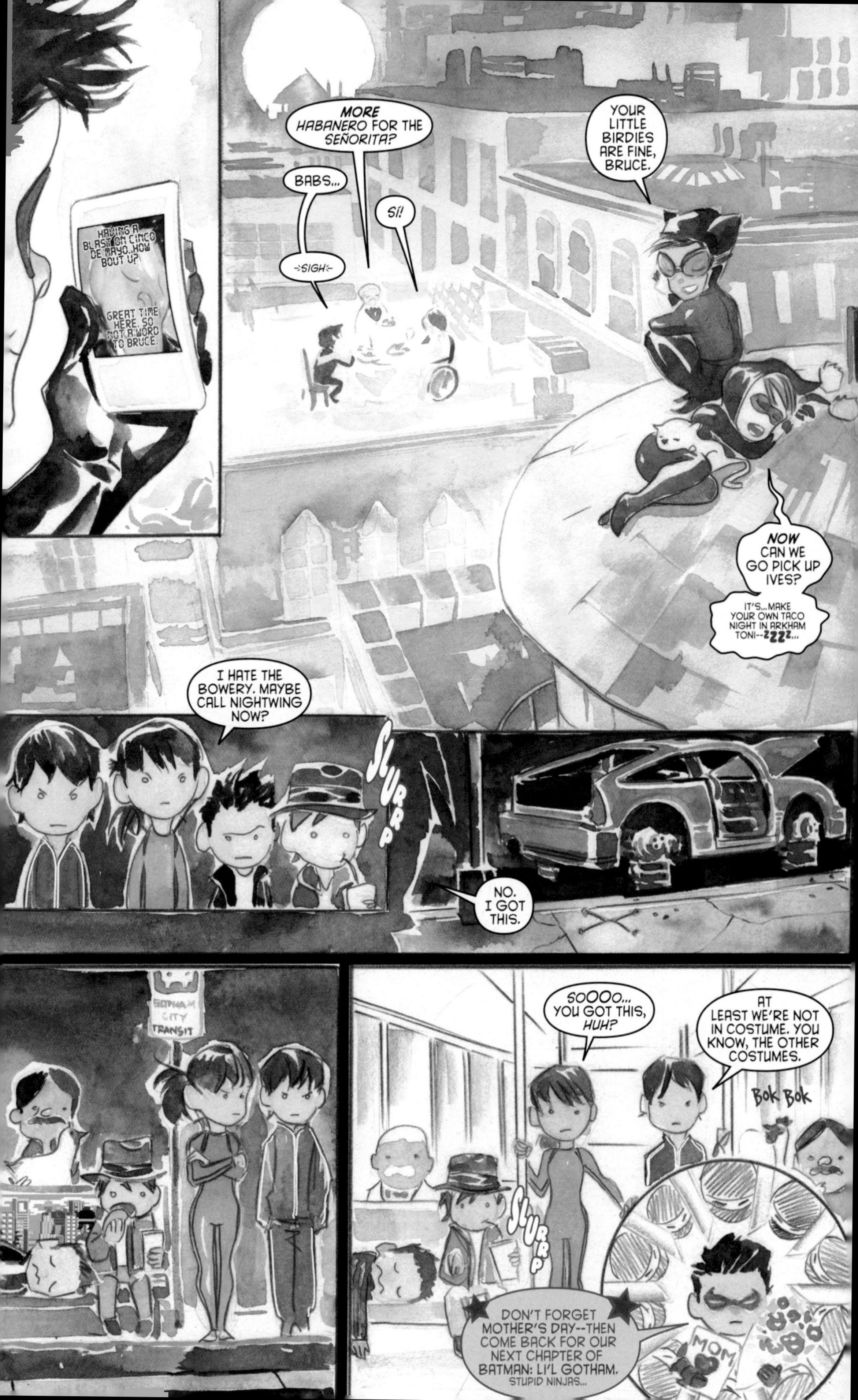

HAVING A BLAST ON CINCO DE MAYO..HOW BOUT U?
GREAT TIME HERE. SO NOT A WORD TO BRUCE.
MORE HABANERO FOR THE SEÑORITA?
BABS...
SÍ!
~SIGH~
YOUR LITTLE BIRDIES ARE FINE, BRUCE.
NOW CAN WE GO PICK UP IVES?
IT'S...MAKE YOUR OWN TACO NIGHT IN ARKHAM TONI--ZZZZ...
I HATE THE BOWERY. MAYBE CALL NIGHTWING NOW?
SLURRP
NO. I GOT THIS.
GOTHAM CITY TRANSIT
SOOOO... YOU GOT THIS, HUH?
AT LEAST WE'RE NOT IN COSTUME. YOU KNOW, THE OTHER COSTUMES.
BOK BOK
SLURRP
DON'T FORGET MOTHER'S DAY--THEN COME BACK FOR OUR NEXT CHAPTER OF BATMAN: LI'L GOTHAM.
STUPID NINJAS...
MOM

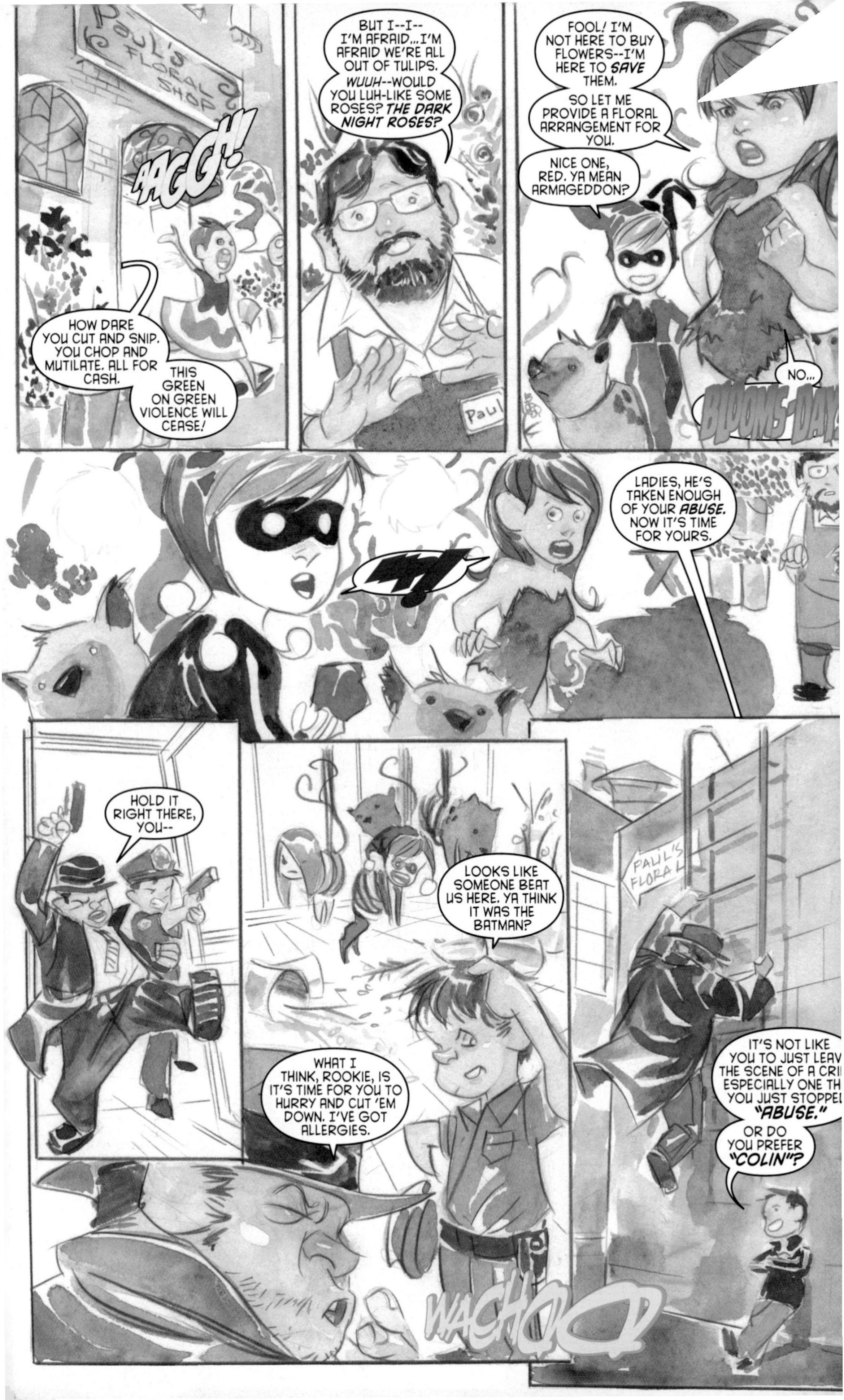
PAUL'S FLORAL SHOP
AAGGH!
HOW DARE YOU CUT AND SNIP. YOU CHOP AND MUTILATE. ALL FOR CASH.
THIS GREEN ON GREEN VIOLENCE WILL CEASE!
BUT I--I-- I'M AFRAID...I'M AFRAID WE'RE ALL OUT OF TULIPS. *WUUH*--WOULD YOU LUH-LIKE SOME ROSES? ***THE DARK NIGHT ROSES?***
Paul
FOOL! I'M NOT HERE TO BUY FLOWERS--I'M HERE TO ***SAVE*** THEM.
SO LET ME PROVIDE A FLORAL ARRANGEMENT FOR YOU.
NICE ONE, RED. YA MEAN ARMAGEDDON?
NO...
BLOOMS-DAY
LADIES, HE'S TAKEN ENOUGH OF YOUR ***ABUSE.*** NOW IT'S TIME FOR YOURS.
HOLD IT RIGHT THERE, YOU--
LOOKS LIKE SOMEONE BEAT US HERE. YA THINK IT WAS THE BATMAN?
WHAT I THINK, ROOKIE, IS IT'S TIME FOR YOU TO HURRY AND CUT 'EM DOWN. I'VE GOT ALLERGIES.
PAUL'S FLORAL
IT'S NOT LIKE YOU TO JUST LEAV THE SCENE OF A CRI ESPECIALLY ONE TH YOU JUST STOPPED ***"ABUSE."***
OR DO YOU PREFER ***"COLIN"?***
WACHOO

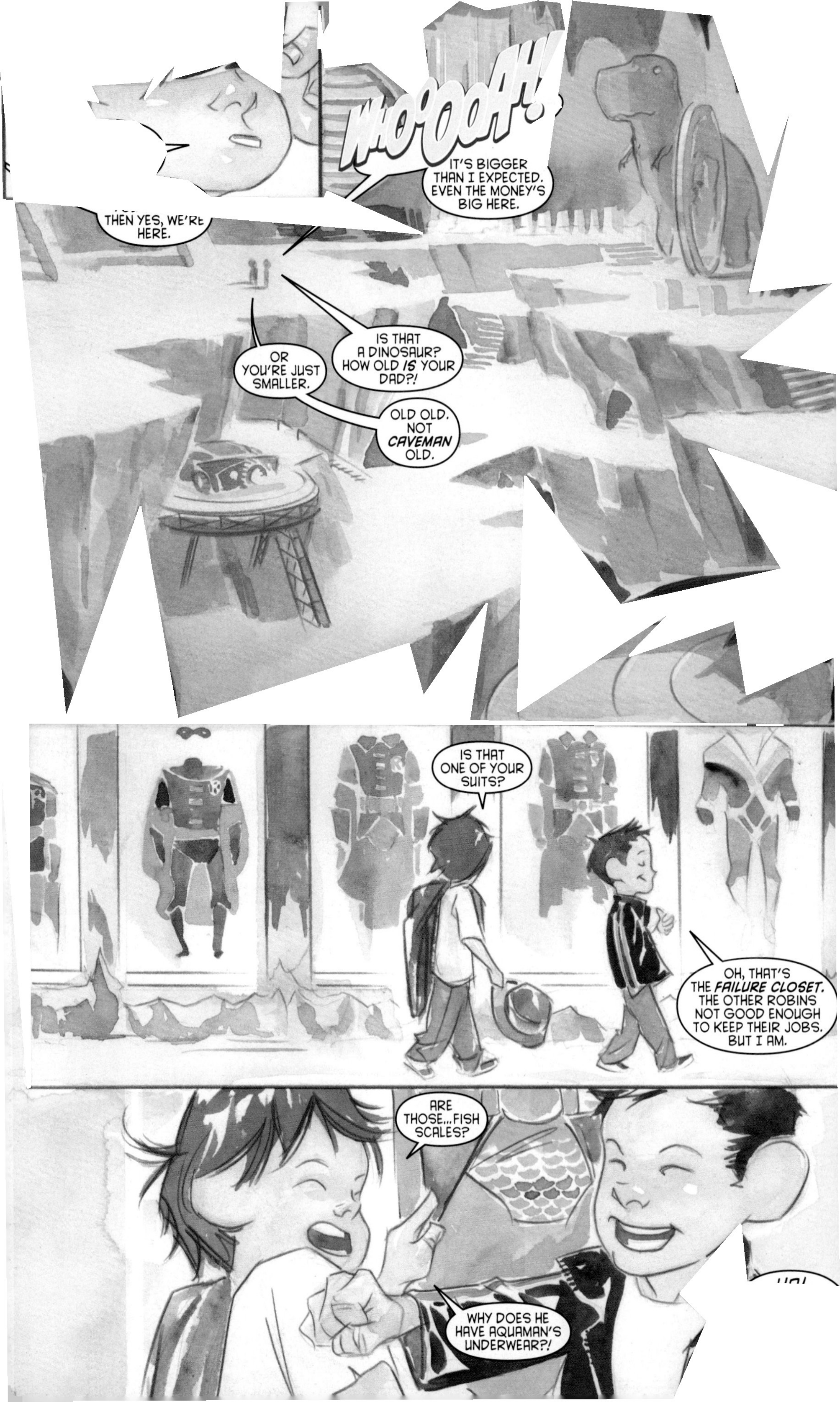
WHOOOOAH!
IT'S BIGGER THAN I EXPECTED. EVEN THE MONEY'S BIG HERE.
THEN YES, WE'RE HERE.
IS THAT A DINOSAUR? HOW OLD *IS* YOUR DAD?!
OR YOU'RE JUST SMALLER.
OLD OLD. NOT *CAVEMAN* OLD.
IS THAT ONE OF YOUR SUITS?
OH, THAT'S THE ***FAILURE CLOSET.*** THE OTHER ROBINS NOT GOOD ENOUGH TO KEEP THEIR JOBS. BUT I AM.
ARE THOSE...FISH SCALES?
WHY DOES HE HAVE AQUAMAN'S UNDERWEAR?!

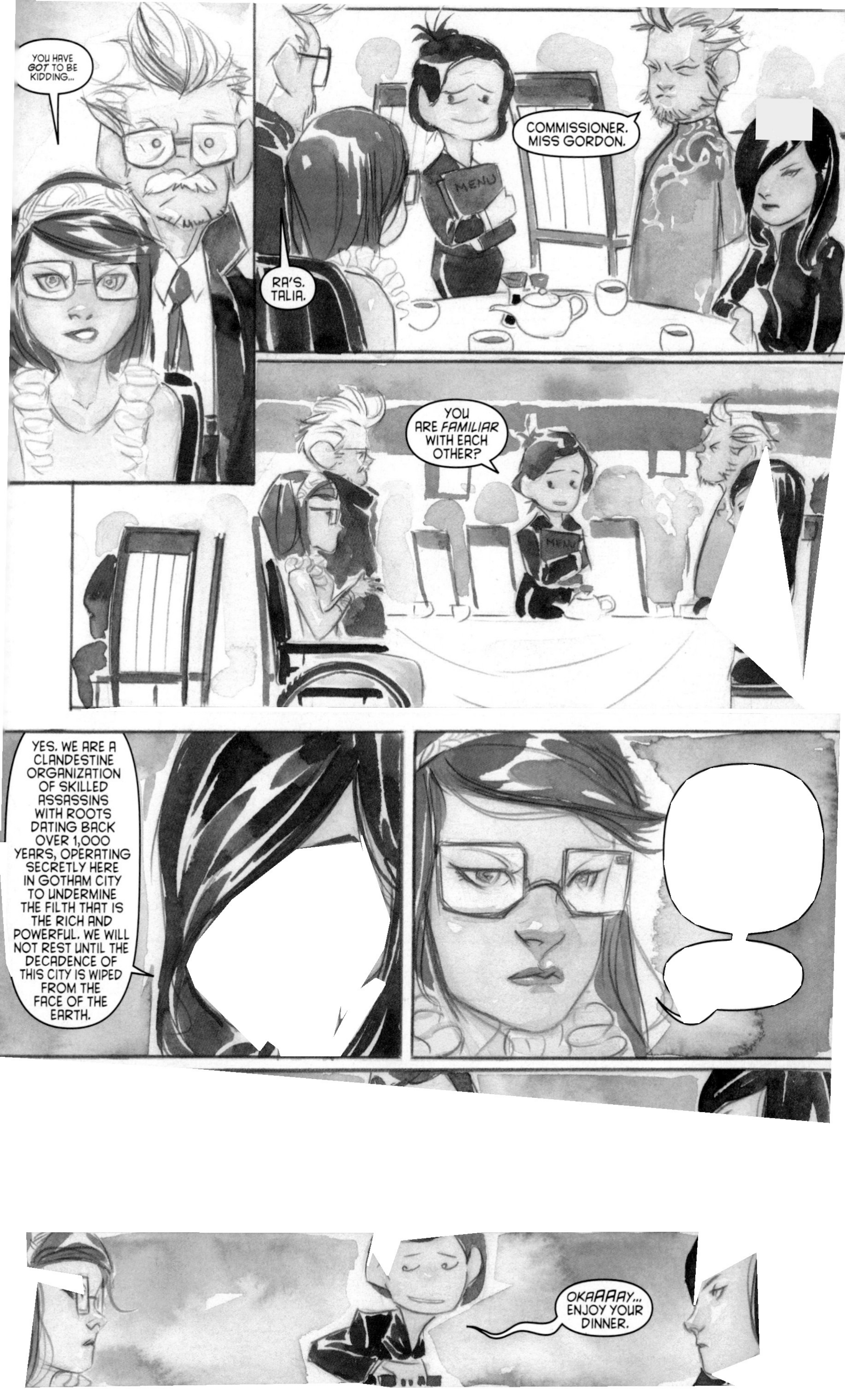
YOU HAVE GOT TO BE KIDDING...
COMMISSIONER. MISS GORDON.
RA'S. TALIA.
YOU ARE FAMILIAR WITH EACH OTHER?
YES. WE ARE A CLANDESTINE ORGANIZATION OF SKILLED ASSASSINS WITH ROOTS DATING BACK OVER 1,000 YEARS, OPERATING SECRETLY HERE IN GOTHAM CITY TO UNDERMINE THE FILTH THAT IS THE RICH AND POWERFUL. WE WILL NOT REST UNTIL THE DECADENCE OF THIS CITY IS WIPED FROM THE FACE OF THE EARTH.
OKAAAAY... ENJOY YOUR DINNER.

Batman: L'il Gotham #1 variant cover by Chris Burnam

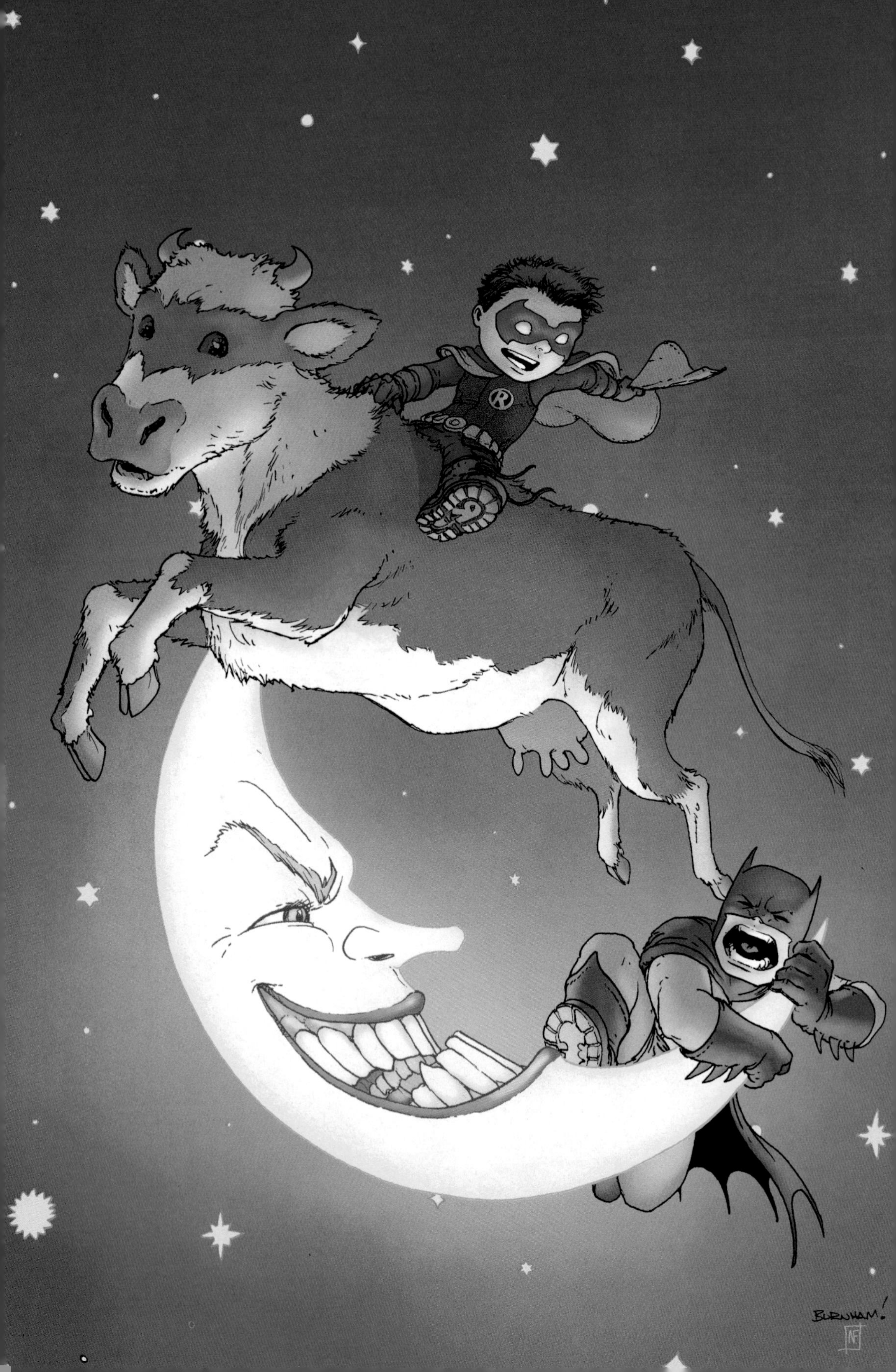
BURNHAM!

Batman: L'il Gotham #1 digital cover by Dustin Nguyen

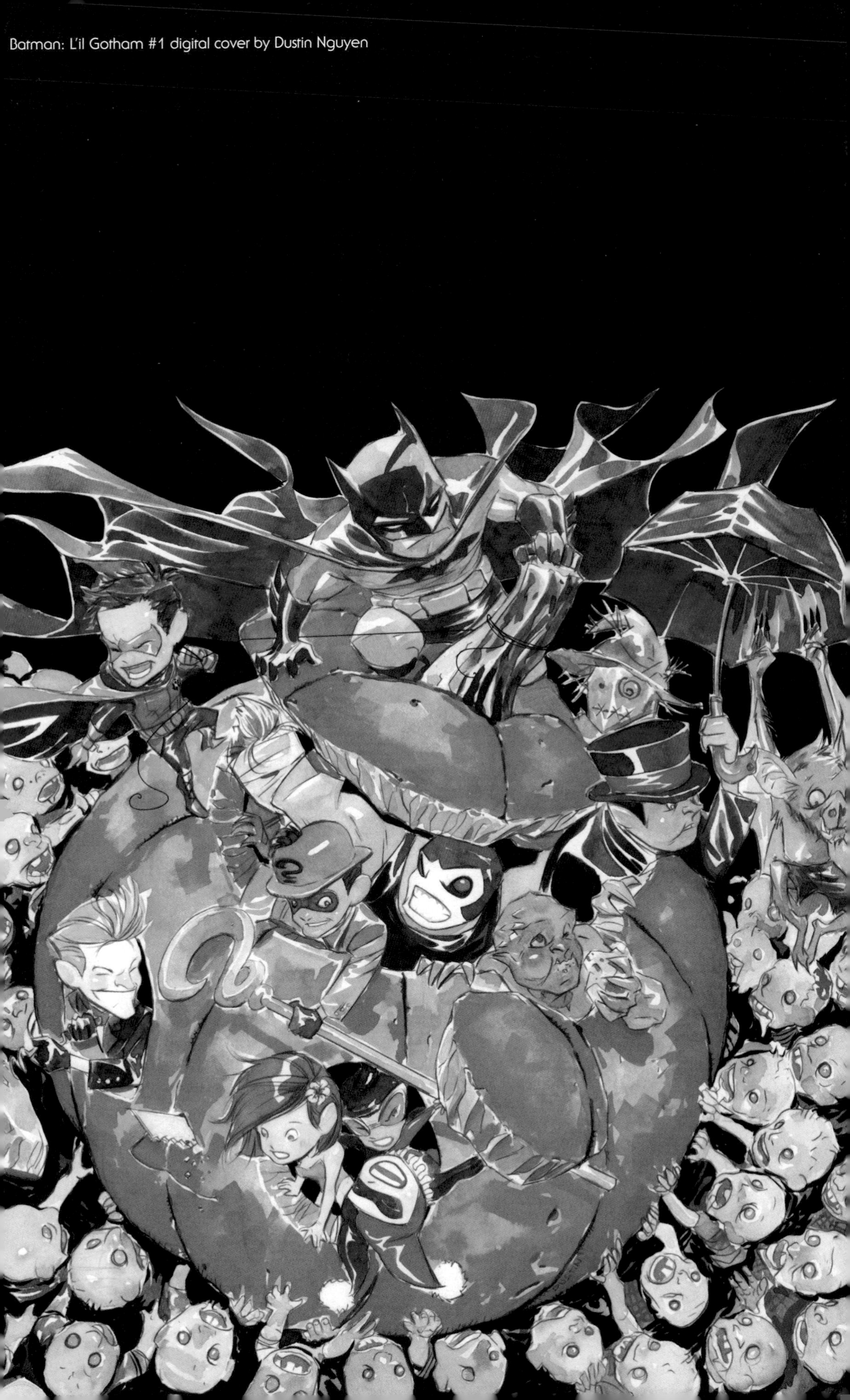

Batman: L'il Gotham #2 cover by Dustin Nguyen

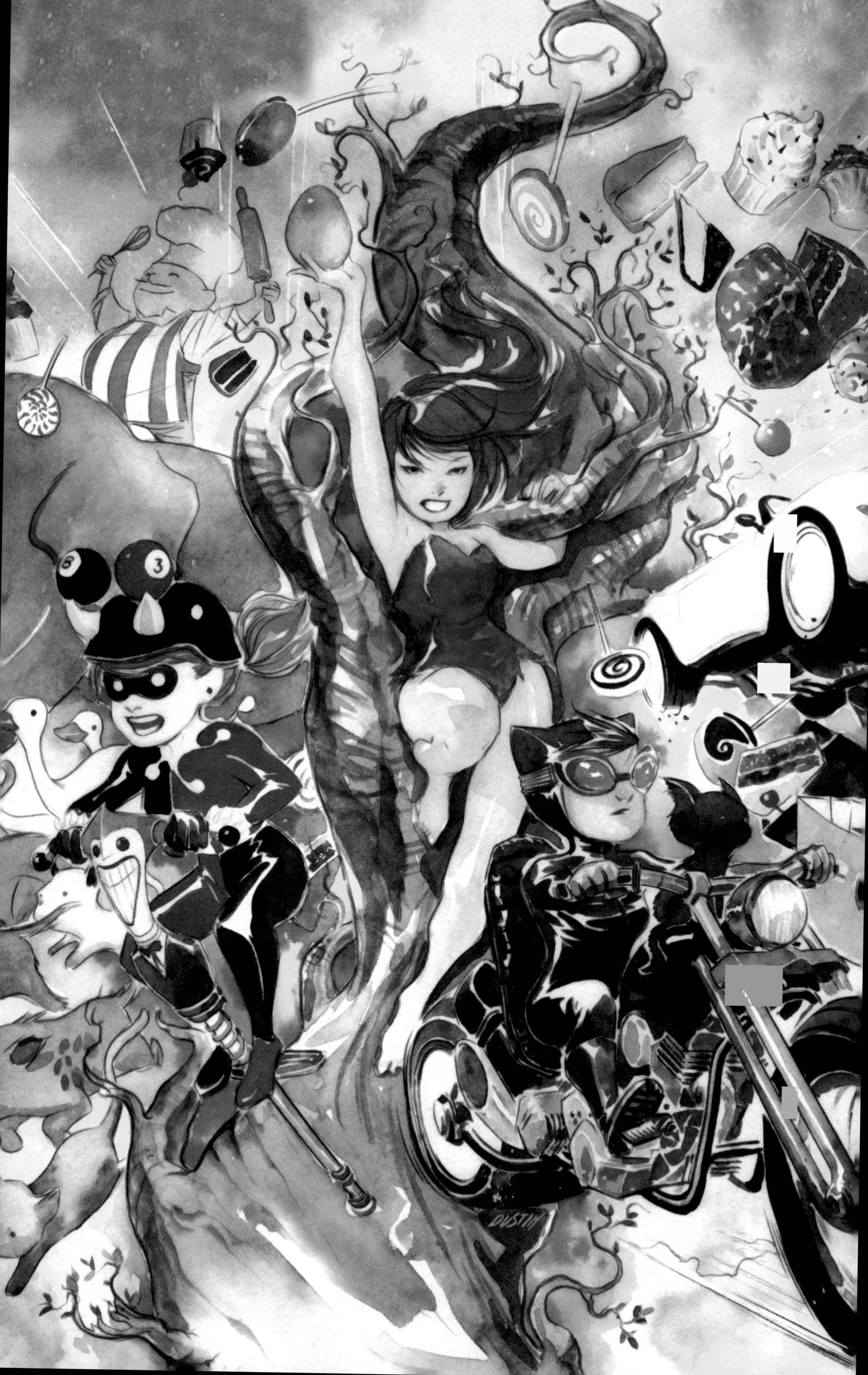
DUSTIN

Batman: L'il Gotham #3 cover by Dustin Nguyen

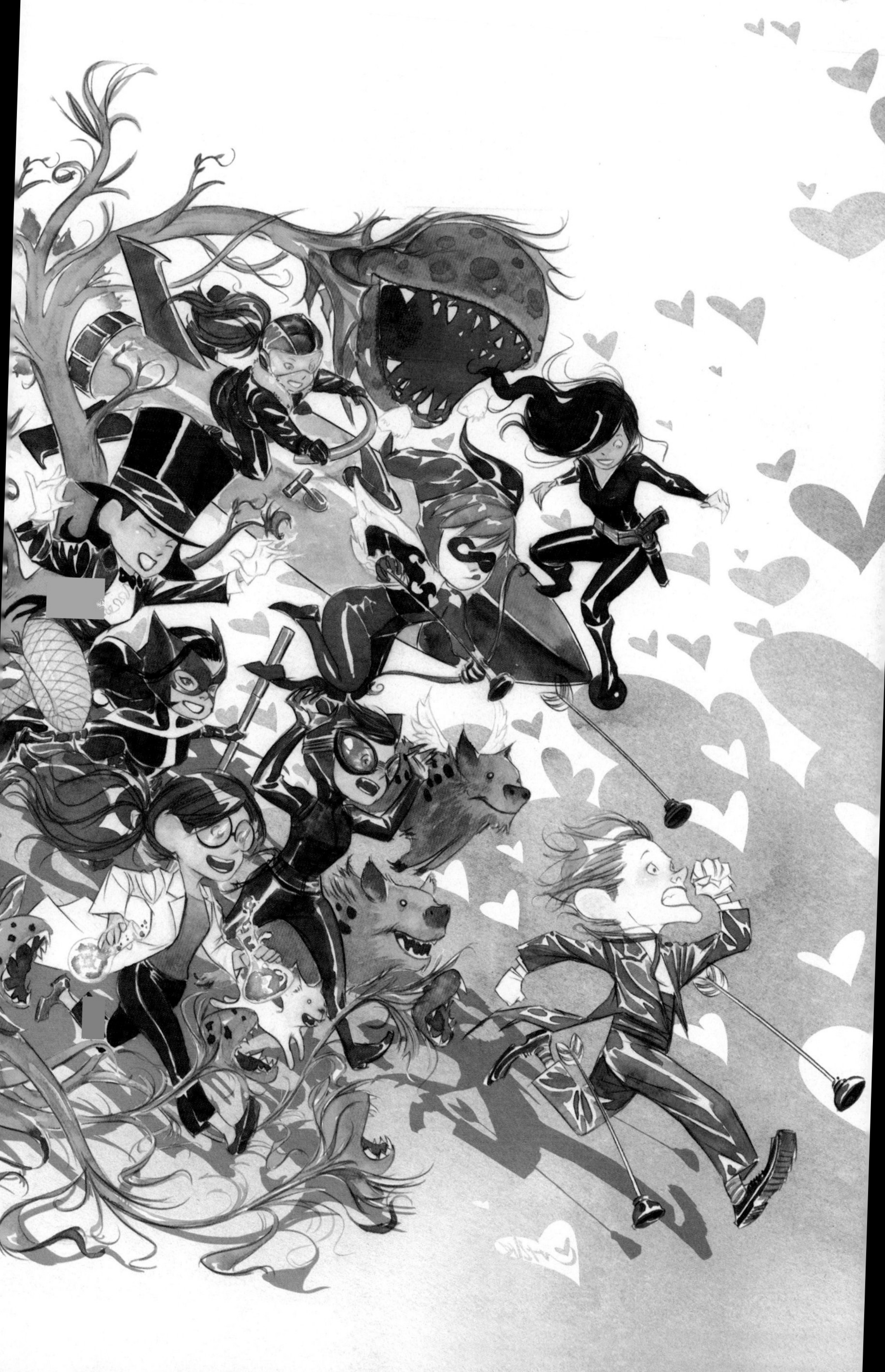

Batman: L'il Gotham #4 cover by Dustin Nguyen

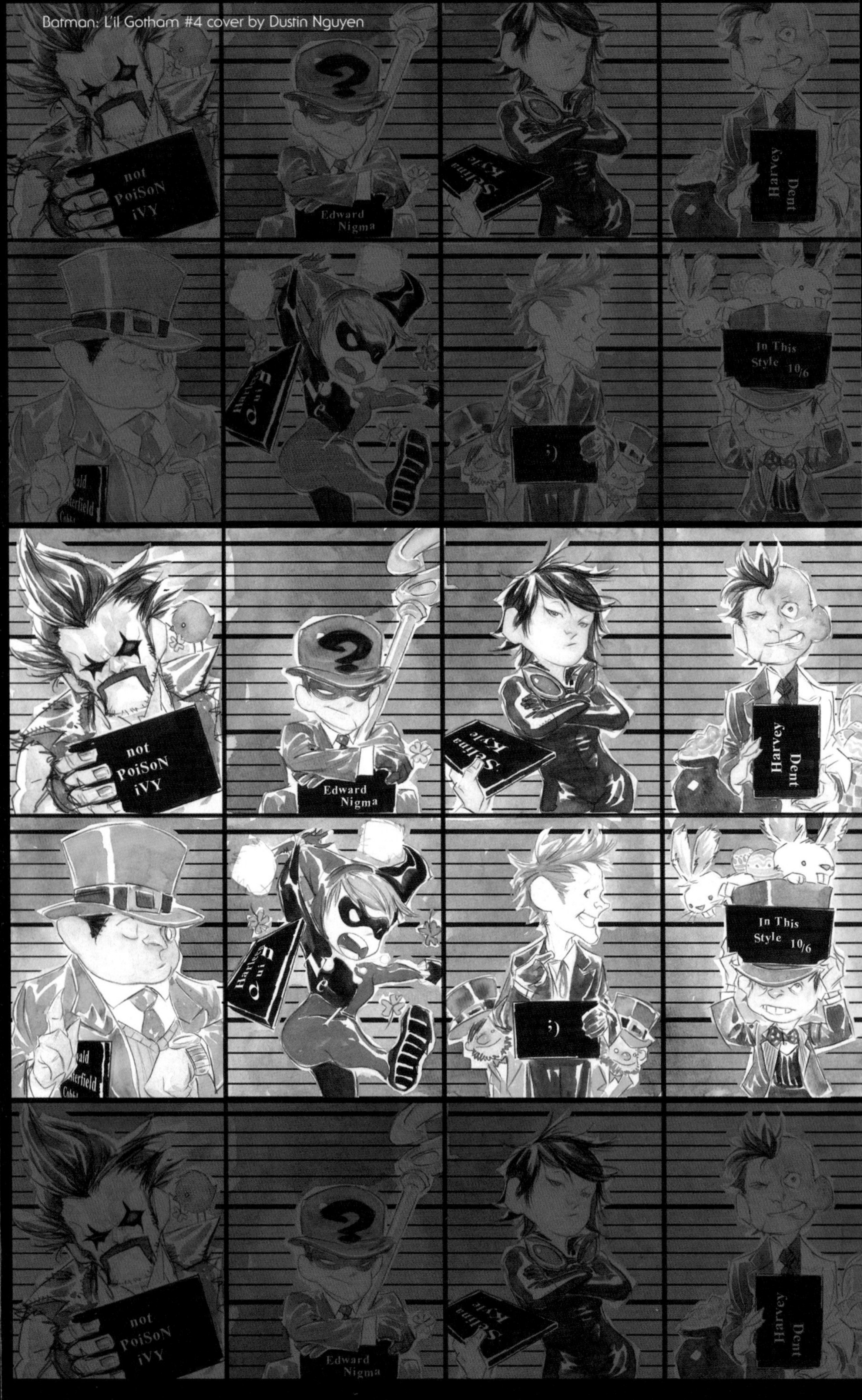

not PoiSoN iVY
Edward Nigma
Selina Kyle
Harvey Dent
In This Style 10/6
;)

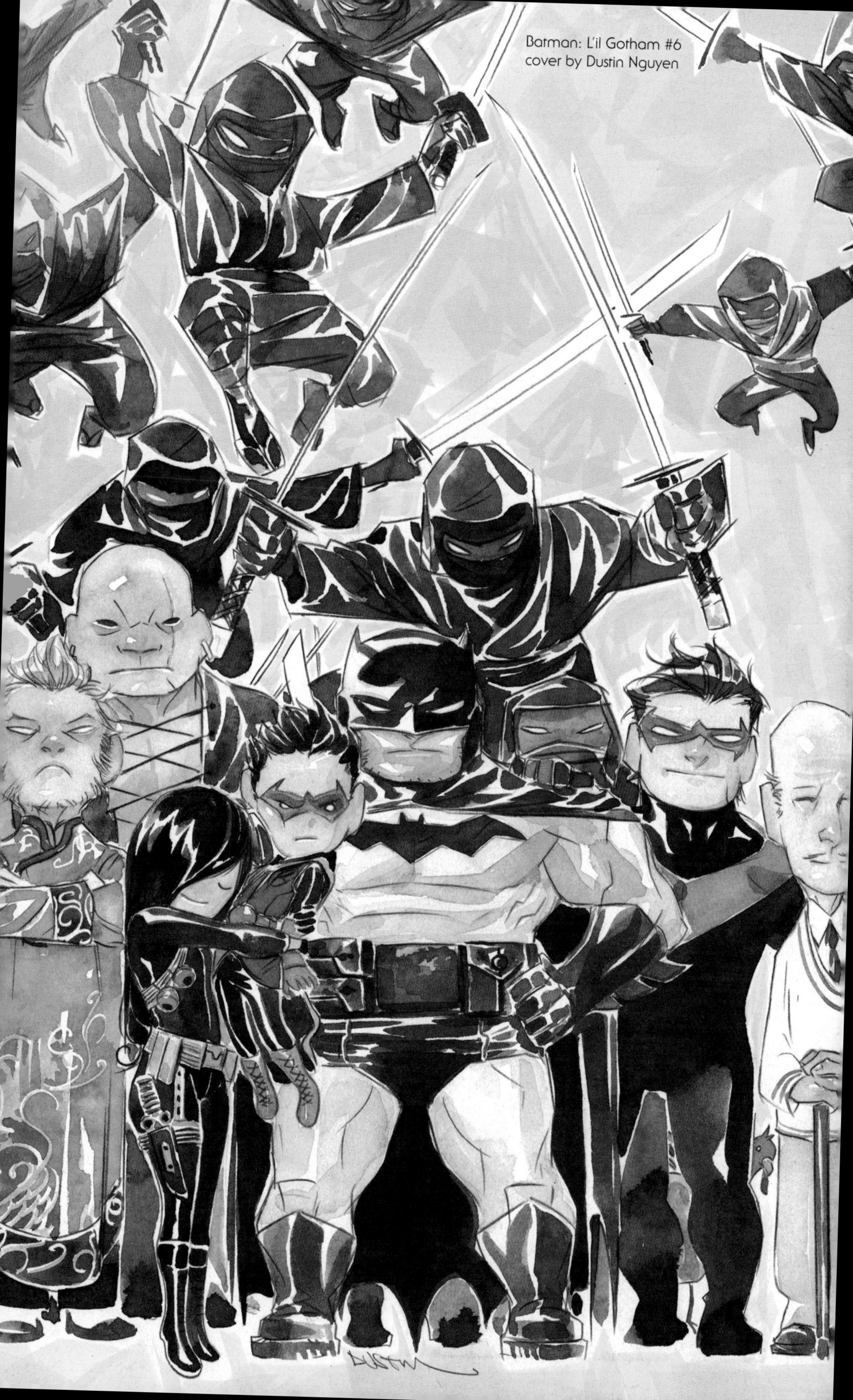

Batman: L'il Gotham #6
cover by Dustin Nguyen

Batman: L'il Gotham #5 cover by Dustin Nguyen

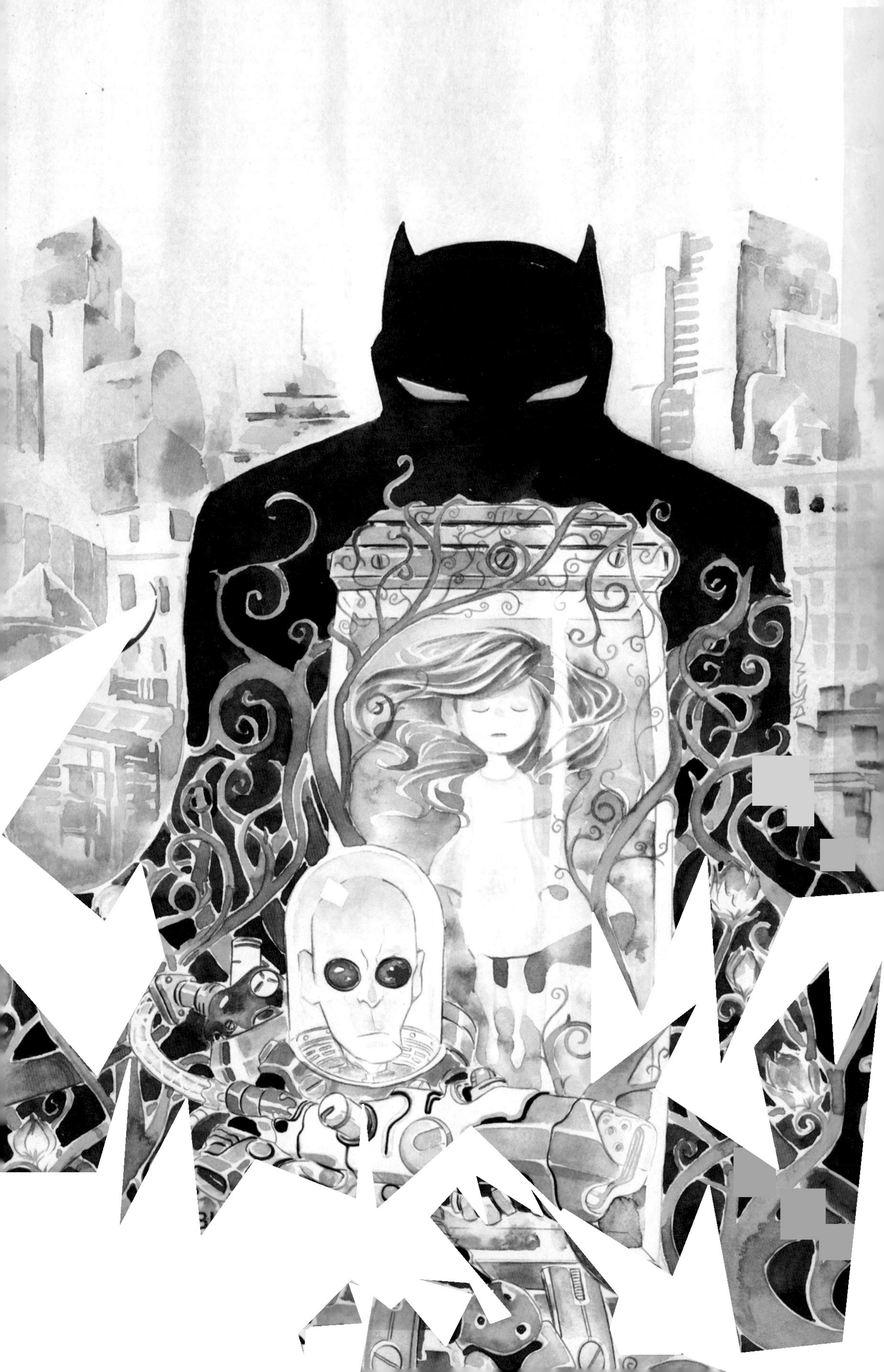